D0340146

SUPERSTAR

ALSO BY VICTORIA GOTTI

| | |

The Senator's Daughter

Women and Mitral Valve Prolapse

I'll Be Watching You

VICTORIA GOTTI

—A NOVEL—

SUPER STAR

CROWN PUBLISHERS
NEW YORK

Copyright © 2000 by Victoria Gotti

Published by Crown Publishers, New York.
Member of the Crown Publishing Group.

Random House, Inc.
New York, Toronto, London, Sydney, Auckland

CROWN is a trademark and the Crown colophon
is a registered trademark of Random House, Inc.

Printed in the U.S.A.

Design by Karen Minster

Library of Congress Cataloging-in-Publication Data
Gotti, Victoria.
Superstar / by Victoria Gotti.—1st ed.
1. Motion picture industry—California—Los Angeles—Fiction.
2. Hollywood (Los Angeles, Calif.)—Fiction.
3. Infants switched at birth—Fiction. I. Title.
PS3557.O82 S86 2000
813'.54—dc21
99-086320

ISBN 0-609-60242-X

10 9 8 7 6 5 4 3 2 1

First Edition

TO

My father, John, for his strength, amazing discipline, and the encouragement to continue fighting life's toughest battles.

My mother, Victoria, my best friend, for her unconditional love and compassion.

My siblings, Angel, John, and Peter, for their support, laughter, and wonderful words of wisdom in my time of need.

My husband, Carmine, for his much appreciated praise
and unrelenting belief that
"no matter what—I will, in fact, meet my deadline."

The two angels in my life, Frank and Justine—
their memory is emblazoned on my psyche.

And to my greatest accomplishments—my children—
Carmine, John, and Frank. Their love, respect, and friendship
are key to my mere existence.

ACKNOWLEDGMENTS

No cleverly woven tale is the sole creation of the author. The initial concept, background, and imaginative insight are basic fundamentals toward its success.

I would like to thank the following:

My agent, Frank Weimann, for his keen insight and remarkable direction.

My editor, Bob Mecoy, an incredibly gifted man, for his stellar performance and the countless times he addressed me as "kiddo" and managed to keep me focused, despite the pressures and insanity of the outside world.

Publicist extraordinaire   Rachel Pace.

"The King of Book Covers"—Whitney Cookman.

The indescribable, technological advances of the Internet—for affording me the luxury to travel the globe while sitting at my office desk.

Attorney Jeffrey Lichtman for his wealth of knowledge inside "the well of the court."

Dr. Martin Handler for his explanation of the mechanics of the human heart.

A list of literary accomplices during my tedious, often tiring hours of research on manic depressive disorder: *An Unquiet Mind, A Brillant Madness,* and *The Broken Brain.*

And to countless other authors who have essentially "paved" the road of enlightenment and offered hope to writers, both struggling and successful, to move forward, be persistent, and eventually conquer—Sidney Sheldon, David Baldacci, Jackie Collins, and Mary Higgins Clark.

SUPERSTAR

PROLOGUE
Cedars-Sinai Hospital, 1966

The babies were born ten minutes apart. Two girls, one vibrant and healthy, the other feeble and frail. The difference was startling, especially under the glow of the hospital nursery's fluorescent lights. Nurse Patricia Hanson had strict orders: Act quickly and discreetly. She waited impatiently as the nurse's aide filled cabinets with a fresh supply of formula. When the young aide was finished, Hanson told her, "Go to 210 and check on Mrs. Murphy. She's been complaining of heavy bleeding." As she reached the door of the nursery, Hanson called out to her, "If there's any cause for alarm, notify me immediately."

Patricia offered a phony smile and nodded as the young woman turned to go. When the door closed, her face pinched into a visible mask of terror. Holding her breath, she peeled back the two infants' blankets.

The baby born first was still crying. Patricia brushed her finger across a soft rosy cheek and the baby turned her head toward it, mouth working. She repeated the gesture on the second infant. No response. Patricia looked at the monitor. The vital signs were normal, but the infant wasn't moving. She touched the tiny hand, but still the infant didn't respond.

How could she have agreed to carry out such an abominable act? How could she play God like this, forever altering the lives of these two baby girls? Guilt stabbed her heart. Could she possibly live with this on her conscience?

Patricia had to fight her heart and act with her head. It wasn't just the money she'd been promised only minutes ago—it was the right thing to do in so many ways. The healthy infant had been born to a single mother with no means of support. Born to Roger and Lana Turmaine, the sickly baby would never make it. Wouldn't the healthy child be better off with all that the wealthy Turmaines could provide? Only a healthy baby could fulfill the promise that money and power would buy her—did Patricia want to see all that go to waste?

She was running out of time. The young aide could walk back through the nursery door at any moment. Without a second to lose, Patricia slipped the plastic bracelet first from one tiny wrist and re-attached it to the wrist of the other infant, then carefully removed the original bracelet from the second child and secured it to the delicate wrist of the first baby. This quick exchange gave these babies their new identities. And their new destinies.

Each year for the next twenty-one years, money would be deposited in a Swiss bank account set up for her. The payments would continue so long as no one—particularly Lana Turmaine—learned about what happened here today.

Not since Vivien Leigh's performance in *Gone With the Wind* had Hollywood seen the kind of excitement caused by Lana Turmaine's starring role in the long-awaited release of *Tamed,* the new Metro-Goldwyn-Mayer film. Lana was stunning: blond and bold, and, at thirty-three, she was Tinseltown's "Goddess of the Moment." An incandescent beauty with catlike green eyes, a delicate, pert nose, and luscious pouty lips, Lana boasted a flawless hourglass figure that was all the more admirable as it played against the anorexic, flat-chested waifs who had overrun Hollywood, New York, and every other fashion capital on the planet. That Lana had "out-Marilyned Marilyn" was the buzz around her sensuous performance in *Tamed.*

Typically, invitations for run-of-the-mill premiere parties went out by word of mouth, but tonight's event was far from ordinary. The *Tamed* gala was expected to be the party of the decade. As soon as the five hundred embossed cream-colored invitations were delivered, Hollywood's most powerful movers and shakers—the studio heads, producers, agents, and other corporate crème de la crème who made Hollywood soar— brandished them like trophies. It was clear that getting invited to the Turmaine party meant you were Somebody. And wasn't that what Hollywood was all about?

The women immediately booked private appointments at every designer salon along Rodeo Drive. Bob Mackie was big that year, so many of the women came away with purchases that could conceivably be considered risqué, if not obscene, in any town other than Hollywood. Christian Lacroix was making a splash with his puffy taffeta dresses, as was Halston with his stark, sleek tuxedos for women. Everyone else would wear the usual array of little black numbers.

And don't think for a moment that the men, too, didn't hit their custom shops. Sean Connery, Jack Nicholson, Warren Beatty, and even the up-and-coming Richard Gere would arrive in their double-breasted, wide-lapeled, custom-tailored tuxes.

On the evening of the party, the wrought-iron gates to Whispering Winds, the Beverly Hills estate of Roger and Lana Turmaine, swung open and closed as limos, Bentleys, and Mercedes sedans swept up the palm-lined driveway. Tucked discreetly behind six massive white stone columns, the Hollywood-style Georgian mansion could comfortably accommodate the five hundred guests.

Roger Turmaine stood in the grand entryway, flanked by an intricately carved oak door, imported from a church in Tuscany. A medieval stained-glass window crowned the door frame and scattered glints of color down the steps. As the guests arrived, Roger greeted each one personally.

Next to Roger stood his son, Jonathan. The sullen seventeen-year-old seemed to make no attempt to conceal his contempt for this scene as he slumped against the doorjamb, his hands rammed into the pockets of the Oleg Cassini tuxedo that encased his body like a second skin. This was Lana Turmaine's night and Jonathan cared not at all for his stepmother. More than once he was heard asking his father, "Where is the Queen Bee, anyway?"

Jonathan wasn't the only one wondering where Lana was. His father's smile seemed slightly strained as he discreetly glanced toward the stairway to the master suite upstairs and then at his watch. And every guest asked for Lana as they passed through the receiving line—even before they helped themselves to the free-flowing champagne and the exquisite hors d'oeuvres. It wasn't just Lana the Star they wanted; each expected to be touched or affected in some way by Lana's rare ability to seduce, charm, and convince each person she met that he or she mattered—really mattered—to Lana Turmaine. And this human touch was totally sincere. It was no secret that Roger had made Lana, first by encouraging his young protégée—a former legal secretary with acting aspirations—to study acting seriously, and then by shaping every aspect of her career. His box-office track record as a director had gotten Lana the early breaks when he'd declared that they were a package deal: no Lana Hunt, no Roger Turmaine. And by the time Lana Hunt became Lana Turmaine, she was a Star.

Roger had always believed in their marriage because, after all, they were a perfect match for each other—weren't they? Granted, Lana had gotten sidetracked, weakened by booze and pills, but she wouldn't let him down tonight. She couldn't. Despite her promise to keep it together, Roger flashed on other parties, other occasions, when she had dissolved into tears over some imagined slight, or raged at the wife of a studio executive for wearing the same color dress she had, or drunkenly pawed a guest—a handsome European film star—who caught her fancy. But not tonight. This was his party; *his* production.

The main hallway leading to the grand salon was decorated with extravagant sprays of Lana's favorite flowers—delicate pink and creamy white roses—exquisitely arranged. The French doors of the salon opened onto the terrace and grounds, creating a romantic backdrop, as if this, too, were a movie set. Outside, the trees fluttered in the balmy night breeze, and partygoers who cared to wander about discovered that the pool was filled with rose petals and gardenias just as the air was filled with their scent.

The dining room's cathedral ceiling was illuminated by an elaborate Louis XIV crystal chandelier below which tables were decorated with the Limoges china that Roger had given Lana on their wedding day. At each place setting was a special memento of the evening—a small photo of Lana and Roger in a sterling-silver frame.

The orchestra struck up "Superstar"—Roger's customary tribute to his wife—but Lana was nowhere to be seen.

| | |

As he stood in the now-empty marble-tiled foyer, he looked up again at the closed door of the master suite. He felt a sudden hand on his shoulder.

"Pay attention, buddy." It was James Renthrew, Roger's best friend and lawyer.

Roger stared flatly into James's soothing brown eyes and then snapped to attention. He bit down hard on his lower lip and took a long gulp of scotch and soda. He nodded and moved toward the music and laughter. "Not tonight, Lana," he whispered to himself. "Not tonight."

| | |

Lana found comfort in the intense fragrance of forty-eight Black Beauty roses loosely splayed in the Lalique crystal vase that held center stage atop the round Victorian table in her dressing room. A fringed pink lamp cast a halo over the flowers. The attached card read, "Best wishes on your enormous success—the President and Mrs. Ford."

Music and laughter filtered up from the elegant party swirling below, invading the sanctuary of Lana's pale pink sitting room, her side of the master suite she shared with Roger. Intoxicated by the heady scent of the roses, Lana felt protected, safely sequestered from the demands of the crowd, from her duties as hostess . . . from the homage paid to her as the star of *Tamed.*

She studied her pale reflection in the full-length mirror, desperately fighting to ignore the music and laughter from the party below and to still the growing panic that roared in her head. She eyed the bottle of pills tucked in the bottom of her makeup bag. With trembling hands, she reached for them, unscrewed the top, and popped two, maybe three, of the shiny red tablets into her mouth. Her eyes were already swimming in a glaze of the two vodkas she'd had while getting dressed.

An emotional whirligig seemed to have taken up residence inside her. These physical sensations, along with the churning anxiety—the voices in her head—were only slightly eased by the sedatives and alcohol. Lana forced herself to breathe, deeply and steadily. It wasn't helping.

Day after day, she was finding it harder to hold on. Lana felt ripped apart down the middle, and this tear was growing wider.

It didn't matter how successful or how high up the Hollywood mountain she had climbed. She remained haunted by the decision she was being forced to make by the night's end. There was no easy solution—someone would be hurt.

Lana looked down at her hands and thought of her daughter. Cassidy was the only achievement she would never allow to be tarnished. In her child, Lana found solace. Cassidy was only ten, but she'd been born with an extraordinary wisdom. She smiled at the thought of her gentle daughter asleep in the ruffled white bedroom down the hall—asleep, or in bed with her head buried in a book.

Lana sat at her dressing table and removed the pins that held her hair in the chignon her stylist had insisted on forming at the nape of her neck. She ran her fingers through the thick blond hair she had inherited from her Irish father and shook it free. Then she learned forward and ran her sterling-silver boar-bristle brush through it to release any tangles. Pulling her abundant mane to one side, she lifted and folded her hair into a simple knot, pinning it up and away from her face to reveal her soft neck. This simple sweep accentuated the slightly plunging back of her Halston dress, a magnificent white-beaded gown that gracefully draped off the shoulder.

Lana daubed a bit more concealer under her eyes to mask the dark circles and used a touch of gray eyeliner to disguise her dilated pupils. After careful inspection, she added the finishing touch—a pair of diamond-and-pearl earrings, perfectly chosen to complement her gown.

Finally satisfied with her appearance, she walked downstairs.

Roger was waiting at the bottom of the spiral staircase. His lips formed a patient but stressed smile at the sight of his wife as he walked to meet her. He grasped her arm so tightly that she flinched, but he did not loosen his grip.

Carefully, she took each step, grasping the banister with her free hand to steady herself. With eyes half closed and lips set in a delicious pout, she said blithely, "I had a case of stage fright, I suppose."

Lana knew that everyone present would assume she was joking. Everyone except Roger. He knew what it took for her to show up on a set, how she had to pump herself up emotionally *and* physically before stepping before the cameras. He also knew that she saw her appearance at the many social/business functions that make Hollywood run in the same tortured light as her performance onstage or before the cameras.

Lana allowed herself to be pulled along into the clamoring crowd. Her eyes found Jonathan, her stepson, standing with Mike Douglas, Kirk's son—not yet the actor his father was, but who knew? And she spotted Jeff Boyd carrying on a fevered conversation—the two Boyd boys always seemed so intense—with James Renthrew. James. He nodded and smiled in Lana's direction. Perhaps he had picked up a new client. That would be nice.

Roger continued holding her arm in a vicelike grip.

Still Lana smiled.

"Lana," an aging—ancient, really—actress gushed, pulling Lana close to kiss the air at each cheek. "Amazing work, dear. Amazing."

Lana was thankful for the chance to wrench herself free of Roger's painful grasp. She was determined to keep the woman talking until her husband faded from her side. But he wasn't going to be shaken loose before he had his say.

"Look around you, my darling," he whispered pointedly into her ear.

"I've done all this for you. All. Don't forget who made you, Lana. Think twice before you throw it all away."

She couldn't ignore the menace in his voice.

| | |

Cassidy Turmaine was born a princess.

Her mother had dipped her very first pair of shoes in silver, and they were there, along with the silver spoons, a cup, and a rattle, on a shelf in her lily-white bedroom.

Her earliest memories were of the lace dresses that she wore to birthday parties where she and her friends rode on carousels set up next to the tennis courts and the parents drank and made deals by the pool. Her Christmas gifts were beautiful porcelain dolls and life-sized stuffed animals. By the time she was four, Cassidy had learned that if she so much as let out a pretend sob, someone would rush to comfort her.

Her happiest times were when her father carried her on his shoulders and told the world about his beautiful princess's amazing accomplishments. He proclaimed her an "implausible beauty," so much and so often that she sometimes felt herself turn red—blushing, Nanny Rae called it.

Daddy had even turned the huge house into a secure, magical castle just for her and Mommy. He had hired guards and installed lights and alarms all over the house and grounds. He said it was to keep them safe.

And every night at bedtime, he would gently tuck the warm ivory lace blanket up to her chin. She could feel his eyes on her as she drifted off to sleep, dreaming of only happy things—fairy godmothers, magical ponies, and palaces with rooms filled with red lollipops and white roses. Sometimes in the middle of the night, she would wake up and find Daddy sitting beside her bed, just staring. When she asked him what he was doing, he'd say, "Oh, just watching over my little angel." Then he'd sing her favorite song, a Leon Russell classic: "Long ago and oh so far away, I fell in love with you . . ." Daddy said he sang the same song to Mommy when they met.

This was the fairy-tale life of Cassidy, and no one would ever take it away—not so long as Daddy watched over her.

| | |

But tonight Cassidy was too excited to sleep.

When she finally heard her mother leave her room and go downstairs, Cassidy quietly and carefully closed her bedroom door, then tiptoed across the bare hardwood floor to her bed. She pulled back the blankets and climbed comfortably underneath, her body soaking up the bed's warmth.

Music was playing downstairs, and the sounds of laughter and muted conversation drifted upstairs along with the smell of cigarette and cigar smoke.

Cassidy always found it impossible to fall asleep when her parents threw one of their lavish parties. It wasn't the noise so much as the excitement that set her mind racing. Often she would sneak to her "secret spot" behind an alcove in the hall at the top of the stairs. From there she could observe every detail—what each woman wore, the dresses, shoes, the special handbags (Nanny Rae called them *etui*) they clutched, and who was wearing the most sparkling jewelry. Always these women were accompanied by men whom Cassidy saw on TV or in the movies—old men, young, all sizes and shapes. They looked every bit as royal as the ladies on their arms.

For Cassidy, the most important part of hiding in her secret spot was that she was able to see that, no matter how the other women looked, not one of them was as beautiful as her mother. The very sight of Lana gliding down the staircase, so beautifully dressed—like a princess out of one of the fairy tales her Nanny Rae read to her each night—simply delighted her.

Especially tonight, she thought, since Mama had been so sad lately. Cassidy guessed it had a lot to do with the fighting between her mother and father. This seemed to be getting worse, louder and scarier, all the time. Lately her father's fury, his loud, threatening tone, and sometimes even the sound of glass smashing, had shattered all of Cassidy's pleasant dreams. Now she would lie awake trying to anticipate when the storm would hit.

But tonight would be an exception. Cassidy was sure. There would be no yelling, no broken glass, and no sobs. Tonight was a special party in honor of her very own mother! Daddy had planned it that way. He told her so.

Content that Mama was, as always, the most beautiful woman at the party, Cassidy pulled the blankets up to her chin, closed her eyes, let her lips curl into a smile, and let out a sigh of pleasure.

| | |

At four A.M. the last good night was finally said and the last Mercedes or limo or Rolls lazily pulled out of the driveway. Lana walked slowly up the stairs, clutching the polished mahogany banister—but not because she was drunk. She was sober now, hadn't touched a drink since she entered the party. She was just tired, physically and emotionally. She felt hollow, spent.

She stripped, leaving her clothing where it fell, not even bothering to remove her makeup. She climbed into her warm, safe bed. Her eyelids were heavy, half closed as she laid her head against the pillow and squirmed about in search of a comfortable position. Lana remembered then that she'd forgotten to remove her earrings, so she sat up and the silk sheet fell from her flawless breasts. She laid the gems down on the Queen Anne night table, glad that Roger's side of the bed was still empty.

She had to admit that she did not care where he was. She needed to be alone. Throughout the evening, he'd been drinking scotch and was pretty drunk the last time she saw him. Perhaps he would sleep in one of the downstairs guest rooms. She hoped so. As her eyes fell shut, her thoughts were clouded with worry and fear. Had she made the right decision after all?

| | |

He looked around and made sure everyone was gone. He took the steps one at a time, his footprints sinking deeply into the plush wool carpet, the impression of his shoes clearly visible in the deep pile. Quietly he made his way down the hall to the master suite. The doorknob felt cool against the fiery heat of his hand. He opened the door and found Lana asleep, her naked body entangled in the soft sheets. The room was still, so silent only the sound of her soft breathing was audible.

He crossed the room to the foot of the bed and took a moment to examine her in repose. One side of her magnificent face was buried in the soft pillow, her wild mane of blond hair spilling over the side of the bed like melting taffy. He moved closer, his hands now just inches from her delicious lips. She was one of God's greatest creations; such a pity she would have to die.

The crystal lamp on the bedside table glowed softly, creating prisms of light that dusted the room in a warm, soft gold. Gently he brushed a strand of hair from her face. She stirred a bit, and he steeled himself. He summoned up the strength he'd earlier thought was lost. Even in sleep, she could easily arouse him, deliberately seduce him, push him over the edge.

Unable to resist the temptation, he brushed the side of her face with his fingertips. She moaned, and a slight smile curved her lips. His hand dropped to her bare shoulder, his fingers tracing the outline of her neck. Lana opened her eyes, squinting several times in an effort to register his presence.

"It's . . . you . . . hmmm." Her voice was tentative, almost frightened, yet her tone was seductive. She smiled sleepily as she focused her eyes. Then she noticed the dramatic change in his demeanor. Had his emotions perverted his features so completely that his mask of love no longer worked?

A frisson of alarm charged through her body, her muscles becoming so tense he could feel her fear.

Oblivious to her nakedness, she squirmed to the far side of the bed, fighting to break free of the sheets and blankets. He leaned down beside her. His arms hung at his sides. Her eyes dropped to his hands, to the shiny glint of metal.

"The game's over, Lana."

He could see her heart beating in erratic rhythms, hear her as she gasped for air. Screams clawed their way up into her throat.

He aimed the small revolver at her, then announced, "And I've won."

She flung the sheets and blankets away from her body like a matador's cape, then swung her legs over the side of the bed in a futile effort to escape.

He squeezed the trigger so tightly that his finger grew numb. He fired twice. The small .22 could do a lot of damage with minimum effort and noise. The first bullet slammed into her shoulder, the second, her head.

He took a deep breath.

It was over.

Her body dropped beside the bed; her blood splattered over the linens like deep red flower petals scattered across a snowbank. Lana fell to the floor. First blackness—then death.

He slowly turned and walked calmly from the dimly lit bedroom into the brightly lit hallway. He was oblivious of his footprints on the highly polished parquet, just as he was oblivious of the intense stare of a little girl peeping through a keyhole.

Ten-year-old Chelsea Hutton lay stock-still under the scratchy starched hospital sheets and watched the slats of the venetian blind flutter in the breeze. She recited the alphabet backward to herself—as loudly as possible—to drown out the singsong voice of the priest. "This is the Body of Christ. . . ."

She lowered her eyes, averting the gaze of her mother, who knelt piously beside her bed, hands folded in front of her heart.

Father Tom repeated the words of the sacrament, this time more firmly, and touched her lips with the Host. "The Body of Christ . . . take, eat . . ."

Chelsea opened her mouth to receive the wafer and hoped her mother didn't notice the shudder that passed through her body. She returned to her personal Ritual of the Alphabet, which she recited in her head whenever she wanted to shut out the voices of those she could not bear to hear. Real people and the voices she heard in her head. Father droned on, reciting special prayers for healing—"Heavenly Father, giver of life and health . . ."—the Hail Mary . . . then the Our Father.

Chelsea felt the movement as her mother, Maria, made the Sign of the Cross. Father Tom intoned, "In the name of the Father . . ."

Mother, is God really listening?

". . . the Son . . ."

Why won't the devil leave me alone?

". . . and the Holy Spirit."

If God really cared, He'd make the voices stop.

"Amen." Father Tom and Mama spoke with conviction. Chelsea remained silent.

"Chelsea," her mother instructed firmly, "thank Father Tom for coming to see you and praying with you so you'll be in God's hands tomorrow morning in the operating room."

Beads of perspiration formed above her brow. Don't let them see, she said to herself. Chelsea inhaled weakly and whispered, "Thank you, Father."

But she knew that no wafer, no wine, no church, no priest or prayer could save her.

Chelsea tried to be a good girl, but the voices in her head said mean, terrible things. She prayed to God, like her mother taught her, asking for the voices to stop. Often, after school, Chelsea would go inside the empty church to kneel and pray, but this brought no relief from the awful headaches that made it feel as if two giant hands were squeezing her temples.

Just yesterday morning, before she came to the hospital, while Mama was combing her hair, the voices called Mama terrible names. The experience left her with such rage, she'd emptied out the medicine cabinet, then hurled it across the bathroom. The small oval mirror shattered into a thousand pieces.

"It's the devil in you, child," Mama screamed as she dragged her out the door. "You must pray for God's grace!" Mama then announced that she had asked Father Tom to come to the hospital to hear her confession before she went into surgery. "You won't get into heaven if you don't make peace with Our Father."

Once again Chelsea felt the shame, the guilt. The mania would sometimes last for days, followed by a dark, empty cloud. Then all she'd feel was lonely, desperately lonely.

Even before the new boy who sat beside her in school called her "Crazy Chelsea," she knew there was something wrong with her head. The doctors said so. But Maria refused to listen to their recommendations. Nothing could be done—at least not clinically—Mama said. No pill or talk would help. The devil needed to be driven out, and God was the only answer.

Chelsea had heard her mother's litany of threats so often, she could almost recite them verbatim. Not that she dared, of course. Mama would extract even harsher penance if she did. And Father Tom would be there to see that Chelsea never missed a step.

Chelsea could not explain why she was so afraid of her mother's spiritual adviser. Mama always said that Father was a gentle, kind, and loving man. "Straight from heaven," she said. Nevertheless, the very mention of the priest's name had terrified Chelsea for as long as she could remember.

Was it his black cassock? Or the fact that Chelsea had rarely been around men? Mama wanted to know. Chelsea didn't know what to say except that Father Tom was a messenger sent from God and he must know she was a bad girl.

| | |

Chelsea's head wasn't the only part of her that was damaged. She was born with what Mama called a "weak heart." As Mama told her time after time, she almost died when she was born . . . that it was God's gift that she was still alive. But if God was so good and loving, why was life so . . . painful? Why did Mama have to work so hard? Why did they have so little?

Home for Chelsea and her mama was a sparsely furnished one-bedroom flat on the first floor of a dingy apartment building in East Los Angeles, a *barrio* where, as Mama put it, all the "others" lived. Chelsea knew she meant black, Mexican, Latino. The tiny kitchenette had a noisy fridge and ancient stove with only two working burners, and was furnished with two rickety wood chairs and a card table covered with a checkered plastic-coated tablecloth. The living room, which was lit by a single bare bulb hanging from the ceiling, held a tattered convertible couch that doubled as Mama's bed. It faced a black-and-white television with aluminum foil twisted on its rabbit-ear antenna—for better reception, Mama insisted. The bedroom—Chelsea's room—was furnished with a scratched bureau and battered "youth bed," a trundle from a set used by a family in Father Tom's parish. Their children were grown and the main single bed was worn out, so they gave it to the church . . . for Father to give to the needy.

It embarrassed Chelsea that people thought of her and Mama as needy, but she knew that they were.

| | |

Maria Hutton worked as a housekeeper for a single man named Mr. Patrick. Most housekeepers and their children lived on their employers' property, in extra bungalows or separate quarters, but Mama believed only the Mexicans and blacks would live in their employers' houses, so she clung to the one-bedroom apartment despite its roaches and rusty plumbing—despite the downstairs lock that was always broken and the neighborhood where Chelsea was afraid to walk the streets alone, even in daytime.

Mama often took her to Mr. Patrick's house while she scrubbed toilets and floors and cleaned the fireplace kneeling on the bricks. Mr. Patrick's house was on the far fringe of Beverly Hills and it wasn't very large, so Chelsea knew he wasn't a big celebrity like the other people she saw in the movie magazines their neighbor Mrs. Gonzalez always read.

So he wasn't really famous at all—not like she was going to be.

| | |

When the high moods came and she closed her eyes, Chelsea could imagine how different life would be. She'd get an agent—maybe by the time she was fifteen—like her classmate Angela Clementi's older sister. The rest would be a piece of cake. She loved to act—she easily slid into different moods. That's what actresses did, right? Soon she'd be saying good-bye to cockroaches, and the pitiful clothes she had to wear from the Salvation Army and the St. Vincent de Paul Thrift Shop. She'd be recognized everywhere she went, and she'd have a mansion in the *middle* of Beverly Hills and a full-time, live-in housekeeper. And a butler *and* a chauffeur, too.

Then the high mood would pass and Chelsea would remember that Angela Clementi's father was a studio executive and Chelsea didn't even have a father. The voices would start hammering at her until she was either too down to get out of bed or in a wild, screaming rage. That was how she came to sock Angela Clementi in the eye. She just couldn't help it. Why did everyone have so much while she and Mama had nothing?

| | |

Father Tom waved his long bony fingers above Chelsea's head, making the Sign of the Cross.

"Dear God, bless this child, her mother, their home, keep all free from . . ."

What a crock of shit. The strange voice in her head took over, and Chelsea knew a rage was coming over her.

What home? The apartment was far from the cozy comforts of a home—it was a dump!

"All the evil that surrounds all . . ."

What evil? Was it true—were there ghosts? Demons—like the devil? Does he really live inside of me, Mama?

"Protect us from . . ."

Protect us from what? Starvation? Freezing in an unheated apartment?

"We may continue to be your loyal disciples. To love and cherish . . ."

Why not love and cherish a man, Mama? It's been years since you even talked to a man—isn't it time?

"Amen."

Or maybe you could cherish me with that one thought.

When the prayer was finished, Chelsea laid her head back down on the pillow and closed her eyes. Now the cascading questions began inside her, each one moving her closer to fury.

Why didn't they have any money? Why couldn't Mama get a real job instead of always having to clean someone's house? Why couldn't Mama be like the other ladies on the block, the ones who sat outside on the porch late into the evening sharing coffee and gossip? She wanted her mama to get all dressed up and go out on Saturday nights, like other mothers. Where was her father? *Who* was her father?

Chelsea knew the answer. She was a bastard. Mama would never tell her who her father was. According to all the gossip, it could've been any one of four men she'd been seeing.

In her heyday, Maria Hutton was what most people called a runaround, a party girl, who sometimes worked as an extra in B-movies. Chelsea was an accident, but a rude awakening nonetheless. That's when and why Maria turned to God—to cleanse her soul and beg forgiveness.

Chelsea tried to be a good girl, tried to believe in the same God, the same rituals her mother did. But it was easier said than done, especially when Father Tom was so frightening to her. It was becoming more and more difficult for Chelsea to follow her mother to church four times a week, to confession on Saturday, to say the rosary each night in the privacy of the tiny bedroom. Chelsea didn't believe her soul would ever get clean. She opened her eyes now and turned to meet Maria's gaze.

"I prayed for money, Mama. Lots of it. So we could—"

"Quiet, Chelsea," Maria interrupted sharply. "Never ask the Lord for material things." Her mother stopped chewing and rose slowly.

"But, Mama, I want—"

"You will not worship God only when and how it suits you, Chelsea. You need his help."

"Screw your God. Screw you!" Chelsea shrieked. Her eyes, the color of nightshade, sparkled, the manic energy torching her anger.

Maria slammed her hand down on the metal night table beside the bed, so hard it nearly fell over.

"Don't you understand, Chelsea? You *must* pray for the strength to fight your sickness."

Chelsea froze. She felt blood rush to her face; her heart rammed against her rib cage, and for a moment she was afraid to move. Her head told her not to speak, to obediently nod and then sheepishly apologize— but her heart knew better.

Her heart knew what Chelsea Hutton prayed for, knew Chelsea was convinced that one day God would hear her and her prayers would be answered. And when her prayers *were* answered, she would leave home and never look back.

But that was not today. Chelsea felt a piercing pain burn an agonizing path through her heart. Her skin became cold and clammy. She tried to steady her breath: Inhale, exhale, slowly, steady. Then she fainted.

By the time the nurse arrived, Chelsea had regained consciousness and, though sleepy and weak, seemed alert. The physician's assistant found her pulse and respiration to be regular.

She had to have a serious operation. At that moment, she realized that God was punishing her. She was probably dying just like Mama said. She hoped God wouldn't smell her fear.

| | |

"Dr. Garron, you're needed in OR3, stat. Dr. Garron, OR3 stat . . ."

Inside the operating room, an extremely competent team had assembled. There were three nurses, two resident cardiologists, an anesthesiologist, and Dr. Phil Garron, a prominent pediatric cardiac surgeon known for his generosity to poor children in need of specialized heart surgery.

The skin incision had already been made down the circumference of the chest to the breastbone, which had been split with an electric saw. The heart and lungs were exposed.

The surgeon inserted the metal retractor, forcing the edges of the breastbone apart. Then he skillfully opened the pericardial sac, exposing the child's damaged, weakened heart.

"Here's the problem." He looked intently over his mask at each member of his operating team, making sure they were with him as he used the tip of the probe to trace the outline of a severely damaged area on the anterior area of the heart wall.

Dr. Garron looked away, collecting himself. When he raised his head, there was a look of uncertainty in his eyes. These young patients were always in life-or-death situations by the time they got to Phil Garron's table. His talented hands might have made beautiful music or carved paradise from stone—instead, medicine had called him. Garron was usually confident, but this young girl was nearly past saving. Poor nutrition, poverty—children paid for this with their health. Still he had to try.

"Okay. Let's get to work. . . ."

| | |

The doctor avoided looking at the mother as he crossed the waiting room to tell her what had happened in surgery. She was once beautiful, he could tell, but life on her own, raising a small, sickly child, had racked her face. She wore old clothes, a faded navy blue dress with a frayed, yellowed collar, something she'd no doubt picked out from one of the clothing drives. In Garron's locker was a pair of charcoal Brooks Brothers slacks and a matching cashmere sweater. He felt ashamed to have so much.

"Why don't you look at me?" Maria Hutton asked directly. "Is she alive?"

The surgeon lifted his brown eyes to her face. His green mask still hung from its ties around his neck. "Your daughter's a fighter. She's going to make it."

His forehead wrinkled as he pulled reading glasses from a pocket hidden in his scrubs. He studied each page of the report the nurse handed to him, poring through the tangle of medical lexicon. He paused, then went back to the beginning. Something was strange here, he thought. Garron kept searching. Finally he turned back to Maria.

"Ms. Hutton, you said your daughter's blood type was A-positive." His eyes were now wrinkled at the corners.

"Yes, that's correct."

Dr. Garron shook his head. "It's understandable to make such an innocent mistake, given all the stress you've been under."

"No," Maria said. She raised her chin defensively. "I've made no mistake. Chelsea is A-positive."

"The lab results from presurgical work-up are O-negative. You should make a note of this. It could be serious if Chelsea ever needs blood. If I had relied solely on the information you gave us, we would have made a terrible mistake. Thank God one of the nurses had Chelsea's blood profile on hand."

Maria shook her head furiously. "No, Doctor. I've been aware of her weak heart since she was born. I'm her mother. I know. Her blood type is A-positive. I have all of her birth records. I'll bring them to you so you can see for yourself. Your lab must have made a mistake."

"No, Ms. Hutton." Dr. Garron shook his head. "I'm sure of it. There's no mistake. I had the lab run it through twice. These tests are foolproof. They're so new and so accurate that most hospitals aren't equipped to run them. Chelsea's blood type is definitely O-negative."

Maria's face registered shock as the words the doctor had just said sank in.

Dr. Garron gripped her elbow and ushered her into a nearby chair. That's when he dropped the bomb. "In planning how to handle both her blood disorder and the condition of her heart, we had to run a battery of tests specifically for her condition. Then we compared the results to your blood donations. There's no easy way for me to say this, Ms. Hutton, but it is not possible that Chelsea could be your biological daughter."

CASSIDY
New York, 1999

3

This is *all* wrong." Cassidy sighed in disgust. "We want the audience's *sympathy,* not their contempt." The filming of the upcoming special segment for *Up to the Minute* was not going well at all. She shot a look of disapproval at a cameraman perched on the edge of the steps leading to the Plaza hotel's Fifty-ninth Street entrance.

Producer of the nation's most-watched television newsmagazine, Cassidy English continued her pacing as she said in abject frustration, "Mrs. Kornberg is the victim of a shooting, for God's sake! Her husband and her daughter were shot and killed before her very eyes. She's not meeting Nancy Reagan and Carole Petrie for lunch."

Her exasperation was rising. Estelle Kornberg may *be* a wealthy widow, a society matron, but she couldn't look like one on television. Cass continued, "This woman is the *sole* survivor of a madman's random act of violence. So why is she primped and propped to look like she's being photographed for *W* or the Style section of the Sunday *New York Times?* That designer suit is all wrong—the handbag, the shoes—wrong, wrong, wrong! Hell, even her hair, it's teased within an inch of its life! This is unbelievable! Not at all what we discussed in our production meetings for this show." Cassidy waved her outspread arms from side to side in an effort to encompass the elaborate surroundings. "The Plaza hotel, the Chanel suit—all of this is so wrong!"

Other members of the crew, as well as the doorman at the Plaza, watched in motionless surprise as the young producer with the six-figure salary marched across the street, dodging a hansom cab, and approached Mrs. Kornberg. The middle-aged woman was still standing as though she were a mannequin, a phony smile pasted on her face.

Afraid to move, the woman asked through clenched teeth, "What do you want me to do, Ms. English?"

"Here. Put these on," Cassidy replied, handing the startled woman her own conservative black blazer, then pulling off her ballet flats as well. "Think Middle America, Mrs. Kornberg. The viewers need to see you as the survivor against all odds. They want to care about you, embrace you, feel your pain. They want to imagine what you're going through," she persisted. "You need to make them believe in how much you suffered because of the loss of your husband and daughter. They have to understand you were devastated!"

Cassidy paused to collect her thoughts, and then, more calmly, she said, "I realize this is your life we're talking about here, Mrs. Kornberg, but we have to make the TV audience care. They can't see you as just a rich lady who happened to hit a bump in the road."

Mrs. Kornberg slipped off her suit jacket and put Cassidy's blazer on over her silk blouse, then traded her trendy high heels for the slippers. The makeup artist and hairstylist rushed to her side and went to work, quickly undoing their too-fashionable handiwork.

Rudolpho Durban, the director of the piece, stared at his boss with perplexed admiration and dismay. Though they'd worked side by side for two years, and had been intimate for the last one, Rudolpho continued to find Cassidy a mystery. "Working closely with," "being intimate with"—these were not phrases that expressed Rudolpho's (or anyone else's either, he was certain) relationship with this dedicated, driven young woman.

Cassidy English was beautiful, intelligent, and, at thirty-three, one of the most acclaimed and respected producers in the business. Sure, the two of them went out occasionally—took in a movie, shared an intimate dinner at an outdoor bistro, even spent the night together on occasion—but that was as far as Cass would let him take it. Was it that he was an "underling"? She *was* his boss, of course. Maybe he was merely a convenient date. Nevertheless, from the start, he'd sensed that she feared, or was ambivalent about, committing to someone. But though he was hardly a romantic, Rudolpho craved her like a runner in the midst of the Ironman triathlon craves a sip of water. Cassidy had that effect on men.

Rudolpho watched as Cassidy stood beside him while Mrs. Kornberg was positioned for the next shot. Cass's slightly pensive expression held intrigue. Of course, her expression was often remote; secrets seemed to play across her face constantly. The only place Cass seemed comfortable, at ease, was on the set, directing actors, civilians, the camera crew, and production staff members. Everyone at the network credited Cassidy English with *Up to the Minute*'s consistently high ratings and four-year success. Last year's three Emmys only proved it again. In fact, it was Cassidy who had pulled the failing news show from the bottom of the ratings to number one in all markets in less than seven months.

The total transformation of Mrs. Kornberg from well-to-do New York society matron to victim of a horribly violent crime was complete in less than twenty minutes. Satisfied with the softer, more viewer-friendly look of her subject, Cass announced, "Great—now let's move all the equipment across the street to the park. Let's make this a real New York thing."

While some of the crew moaned and groaned, Rudolpho stood planted, a mischievous smile spread across his face. "Well, aren't you the opportunist," he exclaimed. "Taking this woman's story from one spot to another is a good touch, but it's a gamble. You know what happens to journalists who re-create facts to fit a story." His smile widened as she gestured impatiently for him to get moving.

"It's a gamble I'll take," she said as they hurried off to the trucks and cars that would transport the technical crew, the hair and makeup people, as well as Mrs. Kornberg and the reporter who was doing the interview to Sheep Meadow in the middle of Central Park.

"You're never afraid to go after what you feel is right—at least not when work is concerned," Rudolpho quipped wryly.

She caught his little dig and paused before they both approached the waiting car. "A great piece is what's right," she said finally, with a laugh that held a wisp of sadness in its loving mockery, a laugh that sounded for only a brief moment.

"How about dinner later?" he asked nervously. "You're stressed to the max. You could use a break."

Cass instantly nodded. "You're right, I could. But I'm afraid dinner's out of the question. I have much too much work to do tonight. The editing's complete on the teen pregnancy piece we shot last week. I'll need to see it before I can approve it."

Cassidy waved away the car, clearly having decided to walk to Sheep Meadow. Head held high as always, she wore power in her walk, her very demeanor. She was tall—at least five-seven—and her posture projected dignity. She claimed this was due to her faithful practice of Pilates, but Rudolpho believed that in another life she must have been royalty—an Egyptian princess perhaps. Her waist-length black hair, slightly curled at the ends, was shiny and smooth like China silk. Her sapphire-blue eyes and small, near-perfect features completed the look of a porcelain doll.

Over her shoulder, in her most confident voice, she yelled, "Hey! Are you coming or will I be shooting without my trusty right hand?"

His laugh was innocuous, in contrast to how his black eyes bore into her, daring and wishing Cass to respond to him in kind. He was fiercely determined to break down that invisible wall she'd built up around herself. He guessed that her Berlin Wall, as he'd named it, had been there since childhood, probably put in place after the death of her mother.

Yet for all her obvious success and ambition, he knew Cassidy to be insecure on some level. He couldn't put his finger on the origin of her insecurity, he just knew it existed. The shocking murder of her mother and her separation from her father while he was imprisoned had to be part of why Cassidy was so emotionally isolated. But was that all?

Rudolpho also surmised that she distrusted men despite the fact that she also craved their contact. Rudolpho smiled when he thought of their ferocious lovemaking. Clearly she was attracted to him, but despite Cassidy's lust, he sensed that she couldn't let go and trust him. It was almost as if she used her aggression to protect herself from him. Had she been hurt by a man earlier in her life? It was a twisted joke of the gods: a woman with Cassidy's face and body, the intelligence of a Rhodes scholar, and the courage of a ferocious lion—alone. No, it was all wrong. He stared at her as she walked into the park, imagining that she would always be showing him or anyone else her back, and he wondered: What do you keep so secret, Cassidy?

| | |

She was imagining the turbulent, unpredictable, crashing waves of the ocean, the cool warmth of the sea breeze, the balmy presence of palm tress, bent by decades of high winds. The sky was a majestic blue and she was all alone.

Lenny, the show's booker, or story scout, had mentioned the possibility of doing a piece in the South Pacific next month. It would be about the overwhelming exploitation of young boys and girls to feed the country's most thriving industry—sex tours. More specifically, tours for pedophiles. The story would be upsetting, dark and difficult—but it was important. Emmy Award caliber. And when it was wrapped up, Cassidy would steal a few days of solitude, not to mention a chance to experience a true-life escape to the South Seas, a Gauguin trip of her own.

Cassidy took a deep breath, erasing all traces of the ocean, the sea breeze, and swaying palm trees from her mind. She'd pick up her fantasy when the South Pacific piece was set on her calendar. Now she forced her eyes open and cast her gaze on the videotape of last week's segment. She realized the segment needed work and she couldn't sign off on it yet, but she couldn't focus on it—not tonight.

Swinging her legs off the couch, she got up and stood erect at the sixteen-by-thirty-foot window, taking in the magnificent, unbroken view of the venerable Museum of Natural History in all its Romanesque revival regalia. And just below the horizon rolled the verdant green carpet of Central Park. The view from the landmark 1909 Tudor Gothic revival building on Manhattan's Upper West Side was a tremendous perk. The show's parent company—Wometco—had awarded Cass the apartment rent-free a little over a year ago, just after the show won an Emmy for the third year in a row. The spacious two-bedroom duplex was hers for as long as she remained with the company. It was the only taste of luxury Cass allowed herself. While her tastes tended more toward the simple, she realized that, as producer of *Up to the Minute,* she had to maintain a certain image, at least give the appearance of living a certain lifestyle.

Cassidy let out a long sigh as she padded barefoot across the living-room floor to the airy country kitchen. She rarely used it as intended, but she did find an uncharacteristic comfort in just knowing she could "cook in" if she wanted to. Its walls were colored bright yellow and pink. The remains of tonight's Chinese takeout were still strewn across the counter, along with a pile of phone messages, some old bills, and, of course, the letter from James Renthrew, her father's longtime friend and trusted attorney. She picked up the creamy bond envelope, pulled out the notecard, and reread the handwritten request:

Dearest Cassidy,
    I am writing this note to inform you that your father is ill. It's his heart. His only wish is to see you once again.

Please find it in your heart to comply and, perhaps this time,
learn to forgive him.
          Sincerely,
          James

Shock? Disbelief? Anger? Yes, all three. She hadn't heard from the man she had called Uncle James in years. He had taken her to lunch once at least ten years ago, when she was at NYU. She hadn't heard from her father, not since he was released from prison. She hadn't seen him face-to-face since he was led away in handcuffs from the courtroom after being convicted of killing her mother. That image remained, a grainy pixel, always shady.

That part of her life was long buried, filed in her mind under the letter *T,* for trouble. Still, that notion did little to lessen the pain and grief—not to mention the guilt. Cassidy English was no longer ten-year-old Cassidy Turmaine, no longer Daddy's little princess.

She looked out across the darkened treetops of Central Park and was transported back more than twenty years. In one evening, her life had changed forever.

The castle other people called a mansion had become quiet, too quiet, and scary. Cassidy would shiver in her tightly made bed, letting only Nanny Rae comfort her. The middle-aged Irish woman would rub her back and tell her that Mommy had been sent to the angels. When Cassidy asked where Daddy was, Nanny Rae said he was being punished. "You should pray for your dad," she would add.

Cassidy would then get on her knees on the hardwood floor and pray, talk to God and ask him how Daddy could do such a thing, when he loved Mommy. Nothing made any sense.

But her prayers were always filled with clatter. She tried to concentrate on the conversation with God and all she could think of was the fights, the smashing crystal. And the sound of the party night that sent her mommy to heaven.

One day Nanny dressed her in the navy blue velveteen dress Daddy had always loved. It had white lace around the collar, just a little band that stood up around the neck, and matching lace that cuffed the sleeves. White tights, black ballet shoes—they even had a tiny string that Nanny tied into a bow. Helping Cassidy to dress, Nanny Rae kept talking to her, telling her that a man would be asking her questions about the night "of the party." Cassidy was not to worry, she should just tell the truth. And Uncle James would be sitting right next to her to help.

"And you'll come," Cassidy clearly remembered asking.

"I'll be right outside."

They were driven by Uncle James's driver—Flax, he was called—a black-haired man who always had the nicest way of talking—Nanny called it a brogue. Flax drove them to a big gray building. Is this an airport? Cassidy wanted to know, because they had to go through one of those machines that beeped when Daddy forgot to take his keys out of his pocket.

"No, darlin', this is a courthouse," Nanny told her.

Over the years, through therapists specializing in recovered memory and endless conversations with Nanny Rae, Cassidy tried to remember more. Through hypnosis, she remembered only one thing about her mother's murder: seeing gray wingtip shoes with red stuff—blood—on them, shoes that made crunching sounds on the floor as they went by her room. Everything else was lost to her.

How odd, one therapist said, that she could remember that one detail of her mother's murder but nothing of the deposition. Eventually she had to put *it* behind her without knowing exactly what *it* was—only that her deposition had been the clincher that had sent Roger off to jail. Manslaughter, Cassidy would learn later.

She had not seen her father face-to-face again. Ultimately—almost twelve years later—Roger had been acquitted on a retrial. Blood samples from the scene were analyzed using DNA testing procedures not even developed at the time of the original trial and were admitted into evidence. One sample, it turned out, matched neither Roger's nor Lana's DNA. It also came out that faint bloody fingerprints, found across the room from where Lana's body lay, had not been introduced into evidence during the first trial. Because the prints were too smeared to get an identifiable reading, they'd been ignored by a novice criminologist who had thought someone investigating the murder had made them since they were so far from the body. Though the new evidence didn't point at another killer, the second jury found too much reasonable doubt to pin Lana Turmaine's murder on her husband.

For many years, his freedom meant little to Cassidy.

| | |

Roger had been out of jail for eleven years—long enough to make a comeback in films and write a book that declared his innocence.

Not once during this time had Roger reached out for Cassidy. She ached for her father's love, her father's charmed presence, the magic that surrounded him in her memory—fairy dust, she'd learned to call it. But she never blamed him. Whatever she had said in that courtroom had sent her father to jail, and when her father was released, he'd made it abundantly clear that he wanted no further contact with her. James Renthrew was the only one who'd faced her, the one who had explained it to Cassidy, saying: "Your father is deeply shamed, and feels that he would not be able to look you in the eye."

At the time, Cassidy felt sorry for her father and accepted James's explanation. But now she was just angry and bitter. What about *her* feelings? What about his duty to her? What about the princess he had left behind?

After her father went to prison, "home" for Cassidy was Uncle Jeff and Aunt Bev's two-story ranch in the Valley, far from the glamour of Whispering Winds.

Sister and brother, whose age difference already precluded much closeness, grew further apart. Jonathan had been sent away to boarding school, spending only one weekend a month at home. Had she been older, Cassidy realized early in therapy, she would have been sent away, too.

Uncle Jeff was no role model for Jonathan. Although he called himself an accountant, he did not seem to work much. Aunt Beverly was a stargazer, the typical middle-class woman who had "gone Hollywood." She only wanted to get invited to the right parties, and she was not above using her relationship to the Turmaines, twisting her loyalties, to fit the crowd. Cassidy had overheard Beverly damn her father as a murderer one night and defend him the next at another gathering. Beverly had neither time nor patience for her niece and nephew. She had made that very clear on many occasions.

Uncle Jeff's "part," Cass found out, involved neither concern nor compassion for either his brother's well-being or that of his niece and nephew. Her aunt and uncle's compassion was derived from a check—a hefty sum, delivered the first of every month to care for Cassie and Jonathan. That is, if you could call it "care." In truth, Jeff and Bev were little more than baby-sitters. However, James Renthrew had remained a constant figure in both Cassidy's and Jonathan's lives. If there was a drama production at school, a moving-up ceremony at the end of the year, or even a parent-teacher conference, James served as Roger's stand-in. And he kept his surrogate role even after Roger's acquittal.

James had assured her that his years in prison had hardened her father, made him into a different man. Still, Cassidy had longed for the hero she remembered, and she blocked out the truths, the accusations against him, perhaps even her own memories about the murder and its aftermath.

But Roger never made a reappearance in her life. No cards, calls, or letters. What she knew of his life, she learned from news stories. He refused her requests to visit as she got older. He returned her letters unopened.

And now when she thought she had control of the demons from her past, her father, the high and mighty renowned feature-film director turned producer then studio head, had come back to haunt her. Although the note was signed by James, the message, of course, came from Father. Clearly, his pride, not to mention his ego, wouldn't allow him to grovel—certainly not for her approval or forgiveness.

| | |

Roger Turmaine was passionate about his profession. He was renowned for his eye for detail and ability to bring together top actors, writers, designers, and cinematographers to get blockbuster feature films to the screen. *Tamed*—his last film with Lana—was still an international cult favorite. This drive to create quality feature films à la Lumet and Coppola with a splash of Hitchcock flair had kept him vibrant, even while in prison, where he devoted himself to scripting the movie he would release two years after prison. *What She Knew*—his apologia—was a thinly disguised story of what Turmaine wanted to believe had happened on that fateful night, with all the glamour of a heroine who was a Hollywood legend; the voyeuristic attraction of her adultery, her drug addiction, the inside look at celebrities—how they really lived and partied, the still-unresolved mystery of who had really killed Lana that night.

The success of *What She Knew* wiped out all of the distrust and any revulsion the public might have felt toward the filmmaker. Roger Turmaine had regained his magic. He was no longer infamous; he was famous. Once again he had the respect of his peers and the attention of moviegoers.

| | |

Cassidy thought about the turn of events that had led her to this point in her life. How ironic that despite her own resistance—her inner protests—she had always gravitated toward a career in the film industry, just like her parents.

Originally she'd planned to be an artist. Creative, yes, but definitely not moviemaking.

Naively she thought she could shed her connections to her family scandal if no one knew who she was. Hence the name English. She had chosen it for herself when she was thirteen, though she wasn't able to make it hers legally until she turned eighteen.

Furthering her drive for independence, Cassidy had moved all the way across the country, as far from the movie business as possible, and enrolled in the School of Fine Arts in New York. In her sophomore year, she briefly dated a much older drama professor who, after she innocently confided her heritage, relentlessly pressured Cassidy into acting. He eventually pushed her in front of the camera as the lead in a low-budget independent film—a love story, no less. Cassidy was not so naive as to be unaware of his hopes to use her Turmaine name as a bridge to the big time. She was, however, curious to learn whether or not she had her mother's acting talent. The film's heroine was an icon, rather like the doomed party girl Edie Sedgwick, always where the action was, but an isolated figure who pulled those around her down.

When Cassidy viewed the finished product, she was embarrassed—horrified—at what she saw: an awkward young woman trying too hard to act natural. She looked uncomfortable and was unconvincing.

But she *had* inherited Lana and Roger Turmaine's passion for film. Cassidy's drive could only be genetic. She was a product of their union as much as of their sad and ugly dissolution. Ironically, her intense ambition was the only thing she and Roger had in common.

Eventually Cassidy dropped out of the School of Fine Arts and devoted her time to going to hundreds of movies. She rented videos of her mother's old films and others her father directed. She supported herself with an assortment of menial jobs—waiting tables in a Greenwich Village bistro, passing out perfume samples at Macy's during the holidays, stretching canvases and cutting mats for a framer in Soho, and selling zeppole at street fairs.

Occasionally she would summon the nerve to contact her father, who by then was back in Hollywood, but he never returned her calls or responded to her letters. Cassidy marked time until she turned twenty-one, when she would inherit some money left in a trust to her by her mother.

As soon as that money was in her hand, Cassidy applied to and was accepted into NYU's film school and soon found that she not only loved film but could make wonderful things happen on film—from behind the camera. She attended classes at night. Meanwhile, she continued to work as a gofer anywhere she could get work, mostly for independent production companies contracted to produce commercials and documentaries.

Utterly fascinated by the art of filmmaking, she made her first documentary, *Letting Go,* in 1990 using the last of the money her mother had left in trust. Cassidy's style was imprinted on the documentary. It was super-realistic, bordering on film noir, taking the viewer "inside the belly of the beast" as it exposed the horrific story of one man's battle with AIDS. It won the Sundance award for Best Documentary, the East Hampton Film Festival's award for Best New Director, and was included in the New York Film Festival that year.

The success of *Letting Go* was followed by numerous job offers from a variety of production companies. Among them were a cushy executive position at Francis Ford Coppola's Zoetrope Studio and an opening as an assistant producer at *60 Minutes.*

Working for Coppola would bring Cass's wildest fantasy to life, but it would also require a move back to L.A., forcing an emotional reunion with the past she diligently reminded herself to forget. And so she opted to remain in New York, taking the position at *60 Minutes.* In less than two years she would be eagerly sought out by more than a half dozen top-rated programs.

Cassidy's move four years ago to *Up to the Minute* was by far her most rewarding and lucrative decision. Now here she was, hugging a letter to her chest, hoping miraculously for some guidance. Should she indulge her father his last wish? Should she risk the serenity that she had so carefully forged? Or should she toss the note in the garbage and pretend she hadn't read it? She gave it a moment's thought, then opted for the latter. After all, pretending was something she'd easily perfected. Making believe that her fairy-tale childhood hadn't come to an abrupt halt was a feat she'd taught herself to do very well.

After years of thrashing around in the messy closets of her mind and in the pristine offices of assorted Park Avenue therapists, Cassidy had realized it was easier just to close the doors. She would never forgive her father for abandoning her. She would never forget her mother for loving her.

With these two mottoes emblazoned on her psyche, it was amazing how easily the other pieces of her life had been sorted out.

As she worked to rein in her emotions, her thoughts were interrupted by the abrasive ring of the intercom. The sound slammed against her brain with such unexpected force that Cassidy felt thrown against a wall. Her shoulders tensed, then jerked, shrinking at the base of her neck as if she'd been suddenly shaken awake from a nightmare. There was no doubt who her visitor was.

The imbalance in their daytime partnership didn't apply at eleven P.M. At night the playing field was leveled.

"Cass." Rudolpho's comforting voice echoed over the call-box. She felt her heart slow down, her mind snapping back into full awareness. "Ring me up, Cass. We need to talk."

Uh-oh, talk—not a good word in this context. While Cass loved their physical relationship, Rudolpho wanted more. He wanted to relate, to bond—all those stupid words the world erroneously thought were used only on women. The worst word Rudolpho used was *commitment,* as in "Why can't you make one?" It drove her crazy. She would not talk tonight. "Actually, I was just getting into bed," she lied into the metal box. "Now isn't a good time. Maybe in the morning—at the office, before—"

He wouldn't let her finish. "Buzz me up, Cass." A pause, then: "I'm not leaving." His voice was shaky—a tone not unfamiliar to her. The cold hand of panic grabbed Cass's gut. She opened her mouth to protest, then realized it was no use. Rudolpho simply would not go away.

| | |

Soft moonlight filtered into the large though sparsely furnished bedroom, illuminating Rudolpho's peaceful form entangled in velour blankets and cotton sheets. Standing at the foot of the bed, Cass set a lingering gaze on him. He looked so still, so tranquil, his body so at ease. It was a far cry from their earlier lovemaking, which had been, as usual, fast and furious. She had never been more physically compatible with a man.

Invariably, their mutual hunger for the other's taste hurled them together. Then, without fail, as they basked in the afterglow of passion, Rudolpho would start to speak, asking questions, demanding answers—though she could offer none.

This was Cassidy's game. She set the rules. The man in question might *think* he had a chance at checkmating her, but it never happened that way. It had happened once; she let the guy be in control—no more. Never again.

Still studying Rudolpho's sleeping form, Cassidy quietly slipped into her plush terry robe, then walked from the room. Closing the door softly behind her, she wandered through the rooms of her home, as restless as a ghost in chains. Tonight she hated her apartment, which at one time had afforded her privacy and a tranquil existence. Now she hated its coldness, its protective shield from the outside world—from L.A. Tonight Cassidy despised its silence, which enveloped the walls and stretched through three thousand square feet of space, so still, she could hear the blood pumping through her head.

She found her way through the kitchen and unlocked the door to her private sanctuary. This room, her office, was dominated by the regal portrait of her mother commissioned by her father the year after he and Lana were married. Cass slipped into the high-backed desk chair and reached for the telephone to check her voice mail. Surprisingly it didn't amount to much: one call, no message, just a click, then a dial tone.

She wondered if her half brother, Jonathan, had been summoned to their father's bedside, too. Cassidy was aware that he had insinuated himself into their father's business. She'd seen pictures of them together in the trades. Knowing Jonathan, he was simply on standby, waiting with bated breath to get his hands on Roger's vast fortune. She hated thinking ill of her half brother, but the truth was, they had never been close. In fact, he, too, hadn't spoken to Cassidy in years.

Jonathan was seven when Cassidy was born. From the moment her memory began, she was aware of his hostility, even hatred, toward her. Her half brother's antagonism went deeper than the classic bitterness and jealousy that went on when a boy's father divorced his mother to marry someone "younger, thinner, prettier." Lana was all these things and more. And for Jonathan, Cassidy represented the final, undeniable split between Roger and his mother, socialite Betsy Vanderleer Turmaine.

But beyond that, Cassidy was the major factor standing between Jonathan and his father's wealth. Of course, it wasn't until Cass was older that she realized that Roger Turmaine would be worth millions of dollars when he died—much of it money from investments made when Lana was alive. But more than that, Cassidy guessed Jonathan resented and envied her, Cassidy's, success, a success she had earned independently of their father.

After a tumultuous adolescence and early, violent marriage, Jonathan had not achieved much on his own. He'd had a short-lived career as Roger's protégé, but now he was little more than a gatekeeper at Desmond Films.

Three years after Cass left California, Jonathan met a wealthy woman twice his age, fell in love, married, and moved to Chicago. Several times Cass tried to contact him, first by mail, and then, when he didn't reply, by telephone. That conversation was a mystery to her then, and it remained so now.

"Don't contact me anymore, Cassidy," Jonathan had said harshly.

"But—" she protested.

"No, stop. I have reasons."

"What reasons?" she persisted. Before he could say anything, she added, "If you don't tell me now, I'll show up, I'll harass you if I have to. Jonathan, we were kids together. What's wrong? Tell me and I'll make it up to you."

"You can't. I mean, it's not you. . . ."

"What, then?"

"It's Father," Jonathan sighed, with apparent resignation. "He says I should have no further contact with you."

"Jonathan—why? That's crazy," was all a stunned Cassidy could say.

"It's better this way."

Shocked and devastated, Cassidy backed away. She couldn't handle any more rejection.

Two years later Cassidy was browsing through *Town & Country* magazine, and there was Jonathan standing beside dear old Dad, looking so at ease. These days there were few magazines she could browse through and not see a picture of the two of them together.

Funny, but as she sat at her desk, remembering, she began to see analogies between the young children they once were and the adults they had become. Both she and Jonathan had been scared—terrified beyond belief. Was it really their fear that had not only blown apart the entire Turmaine family, but that, even now, still kept them tied to each other despite being separated by time and distance?

At that moment, the awful pain, ever present in her heart, seemed to lessen, and with a clear mind-set, she made her decision.

Cass exited the office, then quietly, so as not to wake Rudolpho, made her way across the kitchen. She dug through the garbage for the note from James, and when she found it, she cleaned away all traces of tea leaves and Broccoli and Tofu in Garlic Sauce with a dishcloth. Once again she clutched the paper tightly in her hand, so tightly it bore the impression of her fingers.

She returned to her office, ready to place a call to James. It was still early on the Coast. Dredging up old memories caused Cass pain. She looked toward her mother's portrait, at the angelic yet somewhat defiant pout on her mother's beautiful lips. Cassidy was ready to see her father, even if he was using the heart attack as a ruse. Her father wouldn't have been able to rehabilitate his career if he weren't a master manipulator. But Cassidy was confident and centered enough to know he couldn't throw her off balance—no one could.

Yes. She would go. She would grant her father his wish and, at the same time, settle some unresolved matters between them. Then she would be free.

The Funky Monkey, a trendy dance club tucked into the Hollywood Hills, was busy for a Thursday night, but the press of the crowd and the usual blare of the hip-hop music was white noise to Chelsea Hutton. From her perch at the bar, she scanned the dance floor crowd—music video directors, film executives, models, starlets, and bored Beverly Hills housewives. The usual. The dimly lit room made the writhing bodies seem unreal, shadows against a black backdrop. Chelsea felt caught between two worlds.

She sipped the vodka martini the bartender had placed before her. She couldn't remember whether it was her third or her fourth. As her late husband, Edward Paul Kincaid III, had always said, for a woman, she could sure hold her liquor. Chelsea knew her meds helped keep the alcohol at bay, but she had never shared that fact with Edward. He wouldn't have understood.

The one thing Edward did understand was that she had needed him. He was twenty years older than she, dull and obsessively jealous. Logically, she might have felt a sense of relief—the loss of a huge burden—at his death. But she really missed having the dinosaur around. If nothing else, she would never forget the way he rescued her from the nowhere life of a sometime model/occasional actress and sometime cruise-ship hostess. She'd managed to leave the roach-infested barrio of East L.A., but by the time she met Edward, hadn't gotten any further than a cookie-cutter box of an apartment in West Hollywood, off Santa Monica Boulevard.

Anyone else would have been satisfied, living comfortably on what she made on her eclectic jobs, but not Chelsea. She wanted more. Much more. She truly believed that all she needed was a chance—access to the bright lights of Hollywood—and she could make it on her own.

Edward became her ticket from nowhere. He gave her access, but he also taught her how to live beyond her means.

They met on a luxury liner, *The Ice Princess,* that traveled from California up to and around the Bering Strait, through the armpit of Alaska. That's what Edward had called it. She was a hostess; he, a passenger, a recent widower who hardly seemed to be grieving. It was not hard for Chelsea to clinch him. After two marvelous weeks on the Pacific, with Edward promising his undying love just to be in Chelsea's company, they returned to Los Angeles.

Chelsea could not believe the luxury Edward was accustomed to, from his Bel Air mansion to his cream-colored Bentley to his membership at the the country club. Chelsea was transported into a life she'd never imagined: old Los Angeles money. Very old.

Edward took her in, showered her with expensive gifts, and showed her his world. She took to it like a natural. As one of his many enterprises, Edward was an owner of one of the biggest modeling agencies in the country. He immediately introduced her to the major photographers in Los Angeles and New York and put together an incredible portfolio for her. Before long, Chelsea was in front of the cameras—a new face, sexy and seductive. On the runways she was elegant and graceful. And each photo shoot became another stepping stone toward the big screen.

Unfortunately, Chelsea didn't know that even the rich can live a life of smoke and mirrors.

When Edward had a stroke and died, she learned quickly that he owned only a very small piece of the modeling agency, and that the bulk of his lifestyle had been fueled by the recent sale of his life insurance policy. He had run through his "old money" years ago. Upon his death three months ago, the bank had reclaimed the mansion, which ended up being mortgaged to the hilt. Once again, Chelsea found herself on her own and nearly destitute. The only concrete evidence of her ten-year marriage to Edward was their daughter, Isabella.

Chelsea scanned the bar and dance floor with half-closed eyes. The squat man with the heavy accent was still watching her, hoping she'd change her mind and accept his offer of a drink, perhaps a dance. She pretended not to notice his deep-set, obsidian brown eyes, and instead she searched desperately for Joe, Tom, perhaps Mike. She picked up her cocktail glass, toyed with it for a minute, then anxiously slugged back the rest of her drink.

She was definitely out of her element. Chelsea Hutton had socialite written all over her, from the perfectly coifed hair and the expensive Armani suit, right down to her thousand-dollar Manolo Blahnik pumps. But walking through the brass doors of the Funky Monkey meant shedding her perfect image. She liked spice and variety and could fit in anywhere she might find it—and she'd always had a weakness for a good-looking man.

"See any lucky candidates?" It was Tina, a B-actress and not a very good one, who invariably showed up wherever Chelsea landed, usually the Funky Monkey. Tina was a hanger-on, the worst kind of wanna-be, and Chelsea wondered how it was the tired blonde always knew where to find her.

Not the one I want, she thought, but instead she said, "Not tonight, I'm afraid." She was careful not to slur her words as she wiggled off the bar stool. She reached into her purse, pulled out a fifty-dollar bill, and left the usual hefty tip. A lady never drinks enough to lose her manners. Edward taught her that.

Hot, drunk, and discouraged, Chelsea stepped out of the side exit of the club into an alley the valet used to park cars when the front lot became too congested.

That's when she spotted him, leaning on the hood of his 2000 S Class Mercedes. He smiled.

When he looked at her this way, there wasn't much she wouldn't do for him.

During the last year of his life, Edward had been withdrawn. Isabella had been her only company. Chelsea had taken to trying to keep busy, sometimes even wrangling invitations to A-list parties on studio lots where she had a few minor but not altogether forgettable parts. She was looking for someone, something. She didn't know what that something was until the man with the unspeaking eyes and drop-dead smile came along.

As she approached his car, Chelsea could already feel his lips on hers, his soft hands, manicured fingers roaming her entire body.

"Get in," he said. She needed nothing more.

"When did you get into town?"

"This morning," he replied as he opened the passenger-side door.

"How did you know I'd be here?" She spoke barely above a whisper, fighting hard to steady her speech.

"You're a creature of habit. It wasn't hard to figure out." He leaned against the vehicle, his eyes tracking hers as she moved long, bronze, naked legs, one at a time, into the car. She smiled; the anticipation was hotter than the actual sex, she'd always thought.

As she fell into the deep pocket of the Mercedes's front seat, Chelsea's eyes fell on the *L.A. Times* on the dashboard. The headline read: WEALTHY CONTROVERSIAL STUDIO HEAD SUFFERS HEART ATTACK. Below it was a black-and-white photo of Roger Turmaine the last time he'd been seen out in public, just two weeks earlier.

A frisson of electricty ran through her body.

"What's wrong, Chelsea?" The man's voice expressed concern.

She didn't answer. Her heart pounded in an erratic rhythm and she began gasping for air.

5

Jonathan Turmaine shifted his attention from the monotonous drone of CNN to the voice on his answering machine. He hadn't even heard it ring.

"Jonathan, it's James. Roger doesn't want anyone to see him in the hospital. He scribbled a note asking me to contact you and Cassidy. He wants you both to convene at his house. Be there Monday."

The message clicked off. Jonathan turned back to the television.

Almost as if it were scripted, CNN announced that his father was in the hospital. The reporter spoke over a montage of clips—the wrought-iron gates at Whispering Winds, then his father with his late stepmother, Lana, followed by shots of Roger coming out of the courthouse with James, Roger on the set of some movie, entering the Academy Awards with a stunning redhead on his arm, the standard Great Celebrity treatment. "Tonight the film industry prays for the recovery of one of their great leaders, Roger Turmaine, who reportedly suffered a heart attack early Tuesday after his morning swim. He was found at poolside by his housekeeper, Rae O'Dwyer. A spokesman for Turmaine's production company, Desmond Films, said that Mr. Turmaine is in guarded condition at Cedars-Sinai Hospital."

Jonathan tuned out the narrative on the television. How could he be home by Monday if he's that sick? Of course, he knew his father better than the best doctors at Cedars-Sinai did, certainly better than any heart surgeon. If Roger Turmaine wanted to see his son and daughter at home on Monday, then by God, he'd be there.

Jonathan sat, propped up on the couch, his eyes glued to the television, intent on the shifting images as the memories played out in his head.

||||

He was sixteen years old, and their loud, angry voices had begun to wake him in the middle of the night with regularity. All was not well in the magic kingdom that his father had built for his lovely bride. Jonathan would creep along the upstairs hall to listen. His father's rage seemed to know no bounds, touching even his beloved Lana.

There they were at the Academy Awards, Lana and Roger at the podium. Lana had won Best Actress for Child of Mercy. *Roger held Lana around the waist in the same way that Lana gripped her gold statue—tightly, possessively. Jonathan remembered that night vividly. He'd been in the audience.*

||||

CNN jumped forward in time, showing footage of Roger at a charity benefit seated between the governor and some other politician. "Roger Turmaine is a major contributor to the Democratic Party as well as a personal friend of many of the country's most noteworthy politicians." The images on the screen shifted again, to a series of charity events hosted by various luminaries of the entertainment industry: Roger with Bruce Willis and Demi Moore at an AIDS benefit; with Alec Baldwin and Kim Bassinger for animal rights, and then with Arnold Schwarzenegger to raise money at a celebrity golf tournament for juvenile diabetes. "The legendary studio head is equally generous with various charities and is rumored to be one of the country's biggest philanthropists, though any donations he has made remain anonymous."

The commentator continued, "The question in the minds of everyone in the entertainment industry is who will take over Roger Turmaine's position as head of Desmond Films, a subsidiary of Colossal Studio. Turmaine has worked occasionally with his son, Jonathan, who seems to be waiting eagerly in the wings. Industry insiders, however, wonder if he can handle the responsibility of a billion-dollar-grossing production company. In the past, Jonathan Turmaine was associated with Hollywood's bad boys, the likes of Charlie Sheen, Christian Slater, and Robert Downey Jr., and has been known to have problems with prescription drugs, so his leadership is doubtful. Turmaine's daughter is Cassidy English, the Emmy-winning producer of the television newsmagazine *Up to the Minute*. While Turmaine and his daughter have been estranged for many years, she is also in the running, say some Hollywood insiders. At stake, industry sources say, is who is most capable of dealing with studio head Jack Cavelli. Cavelli, of course, isn't talking. If Turmaine dies, there's going to be a storm at Desmond. And if he lives, anything is possible."

The talking head shifted his eyes to a different camera.

Jonathan steeled his eyes toward the television. Jonathan would take over. There were no other options. Ties to Cassidy had been severed years ago. Eerily, he heard James's voice: "requesting that you *both . . .*"

She was coming back.

But Jonathan was Roger's rightful heir. Cass was—had always been—an outsider. Jonathan *had* made sure of that, hadn't he?

| | |

A year after his father began his jail sentence, Jonathan, then eighteen, was arrested for possession of cocaine and a cache of prescription drugs, and was expelled from the posh boarding school he'd been attending. Caught red-handed, he had little choice but to plead out and, as Uncle Jeff had said, put himself at the mercy of the court. Jonathan wasn't aware of what went on behind the scenes, but something *must* have. Despite the quantity of drugs involved, the court ordered him into rehab, citing the fact that this was his first offense and there were "extenuating circumstances"—namely, his father's conviction in the murder of his stepmom. Jonathan took advantage of the court's leniency and demanded that he be sent to the best facility his father's money could buy. But when Uncle Jeff notified his father in prison, Roger's response was, "He got himself into trouble; it's up to him to get himself out. I won't pay. Besides, I know the statistics. It'll be money wasted. That boy'll never amount to anything."

Well, Roger had been right on one account: Only three percent of addicts who enter rehab remained clean. Despite the odds against him, Jonathan managed not only to get the studio to pay his way, but to get through the program at Hazelden. That's where he met Barbara, and they married soon after. The heir to a pharmaceutical fortune—how perfect.

But like most of Jonathan's plans, his perfect marriage didn't work, either. Barbara divorced him after two years, when she discovered that he had been pilfering money from her bank accounts. Head hanging, Jonathan returned to Los Angeles and begged his father, who had recently been acquitted on retrial, for a position at Desmond Films.

That's when Jonathan pointedly told Roger that his beloved Cassidy had changed her name to English.

Jonathan had wormed his way into his father's world. He was there as his father reclaimed his fortune and his position of power as head of Desmond. Admittedly, Jonathan did little more than take notes in meetings and deliver messages for his father, but he was in. And now it was time for him to assume the mantle. No one was going to stop him.

| | |

Headlights illuminated the fog. Through the banks in his mind, he saw her running toward the columned porch of the mansion. Arms and legs pumping, she took the front steps two at a time. She was screaming but he couldn't hear her, for the wind whipped the cries from her lips. Silence prevailed and time was stilled.

The night played out in slow motion, like an old movie. She came alive each night in his dreams, an angel, an apparition. The golden hair. Dressed in a long white gown, with swirls of snowy, silky fabric floating gracefully about her perfectly shaped body. The look of pity on her face, then the sound of her laughter as she taunted him with rejection. But all of it paled in comparison to the horror he saw in her eyes just moments before she knew she was going to die. And it was that moment that simply delighted him.

He tipped a flask to his mouth, pocketed it, then waited. His heart pounded up into his throat.

He tried to put Lana out of his mind. And at times he even managed a full night's sleep, free from the haunting nightmares of her. But alas, she was stronger than he. She always prevailed.

There was a fine line between love and hate. Which was it he had felt for her? He could never be sure. And still, more than twenty years later, he felt the pain, the stings of humiliation. And now with Cassidy coming back, the nightmares haunted him even awake. He couldn't function—couldn't go on with his daily life.

He mopped the beads of sweat from his brow with a handkerchief and took another swig from the flask, then took in a deep, cleansing breath. He held it, then released it, exhaling in satisfaction.

Even now he imagined Lana's perfume, still permeating the air. Her very essence was enough to drive him mad with desire, and rage. A passionate mixture with deadly results.

As he climbed each step, he heard the music begin in his head, then grow louder and louder, over and over. Then the laughter again; last the shame. He inhaled deeply once more, closed his eyes, and fists clenched at his sides, he whispered, "Lana, I won't let you destroy me. There will be no more games. I will not be the loser. You can no longer choose."

But he'd never considered that even after he killed her, Lana would continue to consume him.

Cassidy sat for a while at the entrance to the estate, studying the place where dreams were born but where heartache often won. From this vantage point, Hollywood seemed a mere backdrop to Whispering Winds—exactly as Roger had ordered it designed.

Cassidy had always wondered why Lana did not put her mark on the house or even the grounds. Now, returning after so many years away, she realized why. The valley that was the heart of Hollywood was like a basin at the foot of a magic mountain. The mountain, all desert and palm trees, had merely sprouted the white letters that rose above, screaming out *Hollywood* since 1923.

Down below, all looked perfect: the houses, the streets, the palm trees. Not necessarily as God made them, of course, but never mind; here the faces were wrinkle free, the skin taut. Clothing, it went without saying, was the fashion of the moment.

But Cassidy wondered, What did the mountain see? Lilliputians swarming on four or five blocks—preferred blocks—then commuting on horrifying mazes of cement arteries all leading to or from the studios. The people were driving brightly colored cars, smiling, laughing under a perfect blue sky, living perfectly staged and scripted lives. The mountains just lay back against a sky once azure, but now, who knows? It depended on the day. The desert sky at night was almost heaven on the mountain, while in the basin the lights housed the young, and not-so-young, stretching toward stardom, trying desperately to hold on to the fleeting measure of their worth. Some merely skirted along the lights of fame. Some made it, some died, burned out by the lights of fame, by all the perfection.

And all the while, the mountain, so impervious—detached— looked on.

And "detached" was key—the first Turmaine had very cleverly captured the essence of perfect detachment. Whispering Winds was set far back in Bel Air—no corner lot here. One had to work to get to see the Turmaine shrine, climb up and up and around other, lesser, houses to find a mansion that bathed in the aura of the mountain and its desert and palm trees and woods.

Cassidy realized this ingenious aspect of the estate, images in her mind flashing from the past to the present, back and forth. Reality against fantasy, and back.

From the car, she could see the light through the front window of her father's study, nearly hidden by the dense shrubbery that had grown over it in the years since Lana died.

Despite the seventy-degree temperature, Cassidy felt cold. A chill rushed through her body. What *should* she feel? What would someone else in her position feel? Cassidy searched herself but felt no reaction other than fatigue, tainted by anxiety—just enough to feel unpleasant, uncomfortable.

The light in the master bedroom flashed on, illuminating the entire second story. A blinding brightness beckoning her to come inside. She was drawn momentarily to the warmth of the glow inviting her in like a moth to a flame.

It was here that it happened. The tragedy that took her mother from her and changed her life forever. Could she ever look past it? Would she ever forget Lana's beautiful form sprawled out on the oatmeal-colored carpet, surrounded by blood?

Cassidy squeezed her eyes closed, warding off the horror, praying that the film would not roll through her mind's eye. Still the pictures, like crime photos, flashed into consciousness. She'd found the photos themselves years later—on microfilm in the NYU research library. Lana, lying naked on the blood-splattered carpet; the walls grotesquely smeared with handprints as her mother attempted to flee her killer; bloody bedding . . . horror.

Bits and pieces of memory intruded on her like charred ash from a burning building. Through the years Cassidy had had many dreams of being a small child again in this house, only to awaken to her own screams of fear and loss.

Her whole body shook; her heart began pounding erratically, skipping beats. She gasped for air. Cassidy recognized the all-too-familiar symptoms of her anxiety mounting and getting the best of her. Breathe in; breathe out. She kept her eyes closed and forcefully replaced the horrible mental pictures with an image of a great white horse, running free across some meadow, in a place that was very green. One big, deep breath. She'd be all right.

| | |

Cass was greeted at the door by a familiar face, Nanny Rae—just Rae now. She and Rae had been in touch on and off for several years, but distance had kept them apart—distance, and Roger Turmaine. Rae's once-glistening black hair was now mostly gray-white; her once-slender form, now round, looked nothing like Cassidy remembered. Only her eyes looked familiar—still sparkling blue.

"Dear child—look at you. Even more beautiful than I imagined." The hint of Irish brogue still resonated in Rae's speech. The older woman pulled Cassidy toward her, into her deep bosom. Rae squeezed her tight, her protective embrace so familiar to Cassidy. A scraped knee, a broken doll, a dispute with another child at school—Nanny Rae had always made everything better, with a batch of her homemade chocolate-chip cookies, a glass of warm milk, and one of her warm bear hugs.

This moment with Rae made her feel safe and secure, but Cassidy reminded herself that the feeling would not last. Once she got past Rae, walked the vast hall, and began to peruse the rooms—all of which held so many memories, some good, most bad—she knew the trembling and uneasiness she'd experienced earlier would return. She stood numbly in the entryway until Rae pulled her inside.

"But my bags?"

"Don't worry about them. We'll get someone to bring them in later."

Cassidy looked over her shoulder to her small rental car, parked outside the estate's ten-car garage. The dark-gray Lexus looked like a wayward sheep, separated from the herd. Inside the garage, Roger would no doubt have a new assortment of the vintage luxury cars he collected, which already included a Tucker and a DeLorean. Roger was singular—some might say excessive—in his interests.

Once inside the marble-tiled foyer, Cassidy looked nervously up the spiral staircase. "Is he . . . is my father . . . ?"

Rae squeezed her hand. "He's asleep, dear," she said, her tone comforting. "I'm afraid your reunion will have to wait till morning."

"And Jonathan?"

Rae's expression gave nothing away. "He arrived a few hours ago, then went out. He indicated he'd be back late."

Cass was torn between the desire to see him and relief that she had a stay of execution. It was hard enough to enter the house; confronting her half brother was an added weight she didn't know whether she could sustain.

"Would you like a cup of tea? I could fix us a warm brew of chamomile—two teaspoons of honey."

Cass relaxed into a smile for the first time since arriving. "You remember."

Rae put one hand on her hip, tilted her head to the side, and rolled her eyes. "How could I forget? I made it for you each night before bed."

Cass followed Rae past the hall, through the mudroom, and into the enormous country kitchen. She looked around, really seeing it for the first time, realizing how dreary and dark it all was: the cherry-wood cabinets, the matching island strewn with newspapers, no doubt of a financial nature—the *Wall Street Journal,* the *New York Times,* the *Los Angeles Times*—along with the entertainment industry trades—*Daily Variety* and the *Hollywood Reporter.* Cassidy had the very same subscriptions at home.

The antique table and Chippendale chairs where she had had breakfast each morning as a child now looked stark, barren. The gloominess, the darkness of it all suddenly made her want to cry. For the life of her, Cassidy had never understood why Rae came back to work for her father after the acquittal. It had stunned her, even made her angry when she heard the news from James. She'd felt betrayed. She'd even thought of cutting off their communication. Now she was glad she hadn't been rash, for the fact was, Rae was a link in the chain that led from Lana's death to the present. She was an essential piece in the Turmaine drama, as long as it played.

Rae must have picked up on her mood, for she grabbed Cass around the waist and led her toward the kitchen table. "We'll share a pot of tea and some good conversation. I want to hear all about New York."

| | |

Later that night, Cass lay awake staring up at the ceiling. Rae had first directed Cassidy to her childhood room, but Cass didn't have the stomach for that barrage of memories, so she asked if she could stay in the guest wing instead. Now she regretted being so far removed from the main part of the house.

Her emotions vacillated between worry and anger. How sick was Roger, really? Would he die without her getting a chance to see him, to say something after all these years? Would there never be closure?

Just as if she were ten again, she crept out of her room and down the hall. The door to her old bedroom was closed and she gently turned the knob. Feeling for the switch, she flipped on the light.

Her eyes darted around the room, studying every facet—every nook and cranny. The furniture, the lavish white draperies, even the custom-made silk moiré comforter were the same as when she'd left. It should have soothed her, the way it had when she was growing up; instead it only reminded her of pain—an ineffable sense of loss.

Her mother was everywhere she looked—in the white rocking chair where she'd sit, endlessly sifting through Cass's baby album; in the chair sitting in front of the antique vanity where she'd taught Cass how to apply lipstick; even at the foot of her white spool bed where she'd perch for their nightly "girl talks."

Cass took a slow, deep breath, then exhaled slowly.

I only have to get through the visit tomorrow. Father and I will talk, then I can go home. Aside from saying good-bye, there is nothing to keep me. I no longer belong here.

She turned toward the door and switched off the light.

As she walked quietly down the lonesome hallway, Cass once again felt chilled. She could hear the trees sway against the house, but the sounds and smog of Los Angeles down below felt far away.

Down the hall, she heard her father pacing around his bedroom. Well, at least he was well enough to move around. And there was no indication that a nurse or aide was present, so that answered one question: Roger wasn't dying—yet. So either he really had had a scare, which had prompted James's note, or . . . he had another agenda. Roger was full of ploys; Cass could count on that.

She returned to the guest wing and climbed back into bed, pulling the blankets up to her chin. Her body tried to soak up the warmth. She tossed and turned and finally fell into a fitful sleep and began to dream.

| | |

She sits anxiously in the stark examining room, watching with tear-filled eyes as a surgical nurse prepares an intravenous line.

The words spill out: "I'm . . . all alone . . . my baby . . . I waited . . . He promised."

"You're a tramp—how else could this have happened?" Beverly Turmaine stared angrily at Cassidy. "You're just like your mother, a whore! You have her ways. You'll pay for this!"

"Please, Aunt Bev, I didn't mean to . . ."

Moments later, Cass feels the doctor, his cold, probing hands inside of her. Twisting, scraping, and pulling. There are other voices in the room, but she can't make out the faces. Everything is a blur, moving in slow motion. The overhead light is blinding, and then she sees Tom beside her. His image disappears. And she is alone.

| | |

Was she awake? Still dreaming? Her head seemed welded to the pillow. She heard the footsteps in the hallway again, the sound amplified as they approached her room. Cass raised herself up on one elbow in anticipation of a knock at her door. The footsteps halted and then grew distant again, in retreat.

Then she heard the sharp slam of a door down the hall, and seconds later, the percussive blare of music. So familiar; so terrifying. And in her mind she sang the words: "Long ago, and oh so far away . . ."

| | |

He dropped her off near dawn in front of the Beverly Wilshire, where she was staying. Temporarily, Chelsea reminded herself. She'd have to get out of here soon. It was just a matter of time before the manager would ask for payment. But she had some calls to make.

From the moment Chelsea saw the newspaper headline, she was able to think of nothing else. She decided to blow off the "audition" her agent had scheduled with the casting director of a pilot and make some calls instead. Her thinking was twisted—a sure sign, her psychopharmacologist had warned her, to take it easy, take the tranqs along with the Depakote for a few days. This new mood stabilizer she was taking was easier on the organs, but it didn't seem to work as well on her mood swings as some of the other medicines she'd used.

When she started going into a high, she no longer felt human, but rather supernatural. She could paint pictures, write songs, devour novels, and work nonstop at the studio for days on end. She forgot to eat. Sleep was not a requirement. The higher her illness took her, the more her body and brain called out—*More, let's do more*—and drugs were but one of the things she indulged in. When a high took her away, she'd buy—it didn't matter what—jewelry, clothing, shoes, CDs. When she eventually crashed, she would have to drag her ass back to the stores to return everything. It was amazing that salespeople hadn't figured her out yet, but then, even when her soul was black, her heart on the floor, Chelsea knew how to manipulate.

She was particularly adept at maneuvering things her way when she was on a high cycle. Mostly she manipulated men. During those times, she couldn't get enough sex, often juggling two, maybe three men in a day. Sometimes she heard her mother's voice, shrilly reminding her that she was the child of the devil, that she was damned, possessed by evil. But most of the time she remained detached. She even kept a list of men she partied with—her slumming list. These were always younger men, of many backgrounds, each with his own style. Where they came from didn't matter. Sex was sex. Men were to be used.

Sometimes the sensations intensified beyond what she considered her usual mania. She'd begin to see things, hallucinate. She would make up entire scenarios that involved imaginary people. Sometimes these scenes included torture or murder, and she'd cower under her blanket, paralyzed by her own fantasy. Often to "protect herself," she'd break out of this mode and become violent—harming herself or even threatening strangers once she got out on the street. Inevitably she would go into a manic psychosis, needing help and medication to bring her back to reality.

Sometimes she'd end up in the emergency room on her way to the psych ward at Cedars-Sinai. When this happened, her on-and-off psychiatrist would be called in. Then he'd start up with the same conversation. "You must go on Lithonate or Haldol," he would say. The hip, new generation of mood stabilizers were less toxic than lithium. But Chelsea would not take the medication. If she lost her highs, she'd have nothing:

Life would be gray; she wouldn't be unique; her sexuality would diminish—no way.

Today she was on the high end of her emotional spectrum. The news about Turmaine screamed out to her—an invitation to finish the "conversation" she'd started a few months ago in his office at Desmond. She'd waited for a sign of when to put the rest of her plan into action, and this, indeed, was her sign: He was about to die. It was time to get her just deserts. No more B-movies for her. Especially now that Edward had left her with nothing but debt.

Hollywood, the land of dreams and promise, had, in reality, been her personal hell. Chelsea thought of all the ways in which she'd compromised her dignity since leaving Maria and East L.A. How full of plans that little girl had been, how big her dreams. Step by step, the ceaseless striving to be noticed, to have impact in this unreal town had worn her down like a file gnawing away at steel. When was it she'd become a whore—no, she corrected herself: a courtesan. She knew the difference between the two. Whores rarely got ahead. They spent their money on drugs and alcohol, they hung out in seedy nightclubs, and they belonged to greasy, greedy pimps. Courtesans slept with wealthy, influential men, used their money wisely, and played and lived by their own rules. Courtesans were not abused or degraded, and throughout the years, some had even changed the course of history.

Chelsea reasoned that her fate had been sealed the day she was born, the moment someone switched her, the daughter of Hollywood royalty, with the bastard baby of Maria Hutton. She had no choice; the years devoted to lowering herself had been preordained. But now the end was in sight.

Chelsea knew her own downfall, the insanity she'd been born with, ruled her, but she resisted—denying, lying about it, going from shrink to shrink, waiting for the one who would corroborate her belief that her emotional disorder fueled her talent. It was necessary for her to succeed. That doctor had not come along yet, but the chaos about to descend on Roger Turmaine's dynasty at Desmond offered, she was certain, one opportunity. She didn't know what exactly, but there was a chink in the Desmond/Turmaine wall and she was going to slip through it.

Chelsea went into the bedroom, locked the door, and took the newspaper clipping out of a manila envelope. She spread it out on the bed and studied it. She remembered the day she figured it all out. It was only a few months ago, right after her mother finally died. It had taken Maria months, years to die. She did not go suddenly like poor Edward. No, Maria had chosen to torture Chelsea right up until the last moment of her poor, miserable life, coughing her way through middle age, dying a slow, deliberate death from emphysema.

Father Tom said Mass for Maria and officiated at the burial ceremony that no one had cared to attend. All these years later, he still gave Chelsea the creeps.

Afterward, Chelsea returned to her mother's squalid apartment, where she had lived as a child. She wanted to simply burn the entire contents but thought better of it, hoping against hope that Maria had a life insurance policy buried in all the mounds of papers in her bedroom.

Chelsea didn't find an insurance policy. But she found something even better.

February 18, 1987

TO: *Lawrence Hibbel, Esq.*
REGARDING: *Maria Hutton vs. Lebanon Hospital*

Careful investigation of birth records for April 1966 indicate there is only one individual who could be the biological match for Chelsea Hutton. Her biological mother is Mrs. Lana Turmaine, now deceased.

Her attorney would like very much to settle this matter out of court.

Please contact my office as soon as possible.

Sincerely,
Charles Kaplan
Attorney for Lebanon Hospital

Chelsea leafed through the other correspondence and documents in the box. She came upon another letter from the hospital suggesting the case be settled for $750,000. As Chelsea dug deeper into her mother's files, she found more than twenty-five uncashed checks accompanied by letters from Turmaine's attorney, each memo indicating that the check was "for the child's welfare."

Chelsea flashed on her dismal childhood—the thrift-shop clothes and donated toys, her mother's vicious accusations. When pictures of

Cassidy Turmaine's sixth birthday party were in the newspaper, Chelsea was fascinated by the carousel right beside her house. Maria had taunted her mercilessly. "So, missy. You think you should have been invited just because you were born on the same day. Do you really think the little Fairy Princess of Hollywood would have anything to do with you?"

Three-quarters of a million dollars would have made life much easier for Chelsea.

Chelsea studied the letter from the hospital and began to put the pieces together. Hah—the checks were to shut her mother up. But these people hadn't counted on Maria Hutton's God—or her incredible capacity for denial.

Chelsea felt the adrenaline rush, knowing this would tip her body's balance despite the lithium. She sat back on her heels, papers strewn around her on the bed, and considered her options. Soon ideas were flitting through her brain. Hadn't Lana Turmaine been married to Roger Turmaine, the famous director? Obviously he would want this little mistake buried. And he was still alive.

Chelsea was transported to the fantasies of her youth, when she would try to wish away the poverty and squalor of her surroundings, when she imagined herself a little rich girl. And to think she was really Lana Turmaine's daughter!

Hours later, just before midnight, Chelsea fell asleep on Maria Hutton's decrepit bed, papers and checks strewn around her. And by the next evening, Chelsea had come up with a plan.

It was after hours—eight o'clock, to be exact—and Century City Towers, L.A.'s monolith, was nearly empty. Few of the office windows were lit. Chelsea could discern the random pattern the cleaning crew followed by noting which floors were lit versus which were dark. Roger Turmaine's business address was no secret. She entered the lobby and told the guard she had an appointment with Roger Turmaine. "I'm his daughter," she said, not giving her name. The guard spoke briefly into the security phone and Chelsea could hear Turmaine's exclamation. All of Hollywood knew Turmaine and his daughter were estranged.

Before the guard could stop her, Chelsea jumped into the elevator.

So far, so good. The Haldol she'd taken worked very quickly. Chelsea had started back on lithium, determined to stay level-headed and keep her manic mood swings at bay.

The Desmond Films logo, an elegant castle against a backdrop evoking ancestral Ireland, was painted in gold lettering on the heavy glass doors. As soon as Chelsea approached, a buzzer sounded and the security lock released. She opened the door and followed the corridor lights to the northwest corner of the floor.

"Cassidy!" Turmaine spoke sternly from his office before she reached it. "What—" Chelsea heard wheels of a chair quietly turning. She sensed Turmaine walking toward the door. Steeling herself, Chelsea closed her eyes and in that brief moment visualized all the things she wanted for herself.

"What the hell!"

Chelsea opened her eyes to find the man in all the newspaper clippings and magazine pieces facing her. He had removed his suit jacket; the pale pink-toned dress shirt was starched to perfection. His gray pants fit his slim waist and fell precisely in a very slight bell-bottom to the tips of his tasseled black loafers. There was no more time to study the man's clothing because his black eyes pulled hers to look at his. We look alike, she thought, but he left her no time to speak.

"Who are you?" he growled, taking a step toward her. Instinctively she stepped back.

"I'm your daughter." Chelsea fumbled with the clasp of her knock-off Chanel tote, where the papers to prove her paternity were stashed. But her hands were sweaty.

"Get out of here, young lady. I'll have you arrested, immediately," Turmaine said, already behind the reception desk, obviously about to call security. Chelsea reached down inside herself for every ounce of courage, strength, and drive she had.

"Please, listen to me." Strands of her honey-blond, straight, shoulder-length hair were glued to her face with perspiration.

Turmaine hesitated. Then, more calmly, he said, "Please take a seat while I make a call."

Chelsea watched as the powerful man sat down and spoke quietly and quickly into the telephone. She couldn't hear a word, yet she sat across from him not five feet away.

"I'm afraid I don't know your name," he said getting off the phone.

"I'm Chelsea Hutton," she said. She reached to shake his hand and he complied. Chelsea sat in a red buckskin chair with brass bolts, the soft fabric whispering against her stockings as she crossed one leg over the other.

"Ms. Hutton"—Turmaine's voice was calm, quiet—"my attorney is on his way. But I'd rather straighten this out between the two of us." He paused.

Chelsea thought how smooth he was—how persuasive, even charming. It was no wonder Lana fell for him. Lana Turmaine, her mother; Chelsea felt herself awash in heat at the very thought of it.

Roger leaned his elbows on the massive redwood desk as two phones rang at once. The fax machine spewed paper into its tray. "What I'm trying to say, Ms. Hutton, is just tell me what you want and let me see if I can make some sense of this unfortunate . . ." He fumbled for the right word. "This mishap."

"Would you like to answer that?" Chelsea nodded toward the one line that was still ringing. It was making her head throb. It was time for another tranquilizer and probably the last three capsules of today's lithium. For a moment she considered excusing herself but decided to stay with Turmaine right here, in this moment.

"No, they'll stop. Could you answer me?"

Chelsea forced herself to ignore the anxiety in her solar plexus, collecting like dirty water in a still, quiet pond. "I guess I'm here to meet you, first of all, and then to . . ." Chelsea noticed Turmaine's silver hair had no dark roots—there was nothing artificial about his handsome features. He was drop-dead gorgeous. Chelsea felt proud. Here was a man she'd always dreamed of as a father—rich, successful, handsome, famous—and now her dream had materialized. It was a miracle. Suddenly she heard Roger's words pierce her cascading thoughts.

"You are not my daughter. If you continue this charade, this obvious con game, I'll press charges."

"But you don't understand," Chelsea said as she pulled the papers from her bag. This time she extracted the file, but the man stood, pounded his fist on his desktop, and then waved his finger in her face.

"Who put you up to this?" She assumed that Roger, like all successful men, had made many enemies. It was within the realm of possibility that someone might try to set him up, extort from him, plant a scandal—any number of things.

"You don't understand—" Father, she wanted to add, but she checked herself. No, he wasn't ready to accept her yet. She'd have to help him arrive at the truth gradually.

Footsteps padded quickly down the gray carpeted corridor. A man around Roger's age pushed aside the lock of brown hair mixed with gray that had fallen over his eyes.

"What's going on here?"

"Thanks for coming so quickly. Ms. Hutton, this is my attorney, James Renthrew. James, maybe you could take over this . . . disaster."

"Take it easy, Roger," the lawyer interrupted. "Get a bottle of water from Miriam's refrigerator. I'll handle Ms. Hutton."

Chelsea recognized his name as the signer of the checks she had found. She cringed at the way this man said her name. His words felt like talons digging into her shoulder. The attorney was tall and handsome, in a dark, Mediterranean way. Still, unlike Roger, he did seem soft, approachable.

As Chelsea was trying to stay focused, Renthrew took a large check recorder from his briefcase. He scribbled a check and threw it at her. She saw it was for one hundred thousand dollars. He handed her a hand-written letter, which she recognized immediately as some form of agreement. Some legal deal to get rid of her.

A foggy feeling was beginning to take over her, and Chelsea realized she wasn't going to get anywhere this way. She ripped up the check and the letter. Standing, she leaned over the desk, allowing her salon-tanned, perfect apple-shaped breasts to spill from her blouse.

"Keep it, Mr. Attorney. I'm not going to be bought." And I'm not going away, she thought to herself.

"Just out of curiosity," she said pointedly, throwing her tote bag over her shoulder, a gesture that spoke of more confidence than she really felt, "if Roger Turmaine has nothing to hide, why would you try to pay me one hundred thousand dollars? And why did he—you—send seven hundred and fifty thousand to my mother?"

Not waiting for a response, knowing deep inside Turmaine would never listen to her, that she'd never know her father, Chelsea turned her back, posing just long enough to give the lawyer a good glimpse of her ass. "She never cashed them, you know."

Then she left, closing the heavy glass door with its gold-leafed logo behind her.

| | |

Freshly showered, and dressed in a simple black Valentino nightgown, Chelsea padded across the floor to the bathroom vanity and was putting the finishing touches to her appearance when there was a knock at the door. She checked her Rolex, a gift from Edward. At least *it* was real.

Chelsea answered the door, and to her surprise and shock, she came face-to-face with her ten-year-old daughter, Isabella, and her au pair, Jesse, a thirty-year-old Polish immigrant whom Chelsea had hired just days before she gave birth.

By the time Bella could speak, she was calling Jesse "Mama," yet rather than feeling compelled to defend her motherhood, Chelsea was comforted by the knowledge that her child was loved and could love. She was confident that, with Jesse's guidance, her daughter would grow to be a responsible, moral human being. Isabella represented the good in Chelsea—the part that yearned for what was right for her daughter. When Edward died, Chelsea had needed time to untangle the financial fiasco of his estate, something she could not do with her child underfoot. As a temporary solution, she had begged Jesse to take Isabella into her small but tidy house on the outskirts of Los Angeles, near the desert, where she continued to live now.

"Chelsea . . ." Jesse started to speak, but Isabella interrupted.

"Don't be mad, Mommy. This wasn't Jesse's idea. I wanted to come."

The child's wild mane of blond curls fell inches past her waist; her expressive green eyes were open wide with excitement. Bella was tall for her age and already showed early signs of puberty. She bore what Chelsea now knew was a strong resemblance to her grandmother, the great Lana Turmaine. She was *that* beautiful.

"You shouldn't have come without calling me first," Chelsea said sharply, not even trying to conceal the edge of anger in her voice. Bella's presence could be disastrous. It could destroy her carefully calculated plans for her long-awaited meeting with Cassidy English. Cassidy was Chelsea's only hope now, and their encounter simply could not wait.

It wasn't his three-thousand-dollar Italian suit or the obvious charisma. It wasn't even the remarkably handsome, finely chiseled features of his slightly weathered face, or the contrast of his glistening black hair, sprinkled ever so slightly with gray, against sharp emerald-green eyes. No, the present commotion at the Chateau Marmont was caused by the man's evident power.

He would be equally appealing out of the expensive armor he wore. He had no prestigious title, not even a political position, yet his power was incalculable, allowing him to influence presidents and CEOs around the globe. Few were beyond his reach, including Wall Street movers and shakers and Washington political titans.

But Jack Cavelli could wine, dine, and shine with the most pristine members of society as well. He'd educated himself in literature and the arts and had become a noted collector of modern paintings, purchasing the works of Rothko, Pollock, and de Kooning before the world at large had dubbed them Abstract Expressionists. He was fluent in six languages, including French, Spanish, Hebrew, German, and Arabic. And he played golf with the pros. He had been last year's champion in one of the big amateur tournaments at the Beverly Hills Country Club.

The list went on and on. As CEO and chief stockholder—he held seventy percent of the stock—of Colossal Studios, Cavelli was able to afford himself such amenities as a fleet of private jets, and homes across the country, including in Aspen, Newport, South Beach, Manhattan, and, of course, Malibu. The condo in Center City was owned by the studio. There was also a place in St. Bart's, a villa in Tuscany, and a collection of vintage cars. Indeed there was only one way to describe him: the sum of his parts.

Omniscient. Omnipresent. Omnipotent.

He was the most dangerous, influential, ruthless, clever, and ambitious person in Hollywood.

At forty-nine, he had never married. He believed passionately in the sanctity of marriage—that was only one of his incongruities. Jack was a complex person. He was much too politically correct to even consider the many women he "befriended" as items to be added to his list of luxuries, yet in a way he owned them also, because all of them had given their hearts—some their identities, even their souls—in the process of loving Jack Cavelli.

Like many successful Hollywood businessmen, Cavelli had first arrived on the West Coast with the hopes of becoming the next Marlon Brando. Twenty years ago he was an actor, a pretty-boy hunk, vying with the likes of Harrison Ford, James Caan, and Robert Redford for roles. Hyped by overeager handlers, he ended up with thirteen hit movies, the twenty million dollars he'd been paid for acting in them, plus two Oscars behind him by age twenty-nine.

But Cavelli was smart enough to quit in search of bigger and better things, which meant, of course, money.

In 1989 Desmond Films, once part of the top three moneymakers in Hollywood, released a string of expensive flops. In very little time, the company's stock careened into a downward spiral, bottoming out at a dollar a share, down from $5.50 at its peak. Roger Turmaine needed the cash. And fast. When Jack Cavelli called and said he'd like to help, Turmaine didn't hesitate.

In less than three years, Desmond Films was back on its feet, running neck and neck with Miramax and New Line Cinema. Today it was number one. And Jack Cavelli intended to keep it that way. Desmond was a boutique shop, one where, once Roger was out of the picture, Jack could have creative input, where he could see to it that talented people could make the kind of movies the giants wouldn't touch, with budgets most independent producers couldn't raise. It also couldn't hurt to write off a few of the Desmond losses.

Nothing would pull Desmond or Colossal from the top of the industry, certainly not the snot-nose heir of an aging, over-the-top, budget-breaking, old has-been like Roger Turmaine. Jonathan Turmaine would be kept on a short chain, so short he could only hurt himself.

| | |

The five men waited until Jack was seated before seating themselves at the large round table in the center of the private dining room. They moved like marionettes—pull the strings and their arms and legs flailed. The five men were the most powerful players at Colossal. They did not exactly *fear* Cavelli. Jack was supremely confident and had no need to surround himself with toadies and weaklings. The subordinate manner in which they behaved was a by-product of respect, admiration, and also instinct—the pack's behavior toward the Alpha male. If any employee, from division head to mail clerk, feared Cavelli, it was because he or she was not giving their all to Colossal. That was all Jack required.

Jack began every corporate meeting—even the annual stockholders' meetings—with the same spiel: Working at Colossal was a lifestyle, a journey. There was no room anywhere in the company for slackers, hacks, wanna-bes, sycophants, or grade-B talent. But not this time.

The men who surrounded Jack now were quiet because they knew momentous change was in the wind. And each division head wanted to listen carefully, to make sure he contributed his all, one hundred percent, to the next problem to be solved.

This group of high-powered businessmen saw their intelligent, gifted leader as an icon. They looked to Jack Cavelli for direction, in both their professional and personal lives, but for all the high standards he gave his staff to emulate, Jack Cavelli had a ruthless side. He had no tolerance for double-crossers and never forgot a slight.

Jack Cavelli had matured in a system that initially used gangsters to make Hollywood magic. Intuitively, he kept what worked about the old system and made it his own. Early in his tenure at the helm of Colossal, one of the top moneymaking actresses under contract, Holly Hayes, a red-haired beauty who handled dramatic roles as easily as comedy, forced the studio to let her out of a three-film contract on a technicality. Subsequent lawsuits, including a class-action suit on behalf of the trade unions that had lost jobs and money from the cancellation of a big-budget comedy that was already in production, cost the studio plenty.

This was not something Jack would let pass. He waited patiently for payback time. And it came in the form of Holly's daughter, Daryl. The young Ms. Hayes ran with other members of second- and third-generation Hollywood—Bridget Fonda, Drew Barrymore, the Sheen boys. As beautiful, and apparently as talented, as her mom, Daryl had signed a deal for a thirteen-week Colossal TV series, rumored to be another *Dawson's Creek*. But she never even made it past the pilot. After months of pre-publicity and taping, Jack ordered Daryl removed—on a technicality. She used drugs but was not a heavy hitter. Drugs or alcohol never interfered with her work. But one day after the pilot was in the can and the first episode of the show was being edited, Daryl was given a random urine check—standard boilerplate language in her contract allowed this. Daryl's urine was, as they say, "dirty."

Everyone knew the night before had been the star-studded wedding of rock superstar Oscar Grant and supermodel-actress Susan Starr. There had been drugs, sure—a little cocaine, maybe some pot—no big thing. Everyone also knew that Daryl Hayes's first and last shot at stardom was gone. Wiped out. Dead before she got started. This was Jack Cavelli's revenge. You could always count on it.

| | |

Once the five men were seated, the maître d' handed menus around, giving Jack the only one that included prices. Drink orders were taken—mineral water for everyone except Jack, who drank hot water with lemon.

"Gentlemen, we all know why we're here. There's no need to beat around the bush."

As always, Jack's voice was very low, causing each man to lean toward him and to concentrate only on him. When one executive pulled his chair closer to the table, the noise caused the others to glare at him.

"Roger is going down. He may recover, but he'll never be able to work again. The whole industry, myself included, will suffer a great loss when one of the greatest is forced out to pasture. Still, the company's best interests must be taken into account. We simply cannot allow Roger's son, Jonathan, to take over Desmond. It's just too big a risk for Colossal. Among other things, *Dangerous Intentions* is overbudget and behind schedule. We need a quick, risk-free plan to either save or scrap the film, and then make the moves to collapse Desmond into the larger corporate body. Without Roger, there will be no more need for Desmond Films. I'm sure we're all aware there is much more than that at stake."

The men nodded in agreement. The treasurer, Phil Brophy, enunciated his assent with a resounding "You got that right!"

"I intend to call a board meeting," Jack went on. "All issues will be addressed. In the end, Jonathan Turmaine will be rejected as his father's replacement. I'm sure there are many big names Roger could bring on board, though given such short notice and the critical state of production . . ."

Jack let the problem hang there, a football thrown in slow motion, mid-flight. Which man would catch the ball and run with it? The charismatic eyes touched each individual's face.

"Spielberg is great with these epics," said Joe E. Lavin, who was the newest on board. "Look at *The Last Emperor*. Maybe he's got a protégé."

"Not bad, Joe," Jack said. "Manny, get on that."

Emanuel Estevez, head of Creative Affairs, made a note in his palm-sized Wizard.

Jack took a sip from the diamond-patterned white-on-white china teacup. "One thing I know. *Dangerous Intentions* has got the right stuff. Everything about it screams awesome."

"Not to mention Oscar," Manny chimed in.

"Right. So let's do it."

A waiter stood just a few feet from the table. Jack nodded to him now.

"Jonathan Turmaine is history. I suggest he be kept off the set." And then his gaze shifted to the waiter. "Shall we eat? I'm famished."

| | |

Killing her when she rejected him was, to his shock, the one experience that had brought back that first great sexual high. Now knowing he could soon relive the experience kept him in a constant state of arousal.

Women had always been his forte, and his weakness. From the very first time, he had discovered a rapture, a sense of power he'd never before imagined.

He was only twelve, an orphan at a home in Brooklyn, when Liza had enticed him. Liza was a dazzling mix of Latino and Native American, and, at fifteen, older. She pulled him into the pantry off the kitchen of the orphanage. She asked if he wanted to touch her. He was afraid, but he let her place his hand to her breasts, which were surprisingly full. Then she guided him below her waist and beneath her skirt. He smiled. They both smiled. His body grew hard, and tense, and he followed Liza's lead. That's how it started, and it didn't stop until the nuns found out.

Then he was really out on his own. Sister Mary Elizabeth ordered him to pack his belongings—and leave. Before dinner. No other orphans' institution would take him, she said. He was too sinful, too immoral.

Before he left the asylum, his only home since he was six, Carrie, the Negro cook, gave him two peanut-butter sandwiches and a hard apple. "Don't let Sister know," she cautioned. Then she handed him two subway tokens and a fifty-cent piece. "You may need these."

He spent his first night out in the world sleeping on the A train and dodging the transit police.

Liza had set the standard for all those who came after. Every encounter after that only fueled his addiction and whetted his sexual appetite. It didn't take him very long to realize he needed money to please his extraordinary women. Only perfection could fill his insatiable appetite.

He found his way into a local Brooklyn gang doing odd jobs, mainly running numbers for the neighborhood big shot—Mickey Finns—perfecting his skill with each pickup and drop. By the time he was fourteen, he considered himself the best "runner" in the business. His services were in demand by every tough guy on the streets. Of course, control of his services was a "territorial thing." One man couldn't touch another man's protégé. To do so meant a street war, a demonstration of raw power. When an all-out battle was fought for his loyalty, he was proud. For the first time in his miserable, poverty-stricken life, people actually thought he was worth fighting over.

He went to the man who was left standing—the one who hadn't been assassinated. In six months, he was given his own piece of the action—Valentine's, a small bar on the Lower East Side of Manhattan. It had been a speakeasy during Prohibition.

He figured out he wasn't alone in his hunger and thirst for women, so he made Valentine's into a place where gentlemen could come and admire or touch the beautiful women—his women. Soon, important men—politicians, celebrities, players—came from all over the city to watch the girls he had handpicked.

Each time he witnessed one of his women turn on a man, he saw Liza. Like a junkie who can't forget his first fix, he was forever trying to get back the feeling of the one that turned him on, jump-started his habit. And like any addict, he would discover that he couldn't get back that feeling, no mat-

*ter how many women he had, or how often. The more women he had, the
more the fire raged within him.*

No one seemed to measure up to Liza. Not until Lana.

| | |

Cassidy woke to a knock at the door. Then Rae appeared.

"May I get you anything? Perhaps a cup of strong coffee?"

Cassidy rubbed the sleep from her eyes, let out a big yawn, then half
smiled.

Actually, a one-way ticket back to New York would be perfect.

"No, Rae. I'm fine." She raised herself up on one elbow and wearily
eyed the clock on the nightstand. "Shit. I overslept." Cass kicked the
blankets off and jumped up, the bare hardwood floor cold against her
feet. "I'll be down shortly, Rae. I just need a few minutes to shower and
put on my face. Is Jonathan downstairs?"

"Yes. He and your father just sat down for breakfast."

"Father? But I thought . . ."

"Oh, my dear, this is his first trip downstairs since he came home
from the hospital. He actually walked downstairs under his own steam,
though Lord knows how we'll get him back up. He did not, would not,
greet you from a sickbed. Not after all this time."

Once Rae had closed the door behind her, Cassidy stared at her
disheveled reflection in the free-standing full-length mirror beside the
dresser. She shook her head. "Ugh. It's going to take more than a shower
and some makeup to make me presentable today."

So—Jonathan was awake. That was a first. If the gossip columnists
were correct, her half brother tended to party all night long and sleep all
day. Even as an adolescent, he would sleep well into the afternoon, given
the chance. Drugs and alcohol took their toll. Cass tried to remember
the last time they'd seen each other. Before he married that woman—
what was her name? Like everything else unimportant, Cass had deleted
the information from her memory. Barbara something. Anyway, she was
about to see him now—her secretive, dark, almost scary half brother.
And her father? What was she going to say to him? How could she face
him after all these years? And where, by God, was her anger?

Oddly, it was not fear of her father but thoughts of Tom, her first
love, that infused her with anxiety. Her dream from last night came
flooding back:

She had just turned eighteen. One month after graduating from high school, she met Tom Gleeson, a sophomore at UCLA. A star of the varsity football team, he was handsome, witty, and possessed a killer smile. Cassidy was instantly smitten. Tom came from a wealthy family and had great expectations to one day join his father's prestigious law firm. Cassidy, on the other hand, hid her upbringing, hiding her family's infamy behind her newly adopted name of English.

Over the summer and into the fall, their relationship grew more intense as they shared romantic dinners at outdoor cafés, Saturday matinées, even an overnight stay in San Francisco. Cass reveled in Tom's company and dreamed of the day she would introduce him to her father, who was still in jail. Tom was everything her father had taught her to look for in a man—compassionate and caring, affectionate and funny, tender and loving.

Three months to the day after they met, a visit to the free women's clinic confirmed Cass's suspicions: She was pregnant. Cass was overwrought with doubts and questions.

But when she told Tom, he calmed her, reassuring her that everything would be all right. He would tell his parents when he returned home. And with or without their approval they would be married.

The following night, Cass met Tom at the UCLA library. He seemed distant, even annoyed, at her surprise visit. It wasn't the same Tom. His eyes were cold.

The table around him was littered with books—definitely not typical of Tom's study habits. "I told you I had to work tonight. You can't just interrupt me whenever you want to—little Ms. English wants attention, I've got to jump? Is that it?"

Later Cassidy would remember that moment as a continuance of her father's cold, contemptuous look at her as he was taken away to jail. The two moments collided and the pain Cass felt was old, new, never-to-end hurt.

"Tom, I . . ." She pulled out a chair at the table and was about to sit down but thought better of it. Angry, dull, cold blue eyes frightened her away.

But the next day, Tom came after her, obviously feeling guilty, and apologized. "I'm just scared, Cass," he said quietly. His arms encircled her; his chin rested on the top of her head, calming her quaking.

"It's all right." She wiped away warm tears. "I'm scared, too. But we'll be okay. You want to get married, right?" She kept talking. "I mean, you don't want to—"

He kissed her. She relaxed into his familiar form. They made arrangements to meet on Saturday, two days hence, at LAX.

"There's a seven-fifteen A.M. flight to Vegas. Let's do it in style." Tom's wry smile warmed her.

| | |

Cassidy had tossed and turned in bed that Friday night anticipating the wonderful life with Tom and their baby. Boy or girl? It didn't matter. It would be a blessing from God—a reward for all the painful memories. She imagined tiny fingers and tiny toes, perfect features, expressive light-blue eyes like Tom's, or perhaps dark sapphire blue like her own. And the delicious, delightful sounds of cooing.

At five A.M., unable to close her eyes, Cass got up and packed her overnight bag. She thought about leaving Uncle Jeff and Aunt Bev a note but then decided against it. Nothing would spoil her trip with Tom to Las Vegas—nothing would ruin their perfect wedding.

She picked up her suitcase and moved quietly past her uncle and aunt's bedroom. She crept out of the house and took the six o'clock bus to the airport. When she arrived at the terminal and made her way to Gate 23, she saw that Tom hadn't arrived yet. She was early. Cass sat down in one of the vinyl chairs facing the concourse.

I'm finally going to be happy. Six-fifteen . . . *Tom and I will live in a small house with a white picket fence . . .* Six-thirty . . . *I'll get pleasantly plump while cooking meals for the man of my dreams . . .* Seven o'clock . . . *And when the baby is born, I'll tell it so many wonderful stories about its father . . .* Seven-fifteen. Still no sign of him. Cass's eyes darted frantically around the terminal. *Maybe he got lost? Perhaps I heard wrong. Did he say seven-fifteen or was it eight-fifteen?* She started to panic. She called his room at the dorm. No answer.

He's on his way—he's just running late. It doesn't matter; we can catch the next flight.

At nine o'clock that evening, Cass took a taxi home. Whatever made her think Tom would elope to Las Vegas, of all places? Years later she would realize he'd tried in his way to joke, to tease, to let her know he wasn't serious. He was ambivalent. She could hear that in the joke. But she didn't consider the force of his fear.

When she arrived home, Uncle Jeff was standing in the foyer, arms folded, with Bev behind him. Cass sensed they'd been standing there anxiously for a long time. But she didn't confuse their questions with concern. Jeff and Bev just didn't want any trouble from her father.

"Where have you been?" Uncle Jeff rarely raised his voice, but now he growled. His eyes were on her suitcase. "What's this about, Cassidy Turmaine?"

The old Cassidy Turmaine, the one who left this house before dawn, would have confronted Jeff about his attitude immediately. That Cassidy had a lot of Roger Turmaine inside her. But this new woman, born during that painful day at LAX, didn't know how to care for herself, so she just told him the facts.

The words just spilled out. "I'm . . . all alone . . . my baby . . . I waited . . . He promised . . ."

Cass locked herself in her room for two days, listening to the ongoing arguing down the hall.

Jeff: "My brother will be furious. He'll think I've failed him."

Bev: "It's not your fault. The stupid kid got herself knocked up!"

Jeff: "He's calling in two days. I'm afraid of what he'll do when he finds out."

Bev: "He doesn't have to find out. We could handle everything ourselves."

On the third day, Cass finally managed to dress and make it down to breakfast, but nothing could prepare her for what she was about to learn. Resting on the kitchen counter was the *L.A. Times* turned to the Society page. The caption said: "Tom Gleeson, son of famed defense attorney Adam Gleeson, and his fiancée, MariLee Wilson, at opening of the new Martin Scorsese film." There was a photo of Tom. He was smiling, holding a brunette with a pretty face close to him with one arm wrapped around her waist—the other waving to the photographer. He looked so happy.

At eight o'clock the next morning, against her will, Cass was taken to Memorial Hospital, admitted under an assumed name, and immediately given a Valium drip to calm her.

Awareness came in the form of horrendous, clawing, stabbing pain. She tried to scream, but no sound came. The dryness in her throat was unbearable. Her arms were strapped to metal rods attached to a gurney; her legs were raised, heels pushed into stirrups on either side that forced her knees apart. The overhead light was blinding. Her body was racked with pain. The nurse gave her more sedation, but she desperately fought the overwhelming feeling of encroaching sleep. She needed to fight, to save her baby. Tears stung her swollen cheeks, but still the sobs could not come.

The doctor's eyes above the green surgical mask were kind but wary. Then the pain between her legs and in her belly began again, this time as a throb. The pain had rhythm—stab, throb, stab, throb.

"Are you in pain?" the doctor asked. And without waiting for a reply, he applied something cool and wet. She was numb. Outside. Inside she was deadened. What a perfect combination.

Cassidy closed her eyes and tried to think herself far away. But a shift inside her body was too strong—it brought her back into the moment. Something was wrong. She could feel it. She remembered nothing after that.

Later that evening Cass awoke to find standing at the foot of her bed a white-clad apparition with a stiff, pointed white cap perched precariously atop a taut white bun. Silhouetted in the fluorescent hall lights, this tall, ghostly being seemed to be studying notes on a clipboard. "What happened?" she whispered.

"Oh, you're awake." The specter peered at Cass over her wire-rimmed half glasses. "I'm Miss Carpenter, your private-duty nurse." Then she told her young patient that her womb had been perforated during "the procedure" and that it had taken a team of seven doctors working for four hours to stop the internal bleeding and save Cassidy's life.

"You're going to be just fine, darling," Miss Carpenter said softly with a gentle smile. "You're out of danger now. You're very lucky to be alive."

"No," Cass murmured. "I should die. . . ." Only later did she realize that it was simply not her time. The agony of losing Tom, along with the unbearable feeling of emptiness in her womb and the terrible sense of complete loneliness, found its spot in her soul. From that moment on, Cass knew she must never allow herself to love again.

Two days later, Cass signed herself out of the hospital against doctors' orders, and with two hundred dollars in her purse, she bought a bus ticket to New York City.

How do you dress for your father when you haven't seen him in more than twenty years?

Cassidy stared at the clothes she'd brought with her from New York. Everything she had with her was wrong. She shook her head at the irony of the situation and finally chose a light-blue TSE cashmere sweater set, taupe cashmere-and-wool-blend Dolce & Gabbana slacks, and her J.P. Tod's black driving loafers. At the last minute, she put on the pearl choker and earrings. Lana's. She wondered if her father would remember—his gift to Lana on the day Cassidy was born.

As Cassidy approached the dining room, she made eye contact with Rae, who seemed to be standing by the French doors to offer support. Rae smiled warmly at Cassidy, nodding her head.

Cassidy nodded in return and steeled herself. She wasn't quite sure why she felt so near to tears. He was only her father, after all.

Then she saw Jonathan. Her half brother wore his dark hair in a too-long Hollywood cut that covered most of his face. When he glanced up as she entered the room, she still could not see his eyes.

"Hi," she said almost inaudibly, still looking at Jonathan.

Her father now spoke. "Well, well . . ." Was he smiling? "Please forgive me if I don't get up."

Cassidy looked at her father and saw the same proud forehead, the same piercing blue eyes, the same sharp cheekbones that she remembered. The hair had gone silver, but there was no mistaking him. His voice was still the smooth baritone she heard in her dreams. Roger motioned to a seat to his right, the one to his left already occupied by Jonathan.

Head high, Cassidy slowly crossed the room, taking purposeful steps so that she did not quake. She wanted instead to show these men who were her only family that she was in charge of herself.

She sat down beside her father, delicately placed the heavy linen napkin on her lap, and then looked right at him. "Good morning, Father."

Roger smiled and said, "Good morning, Cassidy. I'm glad you came." Then he turned to Jonathan and prompted, "Aren't we glad that Cassidy is here, Jonathan?"

Jonathan glared at Cassidy and said in a tone that mimicked their father's, "Of course. Nice to see you, Cassidy. It's been a while."

Cassidy accepted the coffee placed before her and took a sip.

"How civilized," observed Cass, gazing at the elaborate breakfast. There were scrambled eggs, Belgian waffles, fresh fruit, and homemade croissants, each delectable food served on an antique sterling silver tray. The table itself was set with fine bone china plates, cups, and saucers.

Their meeting would not be cordial. Cass sensed the chill in the air immediately. As for her brother, she was too full of anger to even consider reconciling. Her father, on the other hand, seemed mild, even somewhat meek. Her shock at his frailty must have registered on her face, because his usual placating manner took over.

"You look almost as good as I feel. The doctors argue I should take it easy—stay away from work. In fact, they contend I should be confined to bed." He waved his hand in the air, as if to swat away all three assumptions. "I disagree. I feel fit and healthy. I wasn't sure what your favorite breakfast foods are these days, so I had the cook prepare a little of everything."

"It's enough to feed an army," Cass replied.

The room was silent, and then, as if this were an everyday occurrence, the three of them breakfasting each morning like an ordinary family, Roger and Jonathan resumed their conversation, discussing, of all things, Cassidy thought, the film *Dangerous Intentions*.

They traded insults about the new director, recommended by Colossal head Jack Cavelli.

"He's too goddamn flamboyant. His earlier films are evidence of that," said Roger flatly.

"I agree. Everybody in the business knows he's a quack—a complete loony tune. But that's why I think Cavelli put him in."

"Cavelli has no power in this situation," Roger rejoined. "It is our choice, and I say no to Duckerman. I want you to call Sneed at CAA today and see if that young guy is free—the one who did the fabulous remake of *Dial M for Murder.*"

They had not been together as a family in more than twenty years—not since Lana's murder—and here the two men were talking business . . . just like they did every morning!

Cassidy studied her father, trying to decide how she felt. Angry? Heartbroken? As he sat beside her, willfully treating their reunion as casually as possible, she felt distrust, even disgust, begin to rise up her throat.

Was he really even sick? While, yes, he did look a bit pale and considerably older, Roger didn't strike her as near his deathbed. But then again, he was rather protean in his energy, especially when it came to work.

And although his manner was always perfect, in control, Cass immediately sensed his nervousness. She turned her attention to Jonathan. Unlike their father, the younger man seemed cool, collected, even annoyed at her presence.

Cassidy returned her attention to her father. His expressions were expansive; his appetite, huge. As he spoke, the Roger she remembered returned—dominating the conversation, subtly insulting Jonathan, banging his fist on the table to punctuate a point.

How gullible she'd been, Cassidy realized. And what a fine performance Roger was giving. Meek—bullshit. Frail—hogwash. She realized the entire presentation was only a facade. Underneath the carefully contrived performance, the truth lay, so on an impulse she asked, "What's this all about, Daddy? Can you please tell me why I am here?"

Roger lowered his gaze and his smile shifted to a slight frown. "What, I can't be happy to see my daughter? Hell, how long has it been?"

"That's not what I meant and you know it." Now Cass stared at him intently. "I received a note from James. In it he wrote you were very sick, and I stress the word *very.* Now, sitting here, I'm convinced all of it—the note, your illness—is nothing but a hoax. You obviously must have some other plan."

Cassidy looked from her father to her brother. Her brother stared back, a gloating smile on his lips. Her father's face went steely.

These two men, these virtual strangers, composed her entire "family." And she had no idea what either of them was thinking.

"If you don't explain what is going on, I'm going to catch the next flight back to New York." As she stood, Roger took her arm.

"Sit down." This time all trace of civility had vanished from his tone. Instantly she felt like a small child again, obedient and afraid.

"It's true . . . all of it. I am ill. The letter was not a hoax. Physically I've suffered a great blow; mentally, an even greater one." Roger spoke seriously. He stood and walked to the window. Then he turned and stared only at her, as if Jonathan were no longer in the room.

Cassidy felt the penetrating gaze of her father's intense blue eyes. She searched to find in them some lost memory that would close the gulf between them. She had been around the entertainment industry long enough to know that even the most stolid network executive was not above employing theatrics, even histrionics, to win a point. She resented that her father would resort to ploys to get her attention.

"I may not be as frail as I have led the public to believe," he continued solemnly, "but I did have a heart attack, and I don't have the stamina to get *Dangerous Intentions* made. And this movie is going to be my last. It has to be fantastic."

And then, like the crashing sound of thunder, his next words hit her. "I want you to take over for me. You're the only one I trust to do it right, Cass."

Will you be home for dinner?" Serena asked as James headed for the door.

"I'm not sure. It depends on my summation today," he replied. "If I feel confident, we go out and celebrate. If I don't, we stay home."

"So you're telling me I have to pray for a miracle to get a free meal?"

They both laughed. Serena was an attractive forty-four-year-old woman with a curly mop of red hair, expressive hazel eyes, and an incredible body. And according to James Renthrew, the sun set and rose around his lovely wife.

James, who had been compact and well built when they were married ten years ago, was now middle-aged, with ordinary features, lack-luster brown hair, dark eyes, and an average-to-slightly-overweight build. And yet he had still been picked recently by *USA Today* as one of Hollywood's top ten most alluring men. The list, which excluded actors, was similar to *Esquire*'s annual "Women We Love" piece. The reporter had written, "With looks that might be average on another man, Renthrew has an intuitive intelligence that seems to leap out at you from eyes dark and sparkling as raw diamonds." Serena had teased him mercilessly.

Now sixty-one, he was considered one of the foremost entertainment lawyers in the country. He became a partner in Diamond, Phillips, Rosenberg, and Renthrew in 1978 at forty years old. It had been his performance and the outcome of one particular case that sealed his bid for partner: Roger Turmaine's appeal, which resulted in his acquittal. James was known as a keen and cunning lawyer, yet it was his sincere love for and incredible knowledge of law that had guaranteed his place at the top of this competitive world.

Diamond, Phillips, Rosenberg, and Renthrew, with offices in Los Angeles, New York, London, and Tokyo, was highly respected internationally. Clients included most of the top entertainment figures, who demanded and received a hands-on approach from the firm's most highly "connected" attorneys. Agents, as well as their clients—rock stars, actors and actresses, directors, singers, even professional athletes—turned to the firm for everything from contracts to nuisance suits. James had successfully represented Patrick Keen when he was caught with a prostitute. He also won a seven-figure settlement for a former child star whose longtime manager had not only "invested" the bulk of this young man's earnings from a long-running sitcom and feature films in his *own* offshore bank accounts but had also taken sexually explicit pictures of the boy, which he'd shared with a coterie of pedophiles. He'd even managed to keep that aspect of the suit out of the press. Directors, producers, and studio heads all put their stock and trust in the firm when closing major blockbuster deals.

James had joined the firm right out of UCLA Law. At first the other attorneys took pitiless advantage of him, giving him all the menial jobs they themselves couldn't be bothered with—researching cases, briefs, working out details on boilerplate clauses. It was high stress, 24/7, but James was determined. By the end of his second year with the firm, he knew each attorney's individual cases inside and out. Not one fact got past him.

On the morning of Christmas Eve, 1965, James arrived at the office at seven A.M. With nowhere to go, no family to celebrate the holiday with, James had decided to get some of his paperwork out of the way while the office was quiet.

When he picked up the phone, the caller sounded familiar.

Flora Robbins's voice was ubiquitous in Hollywood. She was the agent for Tennessee Williams, one of James's favorite writers. "Young man," she replied to his hello, "get me Phillip Rosenberg, immediately."

Before the days of "patched in" calls, beepers, and cell phones, there was the human equivalent—a law clerk. James explained that Mr. Rosenberg was out of town until after the New Year. "Is there any way I can help you, Ms. Robbins?"

She paused.

"I'm pretty current on all of Mr. Rosenberg's cases," James rushed to say.

"This can't wait. I have a new client with an offer for a directing deal from Warner Brothers. I need help. Legal advice."

James encouraged her to give him the details. That call made history—at least for James.

James managed to settle the issue with Warner Brothers' legal department before the day was out. The agent's new client, Roger Turmaine, showed his gratitude by sending James a bottle of extremely expensive scotch. James's call to thank him led to drinks at the Polo Lounge, which led to lunch.

The two young men were nearly the same age, and shared the same aggressive ambition to get ahead. And both had.

A few weeks later, James introduced Roger to a young secretary in his office—Lana Hunt. By then, James and Roger had already become best friends and professional allies. Roger asked James to be his best man at his and Lana's wedding.

Ultimately, Roger had Lana's legal matters taken over by the firm. Roger Turmaine became the first of James's youthful celebrity clients. Eventually he cornered the market on the contract issues for Hollywood's young set. Sutherland, Sheen, Peter Fonda, Michael Douglas—all of them had their entertainment legal matters handled by James.

But like Roger, James wasn't satisfied with his early accomplishments. His ambition continued to climb, driving him onward.

| | |

"I'll call you from the office around noon," James yelled over his shoulder.

James and Serena had met eleven years earlier at a lavish party Roger had thrown in James's honor after he successfully blocked a rival studio from hiring one of Desmond's leading ladies.

Serena had been the star of a popular television sitcom, until she came down with pneumonia and had to be hospitalized. It cost the sitcom a ton of money and ultimately she was fired. James had discussed the possibility of a lawsuit with her that night, and the following morning Serena was in his office.

James won the case and Serena was awarded two million dollars. The network got nailed, Serena got the money, and James got the girl. They were married the following year. And in spite of their nearly twenty-year age difference, theirs was a happy marriage, something James considered a rarefied product in La-La Land.

He cautiously backed his new BMW out of the garage.

The cell phone built into the dashboard rang sharply. Still looking back over his shoulder, he reached out and pressed send.

"James, it's Jonathan."

"And good morning to you, too!" James responded. He could hear the agitation in the younger man's voice. Something was terribly wrong.

Jonathan cleared his throat and continued, not even acknowledging James's greeting. "That bitch is back . . . that . . . that . . . she . . ."

Immediately, James knew what had prompted Jonathan's call. He struggled to stifle a laugh. "That's hardly an appropriate manner in which to describe your sister."

She had never replied to his note, but James had been certain that Cassidy would come to her father's side. In fact, he'd expected this call. Even as a child, Jonathan had always been obscenely jealous of his half-sister, always obsessing over all the attention she'd received from Roger.

While still in the hospital, Roger had revealed his intention to put Cassidy in charge of *Dangerous Intentions*. James's first words were, "I don't think you can 'put' Cassidy English anywhere." His second words were, "Jonathan is going to go ballistic."

Calmly and confidently, Roger had replied, "He's impossible, unpredictable—a virtual time bomb, everything Cassidy is not. This project is too important to me. I've given it careful consideration. Cassidy is my only choice."

"What if she refuses?"

"I won't let her," Roger shot back. "She owes this to me. She is, after all, my daughter."

James had no response.

Now, however, Jonathan was freaking out on the other end of the phone. "I need to know what my legal rights are." His tone was desperate. "I will *not* allow Cass to take what's rightfully mine. I've worked beside him for years."

You've worked because of him, James thought, but dared not say.

James barely tolerated Jonathan Turmaine. He didn't respect him, didn't like him, any more than Roger did. The only reason James had any dealings at all with him was because of his long-standing friendship with Roger. In addition to the occasional DUI and bar brawl to be hushed up, James had been called in twice to represent him in what were politely referred to as "nuisance" suits. Jonathan had battered his wife, a lovely woman, and barely a year ago he had savaged a girl—a teenager— he'd picked up at the Viper Room.

Jonathan was a lowlife, a user, too eager to get ahead on the laurels and hard work of others, in particular those of his father. James also agreed with Roger that Jonathan couldn't be trusted—from either a personal or a professional standpoint—to carry the delicate business of Desmond Films into the future. He was a loose cannon.

As it was, even without Jonathan to disturb the delicate balance, James Renthrew, Desmond, and Colossal were not a happy match. There were too many ambitious men, too many egos in the mix.

"I know the business," Jonathan was saying. "I want the movie. You've got to help me. His judgment is clouded. I'll, I'll . . . I'll take it to court."

"On what grounds?" James asked flatly.

"On the grounds that my father's mentally incapable of making rational decisions, given his poor physical state."

This time James did not stifle his laughter. "You'll be thrown out of any courtroom. Anyway, you'll never get anyone to represent you. I certainly won't. Look, I'll be by around noon. Tell your father I need to speak with him."

Without waiting for further comment, James hung up.

| | |

Cassidy was having a cup of tea in the large, now-empty solarium of Whispering Winds. Preferring not to be served by the fleet of servants, she was relishing the alone-time in the sun-filled room, one of the happier places in the big house. Her head was still reeling from her father's pronouncement earlier that morning.

Spread out before her were the daily trades. Each carried the same story, straightforward and to the point, obviously leaked before Roger had broken the news to his offspring. She picked up the copy of *Daily Variety* to see how Army Archerd had run it.

It's rumored that any minute now, Roger Turmaine
will announce that, due to his recent heart attack, he is

stepping down as head of Desmond Films. Usually well-informed sources say that effective immediately, his daughter, Cassidy English, will take over all business deal-ings, including completion of the much-talked-about *Dangerous Intentions.* Turmaine has called the $75-million-dollar film noir his most personal creation and the high point of his career. If Turmaine puts the project in Cassidy's hands it will be the most profound expression of trust and admiration a father can bestow on his daughter.

The column went on to spin the rumors circulating about contro-versies over casting. "It's said Ms. English will have total creative control, including casting of the coveted lead female role, but those in the know wonder whether Jack Cavelli may have some ideas of his own."

Cassidy hadn't even accepted her father's request and the news was already on the street. The nerve of him. But it wasn't a request, was it, Cassidy thought. It was a demand. And he had probably had this leaked to force her hand.

Her stomach churned. Nausea enveloped her. Why on earth was she allowing all of this to happen? Why couldn't she just tell her father no? Was her guilt—and Roger's ability to use it—the reason she felt so defenseless?

Before the trial, Cassidy had been well coached by Roger's team of lawyers, but once she got up on the stand, the prosecutor's cross-examination had given them all they needed—a witness, albeit a terrified ten-year-old child.

Cassidy testified that she'd woken up to a man's voice, then she heard two shots. She said she was afraid to open the door, so she peeped through the keyhole and all she could see was shoes with blood on them. Then her father was in her room, holding her.

The prosecution had picked holes in her story so it eventually came out sounding like she saw her father run from her parents' room down the hall to hers.

Roger's insistence that Cassidy could attest to his innocence had backfired and he went to jail.

In time, Cassidy had come to hate her father for forcing her to tes-tify. Worse than that was the guilt that coiled inside her, a tangled mass of dark, impenetrable feelings from which she was never free.

Right now she felt numb, disconnected, functioning on remote control. This suited Cass just fine, as she could only imagine the anger that was sure to engulf her later.

He's done it again. He's won. I was prepared, focused, determined to hold my ground, and somehow he still managed to come out on top. Remain in L.A.? Run a studio? Complete his most personal film with all of Hollywood watching? Oh my God, this is sick.

| | |

Her pediatric nursing had stopped when Cedars-Sinai started an investigation into the switched Turmaine and Hutton babies. The mistake in blood typing for one of the girls had tipped the ethics committee off. Patricia had disappeared. It was easy. She had plenty of money, and she had no family—her drinking had scared them all away. But in time the money ran out. The checks stopped coming, and what she hadn't drunk up, she'd gambled away. She tried working part time through an agency, working private duty a week here or there when someone was just out of the hospital, taking the overnight shift when a family wanted private twenty-four-hour care for their loved one. But her arthritis got bad—rheumatoid arthritis. It was stress related. She tried the new class of medicines—the nonsteriodal anti-inflammatories—and had injections administered to her back periodically. But nothing worked. Patricia Hanson knew why. She was riddled with guilt—aching with it, literally.

So when she read in the gossip columns that Roger Turmaine was handing over his business and, assumedly, his fortune to his "daughter," Patricia saw it as a signal from her Higher Power. She had been in Alcoholics Anonymous just shy of one year, and it was crucial to her sobriety that she clear up the wreckage of her past—all of it. The Ninth Step was: "Make direct amends to such people wherever possible. . . ." She could hear her sponsor's voice, firmly talking about how it's the *duty* of recovering alcoholics to apologize to everyone they hurt by their stinking thinking, their drunk behavior.

She had talked to her few surviving family members and a couple of coworkers who had been subjected to her alcoholic behavior. It had been uncomfortable, but once she'd started talking, she had to admit she did feel relief. The only thing that still gnawed at her gut were the babies. She knew that it was imperative for her to make amends to these babies, now grown, who she had switched for a few thousand dollars. The checks had stopped coming years ago, as agreed, but there hadn't been a day that she had not thought about the lives she had affected by her avarice. If she could just clear up this issue, her slate would be clean, her conscience clear, and she could look people in the eye again. She could rejoin the human race.

In the movies, alcoholics didn't have to make amends, they just stopped drinking and everything fell into place. But this was the real world. It had taken her the past eleven months to work up to it. So when she saw the newspaper article about Cassidy English, Roger Turmaine's daughter, taking over her father's business, she knew that it was time for her to take that last, big step.

Finding him was easy. He was exactly where he'd lived all the time he'd sent the checks. The phone rang a few times. Patricia realized that a machine might pick up. If that happened, she'd write a letter. But eventually a woman answered and Patricia left a simple message: He should call her, as soon as possible. When asked what company she was from, Patricia simply said he would recognize her name.

Jack Cavelli's business offices occupied the entire penthouse of the newly built Colossal building, located in Silver Lake. To get to Jack, one passed three small, utilitarian offices where secretaries, assistants, and production personnel worked behind glass walls. On one side of Jack's office were windows so high up that the freeway below might as well have been in cyberspace—down there was virtual reality. Real life, to Jack, was contained here. The interior wall of Jack's inner sanctum was a pane of one-way glass. From there he could keep an eye on his employees without them seeing him. At the far end of the outer wall was a locked door that opened onto a small iron spiral staircase. On the lower level, tucked between the penthouse and the seventy-fifth floor, was another entire floor, a loft that Jack called his pied-à-terre.

Decorated with massive pieces of rare modern art and sculpture, the loft was hardly a crash pad. Here the lighting was muted; furnishings comfortable yet chic. The loft had a state-of-the-art screening room, maid's quarters, a sauna, full kitchen, formal dining area and bedrooms, plus a private elevator to the basement garage. Five hundred square feet of this space had been closed off to house the sound system that piped music throughout both office and loft. Jack was surrounded by music. Everywhere—jazz, opera, Gregorian chants, Brecht, and, on a lighter note, Mozart and Bach—music for every mood.

Today he sat still, behind the mammoth mahogany desk designed especially for him. Rapt in thought, he twirled his favorite black-and-gold Montblanc pen. This was the first gift he'd received from her.

"For good luck—for good health—most of all, for great success," the card read. "Every time you sign on the dotted line—think of me."

Even now, more than twenty years later, he could still hear her soft, musical voice; imagine her angelic smile.

There was a knock at the door and seconds later his secretary, a middle-aged, efficient, and well-organized woman, entered his office.

"Not now, Sharon. Whatever it is, I'm sure it can wait until after the board meeting."

The board of directors consisted of Jack Cavelli, Roger Turmaine, James Sheldon, John Latham, and Foster Nickerson. Foster was an L.A. banker who had participated in the company's recapitalization more than twenty years earlier—a recapitalization that relaunched the studio by replacing the studio staff from the mailroom clerks to the CEO. This was also when Colossal acquired a majority stake in Desmond Films.

"I think you should see this, sir." Sharon reached for the remote control on his desk and aimed it at the large-screen television discreetly hidden behind two 1920 art deco panels, designed for the elevators of Harrods department store in London.

The picture on the television set flashed to a perky blonde saying, "Roger Turmaine has issued a release announcing he will in fact turn over full control of his business dealings to his daughter, Cassidy English. Most recently, Ms. English has been executive producer of *Up to the Minute,* the number-one national TV newsmagazine. How will this announcement affect the entertainment world? Stay tuned. At six o'clock we'll have much more on Roger Turmaine's decision, the future of Desmond Films, and a feature on Cassidy English. Live from Beverly Hills, I'm Diana Long."

While the reporter spoke, pictures flashed across the screen: a frail Roger Turmaine, followed quickly by a shot of a smiling dark-haired woman, whom Jack recognized as Cassidy English. She was extremely photogenic and looked like a dark version of her mother; Lana was fair, Cassidy was dark—the positive and negative of a woman's photograph. Jack resumed his reverie of that woman from twenty years ago.

"Hold all my calls. I don't want to be disturbed."

"But the board meeting is in ten minutes."

Jack dismissed her with a look, then turned his attention back to the screen.

Under different circumstances, Jack would have welcomed Cassidy on board at Desmond. He knew her work—she was extremely talented, adept at putting disparate components together to come up with a smooth production.

God knows Desmond, and Colossal, too, could use someone like her.

Unfortunately, that no longer suited Jack's purposes. He wanted full control of Desmond and its properties. Cassidy English would be an obstacle in his path to collapsing Desmond into Colossal.

| | |

"How could you do this to me, Dad? I've worked so hard. . . . I earned it. I deserve to be the head of Desmond." Jonathan was drunk, and had been since noon.

"It's simple. You don't have what it takes. Look at you—ask me why I chose Cassidy over you." Roger spoke calmly, firmly.

"Goddamn you!" Jonathan caromed into the mahogany refectory table behind the couch, shaking the Tiffany lamp that rested there and causing it to spray prisms of colors across his face. The light only intensified the rage pulsing from his pinpoint pupils. "This is MINE! I worked for it. I was here . . . I . . . I . . . I stuck around and worked my ass off for you. I put up with . . ." His voice cracked as he caught his breath. He forced his words through clinched jaws. "She's done *nothing* for you. . . . She didn't earn it! She'll crash and burn! I'll make sure she—"

A door slammed, muting the angry voices from the study downstairs.

Cass had been keeping a low profile, staying in her room, out of range of Jonathan's fury. It had been so palpable at breakfast. She stumbled into the bathroom, to the sink, and turned on the faucet. The water ran cold and she splashed it on her face. She could picture her father's face, his proud, unyielding eyes, his cleft chin, as he maneuvered his children, forcing them once again to be archenemies, rivals for his attention, his affection, and now his power.

All at once bile rose in her throat. She splashed more cold water on her face, grabbed a towel, patted her face dry, and then stared at herself in the mirror. Her own mature reflection faded and in its place she saw the terrified, lonely young girl she had been, fully dressed in black, her face covered in tears. She was holding one rose as the sound of the priest's words slammed through her tiny body.

May the almighty Father, the Son, and the Holy Spirit . . . The longer she stared, the clearer the image became: The ten-year-old girl, with the empty eyes and hollow heart. The little girl whose face was pinched into a visible mask of terror. The black limousines, the red roses, the sobs. All followed by a resounding silence.

The vivid details and emotions rushed back to her. Cass clearly remembered the cold, dark blue of her father's eyes, like the unseen side of the moon. Then hours later, back at the house, the two detectives leading him away in restraints.

"I didn't kill my wife. You've made a terrible mistake. She's just a child, she doesn't know what she's saying." Then he was forced out of sight, receding like a wave. The squad car pulled away and Cass felt the sting of the tears on her cheeks.

"Daddy, come back. . . . I'm sorry . . . please. Please come back!"

"Cassidy? Are you okay?"

The images in the mirror vanished; in their place she saw Rae, reflected, standing in the doorway, frowning.

"Oh, I'm fine, Rae. . . . I think I'm still getting over the shock. I just don't know what my father is thinking."

"Maybe you should lie down." She stabbed a thumb over her shoulder. "Don't worry about the others downstairs. Tune them out."

But Cassidy wasn't listening anymore.

The guilt inside her collided suddenly with her independent streak, her self-esteem. *Was she crazy?* She'd never let anyone—not even her father—push her around.

"Rae, I've got to get out of here for a while. If they ask, just tell them I went for a drive." Then Cassidy grabbed her bag and slipped out of the house and into her rental car.

| | |

James stood at the massive entryway of Whispering Winds. He could hear Turmaines, father and son, arguing again.

"How could you screw me like this? I've been at your beck and call for the last ten years. This just isn't fair!"

"Jonathan, we both know you are not executive material. If it weren't for me, you—"

"If it weren't for *you*, my life wouldn't have been the bloodbath it's been. Do you know how humiliating it is having you as a father? It's all your fault."

"How dare you? I didn't *make* you drive drunk, or beat your wife . . .

or alienate everyone who's ever worked for or with you. No. Your mistakes are your own damned fault. You're just proving once again how incapable you are of acting like an adult."

Rae led James into the study. She didn't bother to excuse the verbal violence bouncing off the walls. No one said anything while James settled into an Eames chair that matched the one Roger sat in. Jonathan was sprawled out on the red leather couch. James noted that he had at least taken his shoes off.

Rae tried to pretend the scene was normal. "Does anyone need anything? James? A drink?"

James shook his head. Roger was looking a little better. All the excitement—even the arguing—was bringing him back to himself again.

"I cannot believe what went on here today. Roger, were you going for shock value? Because if you were, I can tell you firsthand, you succeeded," James said, trying to defuse some of the tension in the room.

"James, you know that wasn't my plan. I can assure you my intentions are good."

"They always are." James paused, then looked around the room. "Where's Cassidy?"

Rae cleared her throat apologetically, then said, "She's gone. She ran out of here just a few minutes ago. Said she needed to think."

Rae's revelation brought all three men to their feet. Roger was the first to speak.

"Why did you allow her to run off? Didn't you try to stop her?"

"Stop her? For God's sake, Mr. Turmaine, she's not a child. Despite *your* strong state of denial, Cass is all grown up and very—may I stress the word *very*—capable of making her own decisions."

All at once father and son began arguing again, shouting insults and accusations at each other. James tried to compose himself by admiring the opulent, lavishly decorated room—his favorite in the mansion. The walls were book-lined and mahogany-paneled, with gilded gold accents trimmed from floor to ceiling. A Tiffany shell lamp and a rolltop desk and chair, circa 1909, evoked a period spirit. The addition of a stone and marble fireplace and an American Chippendale mirror complemented the gentlemanly, low-key look of the study.

"Why don't we all calm down and try to handle this with Cass's best interests in mind." As always, James assumed the rational, in-full-control role.

"I agree," Rae said firmly. She turned her gaze on Roger. "Did you at least discuss this with Cass before the release went out?"

Roger took a step toward her. He smiled, his lips pulling away from his teeth in a predatory grimace. "It's the chance of a lifetime, Rae. How could Cassidy—how could anyone—not want it?"

| | |

The running continued. And it always came down to a woman. He'd hooked up with Helena after finding her crying in the dressing room after her midnight performance at Valentine's. At first, all he offered was a shoulder to cry on. After all, a man couldn't knowingly go after a tough guy's girlfriend. Hell, he'd have to be crazy. But on the other hand, craziness was in his blood. Besides, he never could stand by wringing his hands when in the presence of a beautiful woman who was crying.

Helena, he would learn, was quite an actress. She could cry on cue. All she wanted from him was a little extracurricular activity. And he was restless and antsy, always looking for a high. Alcohol didn't quite do it anymore; besides, "the morning after" was always a bitch. Cocaine gave him headaches, heroin didn't mix well with booze. Maybe "hands-on" adventures would give him that ultimate kick.

So began the sweet late-night meetings with Helena at the fancy penthouse in the Excelsior, paid for by her old, married boyfriend. Together they were TNT—two of a kind. Their affair, like all bad habits, was both illicit and addictive. The risk involved heightened the experience. Until they were caught. How was he to know the landlord was on Tough Guy's payroll? Anyone could have made the same mistake. It was definitely time to get out of New York.

He got his hands on a Saturday-night special. It became his faithful companion. During the day he wore it concealed under his clothing; at night he tucked it under his pillow, fully loaded. Thank God for small favors. As logic would have it, Tough Guy came calling late one night just as the midnight movie was starting. He didn't knock. But then again he wasn't notorious for his polite and proper manners. He was alone. Why was anyone's guess. Tough Guy reached for his gun, wasting no time on small talk. He pulled out the Saturday-night special from under the pillow and emptied it. His instinct had kicked in. He didn't want to die. Shoot first, ask questions later. That's what all the men who hung around Valentine's said. Five of the six bullets hit the target. One left a gaping hole in Tough Guy's face, maiming him beyond recognition.

Much to his surprise, there was no sorrow or remorse—only fear. He didn't want to get caught. It took him ten minutes to pack all of his worldly possessions, then he ran from the apartment. From Helena, from New York. By the time he arrived at Grand Central Station, he realized there was only one place he belonged. The Wild, Wild West.

| | |

Forest Lawn Memorial Park was known for its headstones, monuments, and mausoleums that befit Pharaohs or the resting place of Roman senators. But of all this statuary, none was as beautiful as the Turmaine monument, where Lana lay.

The grass was still dewy beneath Cass's feet, just as it had been so long ago, when mourners had gathered for her burial. Cass could picture the open grave, waiting to receive the white oak coffin, which was decorated with the etchings of two angels bound together by a carved, curling ribbon.

It had been a rainy April morning, yet despite the inclement weather, thousands of mourners milled about the meticulously manicured grounds, hoping to catch a glimpse of all the celebrities and politicians who had come to pay their respects. Reporters, both newspaper and television, came in droves, keeping the proper amount of distance, yet zooming in for close-ups of all the recognizable faces.

There were studio heads, famous directors and producers, movie stars, young and old, the presidents of the entertainment industry unions, SAG and AFTRA, as well as the Directors Guild, not to mention governors and mayors. Even the President had sent an emissary.

And then there was the mass of "little people." Housewives, blue-collar workers, aspiring starlets, ardent worshipers; prop men and grips, stuntmen and wardrobe assistants—all were in attendance to pay homage to "Hollywood's fallen angel."

Through the eyes of a ten-year-old, all of it had seemed surreal. Cassidy was astounded at the immediacy of her memories. It was as if all these years away from Los Angeles had kept these memories at bay. Now that she'd returned, the images of her childhood had come back, replaying themselves and taking her up in their frenzy, a river running out of control.

What had happened to that child?

Cassidy bent to her knees and, with her fingertips, brushed fallen leaves from the cold stone ledge. The feel of the marble sent shivers up and down her spine, as if creating an electrifying connection with her mother.

"She was very beautiful. Don't you agree?" The voice startled her and she nearly lost her balance. Cassidy looked up to see an attractive woman standing just a few feet from the mausoleum. She carried a bouquet of roses, wrapped in cellophane.

Surprised, Cass responded, "Yes . . . she was very beautiful." She got to her feet and smoothed the lines of her black trousers.

The mystery woman's voice was warm as she apologized for the intrusion.

"I'm terribly sorry. I was standing over by that tree and I couldn't help but notice you."

The woman nodded slightly toward a nearby grave site. "I come here often to visit my uncle, and, well . . . sometimes I leave flowers on Ms. Turmaine's grave." Her gaze darted back to Cass, then the headstone. "Out of admiration, out of respect—I guess a little of both. But I've never seen you here, so I was just wondering . . ." Her voice trailed off.

"She—" Cass began, then stopped.

The other woman waited.

"Lana Turmaine . . . she was my mother. I haven't been here in a very long time. The night she was killed. I was there, I . . ."

Explaining herself to a perfect stranger? Because the woman's eyes were warm and her voice was soft and it was so much easier to unburden herself to a stranger than anyone close to her?

"Do you mind if I place these here?" The woman gestured with the flowers.

Cass couldn't help but notice that the bouquet was not one of the cheap ones, bought from the peddlers at the intersection that led to the cemetery. These were perfect, peach and cream long-stemmed roses. Cass knew Lana would have been pleased.

"How kind. Thank you." Cass smiled. This woman emanated sincerity, a comforting radiance putting Cass immediately at ease.

"Do you live in L.A.?"

The woman nodded, then placed the flowers next to Cass's feet.

"Born and bred, I'm afraid."

For the first time since she left New York, Cass felt like laughing.

"I know what you mean."

"Really? You couldn't possibly."

The woman's expression shifted. All warmth, all compassion, left her face, replaced by an eerie coldness. Had Cass not been watching her, she would have thought a different person had taken her place.

Cass's instincts told her to say good-bye.

"I have to get going." She purposefully glanced at her watch. "I'm afraid I'm already late." Cass touched her mother's headstone with her fingertips and turned to walk away. Once past the adjacent plot, she quickened her pace, leaving this stranger behind her.

│ │ │

Chelsea watched as Cass made her way to the rental car at the curb, observing her graceful walk, how she held her head high and her shoulders relaxed. She replayed the conversation between them in her head. Cass was articulate and charming, well mannered and polite. It was easy to be elegant when one is born to wealth and privilege, Chelsea thought bitterly. Right now Ms. Cassidy English retained her role as Roger Turmaine's princess, but that was about to change. The thought of reclaiming her father and all that was rightfully hers was the engine that drove all her days. Chelsea smiled; she picked up the roses—no use wasting good money. The flowers would add spice to her hotel room.

│ │ │

Jack was looking west out the floor-to-ceiling window in his office. On clear days, from this height, he could see the Pacific. Above the smog, above Hollywood down below, Jack let his mind travel.

But then Sharon knocked on his door, interrupting him.

"There's a woman out here who just fainted. She was asking to see you. What should I do?"

"For God's sake, is she okay? Who the hell is she?" Jack was torn between concern and annoyance.

"She said her name is Chelsea Hutton," Sharon said calmly.

Jack moved quickly, and when he saw Chelsea slumped to the floor in front of his assistant's desk, he bent down to her.

Chelsea opened her eyes.

Sharon asked, "Are you all right?"

Chelsea looked embarrassed and tried to sit up. "The heat. I've not eaten today." She waved her hand in a gesture of dismissal. "I'm fine."

"Get her some water," Jack said. Then he helped her up.

Jack stared at Chelsea. "What are you doing here?" He'd never considered that she might come here of her own volition. How stupid he'd been. He had to hand it to her; the blond aspiring star was more than a sexual acrobat. He'd overlooked her brains. No, that wasn't true—it was obvious from the beginning of their affair that Chelsea was no bimbo.

Now Chelsea was moving toward him, the slit in her short skirt parted to reveal one gloriously tanned and perfect thigh. She was in full costume, heavy makeup, long, full, white hot blonde hair, the usual intense stare. Chelsea always made serious eye contact. She defined animal magnetism.

Jack tried to stop himself from responding.

"Well, I see you're feeling better," Jack teased. He turned and walked back into his office, taking his seat behind his desk.

She followed him and perched on the edge of his desk. She then crossed her long, lean legs. Using her luscious, pouty red lips and entrancing, inviting eyes, she moved in for the seduction.

"How are you, Jack?" she purred. "I must say, you do look very different sitting behind that great big desk, in this great big office." She let her eyes wander about the room for a moment before falling on his again. "Sooo . . . businesslike. A far cry from the man I know." She looked up, eyelids only half open. "In the biblical sense, I mean."

Jack considered himself immune to the advances of women. When he wanted a woman, he had her—whoever, wherever, whenever—and on his terms. Inevitably, there were broken hearts, misunderstandings. Many women had tried to lure him, only to be rejected. Just as many had fallen for his implicit as well as explicit charms. His looks, manner, and intelligence were his drawing cards. His power was the trump. Whatever the circumstances that brought Cavelli and a woman together, he remained keeper of the flame. He turned it on and off at will. But once or twice he'd stumbled across an exceptional woman who tested his control.

Chelsea Hutton was a variety of women, neatly rolled into one package.

Over the years, Jack had met many women with the same calling card. All they had to rely on to get ahead was their looks. These were smart, tough women, who were ultimately vulnerable to their own greed and ambition.

Later Jack learned that Chelsea's childhood had been a nightmare, that her break came in the form of a husband, but he died and wasn't as rich as he had pretended.

And then she met Jack. He understood her without having to hear her "real story." No matter who she pretended to be or what lies she told him, Jack saw through it. But there was more to her than her stories, some electrical charge that ran through her. And when she showed him her clips—from her small, bit parts in B-movies—he realized that the camera could sense that charge just as he could.

Chelsea's erratic personality served her in one way. Her performance on the "couch" was always designed—choreographed—to fulfill the fantasy of the director, producer, or whoever could help her. And she acted out each one with imagination and skill, a mixture of Kama Sutra and animal erotica. Her fingers as delicate as wispy rose petals, her lips the press of phantom touches. Men—CEOs, studio heads, producers, directors, and casting agents whose wives had, over the years, grown cold and distant, even unwilling—had found solace, comfort, and pleasure with Chelsea Hutton. She filled the void. And she knew how to keep her mouth shut. She needed no secret black book. Chelsea memorized names and numbers, as well as pleasures and preferences.

She cleverly exchanged her services for favors. Jack knew it was all part of Chelsea's plan. Gone was the sweet, young child of poverty and heartache. In her place was a woman with a mission. "Screw Hollywood and everyone in it at any cost" was her mantra. Revenge was Chelsea's raison d'être.

What mystified Jack was not her quest, but the vengeance behind it, and the explanation for that was one secret Chelsea managed to hide from him. Whatever hurt drove her, Jack sympathized. He, too, had been tested by Hollywood, of course. But he was a winner. That Chelsea couldn't make one single footstep up the mountain made him feel for her. The loser in her might not be the woman he chose to join him in many different places, but it was the part of Chelsea Hutton that he cared for.

Chelsea leaned forward, her face so close to his. He could feel her breath on his lips.

"You look tired—stressed. Perhaps you need some time off. I know this great little Italian—"

"Stop." Jack refused to let her finish. At that moment he realized that she'd come to collect "her favor." The only problem was Jack never mixed business with pleasure. It simply wasn't his policy. A diamond bracelet, a new sports car, even a posh condo on the ocean—all were acceptable favors. But pulling in a marker on his business: forbidden. Jack always made that clear with all his lovers. Chelsea must know he'd been careful not to promise her any work in exchange for—whatever. Hadn't he?

She looked at him defiantly, with expectation. Her cerulean blue eyes were trained on his, and for a long moment, Jack could feel heat and light pass between them—electricity. He sighed. Chelsea just might be the one woman who could force him to break this rule, though he didn't know how or why.

"Just what is it that you want, Chelsea?"

She still sat on his desk, so in an effort to put some space between them, he pushed his shoulders back, nearly burying them in the plush leather back of his chair.

She half smiled, then a moment later her expression grew serious— all business. "Your studio owns Roger Turmaine, correct?"

"In a manner of speaking. Yes." Where was she going with this? He was already committed to hearing her out.

"I know this is asking a lot, but I need a favor." Chelsea kept her elegantly manicured hands folded gracefully in her lap. The star in the deep-red sapphire ring she wore on her right hand seemed to wink at him. Jack knew who had given it to her because that particular studio exec liked to brag about how much he paid for it, and what she had done "in exchange."

"Colossal owns Turmaine's company, right?" The question was rhetorical, but Jack nodded anyway as Chelsea continued. She sat perfectly erect, perfectly still. Chelsea was too savvy to fidget or to exhibit those typically female come-ons—tousling her long blond hair, rubbing the inside of her thighs. Chelsea knew Jack better than that.

"And *Dangerous Intentions* is on temporary hiatus, correct?"

Again, rhetorical. But the questions were leading him. He followed.

"And now that Roger's daughter—what's her name? Cassidy English, right? Well, now that she's taking his place, it's become the hot topic in L.A."

Jack remained calm and collected. "Enough Q&A. What do you want?"

Finally she got to the point.

"I want to play Ophelia. It would make my career."

Jack thought, She really *is* crazy. Ophelia was the naive daughter of an egotistical, money-hungry regent in eighteenth-century Italy. She was demure, fragile, vulnerable; a girl betrothed by her father to an older man. Her intended husband was a known sadist, a member of Italy's version of the Hell Fire Club. The young actress cast in this role was an unknown, purposely so, but she had the Nicole Kidman look—wispy, angelic, untouchable, virginal. Jack had to bite his tongue to keep from laughing.

"The film's already been cast."

"I need this part." Her eyes grew hooded once again. Her face, devoid of all emotion, gave away nothing.

Jack was amazed at the swiftness of her transformation.

"I'm not asking, I'm telling," she said sternly.

And then Jack had the greatest idea.

Cass mingled quietly among the guests, her long, white, off-the-shoulder Valentino gown trailing delicately at her ankles.

AMA—Against Medical Advice—that was the best way to describe the fete Roger was throwing in honor of his still being alive. Though his cardiologist, Rae, and James had tried to reason with him, Roger had been determined to have his lavish party.

Cass knew that Roger must have some other scheme, as yet unnamed, up his sleeve. Why else would he risk his health in front of all of Hollywood?

For the past few days, as Cass tried to explain to her network back home why she was taking the job at Desmond, she watched and waited to see Roger in action. It was clear that he had something to gain from this party; she just wasn't sure what it was.

"I've got hope again," was all he said. "I want to shout it to the world."

And that he had, Cass thought, mixing politely with the crowd. Her feet had already begun to ache in her three-inch Charles Jourdan sandals. She'd lived in New York so long, she had forgotten that women actually wore such instruments of torture. She added the fact that she had to wear high heels to the list of her grievances against the party—and Roger. Cass's grievance list was long enough to paper the room. The patio, for example. Why did Roger have to have the party centered in the same space as Lana's premier party the night she was killed? And the guest list. It included such pains in the ass as short, stupid John Latham. He'd inherited tons of money along with his father's seat on Colossal's board when the older man died. And Jina, Roger's latest bit of arm candy. She looked young enough to be his granddaughter, and Cass had serious doubts that she could piece two thoughts together.

"Why in hell did I agree to stick around for this?" she muttered under her breath, forcing a smile as she stepped aside so that this week's rising star and her enormously wealthy, very elderly escort could make a grand entrance.

But she should stop complaining. The night was a perfect seventy degrees, the barest breeze in the air. Whispering Winds seemed surrounded by a million sparkling stars in the midnight-blue sky. The mansion was decorated with exquisite day lilies, and their fragrance transcended even Cassidy's maudlin mood.

A pristine white runner led the guests from the portico out front to the spacious patio in the back. Round tables were set with exotic white orchids, the Limoges china she remembered from her childhood, and Baccarat crystal candelabras, creating a prism of light that sparkled like diamonds throughout the patio. A Plexiglas platform covered the pool, transforming it into a dance floor. The twenty-piece orchestra was neatly arranged behind it, alternating between romantic ballads and soft rock. Over the past hour, guests had arrived by private plane, commercial jet, and limousine. The Davises, the Lears, the Stallones, the Biondis, the Spielbergs.

Obviously Roger was reveling in the attention he was receiving as Lazarus, the delightful host, back from the dead. All earlier traces of his grayish pallor had disappeared, and Cassidy couldn't help but notice his remarkable smile. Even so, she would have preferred not to attend. Her emotions were off kilter, caught up in a turbulent storm of uncertainty.

All she really wanted was a cup of hot tea and a good night's sleep. But in the end she dutifully put on the elegant white Valentino gown and took her place beside her father. It had been ages since Cass had attended a social event more formal than dinner at the Four Seasons. She felt awkward, out of place among the Hollywood crowd. But so far everything was going smoothly. The drinks flowed, the food was superb, and the praise lavish.

Cassidy noticed that her father insisted on introducing her to each guest as both his daughter and the new head of Desmond Films. Cass, who had played the corporate network game most successfully, found the studio contingent pretty much the same as what she was used to.

There was the female executive eager to score points with her father. "I've seen your work, Ms. English. Very impressive," she cooed, cupping Cass's right hand in both of hers. And the chubby, bald, brown-eyed show-biz lawyer who licked his lips before announcing, "If there's anything I can do for you, legally or otherwise, please feel free to call me at any time."

A stealthy agent who picked his wardrobe from the pages of *GQ* asked if she needed help getting out of her contract with *Up to the Minute*. "Ted and I are like this." He held up two crossed fingers. "I golf with him every Thursday." Cass assured Mr. Aren't-I-Cool that James Renthrew was handling the details. When he turned away, Roger made a ridiculous face behind his back, imitating the agent's snooty manner-isms. Cass broke down and laughed. She couldn't help it. She was not immune to her father's charm.

Two Colossal honchos, Donald Braunstein and Clay Ross, squired her away from Roger to ask pointed questions. What exactly did she know about producing a feature film? Who would direct? Cass respected them for being blunt, and she assured them honestly that she'd fill her father's shoes if she could, and if not, she'd go.

Jonathan never looked in her direction.

Cassidy gave her half brother a wide berth, though she had already noted he was never unattended by gorgeous sycophants. Two in partic-ular seemed to be vying for his attention. But his face remained in a scowl. He had been drunk before the guests arrived and only got worse. She realized tonight wouldn't be without explosions; she only questioned the timing.

Hors d'oeuvres and Crystal champagne were served from silver trays by waiters in black tie and waitresses in black uniforms with white aprons. On the buffet were lavish offerings of fresh fruit, buluga caviar, and a splendid selection of delicious entrées specially prepared by the best caterers in town.

Cassidy watched now as Roger deftly worked the room, greeting associates and complimenting their wives. He remembered the name of every spouse—husband or wife—including newly acquired trophy wives. Cass found his social skills awesome. She knew his grace would be hard to replicate—even for her.

Suddenly a commotion developed at the entrance to the party. Cass saw a man she recognized as Jack Cavelli step out of an ivory-and-tan Bentley. He quickly took the front steps.

Instant pandemonium broke out. Cameramen and still photographers waiting outside the gates—as well as a handful who had gotten past the rent-a-cops and were positioned in the bushes around the doorway—leaped into action. It was clear to Cassidy that Jack despised reporters and their insipid questions as he adroitly sidestepped their mikes and moved behind the columns, effectively blocking their view.

Glancing down the barrel of one photographer's lens, Jack readjusted his bow tie, then smoothed his glistening salt-and-pepper hair with the palms of his hands. Satisfied with his appearance, he entered the melee, flashing a pearly white Hollywood smile, and made his way through the throng.

Compliments from partygoers hummed through the crowd. "Looking good, Jack." "Caught a screening of *Remembering Mama*—the buzz is right. Great job." Others tried for a casual "Let's do lunch soon? I'll have my people call your people."

She glanced toward him and for a moment their eyes met. This heightened her senses and piqued her curiosity. Just then Cassidy saw Roger put a hand on Cavelli's shoulder.

"I'm glad you could make it, Jack." Roger was preening.

Jack shot him a crooked smile. "I couldn't very well miss *the* party of the year. Tell me, Roger, did you plan this from the start?"

"You mean the party?" Roger asked, knowing full well he didn't. "Have you met my daughter?"

Before Jack could nod, Roger ushered him over to the bar, where Cass tried to look busy talking to a well-known screenwriter.

"Cassidy, this is Jack Cavelli. Jack, my lovely daughter, Cassidy." The two made eye contact once again.

Cassidy reached her hand out and shook Jack's hand. "It's a pleasure, Mr. Cavelli."

"The pleasure is mine," Jack said, smiling now more deeply.

"Cass is an amazing young woman. I'm sure you'll have no problem working beside her," Roger was saying.

Cassidy half smiled. "Daddy, please. You're embarrassing me."

"I agree, Roger. She's incredible."

Cassidy cautioned herself to be sensible. Yes, she was elated by the praise, but she was also stimulated by the champagne. She found herself thinking that maybe she was misinterpreting Jack's gaze as flirtatious—

even romantic. He probably was just sizing her up, like all the other studio heads.

Roger spotted James and his wife, Serena, at the front door and quickly excused himself. "I really do need to speak to James. This will give both of you a chance to get acquainted."

Cass eyed her father suspiciously and hated him for walking away, leaving her to make idle conversation with Cavelli. She knew Cavelli. They'd even attended the same industry functions once or twice in New York and at Sundance, but they had never spoken. Right now she didn't like the way he made her feel—off balance.

Jack Cavelli was the most powerful man in the film industry. As powerful as her father at his peak. He was intelligent and influential. Cunning and clever. He was also arrogant and egotistical.

Granted, he was probably the most handsome man Cass had ever laid eyes on, and he certainly wasn't short in the charisma department, either. She guessed he was a lady-killer. She knew the type, love them and leave them. And though she hardly knew Jack Cavelli, she felt herself beginning to despise him. Wasn't he the one who owned the controlling share of Colossal, which made him her boss?

And something else—he aroused feelings she felt were better left undisturbed.

The night grew cold, and Cass shivered a little. Jack drew her satin wrap around her bare shoulders. His hands felt like fire against her skin as they brushed the nape of her neck. The silence between them was stifling. She wanted to run, but she realized she needed to compose herself.

Starting tomorrow, she'd be working for him. Ignoring the danger signals radiating inside her, she decided to break the ice, and began humming along with the orchestra as they played "Someone to Watch Over Me."

Jack smiled a devastating killer smile. His finely chiseled features were backlit by the moon.

"It's one of my favorites as well. Shall we dance?" His green eyes gleamed. Before she could refuse, Jack took her waist with one arm and pulled her onto the dance floor. At first Cass tried to keep her distance, but his grip was too strong and he held her close. She noticed all eyes were now on them. She swept the crowd. There was James, with his wife—both had stopped talking to watch her. Clay Ross had a glassy look. She wondered if he was drunk, or was something else going on behind those steel-cold eyes?

Her gaze rested briefly on her father, who was smiling, chatting, clearly happy and relaxed. And for that she was glad. Then she saw Jonathan drunkenly holding on to the bar with one hand, clutching a drink in the other. She saw hatred, rage, and sadness in his eyes.

Jack pulled her attention back. She felt her legs press into his thighs and her breasts against his chest, followed by the sudden shock of his hand gently brushing the small of her back. It happened too quickly to resist and then it happened in slow motion. His arm was taut around her waist, pulling her even closer, flattening her body against his. He didn't speak, only stared.

She nearly froze in his intense gaze. Her head began to spin and her breathing grew shallow. She fought the delirious sensation. Finally her rational side kicked in. Using both hands, she pressed her palms against his chest, putting some distance between them.

"Please, stop," she murmured.

Still he didn't speak.

| | |

The security at the gate was astonishing. Guests gave names, guards checked lists. Chelsea held her breath as one of the men searched for her name. "Mr. Cavelli's guest," she'd repeated twice. Moments later he nodded, then beckoned the limousine inside. The driver snaked the car up to the front entrance. By the time he got out to open the back passenger door, Chelsea had already exited the car and disappeared into the throng of rich and famous milling about the mansion.

Avoiding the main entrance, she made her way around the side of the colossal building. Whispering Winds, she thought to herself. How pretentious. After sneaking through an open French door that seemed to lead into the solarium, Chelsea found an entrance into the kitchen. Waving casually to a cluster of women dressed in black uniform dresses with starched white aprons, she found the back stairs and climbed them as if she had been here a thousand times.

Upstairs, she perused the rooms and found everything exactly as she'd imagined—just like the pictures she'd painted in her imagination.

The beautiful mahogany furniture, the exquisite crystal chandelier dangling like stars in the night sky over the spiral staircase, lighting the foyer below. Along the walls of the second floor were paintings she recognized; Roger and Lana had obviously assembled some of the finer Impressionist paintings seen in a private collection—a Monet, two Manets, and an enormous Renoir. And one signed Picasso, from his Blue period.

All part of her birthright.

"Soon this will be mine," she said to herself. Very soon *she* would be mistress of this house. Cassidy—the *false* daughter of Roger and Lana Turmaine—would be banished. The bitch would lose her claim to the Turmaine fortune, the Turmaine status.

The heinous switch, made more than thirty years ago, would finally be reversed. Cassidy would have to take over the life of Chelsea Hutton. The *horrible* life of Chelsea Hutton.

Her footsteps crunched softly on the white carpet. Quietly she made her way down the hall. Quickly she checked each bedroom, knocking first, then pushing her head around the door. The third door she opened led her into an elaborate room. It was soft and feminine, and even before she checked the closet and stumbled on the matching Louis Vuitton suitcases, she knew it had to be Cass's room. It was pleasant and inviting, and, above all, lavish. The brass bed had an intricate design on its head- and footboards. Walls of built-in cabinetry, a sofa upholstered in soft gray velour, silk curtains over the double windows, and a bathroom suite—its absolute luxury fueled the rage now building inside of her, bringing to the surface memories of the roach-infested apartment in East L.A., that prison cell where she'd been raised by Maria Hutton. Flashes of her tortured childhood returned like humidity on a summer's night, lashing through her blood and making her feel heavy, weighted now with disgust and anger.

Chelsea forced herself to keep moving, not wanting to be caught in the maelstrom of her thoughts. She couldn't afford to lose her momentum now. She snapped out of the past, then sifted through the expensive frocks on hangers. The closet was full. There were gowns, dresses, and suits from all the top designers. On the floor neatly stacked were at least a half dozen pairs of shoes. Never worn. She opened the closet drawers and thrust her hands into the hill of lacy silk lingerie. Silk nightgowns, panties, bras, and camisoles slipped through her fingers. Dear old Dad must have arranged a shopping spree in Cass's honor—everything in the closet and drawers, including the lingerie, was still tagged with names of shops along Rodeo Drive.

The voices started. *"This should be yours. That bitch doesn't belong here. You do."*

Chelsea shook her head, trying to silence the venomous words before they filled her up.

Watching the clock, she pushed the drawer closed and shut the closet doors. Swiftly she made her way inside the bathroom. In the vanity mirror she glimpsed her reflection and was shocked by what she saw; the effects of ever-present anger had painted ugly lines across her forehead. Wrinkles of age? Worse. Her face, which she knew was otherwise beautiful, seemed marked by her bitterness. But not for long.

On the counter next to the sink was a basket of toiletries—only the finest European lotions and creams, soaps, and oils. Chelsea picked up a bar of lavender-scented soap, held it inches from her nostrils, and inhaled deeply; the fullness of the smell overwhelmed her. She imagined bathing in the large claw-foot tub, rubbing the creamy essence over her entire body. She closed her eyes and imagined the room awash with the warm glow of scented candles. Jack was there and they sat facing each other in the tub. He was reaching for her, desire on his face. Her depression lifted. She was completely relaxed, drifting into a peaceful meditation. She didn't feel the soap slip from her fingers. And when it crashed to the floor, she snapped back to reality.

Quietly and carefully she slipped back into the hallway and tiptoed downstairs. She should have headed for the nearest door. The smart thing to do would have been to make a quick exit and join the other guests on the patio. Instead her attention fell on the half-closed doors of the study.

Quickly she pushed the heavy double doors open, entered the warm, inviting room, and stood before the enormous, Gothic desk, definitely authentic. Chelsea had seen one of these sixteenth-century pieces at another party and had been drawn to its style. Its top was cluttered with unopened mail, scattered files, and newspapers. Among the clutter there were framed photographs and mementos of Cassidy. One photo of a young Cassidy perched high atop a beautiful Arabian horse caught her attention. The sterling-silver-framed picture had collected a patina of dust and Chelsea rubbed her thumb over Cass's image to clean it. She stared at the image of the beautiful little girl, dressed in expensive riding clothes and a velvet cap. Her smile was radiant. How different from the awkward, skinny, sickly creature she had been. For a second Chelsea felt the burning behind her eyes, but she refused to let the tears fall. Instead, she returned the photo, pivoted purposefully, then strode across the foyer to the entrance, letting the heels of her Ferragamo sandals strike the polished marble as hard as possible to chase away the ghosts—and the lingering hurt.

There would be plenty of tears later, only they would be Cassidy's. It was at that moment that the excruciating headache returned, and thoughts—crazy ones—filled her head.

Jonathan hugged the bar as he observed the party from his stakeout position. He was on his fourth or fifth drink—he'd lost count. He felt numb. His surroundings blurred, yet he found relief in this boozy dream state. He muttered profanities under his breath, rehearsing what he would say to the important friends and colleagues of his father who came over to say how good it was to see Roger up and about.

He would make his father pay for freezing him out, for giving the position that was rightfully his to that icy bitch. The "mysterious" Cassidy English, the "myth" of network news—yeah, right. She may have left L.A. years ago, but she was as phony as all the other babes in Hollywood.

He scanned the crowd for Cass and saw her dancing. There were two of her—maybe three. He squinted to make out her partner. When he realized it was Jack Cavelli, he cringed. Even drunk, he could read the look of intrigue in Cavelli's eyes. Jonathan was no fool. Tonight everyone here came to pay homage to her.

Jonathan fumed. No one *ever* took him seriously. They thought he was just some out-of-control asshole out for new kicks, perversions, thrills, and drugs. His current claim to fame was the wild parties he threw at various friends' apartments, entertaining on a lavish scale with free cocaine, cheap women, and loud music. Jonathan was aware that he had few allies here tonight, or at least few who would openly admit it. And funds for his hobbies were becoming scarce since James, that old busybody, had convinced his father to cut Jonathan's allowance to a mere pittance. James's spies had carried back tales of Jonathan's wild partying and aggressive spending. Ha! As if cutting back on his funds would alter his lifestyle. Sure, with less money to spend, parties were a bit less crazy, but overall he still lived by his own rules. No one—not James, not Roger, nor Miss Prissy—could stop him.

Jonathan sipped his drink and wished the night were over. He hadn't wanted to come in the first place. In fact, he'd announced he wouldn't, but after careful consideration he realized that was exactly what Father and Cass wanted. Instead, he decided to make an appearance. Perhaps there was some way he could make something of the evening.

| | |

Chelsea stood on the edge of the patio, momentarily stymied by the sight of the couple dancing cheek to cheek. Then, without another second's hesitation, she strode purposefully to the dance floor and stood inches from the two swaying bodies.

"You probably don't remember," Chelsea began. "We met at the cemetery."

The princess looked stunned. "I . . . I, uh . . . remember your face. What did you say your name is?"

"I didn't," Chelsea replied in an even tone. "Chelsea Hutton." Then she turned her focus to Jack. She had expected to get his full attention, but she didn't. His eyes never left Cassidy's. She was thrown by this and fought to rid herself of that resurfacing sense of inferiority. The need to claim her territory was great.

"I'm Jack's date for the evening."

Cassidy looked startled and awkward. She broke out of Jack's embrace and took a few steps backward. "We were just dancing, Ms. Hutton. Jack was impatient waiting for you. I'll leave you two alone now. Enjoy the party."

"Before you leave, Ms. English," Chelsea said, "allow me to formally introduce myself. I'm the new star of *Dangerous Intentions*."

| | |

Cassidy had grown into a beautiful, sensible woman. Gone were all traces of youth and immaturity. She was a fighter, determined to beat the world at a game she knew little about. And although others might be skeptical, James's money was on Cass. The young girl he'd known and loved avidly had prevailed, with panache, above every obstacle thrust in her way. He took pride in her success. After all, he was owed some amount of credit. For much of their lives, both Turmaine children had been his responsibility, and he never regretted the wear and tear he suffered as a result.

Watching her on the dance floor, he thought her choice in partners was poor. Cavelli was trouble. He made a mental note to discuss this with her in the morning. For now he'd simply allow her to be the belle of the ball.

His gaze shifted to Jonathan. He was staggering and stumbling, obviously stone drunk. The young man was totally out of control. When Roger finally noticed, he would be livid. Somehow he'd have to find a way to get his children under control. This was not a time for the family to waste energy on internecine warfare.

| | |

It was nearly midnight. Jonathan still skulked around the sidelines of the party, brooding, watching. Cassidy was standing just ten feet away from him. She smiled at the guests. He knew she was reveling in his misery, stealing all his thunder. The queen bee, dressed in white from head to toe, surrounded by her drones—the ass-kissers and toadies. Queen bee? Hell, she was a black widow spider.

He got the sudden urge to douse her expensive frock with his drink. He realized this was childish, but he couldn't help himself. He made his way to the center of the dance floor, fighting desperately to steady himself.

Cass seemed surprised—no, shocked—by his appearance.

"Hey, sis. How's it going?"

Cass shot a warning gaze at her half brother. She would not allow him to embarrass her or her father—or himself. In her absence she had missed the evolution of her somewhat rebellious half brother into a vindictive, bitter lush.

A waitress offered them champagne. "Maybe you've had enough," Cass said quietly.

"Maybe *you've* had enough," Jonathan said quickly, and downed the bubbling liquid in one gulp. "I see you've already met"—he turned his gaze to the opposite side of the dance floor—"Jack Cavelli, L.A.'s number-one mover and shaker." Jonathan licked his lips, then smiled. "Yeah, I could see the attraction, Cass. Kinda reminds you of Tom Gleeson. You remember him, don't you?"

At that moment Cass wavered, her legs buckling slightly. Suddenly Jack Cavelli appeared by her side.

"You've had a lot to drink, Jonathan. Why don't you call it a night?" Jack said firmly.

"Go to hell, Cavelli," Jonathan slurred. He turned back to his sister. "You remember Tom, the guy who knocked you up and then dumped your lily-white ass," he said, laughing loudly, unable to stop.

Cassidy's cheeks flushed, but her gaze stayed focused on Jonathan.

"How long did you wait for him at the airport?"

Jonathan was talking, his lips were moving, but Cass couldn't hear what he was saying. She was in a vacuum, shut off from the rest of the world. All Cass saw, all she wanted, was darkness, quiet, sleep. A tumbling rock of a memory, the white, cold clinic, began the avalanche. The memories crashed around her feet. She felt trapped.

Jack took her arm, murmuring that everything was all right, that her brother was obviously raving. The spell was broken and the roar of the party swirled around her. Everyone seemed to be talking at once.

Without a word, Cass moved away from Cavelli toward the house, slowly at first, testing her legs, making sure the tremors she felt were not making her legs shaky. She'd never let Jonathan see the effect of what he had said.

She cut through the kitchen because it was usually the quickest route to the back stairs, but tonight the army of waiters, cooks, managers, and clean-up crew from the catering company blocked her way.

"Excuse me," she said. "I'm sorry." She forced herself to be patient as she made her way through the room. The restaurant-size kitchen resounded with pots clanging, dishes being stacked, loud, sharp calls from the manager to the cooks, the cooks to their assistants. Finally out of the kitchen, Cass picked up speed, holding up her gown to keep from tripping over the stilettos. She ran up the spiral staircase and into her bedroom. Safe. She waited in the dark for her breathing to calm. Then she turned the light on. And screamed.

The once-lovely comforter had been destroyed by fire. A blood-stained frilly nightgown was thrown across the foot of the bed. On the floor was a partially incinerated photo of her mother. Next to it was a note, scrawled in paint, the same color as the stain on the nightgown:

Hey, Superstar, twinkle for as long as you can—
the Turmaines are about to lose another pretty lady.

He edged his way through the crowd, coldly calculating the speed of her swift, graceful strides. It was nearly midnight. Cassidy had fled upstairs, no doubt shaken.

The warm autumn air had become chilly and he was glad the alcohol was keeping him warm. Overhead the sky grew angry. The stars were now covered by clouds and the moon had disappeared before his very eyes.

He stopped at the fountain underneath her window. He waited for the inevitable light to go on, and then he sighed as he heard, as he knew he would, her high-pitched screams piercing the night. He had to move fast.

It wouldn't take long to break her.

The next morning, Jack Cavelli sat looking out over the Pacific from his secret hideaway beneath his beach house in Malibu.

Bordered on the west by the Pacific Ocean and to the east by the Santa Monica Mountains, this scenic strip of beach lies along miles of California's mythic Highway 1. This exquisite piece of real estate provided backdrops for Judy Garland and James Mason—Mr. and Mrs. Norman Main—in Cukor's *A Star Is Born,* and later, for Streisand and Redford in *The Way We Were.* In Hollywood's heyday, movie industry elite built lavish "weekend" homes here to provide escape from work and their fans.

Storms and hurricanes could hit hard here, and flood the low-lying houses, built close together along the road that traced the crest of the Pacific coastline. Newer houses were built on stilts, and weathered wood sidings disguised magnificent mansions as mere beach houses. In these palaces lived the important players of the entertainment world and their camp followers.

So sat the house that Jack built. Behind the simple facade was a multileveled geometric house with an indoor swimming pool and expansive solar windows—all with breathtaking ocean views. Only from the beach could one see the full scale of this four-story structure, which looked like it had grown organically from the rocky cliff. All that could be seen from the highway was a nondescript three-car garage at one side of the wide, paved driveway and a high wall of weathered wood planks fronted by a line of cedars. The actual entrance to the house was secreted on the opposite side, behind a cluster of gigantic yuccas. Huge cacti flanked the humble weathered wood door, which opened into a dramatic yet highly functional entertainment and multilevel living area that included a formal dining room and professional kitchen, separated from the informal living space by a curving caramel-colored travertine marble bar. Beyond this was the pool and, outside on the cantilevered deck, the hot tub.

With the Pacific Ocean as its main design element, the house was decorated in the hues of the ocean, sand, and sky. Mementos from around the world were artfully displayed throughout. Down one floor, a home theater seated a hundred guests quite comfortably and, in the billiard room, players got an underwater view of swimmers in the pool through an aquarium wall. This floor also featured a high-tech multimedia conference room, which opened into Jack's handsome, very private office.

On the first level were the exquisitely decorated guest-room suites, each opening to a lower deck that gave them access to the beach. The top level of the mansion housed the master suite—Jack's haven. It was furnished with a custom-made teak bed with Versace silk openings, an art nouveau desk, animal-print chaise, and a Carrera marble bath with a full ocean view.

Sometimes Jack would sneak away from his guests, through the guest-room floor and out to the sand beneath the lower deck. There he would lean against the stanchions that held his house against the cliff and look out to the unreachable horizon. There he would dream.

Jack had homes all over the world, but Malibu was his private retreat. The salty sea smell and taste of the Pacific Ocean air, the sound of crashing waves, both turbulent and soothing, offered comfort in his crazy, hectic, unpredictable world.

Jack was at work at his desk in his office, reviewing quarterly financial reports from Colossal's diverse divisions, when he heard Chelsea's steps as she approached from the guest-floor below. Those few women who stayed the night were never permitted to roam, and he'd made it clear that they were not welcome in his inner sanctum. That was a given.

Obviously Chelsea thought she was an exception.

This minuscule betrayal was enough to send him over the edge. She approached the desk, stood just inches from him. Her presence caused him to slouch; she was an irrepressible weight on his shoulders, a constant nag. He loathed "the mornings after," when a woman expected to exchange niceties or bits and pieces of pleasant conversation—how beautiful they looked, how wonderful last night was, would she like to join him for breakfast out on the terrace? That's why he usually sent them home in his private limo at evening's end.

When a woman did stay the night, Jack went through the motions just for the sake of peace. There was nothing worse the first thing in the morning than a hysterical woman who felt that she'd been scorned. But today was an exception. Hysterical or not, Jack was determined to bypass the usual ritual and continue on with the business at hand—the studio.

"At last I've found you." Chelsea tossed her head in a playful manner, let out a great peal of laughter. She was still dressed in the sexy black nightgown she'd surprised him with after last night's party at Whispering Winds. She continued to move toward him. Her movements were slow, cunning, and purposeful . . . a cat in heat.

"So you have," he shot back, without even glancing up.

She perched on the edge of the desk, her long, lean legs amply exposed.

He cast a disapproving glance at her well-tanned thighs. He squeezed his eyes shut for a moment in the hopes that she'd disappear. No such luck. He had rehearsed a hundred polite ways to make her leave, yet he had to proceed with caution. He needed her.

Jack would indeed see to it that Chelsea was cast as Ophelia in *Dangerous Intentions*. This way, he would know everything going on during the filming, on the set and off. He wanted to keep an eye on Cassidy English. Chelsea would be his unwitting spy.

He told himself it was all about business, that Ms. English would prove totally inadequate to produce the film. Clearly it would just be a matter of time before Desmond Films would need help—his help. Then he could put Phase Two of his plan into action.

Images from the Turmaine party replayed in his mind. He rarely attended media events. He hated all the ass-kissing, everyone flashing pearly white, phony Hollywood smiles, telling him how great he was. He knew all they wanted was to stay on his good side.

Important Hollywood parties weren't celebrations at all. They were sophisticated rituals of either casting, interviewing, or one-upmanship. The more impressive the host and the guest list, the more despicable the game. It had to be A-list or nothing. Jack chose nothing.

And no Hollywood event would be complete without the beautiful young women—lots of them, lining the walls, draped seductively over chairs, encircling the bar. Window dressing. All searching. Not one, not even established stars and wives of stars, would miss the chance to chat a bit, or at least make eye contact, with Jack. He didn't need to *see* them to know who was there. They were always the same: the pert-nosed red-head in the skimpy rust-colored mini; the short-cropped blonde in black leather—Hell's Angel with cleavage—and, of course, the dozens of Pamela Anderson and Elizabeth Taylor look-alikes. He smiled noncommittally at any woman who caught his eye.

Last night, as he'd worked his way through the crowd to the bar, he passed an exotic brunette with cheekbones that could cut glass. He couldn't ignore the look she threw his way as she ran her long blood-red fingertips seductively through her hair. He was *not* in the mood for a come-on. He'd felt that way a lot lately. He was tired of Hollywood babes. They lacked substance. Their aggressive flirtation invariably came off like an acting exercise with no spontaneity. Maybe it was middle age, maybe not. He just knew there had to be something more that went on between two people.

Jack had almost tried the marriage thing once. She was an English woman who gave new meaning to the phrase "lady in the kitchen, whore in the bedroom." But after six months, she'd turned into a whining, materialistic brat. Not at all what he was looking for.

Jack concluded that he was holding out for a woman who would meet his standards, an intelligent, successful, refined women—a lady—who knew all about the finer things in life. He liked them dressed in Armani, with jewels from Bulgari. He liked them in La Perla lingerie and Manolo Blahnik pumps. He liked them to be worldly and cultivated. He liked good breeding, and he didn't mind spending for it. He also liked compassion, class, and sensitivity, rare commodities among the women he often dated and even bedded.

Cassidy English intrigued him. She was even more beautiful in person than she appeared in the grainy black-and-white photos in *Daily Variety* and on TV. He was mesmerized, entranced by her vivid blue eyes, luminous skin, and the wild mane of black curls that fell nearly to her waist—all set off by the magnificent clinging gown she was wearing.

Ever since they danced, the feel of Cassidy's body against his had wrapped around him like a warm blanket. Granted, she was devastatingly beautiful. Any fool could see that. But Jack was sure this attraction went way beyond the physical. Perhaps it was her face, so full of strength, shining with steadfast serenity; her determination, even her visible vulnerability. Of course, there was also the fact that she could, and did, resist his advances. This left him hungering for more.

He needed to proceed with caution. He reminded himself to stick to his practice of never mixing business with pleasure. It was a shame, though. He flushed with embarrassment at the memory of her face.

He wondered about the brief exchange he witnessed between Jonathan and Cassidy. He felt sorry for her and her obvious hurt at her brother's words. At the time he had wanted to cradle her and rock her back to safety. Now, in the light of day, he had gained perspective. He'd put his compassion aside—after all, business was business.

| | |

"I thought we might have breakfast together." There was a plea in Chelsea's voice and a shimmer in her eyes. Were those tears? "Of course, if you're too busy . . ." Her face twisted into a grotesque mask of anger and jealousy when she spotted the newspaper folded open to Cassidy's picture.

The contrasts between the woman pleading before him and the woman in his fantasy collided: Chelsea, hard, stubborn, and abrasive; Cassidy, determined, ladylike, and brilliant. They were polar opposites. And still he sensed that something apparently linked them together. What? He had no clue.

Chelsea bit into her lower lip, waiting for his reply. He supposed he'd better answer, lest she throw one of her notorious hissy fits, convincing him even more that behind all the glamorous armor, she was, in fact, an errant child.

"I'm too busy." He ripped out the words impatiently. Normally he would have obliged, but today there was no time for chitchat.

She hopped off the desk and stood defiantly with her hands on both hips. "I can see that." She pointedly looked at the photo of Cassidy.

"Oh, come now. You can cut out the charade. There are no strings attached. What we share"—he carefully chose his words—"what we've always shared, is a mutually profitable business relationship. Spare me the histrionics. Jealousy doesn't become you."

Still looking at the desk, she shot him a commanding look. "And spare me the bullshit. I saw the way you looked at her last night. Hell, you might as well have fucked her right there on the dance floor. But Ms. English is too much of a lady to fuck. That is what you're thinking, isn't it? Admit it, Jack." She turned and headed for the door. "Whether or not you're man enough to admit it, Jack, she's already got you."

Only when he heard the door of the suite slam shut did Jack drop his guard. His usual bravado and his smug smile were instantly replaced by all-consuming anger. How dare Chelsea accuse him of growing soft—over a woman, no less. Of course she was wrong. No woman alive was capable of "getting a hold" on Jack Cavelli, no matter how exceptional she was. He went through women like other men smoked cigars. He enjoyed their scent—the more extravagant, the better. And he liked variety. He relished the fire and the smoke. But when the night was over, his pleasure was extinguished.

A woman strong enough to bring Jack Cavelli to his knees? Impossible.

He ran for the door, then hurried down the hall. He caught up with Chelsea just as she was about to descend the stairs. He moved toward her and she started to speak, but he shut her up with a kiss. A kiss that was hard and demanding. She didn't protest, wouldn't dare push him away. Instead, she pulled him closer to her body with urgency and need. Their immediate surroundings meant nothing.

He ripped off his trousers and tore at the buttons on his shirt. Chelsea clung to him, knowing it was not love or even lust, but rather rage that was driving him. He pushed her back against the railing and reached roughly between her legs. He closed his eyes and became a stranger again, just like he did whenever they made love. He tore into her. His rage intensified with each thrust. Passion fueled his anger. He was tearing her apart and Chelsea let him. She bit her bottom lip to keep from crying out.

She knew better than to push Jack. The truth hurt and he was retaliating in the best way he knew how: making love like a wild animal. He held her down, his hands pulling at her hair. Chelsea desperately tried to keep control of herself, to keep from sliding under. Jack cried out when he climaxed, a sad, baleful moan, and then dropped down beside her. Any minute, she knew, he would leave her there, on the floor at the top of the stairs, without a word, expecting her to let herself out. Just like he always did.

Cassidy was amazed at the early-morning traffic on the freeway. It was barely seven o'clock, yet the roads were clogged with traffic, everyone on their cell phones, doing their makeup, listening to books on tape. It was crowded, yes, but people were at a safe distance. What a change from Manhattan, she thought with some relief. Maybe she was going to like living in L.A. after all.

Traces of the previous evening still lingered. The nightmarish vision of her burned comforter, the bloodstained nightgown, the note, scribbled in a jarring script, had all left their mark. She had moved into another room but still could not sleep, despite her absolute exhaustion.

Her father had tried to calm her, saying it was someone's idea of a bad joke. Cassidy just looked at him without saying a word. She knew they were both thinking about Jonathan, his drinking, his rage.

Finally, giving up all hope of sleep, she'd dug her head into a book—*Colossal: The Rise and Fall and Rise Again of the Studio.* If she couldn't get any rest, she could at least bone up on her Hollywood history. If she knew where Colossal had been as a company, she might be better able to understand where it was heading. And be ready to guide it.

And Desmond, for better or worse, was the property of Colossal, which was controlled by Jack Cavelli. Cassidy knew that one key to the success of any project was to know the players. And right now Jack Cavelli was the player to know.

Cassidy wound her way down Sunset Boulevard, looking at the totems to the Hollywood of the past. Sunset Boulevard, once a dirt track linking the burgeoning film studios with the hillside homes of screen stars, had become the center of Hollywood's film industry. Famous nightclubs like the Trocadero, Ciro's, and the Macambo—where young

Margarita Cansino met studio boss Harry Cohen, who renamed her Rita Hayworth—were just a small part of Sunset Boulevard's legend.

"Classic Hollywood"—two words that evoked images of glamour, style, and stars. The thirties and forties had been the Golden Age of Movies. Hollywood studios were dream factories in those days, pumping out hundreds of movies each year to satiate the appetite of the American public. And it had been Walter Pickett, a wealthy vaudeville promoter, who had a vision and chased his dream of owning one of Hollywood's most successful, most productive studios.

On Melrose Avenue, just south of Paramount Studios, on sixty-five acres of back lots and soundstages, Pickett brought his dream into reality. He had strong connections with entertainment industry bigwigs, and in time was able to woo stars like Mae West, Marlene Dietrich, Gary Cooper, and Bing Crosby into his fold. Within two years, a series of mergers and realignments would concentrate ninety-five percent of all American film production in the hands of nine studios—five majors and four minors, including 20th Century–Fox, Paramount, and Warner Brothers. Colossal had held the second position, behind only MGM.

Colossal, under Pickett's rule, consistently made movies that captivated the hearts of Depression-era Americans who sought refuge from those hard times.

From what she'd read the night before, it was clear to Cassidy that the key to Pickett's vision was that he believed characters should be accessible to everyone. It didn't matter if you were an unemployed husband or a pathetic housewife: Pickett put someone you could identify with up on the silver screen. He transformed the lives of everyday Americans and their struggles into myths. If Americans had problems, Hollywood had the antidote. And it worked, allowing Pickett to supersede the likes of Cecil B. De Mille, Samuel Goldwyn, Louis B. Mayer, and Jack Warner. Eventually Colossal became the number-one studio.

But Pickett may have had help. Cassidy had been fascinated to discover how the supposedly legitimate business of filmmaking became entrenched in mob politics.

One of Pickett's longtime associates was none other than the dashing mobster Benjamin "Bugsy" Siegel. Siegel, who had grown up in New York's Hell's Kitchen, started out as an associate of Lucky Luciano and Meyer Lansky. At first he was simply known as a bootlegger, and a killer with an enormous libido. But then Siegel developed a passion for Broadway showgirls and Hollywood starlets. He began hanging out with Hollywood society's elite, including Harlow, Gable, Cooper, and Grant. And soon Siegel made his way into a powerful shakedown business that fed off Hollywood extras and bit players. Quite simply, if you wanted to work, you had to pay. Eventually his control over the "little people" spread up to the moguls. If the big shots didn't pay, their actors and actresses would be forced to walk off sets.

Rumor had it that Siegel was responsible for Colossal's staying power. He was able to clear a path for its rise to the top by instilling fear and respect in the heads of all the other studios. Bugsy had Hollywood by the balls. No studio head, producer, director, or agent had as much power or control over Hollywood's rackets as Bugsy Siegel.

Siegel netted almost a million a year. All of his profits went back into his share of the Hollywood dope and white-slave traffic. Even after his arrest for the murder of Harry Greenberg in 1939, Siegel was afforded exceptional VIP treatment while behind bars. He was granted at least twenty "passes" in a month, enabling him to pop in and out of jail as though it were a hotel. He was seen in town with "players," a few of them "associates" who were known members of organized crime, and the men who managed his money: his banker, broker, and accountant.

And of course he was let out for every important premiere or Hollywood social event.

Soon the murder charges were dropped, and within a matter of weeks, Siegel's friends, among them Walter Pickett, helped restore him to the top of the Hollywood scene.

In June 1947 at nearly midnight, Bugsy Siegel was reading a newspaper in the living room of his girlfriend Virginia Hill's home when a fiery blast shattered the window. Siegel was shot dead, his face veiled in a thick sheet of blood. Three bullets had ripped through his skull.

Pickett was very broken up at Siegel's funeral, mourning the loss of his friend, or so people thought. In truth, what looked like sorrow was really his concern for the future of Colossal. Pickett, however, need not have worried. He would not live to see Colossal's future. In 1954, the year he filed for bankruptcy, Walter Pickett suffered a fatal heart attack.

The studio was left to his only son, Walter Jr.

And the Walter Pickett Jr. she'd been reading about into the wee hours of the night seemed unpleasantly similar to her half brother, Jonathan. Pickett the Younger was spoiled, his tastes extravagant. His business acumen was nil, as was his ambition. It didn't take long for Colossal to fail. The studio closed its doors in 1964, a signal that "Old Hollywood" was dead.

Its resurrection, fifteen years later, was due to none other than Jack Cavelli. Had it not been for Cavelli's millions and keen insight, Colossal might very well have been a dusty memory in the archives of Hollywood legend.

From the start, it was obvious to anyone in the industry that Cavelli was a mastermind. He was the savior, the hero, the studio's Messiah, and his incredible resuscitation of Colossal had earned him the moniker "the Mighty One."

Cassidy made it a point to study Cavelli's role from '84 to the present in intimate detail—the years when Cavelli's power truly became apparent. After all, knowledge was power and power seemed to be all that mattered to Jack. If she wanted to earn his respect and support, she had to be well schooled. More than that, Cassidy wanted to know where Jack was coming from; to get into his head. The last thing she wanted was to be caught off guard again.

She had to think about him only as her adversary, but it was difficult. The whirl around the dance floor, wrapped in his arms, brought forth emotions strong enough to stun her. The warning light inside her head told her to proceed with caution. This is not a man to whom she should be attracted. She couldn't afford to be.

She thought of Rudolpho in New York, her colleague, her best friend, her sometime lover. She had called him yesterday, begging him to come out to Los Angeles to help her with *Dangerous Intentions.* He had agreed but now she wondered if that had been a good idea. She trusted his ability to direct—he'd always wanted to direct feature films—but on the personal side, he was always pressuring her for more commitment. Did she love Rudolpho enough for that? Yes and no. The fact remained that for as much as she could rely on him, know that he was there for her in ways she had never experienced before in her life, she wasn't quite sure if they were meant to be a couple.

But she did know one thing: Rudolpho was absolutely essential for her if she was to make *Dangerous* work and succeed.

Her thoughts returned to Jack Cavelli, and then to Chelsea Hutton. They were lovers. That was obvious. But for some reason they seemed ill-suited for each other. Cassidy laughed at herself. Was she jealous? Nevertheless, the Hutton woman was another of life's cruel jokes.

Their apparently accidental meeting at the cemetery had seemed friendly and civilized, at least at first, yet at the party, Chelsea's performance made it clear that she considered Cassidy an enemy. Friend or foe, the one thing Cass knew was that Chelsea Hutton was definitely a handful.

| | |

Cass was almost to the studio when her cell phone rang and she was "formally notified" that Chelsea was to replace the actress already cast as Ophelia. The poor young actress had been bought out of her contract and the settlement money would come out of the film's budget.

Instinctively, Cassidy knew that Chelsea Hutton was all wrong for the part of Ophelia Rossini. The character was strong, determined, but naive, possessed of an innocent and graceful beauty and the soft-spoken manner of a child. From what Cass had seen, Chelsea seemed to embody a full-blooded passion that was nothing like the fragility of Ophelia.

But Cavelli had already made it abundantly clear that Chelsea was his choice for the role, even though her previous film credits gave little indication that this volatile woman could carry the part. Cassidy was not about to argue with the boss over it—at least not yet. Besides, shooting was scheduled to begin in barely a week, and completion would be impossible if they stopped moving forward to discuss casting this part—as if Jack would "discuss" anything. She couldn't afford a defeat at this point. Thank God at least Rudolpho would be here soon—she needed someone to watch her back.

Cass approached the entrance of Colossal Studios slowly. She stopped at the small guardhouse. Moments later the uniformed guard stepped out. "Can I help you, miss?"

"Cassidy English. Desmond Films."

"Of course, Ms. English." The guard smiled warmly. "Your pass hasn't come in yet, but as soon as it does, I'll notify you." He pushed a button and the gate went up.

"The main building is just up the hill and to the right. My name's Sam. If you ever need me, just call."

Cass returned the smile, then drove slowly past a row of neatly parked trailers, which she assumed were used by writers and directors. She took the first right and ended up on a New York City street. The Theater District, she thought. How authentic. And on her left, downtown—the Village perhaps. Rows of neat brownstones ran down the block. It was an exceptionally well-designed, well-constructed set, and Cass guessed the directors at the studio got a lot of use out of it. In fact, she'd remembered from reading over Colossal's 1999 figures that the New York City set was the most requested for rental from other studios and independent film companies.

She continued right to the main building and drove into the parking lot, surprised to see a spot reserved with her name. So far, so good, she thought, realizing that Roger must have prepared everyone for her arrival.

The main building was a four-story structure with a brick facade and a row of columns. It was stately, elegant, and screamed power, totally unlike her father's soulless Century City office tower.

Cass took the elevator up to the third floor and stepped out into the reception area. A large desk straddled the narrow hallway, occupied by three very busy receptionists. Before she could announce herself, a middle-aged black woman appeared from an office behind the counter.

"You must be Mr. Turmaine's daughter." The woman offered her hand to Cassidy. "I'm Lucy Whittaker, office manager. Let me be the first to welcome you aboard."

Cass smiled, returned the handshake, and turned on her businesslike charm. "I'm very pleased to meet you."

"If you'll just follow me, I'll take you to your office." She led Cass down the hallway to a large pair of double doors. The plaque on the wall said CASSIDY ENGLISH. Producing a key, she led her inside.

The room was large, with a very high ceiling and a wall of windows. There was a huge, leather-embossed desk, a leather sofa, two leather side chairs, modern paintings on the walls, and a conference table with seating for ten. Three walls were floor-to-ceiling bookcases; covering the floor was silk plush burgundy carpeting. Sunlight poured in through high windows behind the desk.

"In the early years, they used this room for private screenings. Mr. Pickett liked the intimate feel. I agree, don't you?"

"This was Mr. Pickett's office?"

"Yes," Lucy replied.

Cassidy smiled, liking the idea of being kept company by the studio's notorious founder.

Lucy went to the desk, showed Cass the intercom button. "If there's anything you need, anything at all, don't hesitate to call me." She checked her watch. "Your secretary, Ally Farmstead, should be here momentarily. I just saw her on her way to Security to get a set of keys for you. I think you're really going to like her. I bypassed Personnel and picked her myself."

"Thank you, Lucy," Cass replied.

"Well, if there's anything else I can do for you . . .?"

"Oh no, you've done so much already."

Lucy crossed to the door. "I'll let you get settled. I'm sure you have a million things to do."

Cass waited for the door to shut before plopping herself down in the chair behind the desk. Her eyes scanned the room, seeing it for the first time, marveling at its size and elegance. She really couldn't believe she was here. For years she'd longed to work in features, but the thought of even being on the same coast as her father had always stopped that thought in its tracks. This time last week she was producing a TV news-magazine; now she was head of a film company.

The door opened and a young woman stuck her head around the corner. "Hi, Ms. English, I'm Ally."

Cass was surprised to see an adorable woman who looked to be about twenty-five or so, with cropped blue-and-yellow-striped hair and a telltale hole in one nostril, no doubt usually filled by a ring. "Here's a set of keys—to this office, the private elevator out back, the file cabinets. Can I get anything for you?"

Cass stood and walked around the desk to shake Ally's hand and take the ring of keys. "No, I can't think of anything right now. I haven't even gone through my messages yet."

"Okay . . . well, if you need me, I'm the top button there, on the left." Ally pointed to the telephone console to the left of the massive desk. "Oh, and there's coffee and tea, and a fridge with juice and sodas, and a bar behind that end of the bookcase."

"Thanks," Cass replied warmly. "I'm sure I'll have lots to do once I get settled in."

As Ally returned to her place just outside the door, Cass returned to her desk to get her bearings. There were dozens of messages to sort through, meetings with department heads and corporate executives to schedule, locations to be approved, screenplay revisions to review, not to mention interviews to conduct with the leading actors and actresses.

"Ally, can I have the escalating advertising and promotional costs, as well as the budget reports for *Dangerous Intentions?*" Cass released the intercom button, buried her shoulders in the leather desk chair, and took a deep breath. Roger's illness and his resulting absence had wreaked enough havoc to gravely jeopardize the completion of *Dangerous.* Several members of the cast had to be replaced, the set designers were threatening to walk off, and then finally, the director up and quit. It was up to her and Rudolpho to get everything back on track and try to have the film completed by the end of the month. Next to impossible. Thank God Rudolpho would be here this evening.

| | |

There was a loud knock on the door, followed by a cacophony of voices. Ally, her secretary, said firmly, "You cannot go in unannounced. Please have a seat in the waiting room and I'll tell Ms. English you are here."

Cass had learned in just these last few hours that Ally was tough, unflappable. So if she was ruffled, something unpleasant was about to happen.

And it did.

The door swung open and Chelsea Hutton stood in the doorway, surrounded by her "people." Ally tried futilely to block their entrance. Eyes snapping, she positioned herself between Cass's desk and the invaders as if to say, You'll have to walk through me first.

Chelsea reached out and pushed past the young assistant. Her nostrils were flared with fury, her eyes flashed firm warning. "Please tell this woman who I am."

Cass was on her feet, hands firmly planted on her desk. A shadow of annoyance crossed her face. She turned first to Ally and shot her a look of understanding. "It's okay. I'll handle this."

Cass smiled. The secretary, still flushed and angry, nodded, then left the room.

Chelsea's two escorts moved into the office as though choreographed. The publicist sat confidently in one of the side chairs, while the manager took the other, pointedly placing his Coach attaché beside his chair. Chelsea settled herself demurely in the middle of the mauve couch—center stage—and casually arranged the side slit of her royal-purple ankle-length skirt so that when she crossed one leg over the other, the silk draped gracefully to expose her matching ankle-length boots. Once everyone was in place, the ersatz star sighed, obviously satisfied with the effect of her grand entrance. Immediately she began to discuss her agenda.

"This is my staff." Chelsea turned to each of the two men who'd accompanied her and eyed them affectionately. "You might know Michael Lott, my manager and agent." The baby agent, as Cass thought of him, smiled uncomfortably. "And Phillip West, my publicist extraordinaire." The publicist, on the other hand, had not stopped projecting confidence and congeniality since Chelsea's intrusion.

"They are to be treated with as much respect and importance as I am." She turned to Phillip and held out her right hand. Immediately he thrust a legal pad at her.

"Phillip has been plotting my publicity campaign and, might I add, he has worked very hard."

Phillip nodded like an obedient puppy. In her entire professional career, Cass had never known a publicist to let the client speak for him. West now did look a bit chagrined.

Chelsea continued. "Here is the strategy he's come up with. We need someone to scout billboard locations. Twenty or thirty spots per major city will be sufficient to start. I'll need some new publicity photos—get me Harry Benson or Patrick Demarchelier. My image will be displayed on each billboard with the caption 'Who is Chelsea Hutton?'" She paused, waiting for Cass's reaction. When she didn't get one, she continued. "By teasing the public, we'll pump up interest in me. I'll drag the movie along with me—you know, right before it opens we'll put up something like 'See her in *Dangerous Intentions.*'"

Chelsea's eyes looked off, no doubt into her brilliant future, Cass thought.

She turned back to Cassidy, her determined eyes dazzling. "We simply can't lose."

Cass could hardly believe what she was hearing. Chelsea wanted Colossal to pay for her to advertise herself—not the movie. What chutzpah! Cass attempted to disguise her annoyance from the others. There was nothing more important to some movie stars than their massive egos, and their dignity, a warning voice whispered in her head. Don't say no to her in public. "I think we should talk about it."

Chelsea straightened. Michael Lott tried to say something, but Chelsea cut him off.

"What's there to talk about? It's what I want." She added triumphantly, "Besides, Jack agrees."

Cass heard the heavy dose of sarcasm in her voice and it made her want to scream. Under any other circumstance, she would have thrown in the towel right then and there, but something stopped her. *Dangerous Intentions* was too important. She would not allow herself to cave in to Chelsea Hutton and her ludicrous demands. Rather than resisting, she would deal with Chelsea as if she were a spoiled child having a tantrum in a crowded store—by placating her.

"Look." Cass concentrated her gaze on Phillip. "I think your campaign has promise. Why don't we sit down and formally discuss it over dinner next week?"

This seemed to please everyone, including Chelsea. Her mood seemed suddenly buoyant; her features became more animated. She stood, then started for the door. Over her shoulder she asked, "When do we begin shooting?"

Cass retained her affability, despite herself. She gritted her teeth. "As soon as all the kinks are ironed out."

| | |

"You can't be serious?" Cass glared at Jack with burning, reproachful eyes. Her lips tightened with anger, her nostrils flared with fury. She realized she was taking an awfully big risk, arguing with the boss, but she was so furious, she didn't care.

Jack seemed unfazed. In fact, Cass could swear she detected a hint of amusement in his eyes.

They had not come face-to-face with each other since last night's party. There was no need to. She had avoided him until now, but she did not know why. From embarrassment, uncertainty, perhaps fear? She guessed all three. Now standing before him, Cass was conscious of his scrutiny. He regarded her with a speculative gaze and she grew uncomfortable, humiliated.

"By giving in to her demands, you're creating a monster," Cass tried again.

Jack remained calm. His eyes bore into her, studying her every movement.

"Ms. English, every starlet who walks through that door is a monster in the making. Who cares about demands? So long as the revenue is high, you turn a blind eye and a deaf ear. The cost of the average film is now north of fifty million dollars. Right now, as it stands, the budget for *Dangerous* is well above that figure—and you haven't even started shooting."

He walked to the window and, with his back to her, said flatly, "At this point a few hundred thousand dollars to publicize Chelsea hardly matters—and we don't, as I recall, have any other publicity plan. To be quite blunt, Roger's 'performance' on this project was really disappointing. In Hollywood slang, he phoned it in. If there's any blame to be laid, it's with him."

"How can you say that? You know my father gave *Dangerous Intentions* his all," Cass spat back. Suddenly she realized that there was nothing she could do about Cavelli's promises to his paramour. She would have to work around her and the publicity campaign. Her heart slowed, the adrenaline stopped upsetting her brain chemistry balance, but instinct told her to remain detached and not let Jack know he'd won this round.

"*Dangerous* was optioned by Miramax three years ago," said Jack, still standing at the window. "When they decided to drop it, it was put back on the market. You know as well as I do, turnaround scripts are very desirable to many studios, which hope that by cracking whatever story problems remain they can get a property that is nearly shootable. Roger picked up *Dangerous* for a song and then threw money at its pre-production. It wasn't as simple to fix as he thought, and he got in over his head." Jack turned. He took a deep breath and said, "None of that is relevant now. What we have to do is make the best of a bad situation."

Cass took a few steps toward him, careful to keep enough distance but get close enough to look him straight in the face. "I don't plan on just breaking even, Mr. Cavelli." Her blue eyes mauled him. "This might be a drop in the bucket for you financially, but for me it's survival. I intend to put everything I have into this film. And I won't settle for second best."

He tilted his brow, looking at her uncertainly. "Are you a gambler, Ms. English?"

She was thrown off by the question. Why was he changing the subject? Jack closed the distance she'd purposely set between them. He was close enough for her to see his afternoon shadow. That he wasn't perfect made him seem more approachable. Cassidy's guard slipped. She couldn't speak, she could only shake her head.

"I don't know if you're aware, Ms. English, but this studio, this company, has been my *wife* for more than twenty years. Colossal is the most important thing in my life. Still I'm willing to bet half of my share of Colossal that you can't meet the deadline."

She wavered a moment, trying to comprehend what she was hearing. "And if I don't?"

"Dinner at the Palm." He shrugged his shoulders in mock resignation.

She stood motionless in the middle of the room. His expression was unreadable. It was difficult to tell whether or not he was joking.

"So now this is a *personal* challenge—correct?"

Jack nodded with a taut jerk of his head. "If you win, Colossal is half yours. If you lose, you pay for my victory dinner." He inched toward her further, closing the space between them. He reached out and caught her hand in his in a gesture of agreement. Obviously he was toying with her, turning up the Cavelli charm to full blast.

She felt the electricity of his touch and she instinctively jumped back. If he actually paid off the bet, she could trade him her share of Colossal for *all* of Desmond.

"So we have a bet?" he asked.

"We have a bet," she replied. If he was serious, he was crazy. If he was joking, she'd be certain he paid up in full when she got the movie out in time. Cassidy had never known a betting man.

| | |

When Turmaine hadn't returned her call after two days, Patricia Hanson couldn't decide what to do next. The longer the news about the movie and the studio stayed current, the more anguish she felt. Her terrible secret was in her face. Her AA sponsor suggested that perhaps opening up this can of worms could create turmoil for the families. Reminding her that while making amends was important, the second part of the Ninth Step cautioned, "except when to do so would injure them or others." Perhaps she should leave well enough alone. But Patricia persisted. It was the drunk in her who could never stop, who never knew when enough was enough, whatever it was—alcohol, sex, shopping, anything on which she fixated.

So when she found Chelsea Hutton's home number in the directory, she left a message on the answering machine saying that she had important information about her father.

The woman called back. "This is Chelsea Hutton," she said.

Patricia saw again the poor, damaged baby with the tag *Turmaine, Cassidy* on her tiny wrist. "I have information about your background that I think you should know."

To Patricia's surprise, the other woman didn't hesitate. It was as if she knew something was awry and had just been waiting for the call. "Where can we meet, Ms. Hanson? I don't think this conversation should happen over the phone."

"All right. Can you come here? I don't get around very well. I'm . . . disabled."

Chelsea Hutton sighed and Patricia heard the unmistakable sound of her dragging on a cigarette. "If it has to be that way. I don't like it, but I'm too curious to stay away, so this better be good."

"Just come, Ms. Hutton. We'll have tea."

"Make it five o'clock. We'll have a cocktail."

| | |

Rudolpho stared out the window of the first-class cabin, thoughts turned inward. He wished the ironies of life would amuse him instead of bite at his insides. He had always wanted to work in feature films, had gone to film school, paying thousands of dollars in tuition just to learn how to direct, and here he was being handed his first picture.

Was Cassidy nuts to give him the job? Did her taking a chance on him mean what he hoped?

When she had called, he almost couldn't believe it. When she immediately offered her family's lawyer to get him out of his contract with *Up to the Minute* so that he could join her, he did not hesitate. How could he refuse? Finally, Cassidy needed him.

Her offer was good, not great, she told him. To keep costs down, she couldn't give him more than $250,000, and no points. But he didn't care. He would have taken the job for free.

The captain turned on the FASTEN SEATBELTS sign and the plane began its descent into LAX. Rudolpho inhaled deeply, then closed his eyes and visualized Cass's face. He thought back to their last night together before she left New York. He had come into her office in her apartment and she'd been annoyed.

"This is private," she'd snapped.

"I'm not violating any rules, am I?" he remembered saying.

"Actually, yes—you're violating my space."

The words had bite in them. He'd felt the familiar frustration. Why could she never let him in?

Well, he thought, she seemed to have changed her mind. Why else would she reach out to him now?

The plane landed five minutes ahead of schedule. Rudolpho deplaned quickly—one of the benefits of traveling first class. He grabbed his luggage from the carousel and hailed a cab outside the baggage claim area.

Soon he was pressed against the rear passenger door of the late-model taxi, his right hand gripping the door handle for dear life, in case the driver, a generic foreigner with no discernable personality, made a quick stop. After all, as a New Yorker, Rudolpho was all too familiar with the craziness inherent in members of the livery trade. Any attempt to suggest that the man stop tailgating or correct his route would be met with sarcasm, or worse, rage. From his years in television Rudolph knew that conserving mental energy was essential—and he wasn't going to expend any now by taking on the driver.

They were on their way to Shutters on the Beach, a resort in Santa Monica. And of course they were stuck in traffic. Sepulveda Boulevard was jammed. So what was new? Manhattan, L.A. Both meant traffic.

The driver finally merged with the freeway traffic. Outside, the dry heat and cloudless skies began to soothe him. Rudolpho actually found himself relaxing. When he left New York it was wet, gray, and dirty—and oh so depressing. In contrast, L.A. seemed like paradise.

They reached the turnoff for Santa Monica and headed west on Pico

Boulevard. Rudolpho traveled to L.A. regularly on business and he always made it a point to stay outside the city. Santa Monica was homier, more down to earth than Beverly Hills.

The driver snaked the cab up to the front entrance of the hotel. Rudolpho shoved a twenty-dollar bill at him, got out, and grabbed his belongings from the trunk. He walked past the bell captain into the colorful lobby, which looked as if it came right out of pictures he'd seen of the Santa Monica beach circa the 1920s. Check-in went smoothly. When the bellhop let him into the small one-bedroom suite, he was thrust back in time. Both architecture and decor were contemporary interpretations of the colorful Southern California style of the twenties. Both the small bedroom and living room had breathtaking views of Santa Monica's famous pier. Granted it wasn't a palace, but it would certainly do. At least until he could convince Cass that they should room together.

| | |

L.A. was a gold mine of women, every one of them hungry. Hungry for him. Eighteen years old and on his own. What more could any red-blooded male ask for? Work wasn't easy to come by; bussing tables and mopping floors weren't exactly his cup of tea. But there were other options. One of them was hanging out at the Tracadero, in the hopes of getting lucky. There was always some bored housewife, or over-the-hill actress, or young woman with a rich daddy vying for his attention. All of them were ready and willing, eager to pay his way and keep him comfortable in exchange for small favors and a minuscule amount of attention.

He was young, good looking, and experienced. He had a college professor's IQ and a gangster's attitude. In just a few short months, he found his way up the L.A. social ladder. He charmed, escorted, and dedicated himself to any woman who could help him. His lady friends dressed him in the finest—custom-fitted shirts, hand-painted silk ties, hand-tailored suits. He wore Chanel cuff links and a Piaget diamond watch. He drove a Jaguar roadster and rented a condo on the beach.

He attended all the important Hollywood parties—A-list all the way. He schmoozed. Even the male power brokers were taken with him.

He never got involved with his female partners, though often they got involved with him. He learned to tune his feelings out and put forth his best performance. He partied all night and slept all day.

Life in the fast lane suited him. And after a year, he became the best actor Hollywood had ever seen. He was the businessman, the garage mechanic, the Wall Street tycoon, the television repairman. The kind, compassionate husband or the cold, calculating boyfriend. He acted each role with precision and talent.

Soon he figured out what he really *wanted for himself, and it wasn't "make-believe." He wanted it all. He wanted to be a star. The world would be his oyster. He would be as powerful as Brando, as effective as Eastwood, and as handsome as Redford.*

Hey, it was Hollywood. Anything could happen—right?

| | |

Morton's on Melrose exuded the very essence of "power" in Hollywood, especially on Monday nights when the crème de la crème of celebs showed up to flex their muscles and revel in their star status.

For the second Monday in a row, James Renthrew had dinner there with Jack. Ever since the Turmaine party, both men seemed intent on keeping an eye on each other. When they were settled at their usual table and their drink orders had been taken, Cavelli said, "Roger's daughter is certainly a powerhouse."

James shrugged his shoulders. "Did you expect anything less? She comes from good stock."

"I had a small run-in with her today in my office." Jack forced a smile.

"And?" James asked, lifting an eyebrow.

"Let's just say I expect a lot of fireworks in the next couple of weeks." Cavelli laughed stiffly.

James kept his smile to a minimum. "I think you've finally met your match, Jack. Cassidy is a very determined, headstrong woman. And might I add, extremely passionate about her work." James eyed Cavelli with admiration. He knew that the forty-nine-year-old billionaire sitting across from him had been quoted in the *Wall Street Journal* as saying he believed the way to success was to hire the best people, then sit back and watch them deliver. He was an accessible, well-liked, and respected leader. As far as James was concerned, without Cavelli, the studio would go under.

But James also knew that working under Jack's rule was going to be one hell of a challenge for Cass.

The waiter returned with two dry martinis.

Jack raised his glass in a toast. "Here's to a good working relationship and continued peace at Colossal. May Cassidy succeed and prosper."

"I'm not concerned. I know she'll do both. But I warn you, Jack, go easy on her. If not, you won't have just Roger to answer to, you'll have me as well."

Just then, James heard a familiar voice, and one that made him hot under the collar.

To his left he saw a group of rowdy men and women, seated at a large, round table just off the bar. Their laughter and obscene comments grew louder and soon the maître d' rushed over. Words were exchanged, followed by the sound of glass shattering.

"Do you know anyone at that table?" Jack asked, who had his back to the group.

"Yes, I'm afraid. Jonathan Turmaine," James said angrily. The lawyer threw his napkin on the table and pushed his way through the crowded restaurant toward the offending table.

James grabbed Jonathan firmly by his right elbow. Through clenched teeth he growled, *"This* is why your father turned Desmond over to Cassidy. Don't you realize how badly your behavior reflects on him?"

"Fuck him! Fuck my fuckin' father!" Jonathan roared. "And fuck Cass-my-ass, too!"

James ignored the obscenity and quickly ushered the younger man outside to the street. The late afternoon sun had disappeared. He hailed a cab, thrust a fifty-dollar bill at the driver, and said, "Take this man to Whispering Winds, off Sunset in Beverly Hills. Get him there safely— no stops. Keep the change for your trouble."

He opened the door of the cab. Reluctantly Jonathan slid inside. Only then did James release his grip on the young man's shoulder.

James leaned into the backseat and said sternly, "One more public display and you're finished."

"What do you intend to do, tell *Daddy?*" Despite his petulance and angry tone, James could see the fear and dismay in Jonathan's eyes.

James leaned in even closer, getting right up in the young man's face, so close the stink of alcohol nauseated him. His voice was cold: "Now, you listen to me. From now on we do things my way. There will be no more parties, no more drugs, and no more spending. It's time you started acting like an adult. It's time you learned to accept some responsibility."

Jonathan's head fell back against the seat. He squeezed his eyes shut and with great difficulty murmured, "How do you suppose I do that?"

His statement hit James as poignant. Jonathan had been stripped, neutered, cast out from the family's "grown-up" affairs. James recognized the hurt beneath the acting-out.

James stood erect and pushed his hands deep into his pockets. "Go home, take a cold shower, and sleep it off. When you're sober . . . then we'll talk."

The lights of the city flickered on brighter against the darkening late afternoon.

"And if I don't . . ." Jonathan's breathing became labored. James realized he was just minutes from passing out. He felt sorry for the young man and couldn't find it in himself to judge him too harshly.

"Go home, Jonathan."

Then James turned and went back into Morton's.

Chelsea was on a high when she left Cassidy's office. She couldn't sit still, so she began walking, up and down Rodeo Drive. She went into every store—Gucci, Giorgio Armani, Chanel, Christian Dior. She'd try on clothes, take them off, and then try on some more. She could practically taste the money that would be hers, and it was delicious.

She strolled the wide sidewalks bordered by palm trees, wandering through the chic designer boutiques, ogling the cornucopia of French fashions, expensive jewels, and exquisite glassware. Everything felt dazzling, delightful. Hers.

No longer would she have to worry about who she was, where she'd sleep, how she'd get along. She was getting closer each day to finally possessing everything she'd ever wanted, and the feeling was electrifying.

She walked the twenty blocks back to the Beverly Hills Hotel—the Pink Palace.

Overhead four powerful flashes of lightning were followed by a roaring roll of thunder. Soon heavy rain began to fall. The sidewalks grew empty, but the streets still bustled with heavy traffic.

Chelsea felt exhilarated. The dark clouds, the messy wetness, and the gloomy feel of it all tickled her senses. She loathed sunshine. Welcoming the storm, Chelsea removed her black leather peacoat, draped it over her arm, and reveled in the cool water splashing over her. She breathed deeply and freely for what felt like the first time in her life.

Compelled to keep moving, she stepped through the hotel's twelve acres of landscaped gardens—lush hibiscus, blooming bougainvillea, and tropical palms. She passed all twenty-one of the hotel's secluded bungalows and imagined them to be secret romantic hideaways for such stars as Monroe, Gable, Taylor, and Burton. She imagined Monroe stealing away to rendezvous with JFK, disguised in large dark sunglasses and a straw hat with a large brim. Perhaps Taylor and Burton spent hours together here while *Cleopatra* was on hiatus, before the world knew the scandal of their love affair.

Chelsea quickened her pace when she passed the legendary pool and cabanas, still one of the most important places to be seen and heard in Hollywood. She imagined young actresses lounging poolside in skimpy bikinis with well-coifed hair and made-up faces, posing prettily and hoping to be discovered. And she walked even further to the Polo Grill and the Polo Lounge, two hot spots at the center of the movie industry's dealmaking. She knew Jack had his "own" table here, as did Roger Turmaine.

She remembered how she'd longed to be a guest at one of those tables. Now, no doubt, she would be . . . if she accepted the invitation. Chelsea smiled.

The rain was letting up, to a light drizzle. Behind the dark clouds, the sun began to peek through. Soon employees and guests began to fill the courtyard, destroying the peace and quiet. This made Chelsea angry and triggered an overwhelming urge to flee. But out of the corner of her eye, she spotted a group of men playing cards under one of the poolside umbrellas. Chelsea could see a large pot of money in the center of the table. Instantly she was captivated. Anything that kicked up her adrenaline easily caught her attention. The stock market, race track, roulette wheel, blackjack table, slot machines—whatever the game, she enjoyed the rush and thrived on the tension. It was a form of instant gratification that precisely suited her impatient temperament. She'd been told once that her passion for gambling was a symptom of her disease, her mania, but she didn't care. She would never want to be cured if that meant giving up the ecstasy that came from living the high life.

As Chelsea entered the hotel lobby, she could feel her energy start to slip and she began to feel anxious that she was going to have another one of her crash landings. As she rode the elevator to the top floor and walked the long hall to the presidential suite, she tried to slow down. She hugged the wall to help her keep her balance. She needed to rest.

Thank God Jack had let her stay in his suite at the hotel. He always kept one on hand for visiting actors or other celebrities. And now that she was his star, he'd set it up for Chelsea to stay there for as long as *Dangerous* was in production. Not bothering to search for the key card, she rang the bell. Within moments her butler, Charles, appeared. Charles, a small Asian man with sharp features, was by nature pleasant, always cheerful. So when Chelsea saw the worried look on his face, she knew something was terribly wrong.

"Ms. Hutton, please understand I did my best to convince her to stay, but . . ." He turned to her and lowered his head. "She's . . . in there."

Chelsea pushed past him, threw her coat and handbag on the sofa, and hurried into the master bedroom. Isabella was sitting cross-legged on the floor. Beside her sat a large bowl of popcorn and her school bag. Her eyes were glued to the TV screen, on some cartoon playing on Nickelodeon. Seeing her mother, the slight, blond girl instinctively cowered.

Chelsea reached for the remote, but Isabella had already switched the TV off.

The little ten-year-old stood and straightened her pleated blue-and-green knee-length skirt, her Country Day uniform. One blue knee sock had fallen down her calf and Isabella struggled to fix this imperfection.

"What's going on? What are you doing here? Where's Jesse?" Chelsea could barely contain herself. From nowhere, a surge of manic energy began to infuse her veins. She could feel her head begin to throb.

"I don't know, Mom," the child replied in a small frightened voice. She straightened her shoulders and cleared her throat. "Jesse said she had to go away." Isabella shifted her gaze to the dresser. "She left a note for you."

Chelsea lunged toward the note. She tore the envelope and unfolded the handwritten letter.

Chelsea,

Had a family emergency. You could not be reached. So I left Bella with Charles. I'm sorry, I had no other choice. I don't believe I will be returning.

     Jesse

Chelsea read the note twice.

"Oh my God!" she shrieked.

Bella froze, intently watching her mother. Chelsea saw the panic in her innocent blue eyes, but she could not help herself. She raged, "What the hell am I supposed to do with you now?" The child turned her body so she could keep her eyes on her. *We look so much alike*—the thought penetrated Chelsea's aura of hate.

Isabella's terror resonated within Chelsea. She saw her daughter's fear, and for one brief moment she remembered herself at ten, lonely and scared, in a dark church, in a tenement apartment. But then the rage returned. Isabella didn't know how lucky she was. the trembling heart that never felt loved, secure, welcome at home. Tough shit! she thought. Chelsea closed her heart to her daughter's unnamable terror.

"I'm . . . I'm sorry, Mommy."

Chelsea could no longer hear the child. She felt strange. Her body and mind seemed out of synch. Her heart raced and she began to sweat profusely. Her body kept moving, but her mind stood still.

Her head throbbed. A headache came on. She eyed the little girl before her. *Who are you?* The voices spoke up. Chelsea began to circle the child, who stood now, without blinking, arms at her sides. Was the girl accusing Chelsea of something? Memories flashed through her, each one more brilliant and vivid than the next: The time she wet her pants in church because Mama wouldn't let her use the public bathroom. Even now she could feel the shame. Or when she accidentally broke Mama's antique clock and was sent to her room to spend three days praying without food or water. Her mother had called her the devil.

These memories suffused her with such rage that she pulled the top dresser drawer out and hurled it against the wall, spewing lingerie and hosiery across the room.

Then the next drawer and the next.

When Chelsea was finished with the dresser, she started on objets d'art, books, a Steuben crystal vase.

Isabella was crying now, standing perfectly still and trying to control her sobs. This fueled Chelsea's fury like a demon that rode her. Her rage ignited.

Chelsea stopped momentarily and looked down at a pair of scissors in her hand. She couldn't remember how she got the scissors, only that the moment demanded a sacrifice. Turning deliberately away from her daughter, Chelsea ran to the closet, jerked the doors open, exposing her afternoon suits, her evening gowns, and street clothes. She tore at the clothes with the scissors. In her mind, she was in Cassidy's bedroom. Those were Cassidy's clothes she saw. She attacked the clothing with a consuming violence. Then she ransacked the shoe boxes, throwing shoes and boxes over her shoulders, stabbing at handbags and luggage.

"Mommy, please stop! Charles! Charles, do something! Mommy's going crazy!"

Charles charged into the room. Assessing the scene before him, he ran to the telephone.

Chelsea, exhausted now, played with the pieces of fabrics that once had been her beautiful wardrobe.

Isabella sat behind a chair in the corner, softly sobbing, holding her knees to her chest.

And that's how Jack found them.

| | |

When she saw how much had to be done to pull *Dangerous Intentions* together and get it before the cameras, and the short time she had to do it in, Cass fought an overwhelming urge to throw up her hands and walk away from it all. However, whenever her concentration wavered, she would remember the bet she made with Jack Cavelli. There was no way in hell that she would lose.

Cass spent the entire morning trying to pick up the pieces from where Roger had left off. The production budget and shooting schedule had to be completely revamped. The script had to be replotted, revised, and broken down into scenes. What complicated the situation even more was the location: *Dangerous* was set in eighteenth-century Venice, Italy, and Roger had barely created one stage set. In order to get production moving, Cass had to figure out how to build a set and have it up and running in less than a week. Once she and the designers decided how to create a backdrop of St. Mark's Square, Cass had to finish overseeing the casting. The lead roles were cast, but now it was time for all the supporting, bit, and extra parts.

At least Rudolpho could take some of the load off her shoulders.

| | |

Cass joined Maggie Winters, a veteran casting director, who had cast a number of successful films for Desmond, and her young assistant, Linda Peters. The two women were sipping coffee from Starbucks cups as they sat at a tiny table stacked with eight-by-ten headshots. Barely noticing Cass as she joined them in their trailer, the women concentrated on a young man with large white teeth, black curly hair, and deeply tanned skin.

"Can you show me more anger?" Maggie asked wearily.

"How's it going?" Cass whispered.

"My headache or these auditions?" Maggie asked. Cassidy had met Maggie at Roger's party. In her seventies, she was exactly what Cassidy was looking for. She was a woman of dignity, and reminded Cass of Hepburn in her later years, with her white hair caught up in a haphazard bun, her faded jeans and workshirt making her appear at ease.

"Do you know Linda Peters?" Maggie asked Cass casually, gesturing to the tiny woman beside her. "This smart young woman is my third eye."

Probably not yet thirty, Linda had enormous green eyes framed by a haircut so short, it looked as though the U.S. Marine Corps barber had styled it. "Linda knows before I do which actor's performance will please me."

Cassidy shook hands with Linda, then all three turned their attention back to the actor auditioning.

The young man's soft, finely chiseled features soon turned dark and abrasive, as he ably followed Maggie's directions.

"Now, that's the look we want." The two women worked like a well-oiled machine. Linda helped auditioners with motivation while Maggie, Cassidy noted, watched every gesture and expression the actor made. Right now Maggie bent her head, taking some notes on his performance.

Cass quietly left the trailer.

| | |

Cass's next stop was the marketing department. She was meeting with Ed Burnbaum, Cavelli's marketing guru.

"Cavelli's guaranteeing twenty million dollars for advertising and promotion. On top of that, *Dangerous* will open on no fewer than twelve hundred major-market screens. Naturally, Ms. Hutton's publicity guarantee will have to come out of this budget."

Burnbaum sat hunched in a chair, a haze of cigar smoke surrounding him. He was a middle-aged, overweight, bald man with greasy skin and beady black eyes. "Here're the fully executed contracts from all the actors. The legal department just sent them over. I hope you don't mind, but I've gone through them to see if anyone has any promotional or marketing demands I need to know about. With the exception of a few clauses, everything seems to be in order. I believe Ms. Hutton is the only one still holding out?"

Cass raised one eyebrow. "What are her demands?"

Burnbaum read through the list. "Accommodations at a first-class hotel should we have to go on location, use of the Colossal jet, a custom trailer, a personal wardrobe allowance, her own makeup artist, hairstylist, and dresser, and a personal assistant."

"What, no personal trainer?" Cass said with an edge to her voice. "Of course, all of it will have to be cleared with Mr. Cavelli."

Burnbaum nodded.

"Move mountains, but I want that contract signed and on my desk in"—she glanced at her watch—"one hour. I don't want any excuse to hold up shooting."

Cass eyed Burnbaum carefully. Instinctively she didn't trust the man. Rumor had it he'd earned his position at Colossal after his model girlfriend, a twenty-five-year-old heroin addict, overdosed and died just after the completion of a low-budget mass-market film the studio was producing. He arrived at her apartment close to midnight and discovered her body. Instead of calling the police, he called the studio. Money-hungry executives set forth a plan to capitalize on her demise by guaranteeing their backers millions of dollars of free publicity when news of her death spread. As a consequence, the film grossed three times the amount projected. And Burnbaum's career was in an upward swing.

"By the way," Burnbaum said. "Publicity left three messages on my desk this morning. They knew I'd be seeing you. Apparently, since your father's announcement about your taking over, they've been inundated with requests for interviews from all of the trades and daily newspapers, as well as magazines and news programs." His features became more animated. "What a coup, huh? We couldn't buy publicity like that. I'll have Publicity contact you directly to set up some interviews."

"Don't," Cass said as a shadow of annoyance crossed her face. "I'm not interested in giving any interviews." She wondered why this man was getting messages for her, and why signed contracts were delivered to him before she had a chance to see them. He wasn't a producer, he was in marketing.

"But it will be good for the film. Cavelli would—"

"This film is not about me. And I won't be giving any interviews. Tell Cavelli that." Cass had no interest in the limelight and preferred keeping her private life private

She skimmed through the contracts and, amazingly, found them satisfactory—no whammies thrown in by actors' agents. She turned to Burnbaum and said, "Remember. Chelsea Hutton, signed and on my desk in one hour."

| | |

When Cass arrived at one of the back lots just before lunch, she was happy to find a construction crew assembling the set. Carpenters, welders, grips, painters, all were hammering, welding, painting, and building. Eighteenth-century Venice was being erected right before her eyes. A city with a magnificent labyrinth of alleys and canals, the cathedral, the bell tower, and the squares—all replicated in seven blocks. Soon gondolas would be floating in a man-made canal, and there would be beautiful shops and marvelous brasseries with dark corners to add a tone of mystery.

Cass spied Brian Williams, head designer, and gave him a thumbs-up. He approached her quickly, pencil and sketchbook in hand. He flipped through the pages for her. Cass couldn't believe her eyes. There were sketches of small villas, a cottage, a chapel with stained-glass windows that would represent Ophelia's family chapel, and a labyrinth of hedges and dirt horse trails created for the landscape of Ophelia's betrothed's palace.

On the last page was a spectacular drawing of the bedroom where Ophelia finally gathers the strength to defy her overbearing, money-hungry father and refuse to go through with the marriage he had arranged for her. There was a polished rosewood bed with a rich brocade canopy and fur covers and linens edged in Venetian lace; an inlaid wooden chest with heavy brass fittings; leaded windows with beveled panes. Every detail was impeccable.

In this last scene, still dressed in the gown intended to be worn at her wedding to the sadistic Doge her father had betrothed her to, Ophelia rushes off to an abandoned one-room cabin she and Carmelo have used as their trysting place. She finds him there, murdered, a jeweled sword, obviously belonging to one of her father's sentries, still buried in his chest.

"I'm astonished. How on earth did you do all of this so fast?" Cass said to Brian.

"I'm creative and a bit eccentric. Plus I stayed up all night," he said with a dramatic shrug of his muscular shoulders.

Cass stepped back and eyed the young man. From the looks of him, she would have cast him as a criminal lawyer in a television series, or maybe a zealous host of a conservative political TV show. "I'm so lucky to have you, Brian. You're a godsend!"

| | |

Next Cass walked into the wardrobe department. The whir of sewing machines seemed in sync with the hiss of the steam irons. She passed the rows of cubicles used for fittings, and for at least fifty seamstresses. She could see that even further past the offices of the wardrobe attendant and costume supervisor, all were busy at work.

The head costume designer, a middle-aged brunette with a warm, welcoming smile, met Cass at the end of the hallway. "Ah, Ms. English, it's a pleasure to finally meet you. I'm Hilary Suazy."

They shook hands.

"I've heard so many wonderful things."

She led Cass inside a large wardrobe warehouse filled with costumes, both period and contemporary.

The group of women and men gathered for the meeting reminded Cass of photos she'd seen of the gifted seamstresses and tailors who worked in the couturier ateliers in postwar Paris. Out of the twelve, there were two men, both dressed in the old-fashioned, formal style— white, starched, long-sleeve shirts and neckties. One gray-haired, pudgy-faced gentleman wore pinstriped suspenders. All of the women were Latinas, except for a tiny older lady with tightly permed dyed blond hair. She wore a black man-tailored suit, with a white pima cotton dress shirt. In contrast, the younger women were clad casually in jeans and T-shirts.

All were seated around a table littered with fabrics, left dangerously close to coffee cups and soda cans. Their chatter as they waited for their meeting to begin was easy and warm. But as soon as Cass entered, the room went silent.

"This is my tailoring staff," Hilary Suazy said, introducing them one by one.

"Don't let me interrupt," Cassidy said in mock sternness. "I can't afford your downtime." The group laughed and the tension eased.

"We have a great stock of period costumes we'll be able to pull from wardrobe for the supporting cast and extras. That'll keep our budget in line," Hilary Suazy explained, directing Cass to a larger cubicle with a drafting desk. "I've put together some sketches for each scene." She handed Cass a sketchbook. "They're in sequential order."

Cass browsed through the pages and was amazed at the beauty and depth of each drawing. She lingered over a colored pencil sketch of a bridal gown, the costume Ophelia would wear near the film's end. The detailed rendering was of a layered ivory lace wedding dress. The picture indicated three separate lace styles for the billowy graceful garment. Cass thought the capped sleeves and high neck of the bodice would be beautiful, especially when made of transparent *peau d'ange* lace.

"She will be wearing a flesh-tone undergarment," Hilary explained. "Look at the veil, tell me what you think."

The veil was actually a simple mantilla of Venetian lace that flowed along the side of the face and fell in graceful waves into a long cathedral train. Cassidy was astonished at the artistry of the creation.

"Are you pleased, Ms. English?"

"Pleased is an understatement," Cass said, impulsively hugging the woman.

By this time next week, they'd be shooting. I may actually win this bet, she thought. It was the first time she'd dared to believe.

| | |

On her way back to her office, she spotted a familiar profile seated in the corner office closest to the receptionist. As soon as she saw Rudolpho, Cassidy realized that she'd been holding her breath, figuratively speaking, from the moment she left New York.

He sat behind a long glass-topped desk that rested on dazzling chrome legs, his nose buried in the script. Cass knew he'd probably read it a dozen times. She smiled. He was a perfectionist in all things, passionate and enthusiastic.

She threw her tired body onto the sofa and let out a long sigh.

"Having a bad day?" He cracked a smile, that impish grin that told her he was ready for anything.

"No. I'm just exhausted. I've been roaming around all day. I haven't had a moment's rest since my father threw me into the river. Thank God you're here." Cass gave him her most winning smile.

"Well, I hate to be the bearer of bad news." He laid the script face-down on the table.

"But?" Cass asked nervously, her smile disappearing. She rose from her seat as if propelled by an explosive force. She began pacing up and down in front of his desk, readying herself for the worst.

"I saw the tape of Chelsea Hutton's read-through today. There's no way it's going to work. She's all wrong."

"But why?"

"First of all, she was all over the place—emotionally, I mean. Her eyes . . . She looked like she was high or something. I don't know. Call me crazy, Cass, but she's not at all convincing as an innocent Italian virgin, either."

She couldn't put it off any longer. She had to tell Rudolpho about Jack's deal with Chelsea. She put her hands on her hips, apprehensive about broaching such a delicate subject. Of course, he'd have a fit. As far as she was concerned, Rudolpho was the most important component of the project. She knew him well—if he didn't think he could make the film a success with Chelsea in it, he would walk.

"I'm afraid we don't have a choice," she said gently.

"Why not?" His eyes were now sharp and assessing as he gave her his full attention.

"Because Jack Cavelli insisted she get the lead."

"Jack Cavelli is not directing this film." The force of his seething reply took her off guard.

Taking a deep, unsteady breath, Cass stepped back and said, "Rudolpho, I've tried to reason with him. There's no negotiating with him on this point."

Looking away, he leaned his elbows on the table and rested his chin in his clasped hands.

"Cass, you know as well as I that if the lead actress doesn't have the right chemistry for the role, the film doesn't stand a chance. I just won't work like that. If she's in, I'm out."

| | |

Twenty minutes later, Cass telephoned Jack from her office.

"I have a problem. My director won't work with Ms. Hutton. The lead needs to be recast."

"Well, that's not an option," Jack said sternly.

"Jack, I know Rudolpho Durban really well. He's perfect for this job." She hesitated, hoping he wouldn't infer too much from her comment. "He'll walk. . . ."

"Then I suggest you start looking for a replacement." The line went dead.

| | |

One of the unpublicized features of certain California hospitals are private suites—bungalows, really, that allow patients, their friends and families, to come and go protected from the prying eyes of the media. Jack was visiting Chelsea in her private suite on the grounds of Encino General Hospital. Dr. Jeffrey Smith, a renowned psychiatrist, led Jack into a discreet conference room.

"I'm afraid Ms. Hutton is suffering from manic depression. She's been aware of her condition since childhood. When she was first brought into my office, she was so hyperactive, I initially thought she was speeding on amphetamines." Dr. Smith put his hand on Jack's shoulder in a sympathetic gesture. "Now, from the medical history she gave me, I've been able to surmise that she's a rapid cycler—her moods can swing from mania to depression within hours, sometimes minutes."

The doctor's diagnosis resonated. It put a label on Chelsea's disturbing behavior.

Remembering walking into her suite at the Beverly Hills Hotel was like recalling a nightmare. He had arrived to find the little girl beside her mother, who lay in a lump on the floor beside her bed. Everywhere lay the slashed remains of sheets, dresses, magazines, pictures—a psychotic mess strewn about the room. Even Chelsea, her hair cut and mangled, had been damaged by her own hand.

Jack had quickly told Charles, the butler, to take Bella out of the room. "Take her for a hamburger, anything. Just get her out of here. And get someone in here to take care of her until I tell you different."

Next he'd gone to Chelsea and gathered her into his arms. She was unconscious. He called for an ambulance and arranged for her to be treated here by Dr. Smith. The doctor—and the hospital—had a reputation for discretion, earned over years of treating unstable celebrities determined to maintain their careers.

Now Jack understood Chelsea and her fevered ways. He was ashamed to admit that he'd actually taken advantage of her mood swings. He may not have known she was suffering from a real mental illness, but he'd known something was wrong. He had used her behavior—had even become turned on by her unpredictable personality.

Jack returned his focus to the psychiatrist. "What's the prognosis?"

Thoughtfully, Dr. Smith folded his arms. "She's been sedated for twenty-four hours now. We managed to get her relatively calm. The course of treatment, as well as her long-term recovery, depends a great deal on Ms. Hutton's willingness to get well." Skepticism edged his voice. "She's already refusing treatment. She will not allow us to admit her and has refused to discuss a protocol of medication and therapy. Our hands are tied. We can't force her into rehab."

Jack detected a hint of sadness in the doctor's eyes.

"So, what do you suggest, Doctor?"

"I'm afraid that's up to you—or her family—to decide."

| | |

When Jack entered her room, Chelsea was sitting up in bed.

"Get me out of here. You can't keep me here against my will, Jack."

Standing beside the bed, he straightened his shoulders and cleared his throat. "No, but I *can* take you out of the film."

"You wouldn't." Her face turned furious.

"Oh?" His tall black-clad figure stiffened. "So far you've got two strikes against you. One more and you're out."

She swallowed hard, lifted her chin, and boldly met his gaze. "What do you mean two strikes?"

"Now the director doesn't think you're right for the part."

"I can play this part, Jack. Promise me you won't pull me out." She sat up and ran her fingers through her new mangled hairstyle. "You have to let me continue," she said petulantly. She swung her legs off the bed and reached for her clothing, which lay across a nearby chair. Without closing the door or turning from Jack, Chelsea slipped out of the hospital gown and dropped it to the floor. She put on her street clothes, marched into the bathroom and firmly shut the door.

Jack heard her turn on the water. He felt sorry for her. Yet could he really count on her? He thought back to her other work. In the past, Chelsea always rose to the occasion. He found himself thinking of Lana. She'd been able to rise to any occasion, too. He had to risk it. He would simply stay close and make sure that Chelsea performed. He wanted her on that set. He needed to know what was going on with the movie. And with Cass.

Chelsea ran a cloth under the cold water, wrung it out, and pressed it to her face. The throbbing at her temples intensified—the voices were back.

She was falling apart—crashing again. But this time there was a lot more at stake. The film, Jack, Cassidy English. She had to hold on; had to stop acting like a raving lunatic. She stared at her reflection in the mirror and, to her horror, realized she even looked like a lunatic.

"Screw 'em." She marched back into her hospital room and stood face-to-face with Jack.

He looked at her. She looked at him. The silence between them was palpable.

"Look, if I promise to take the goddamn medication, can I keep the role?" she said.

He bent his head and studied his hands. "What about the director?"

"I'll handle him. Don't you worry, Jack."

| | |

It was about ten days before Patricia Hanson's upstairs neighbor called the cops. The stench was terrible, she said, but Patricia kept birds—African gray parrots—and they could get too smelly being caged up if she went away for a few days and didn't clean the cages.

The body was found right inside the front door. A clean sheet was thrown over it. The killer was savvy enough to remove the shell casing, and there were too many sets of prints on the buzzer and doorknob to be any good. Someone had shed a few blond hairs. Other than that, forensics turned up shit.

Just another unsolved homicide in the City of Angels.

Roger and James settled in the formal dining room at Whispering Winds, just the two of them side by side at the long banquet table. A veritable feast lay before them—a Limoges tureen of lobster bisque flecked with bite-sized bits of claw meat; an aromatic rack of lamb, a glistening platter of sautéed spinach with garlic, an airy vegetable soufflé, and a basket of piping-hot sourdough bread.

Roger picked at his food, moving it around his plate with his fork. All attempts to make small talk failed.

Finally James said, "What's going on? Why are you so quiet?"

Roger shrugged. "Nothing monumental."

The two old friends dined in relative silence.

As they finished eating, almost on cue, the maid rolled in a cart with coffee in a silver pot, a freshly baked carrot cake, bowls of fresh fruit, and two Kir Royales. There was fresh cream, and whipped cream for the cake, and a footed sugar bowl filled with turbinato sugar cubes and silver tongs.

"No whipped cream for me." James held his hand up to decline.

Roger refused dessert. "Just coffee, please."

James didn't like the way this evening was going. He hadn't seen Roger this despondent since Lana died. James surmised that his ennui must be related to his stepping down from his duties at Desmond. He knew Roger was unaccustomed to having so much time on his hands. After his acquittal, Roger had put together Desmond and he'd been indefatigable. As Lana's death became history, James had watched his dear friend reinvent himself. Only James knew the torment Roger had gone through, even denying himself contact with Cassidy as she went from a child to a woman. He had been determined to see his child only after he'd made amends for what she'd had to go through after the murder. Not that James agreed with Roger's method. But that was Roger's way of dealing with his torment.

The man beside him now was almost unrecognizable. It was frightening. Perhaps it was true that men's personalities sometimes changed with heart attacks. Illnesses could kill you in lots of different ways. So could age. God, James felt depressed. Tonight the huge house was cold and dark and the silence became unbearable. A fire roared in the fireplace, twigs crackling, hissing, sending plumes of smoke up the chimney. The warmth of the flames barely penetrated the chill lodged in the room.

"Jonathan and Cass were supposed to join us. What do you suppose happened?" Roger stared into the flames, a faraway look in his eyes.

James lowered his gaze. "I'm sure something must have come up," he speculated, aware that Roger's pride had been seriously bruised.

"Jonathan . . ." He shrugged. "But it's not like Cass." Roger checked his watch once more. "She's usually home by now." He reached for the cordless phone resting on the table beside his dinner plate and punched in the studio number. The main switchboard transferred him to Cass's extension. He got her voice mail. So he hung up.

Roger shoved his plate away, then rose from his seat.

"Goddamn it. Why doesn't she listen to me?" He paced back and forth a few times, then stood motionless in the middle of the room. "All I ask is that she follow my directions—my very simple directions." Roger spit the words out like stones.

James thought it best not to speak.

The doorbell sounded and they both jumped.

Moments later Rae appeared. The anxious look on her face told them something was wrong. Suddenly a chill blank silence surrounded them.

"There's a police officer at the door, Mr. Turmaine. He'd like to speak with you."

"Is . . . is it Cass?" Fear, stark and vivid, glittered in his eyes.

"No," Rae replied. In unison, both men let out sighs of relief.

"It's Jonathan," Rae continued. "There's been a car accident."

The color drained from Roger's face. He sank back into his chair.

"He's okay, just shaken up and bruised. Apparently he was speeding, driving under the influence, the officer said. He's okay." Rae lowered her eyes. "But I'm afraid the young girl he was with was killed."

James closed his eyes. A sensation of intense sickness and desolation swept over him. He fought hard to steady himself.

"The officer needs to speak with you, Mr. Turmaine. . . ." Rae spoke barely above a whisper. "The young girl was the daughter of Senator and Mrs. Williams."

| | |

Cass was working late again. She glanced at her Cartier tank watch. She had expected Rudolpho to stop by her office and take her to dinner. It was almost eight and still no sign of him. She assumed he was still sulking over Chelsea's performance as Ophelia.

Ally filled Cass in on the schedule for tomorrow morning. Cass couldn't concentrate. She was ruminating. Rudolpho had said, "If she's in, I'm out." And then Jack stood firm: "Then I suggest you start looking for a replacement."

On such short notice, if Rudolpho quit, she might be forced to settle for just anyone. And then she might still have problems meeting the production schedule as things stood. Rudolpho was used to working against the clock and keeping to a tight budget. TV does that to a director. The way her luck was going, she'd be grateful if she got a kid just out of film school.

Earlier she was walking on air, but now a niggling doubt pushed at her brain. Somehow she'd have to get one of them to change his mind. She first considered Jack, so headstrong and egotistical. She shook her head. No way. Jack held all the cards. It was his film, money, and studio. Besides, the change of directors would cost them weeks—and she wasn't losing her bet with Cavelli. It would have to be Rudolpho. He would do anything for her if she'd only give him a small sign of hope. Cass hated manipulation, but desperate times called for desperate measures.

She picked up the phone and called Rudolpho's suite.

"Hello?"

"Rudolpho, we need to talk. I'm willing to make some compromises." Cass tried to sound calm, but she felt desperate.

"Relax, Cass. Things can't be that bad," he said soothingly.

"I can't afford to have you walk off the film. I need you. I swear somehow, some way, I'll get Jack to change his mind."

There were a few seconds of silence, then Rudolpho said, "Uh, listen, Cass, perhaps I was too hasty. Ms. Hutton will make a fine Ophelia. Let's give her a try."

Cass couldn't believe her ears.

"Are . . . are you sure? This afternoon, you stood firm on your decision. What changed your mind?"

"I've been doing a lot of thinking. I don't want to let you down. I'm a good director. I'll get a performance out of her, Cass, I'm sure of it." Silence again, then: "Hey, we're a team, right?"

Cassidy was certain there was more to this story, but she didn't care. She heaved a deep sigh. "Thanks, I owe you."

"Sleep tight. I'll see you in the morning."

| | |

Chelsea lay on her side on the enormous bed, her head cupped in her hand. The beige silk ankle-length Dior nightgown had been a gift from Jack. She felt it appropriate that she wear it as she attempted to "convene" with the man who could furnish her with enough information to keep Jack satisfied. She stroked Rudolpho's naked back while he spoke to Cassidy on the telephone, and now, when he turned his attention back to her, she replenished his glass with the champagne that was being kept chilled in a sterling-silver wine cooler beside the bed.

"Is everything all right?" she asked.

Rudolpho drank deeply and then put one finger into his glass to dab champagne between her breasts. "It is now."

| | |

About nine-thirty, Cass left her office, exhausted and spent. As she walked to her car, she looked up from the parking lot. She could see Jack was still in his office. The lights were on, and his black Mercedes was parked in its reserved space. For a second she thought about going back upstairs and telling him about Rudolpho's change of heart, but then decided against it. It could wait till morning.

She climbed behind the wheel of the gleaming black Porsche, a company car that came along with her new position. She drove down the hill to the exit just past the guard's booth.

Sam flashed her a wide toothy smile and said, "Have a safe trip home, Ms. English."

Cass returned the smile and nodded.

| | |

He watched her leave.

He watched her walk up the sidewalk to her car, her long legs eating up the concrete. Her black hair picked up the bright lights that circled the parking lot, showing rich red highlights. Even in the dark, her angular face and big sapphire eyes were evident. This was a babe, no question. She got into the exquisite black vehicle and she was gone. Five minutes after she'd passed the guard's booth, he walked down the corridor to her office.

Getting in was easier than he'd imagined. He wouldn't have believed the doors still had those old-fashioned locks on them, the ones you could actually open with a credit card. He stood in the center of the large, beautifully furnished room, checking out where best to start.

This babe must be important, judging from the expensive furnishings in her office, expensive digs. Rich, rich, rich. A shame, such a beautiful creature, and someone was going to great lengths to destroy her. But he never got personally involved in the assignments. Hell, the money was too good to let feelings get in the way. The person who had hired him was careful and extremely secretive about all of the particulars. The transaction took place over the phone. The money was wired to his account. There was no face-to-face meeting—just brief, albeit specific, instructions.

He slid the duffel bag off his shoulder, unzipped it, and pulled out a compact camera and a pair of leather gloves. He slipped them on and went to work, sifting through every sheet of paper on her desk, then combing through her files. He photographed all those that pertained to a project titled *Dangerous Intentions*. He stuffed the camera back into the bag. Next, he placed a tiny chip inside the receiver of the phone and screwed the microphone's attachments into the inside of the desk drawer, careful to conceal the tiny wire. When it was securely in place and he was sure it was in working order, he slipped back into the hall and, using his cell phone, punched in the number given to him.

"It's done. I have the photos and the bug is in place. I have everything you need. I can get copies of these documents faxed to you immediately, as you instructed." He waited for a response but only heard breathing on the other end. So he continued.

"It looks like the lady plans to shoot the entire film on the lot. They're pouring millions into a new set. It's just about complete."

The voice on the other end of the line was curt. "You know what needs to be done."

| | |

It was the wild seventies; disco was big. Tons of John Travolta clones in white polyester suits crowded the Hollywood clubs and bars. The Bee Gees were back on top with the phenomenal success of Saturday Night Fever. *The war was over; Nixon had been run out of town. Baby boomers like Spielberg, Geffen, Terrence Malick were climbing, coming into their own.*

He attended Actors West by day and cruised the hot spots at night. Chicks gravitated to him. Some of the older ones—wealthy widows and bored first wives whose ex-husbands paid dearly to be divorced—even paid him to escort them to dinner parties and other social dos. He lived a double life and it suited him just fine. Burning the candle at both ends was a trip. By day he wore his "mysterious, eager-to-get-ahead" hat. He studied hard and perfected each stage performance, and mingled congenially with the students and teachers.

Thanks to those needy older ladies, he had more money than he could have anticipated if he'd had only acting to count on. Auditions were plentiful. He'd landed a couple of industrial films. Even a bit part in an Altman movie. He became eligible to join the Screen Actors Guild and got his SAG card. He was on his way.

And it was a never-ending wonder that a guy like him could not only get ahead but put behind him the hard times and ruthlessness. Gone was New York City. The degrading foster homes, the crazy, obnoxious crowd at Valentine's, Sally and her dead boyfriend. The naive, scruffy kid from the streets, who stole from street vendors and rolled drunks for fun, was long dead.

Yesterday's life was only a memory. Hollywood was a land of hope, promise, and dreams. He knew what he wanted; he knew how to get it.

In a town where the strong devoured the weak, he attached himself to the winners, women like Marjorie Hiller, twenty-five years old, fiery yet mellow, bold yet surprisingly shy. He'd met her on the set of an Actors West production of Hamlet. *She was married to a famous European director, but this didn't stop him from reeling her in with his sexuality, machismo, charm. When Marjorie informed him that she was leaving the director for him, he persuaded her not to—what they had was delicate, he'd said. It wouldn't do to rock the boat.*

Actors West comprised two groups: the Showcase company, the more experienced actors, and the Workshop. He got stuck with the Workshop, those in training. Unfortunately, only those in the Showcase got exposure in the press, in the industry. But he had a plan. The Workshop was about to put on its semiannual production. This season it was Streetcar Named Desire. *A new guy—Richard Gere—was being introduced as the next Stanley. He begged Marjorie to invite her husband. He gave his greatest performance that night and he reveled in adulation afterward. The next day Marjorie phoned.*

"Hubert adored you. He wants you to do a reading for a new movie he's working on. It's not a leading role, but it's a good start nonetheless." Indeed it was. And so began his successful climb up the Hollywood ladder.

Two months later he ended the affair with Marjorie.

He was on his way to being the biggest star Hollywood—the world—had ever seen. At least that was his plan.

| | |

As soon as Cass drove through the gates, the tensions of the day fell away. Despite the bad memories and nostalgia, Whispering Winds had now become a refuge, her sanctuary. When she arrived there, she nosed her car between two Mercedes sedans, one Roger's, the other belonging to James. She checked her watch as she got out of the car and wondered why James was here so late.

As she grabbed her briefcase from the trunk and started across the drive, she remembered: dinner with her father. She was sure he was angry. And he had good reason to be.

How could she have forgotten? He'd made a point of having Rae leave a reminder on her voice mail that morning. But she'd become so engrossed in preproduction on *his* film, no wonder dinner had slipped her mind, she rationalized.

In reality, Cass had counted on an empty evening locked in her room. She needed to go over script revisions, location reports on possible sites for exteriors, and maybe even spend some time relaxing. Now that was out of the question. When she got to the door, Cass took in a deep breath, ready to step into the fray.

She felt defensive and predicted that James would side with Roger. Did her father really want her to head his business, finish his masterpiece, and still show up for dinner at six? She groaned silently, striding over polished hardwood floors to the sitting room, psyching herself up for the questioning—no, interrogation—about *Dangerous*. How are the budgets? How about scheduling? Are the actors compatible? All topics she'd spent the last fifteen hours fixing.

She took one more deep breath. From behind the closed doors of the study, she could hear James and Roger—they were arguing. She managed to sneak past the study. She made it up the stairs and nearly to her room, but from behind Rae's bedroom door, she heard sobbing. Opening the bedroom door without knocking, Cassidy found Rae— on her knees, praying, crying. Cassidy went quickly to the older woman's side. She extended her arms to her beloved nanny and leaned over her. Her long hair flowed along the sides of her face like an opaque black veil.

"Rae, Rae . . . what's wrong?"

Rae looked up at her, eyes dark with pain. "Jonathan was in a car accident."

Cass gasped. "Is . . . is he okay?"

Rae nodded yes and began to speak. The story rushed out: Jonathan's drunken state, the horrible accident, the death of the young girl—the senator's daughter.

Cass was hardly shocked. Her half brother's behavior was destructive and reckless. Sooner or later something tragic was bound to happen.

"Dad needs me."

Rae held out her hand and Cassidy pulled them both to a standing position.

"No," Rae said, tear tracks following the long wrinkles on her dear face. "Leave him be. James is with him. Give him till morning. The shock is still fresh."

| | |

Cass went into her bedroom and stripped off her clothes, leaving them wherever they fell. She pulled her comfortable sweats from the back of the bathroom door and then sat at her desk.

Try as she might, she couldn't concentrate on the documents before her. Jonathan. The young girl. The production schedule. The girl again. Killed. Her brother driving. What must her family be going through? Jonathan had really done it this time. Yet she was sure he felt no remorse. In fact, he was probably still too drunk to realize what he had done.

Ever since they were children, Jonathan had used his father's guilt to get away with murder—literally, it seemed, this time. He had hidden behind their father's wealth and powerful connections, evading the consequences of his recklessness. Money could buy anything, and anyone, and Jonathan's thoughtless romp through life was proof positive of that. He had never paid the price for the wreckage he caused.

This girl's death would, in any other family, be earth-shattering news. But Cass was sure by morning it would be nothing more than a memory swept under the rug. Just another "tragedy" in the annals of the Turmaine family history.

Tragedy. How many times had she heard that word since Mother died? Just the thought triggered such terrible memories. She slumped back in her desk chair, nestling her head comfortably in the butter-soft slipper satin, and closed her eyes. Tranquillity wouldn't come easy tonight. No matter how much her body craved sleep.

Down the hall, she heard movement and loud, sharp noises. Then her father's voice. Her heart fluttered out of rhythm. For the first time since she was a little girl, Cass covered her ears with her hands and shut out the sound.

| | |

"Mommy, do I look as beautiful as you?"

It's her tenth birthday. Cassidy stands in front of the mirror admiring the satin-and-lace dress her mother had presented her with just that morning. It came from Neiman Marcus—hand-delivered, no less.

Her mother is smiling for the first time in days. She still has that funny, minty smell on her breath, and her eyes are wide open and glassy, but she seems happy. She fusses over Cassidy, straightening her collar, buttoning her cuffs. Cass revels in the attention. She desperately wants her mother to wrap her tightly in her arms, but Mama mutters something about wrinkling her dress and messing her hair, so Cass stands still as a mannequin while her mother makes the final adjustments.

"There," she whispers. Her eyes fill with tears. "You are the most beautiful girl in the world."

Cass smiles and hugs her mother tight. She doesn't care about the dress or her hair. She only craves the security and comfort of her mother's warm embrace.

"Lana, where are you?" Her father's voice echoes in the cavernous hall.

The transformation in her mother occurs instantly. Lana closes her eyes, bows her head, and her body slumps in despair. She quickly leaves and Cassidy hears her mother's high heels hurry toward the master bedroom.

Her father is screaming and her mother is crying. Cassidy is covering her ears to escape the noise. It grows quiet for a while. Her daddy is standing in the doorway, only she can't see his face. A door slams and she hears her father's angry voice and her mother's sobs. Cass, terrified, runs to her "secret spot."

| | |

Cass's eyes snapped open to moonlight, and the image of her father's face, hidden in the shadows, burned into her retina. Her mother's sobs sounded in the distance. No, it couldn't be. Perhaps she had dozed; perhaps she only thought she did. She was hearing things—stress could do that to anyone. The curtains moved restlessly in the rain-scented breeze. Cass went to the windows and pulled the casements shut. She threw herself onto the bed, climbed under the blankets, and tossed and turned till she found a comfortable position.

She felt her body relax as she drifted closer and closer toward sleep. The sobs came again. As she listened more intently, it seemed to become louder now.

She slipped out of bed, put on her robe and slippers, and tiptoed out of the bedroom. The hall was still and silent, but in the distance, the sobbing continued. It appeared to be coming from the attic. Deciding to take the back staircase, she pushed open the old wooden door and stepped inside, then quickly mounted the short flight of stairs.

The attic was a single room, about two thousand square feet. The walls were covered with plywood paneling. An ancient Oriental rug, its once-vibrant colors muted by time, was spread over the oak floor. An old potbellied stove on the back wall had wood piled neatly next to it.

In the center, in front of the window, was a long wood table with two benches designed specifically for a child. Just the sight of the room—a rainy-day playroom when Cass was small—brought back so many memories, good and bad. For the most part, this space had become a haven during her childhood. When her parents' arguments became really bad, even her secret spot at the head of the spiral stairs wasn't serene enough, forcing her to run up here. She pictured the scared little child she was, cowering in the corner. Sometimes she stayed in the attic for hours, until the noise stopped.

In the far corner, Cass noticed neatly piled boxes. She approached and saw that they were securely sealed. She opened one, then a second, and began to sift through their contents. All of the objects belonged to Lana—her vanity set, letters, books, small picture frames, including one of Cassidy as an infant on her mother's shoulder.

She rifled through one storage bag stuffed with evening dresses, all either white or blue. Her mother loved blue, particularly the dark hues that complemented her eyes. Suddenly the scent of her mother's favorite perfume hit her in the face, full force. The effect was shocking. When Cass came to the dress her mother wore to the Academy Awards, she zipped the bag back up quickly and pushed it away.

She opened another box, and the glint of gold caught her eye. She reached in, moved the other items away, and pulled out a wood box, delicately hand-carved, about the size of a shoe box. On the front was a brass plaque engraved with the letters *L. T.* With trembling hands and tingling fingers, Cass lifted the lid and gasped. Her body reacted and she shivered even before her mind grasped that this was her mother's personal diary.

She clutched it to her pounding heart and walked toward the window, brushing aside some cobwebs. The cold wood floor penetrated through her slippers and numbed the soles of her feet. Suddenly Cass wanted to be anywhere but where she was. As she started down the stairs, she heard the moaning sound again.

"Help me . . . help meeee." This time the sounds weren't muffled; the words were chilling. The cries were coming from a darkened alcove behind the door. Cass stood still. The noise stopped and silence loomed like a heavy mist.

From a few feet away she could see that the walls were covered with pictures of Lana. The alcove was a veritable museum, a shrine. Even the dim light could not hide the exquisite beauty of her portrait. The photographs were a catalog of Hollywood royalty and ritual: Lana dancing with a fading Fred Astaire, Lana and Roger smiling at each other, standing against a landscape Cassidy recognized as the gardens at the Hotel Bel-Air. Lana, Lana, Lana. Everywhere she looked, her mother's gorgeous face with the sad, deep, beautiful blue eyes, summoned from the dead.

Cass absorbed all of the photos at once. She lightly rubbed her fingers over the images to brush the thin layer of dust away, moving from one to the next.

Sinatra and Lana laughing, seated at a banquette. Probably the Brown Derby.

Lana at the Academy Awards with Roger and a very young Sean Connery. Lana on her thirtieth birthday, her thirty-first, thirty-second. Lana holding Cass the day she was born. Lana gracing the covers of *Vanity Fair, Vogue, Variety.*

As Cass edged closer to get a better view, she accidentally stepped on the frayed ends of a yellowed ivory lace sheet. The fabric fell to the floor and Cassidy choked back a cry, frightened, electrified by the mawkish sight before her—a dressmaker's fitting form, dressed in a blood-streaked white gown. A blown-up photo of her mother's face was clumsily taped to the top, where the head would be.

Cass recoiled in horror before she realized that she was seeing a horrifying mannequin.

She also realized that this meant that the destruction of her wardrobe the night of Roger's party was not just a vicious prank. Obviously someone was going to great lengths to frighten her.

She stared at the form, unable to wrest her eyes from it, absorbing every grotesque detail. She was unable to scream, as if a vise had closed around her throat. Her pulse began to beat erratically. Perspiration drenched her body and she began to shiver. Backing away, she stumbled toward the stairs.

| | |

"My God, Rae, will you listen to me?" Cass cried in a small, frightened voice. "It was here." She stood in the alcove where the mannequin had been just minutes ago. She had dragged Rae from a fitful sleep and led her into the attic.

"It was Mother. . . . There was a sheet. . . ." Cass was breathing in shallow, quick gasps. "There was blood all over her gown."

"Cranberry juice, you mean." Rae leaned forward, her sensible cotton nightgown covered by the white ankle-length terry robe she had grabbed on the way out of her bedroom. The hem of the robe swept the dusty attic floor, stirring up a storm of particles. She put her large, soft hands on either side of Cass's face and held it gently.

"It was only a bad dream, darlin'." Rae's eyes scanned the alcove. "Look around. There's nothing here. We threw that old mannequin out years ago."

"But I saw it . . . right here," Cass cried, her mind a crazy mixture of hope and fear.

"Sometimes the eyes, the mind, play tricks on us, darlin'. It's stress, Cassidy . . . coming back after all these years. You were just looking at all those photos."

Cass showed her the diary. "It belonged to my mother."

"Where did you find that?" Rae asked quickly. Shock flashed across her face. "That's not for you to see."

Cass pulled the diary out of Rae's reach. "But why not?"

"No one should have it except your father. He probably doesn't even know it's here. The crew that came to put your mother's less valuable possessions in boxes must have packed it away." Rae put her hands on her hips and an unreadable expression took over her face. "Cassidy, don't read it. What good could come of it?"

Rae immediately knew this was exactly the wrong thing to say to Cassidy, who quickly sat down, her pearl-pink silk robe opening on the floor like a tablecloth at a picnic. She read slowly through the first few entries. Emotions flickered like shadows across her face, and her mouth twitched as her fingers began to turn the pages.

Rae reached for the small book, grasping for the spine as Cassidy twisted away. Resigned, she spoke softly. "Okay, Cass. But at least get some sleep. The diary will be there tomorrow."

Cassidy felt like a child hiding a forbidden piece of candy. "I'm locking it in my briefcase and taking it wherever I go."

As they reached the door to Cassidy's room, Cass saw worry lines deepen on Rae's face in the pinkish light of the corridor sconce.

Rae touched Cass gently on the arm. "I can't stop you. After all, by rights, I suppose the diary is yours as much as your father's."

"That's right. It is, and it's no one's business that I've found it."

Cass's eyes implored Rae to keep this secret. The older woman kissed Cassidy on the cheek. "Go on, then." Cassidy cracked open her bedroom door. "And Cass," Rae whispered, "if you have that nightmare again . . ."

"It was real. I tell you: I saw a mannequin with Mother's photo and a bloodied gown. I don't care if you don't believe me."

Rae shook her head. "I was going to suggest a sleeping pill."

Cassidy held up the diary. "I've got some reading to do."

Rae sighed and continued her way down the hall.

| | |

Cass skimmed through the entries for the first year, 1970.

"No matter what I do or how tired I am, I never sleep anymore," one entry read. "I've given up going to bed until I can't hold my head up. Nothing helps—not booze, not pills . . . not warm milk. Nothing. My life is a mess . . . my heart is ripped apart. I can't stop thinking that it might be better for everyone if I just didn't wake up at all in the morning. Or maybe I'll just walk out the door and never come back. I'll leave everything and everyone behind."

As Cass skimmed the pages, it became clear that her mother and father's union was volatile, to say the very least. It was a love-hate relationship, with Lana always feeling as if she could never measure up to Roger's high expectations of her. Had that happened to Jonathan, too? Cassidy thought, for the first time, that maybe one reason she was so, well, level-headed was because she had not had much contact with her father over the years.

She concluded from what her mother had written that Roger was by far the more powerful, intelligent, and charismatic of the two. Lana wrote poignantly about her terrible insecurity and feelings of inadequacy whenever she was in his company: "Roger tells me he loves me, and I know he does, in his own way. Sometimes I feel like I'm just another one of his productions and I'll never be good enough." Cass was amazed. Her mother was a legendary beauty, an accomplished actress, yet Lana felt she wasn't "pretty enough, smart enough, or poised enough" to properly complement Roger.

When Cass couldn't bear to read any further, she placed the red ribbon at the entry to May 17, 1971, and closed the book. She turned off the light, but she could not turn her thoughts off.

She was restless. Several times she dozed off only to fall into another nightmare. One time she had screamed so loudly that Rae rushed to her room. Finally, around two, Rae managed to coax her into taking a light sedative, and she settled into a restless drugged slumber. Her mother's diary was clutched to her chest.

| | |

The ringing telephone jerked Cassidy back to consciousness. She woke with a tightness in her head, right across the forehead—the beginning of a headache. Where was she? Why did she feel so disconnected? Then everything flooded back to her: the attic, the mannequin, the diary, the sedative. The phone rang insistently.

Cassidy bolted upright, letting the diary fall to the floor. She shuddered as she picked up the receiver. "Hello."

"Cass?"

"Yes." Her voice was a hoarse mumble.

"I think you better get down to the studio right away," Rudolpho said urgently.

She looked at the clock on the nightstand. It was nearly four A.M. "What's wrong?"

"There's been a fire." Silence, then: "The set. That's all I know."

Time stopped.

| | |

A battalion of squad cars and fire trucks, sirens shrieking and lights flashing, filled the studio lot. The road surface was slick from the rain and Cass slammed on the brakes, stopping just inches short of a collision with a parked car, and leaped out. She tore past security guards, police officers, firemen, reporters, and gawking bystanders holding handkerchiefs to their mouths.

She had expected the worst—and saw it.

Billows of smoke obscured the night sky.

An explosion echoed through the fire and the rain. Flames danced wildly before her eyes—walls of fiery hell. She moved closer. Her nostrils burned. Smoke filled the air and made her cough. She pulled a sleeve over her mouth and nose and kept walking toward the set. Despite the intense heat, despite protests from the officers and firefighters.

"Hey, lady! Get back!" a studio security officer yelled in her direction. "You have to stay back—it's too dangerous."

"Get out of the way!" roared a fire fighter as he ran toward the blaze, a coil of security cable thrown across one shoulder.

Cass ignored them. She was numb; she couldn't think clearly. With eyes teary from the smoke, she saw Rudolpho. He was with the fire marshal and the set director. They were walking toward her.

"How bad is it?" she heard Rudolpho ask.

The fire marshal said, "The entire set is destroyed. A total loss. Nothing left but ashes."

"How long to rebuild it?" Rudolpho asked.

The set director said, "At least three weeks. And that's just the set. I can't speak for wardrobe and props."

"We haven't got three weeks," Rudolpho snapped. "Cass . . ." He reached toward her.

"Any idea who would want to sabotage this project, Ms. English?" the fire marshal asked.

"Sabotage?" Rudolpho raised an eyebrow.

"Afraid so. This is a clear case of arson. It's not the work of an amateur, either. Whoever did this used small amounts of dynamite attached to a timing device."

All three men turned their gaze on Cass. She stood frozen and silent, with a glazed look in her eyes.

| | |

Slowly the numbness began to wear off. Cass and Rudolpho retreated to a spot on the lot away from the fire. He handed her a flask. "Drink this." She didn't bother asking how he'd known to bring the whiskey. She took a long sip, ignoring the awful taste. Her father's voice replayed in her head in an endless loop: "I want you to take over for me. You're the only one I trust to do it right, Cass."

Now she was filled with an overwhelming sense of failure and loss.

The heat before her was so intense, she could swear the flames nearly licked her body. But she felt nothing—no pain. She was insensate.

Then she heard Jack saying, "Are you a gambler, Ms. English? I'm willing to bet half of my share of Colossal that you can't meet the deadline."

Rudolpho wrapped his arms around her and held her. In a comforting voice he said, "Come on, Cass. It's over. There's nothing you can do here. Go home."

The last explosion echoed through the rain and fog and the once majestic set had become charred rubble—all of the hard work and effort lost in the darkness.

In that instant, Cass felt her dreams, her future, burning into nothingness.

No place on earth is as rich or passionate, no landscape as beautiful. And once the love affair with Italy has begun, it's next to impossible to escape the country's charm—its majestic mountains, misty lakes, idyllic islands, wonderful walled villages, and exquisite cities.

The peninsula of Venice stands apart. Rising like a mirage from the waters of the lagoons, this picturesque city of canals and gondolas is unlike any other, a seemingly chimerical maze of alleys, waterways, tiny squares, and bridges all playing hide-and-seek with one another. It is the city of Marco Polo, Titian, and Vivaldi. The Basilica di San Marco and the Piazza San Marco survive, frozen in time, romantic relics of a vast, ardent history.

And with no back-lot set and no time to rebuild, Cass had no choice but to move the production of *Dangerous Intentions* to the *real* location of the story—Venezia . . . Venice.

So here she was in the middle of the historic Piazza San Marco—St. Mark's Square—watching in awe as a production crew—part American, part Italian—worked in seamless accord to again transform the historical plaza into a working movie set in a matter of hours. Not that it was easy. Italy is known for its labyrinth of red tape, yet Cassidy had managed to cut through it in record-breaking time with nonstop calls from the plane on her flight from L.A.

Using her contacts, and the amity earned when she produced a series on the restoration of Venice for *Up to the Minute,* which moved American TV viewers to donate millions to the cause, Cass called in all favors, first from the authorities in Rome, then in Venice. Italian cities still seemed to function as the ancient city-states they once were. It also didn't hurt that, by cooperating with her to make *Dangerous Intentions* happen, the Italian film industry could count on *priceless* press in the U.S. No doubt this altruism, given in the form of expedition of visas, licenses, and assorted permits and concessions from local theatrical and trade unions, would be translated into reciprocity on the American side of the Atlantic.

Now cameras were in position, the lighting calibrated, and the square's pigeons were, to Cass's amazement, culled so that only a small flock remained. The crew had also denuded the piazza of all modern litter—no more butts, no more beer cans or paper coffee cups. The crowd of natives and tourists were corralled off camera, contained by a team of *polizia*, whose handguns seemed so out of place next to the group of extras in eighteenth-century costumes. For now, the plaza belonged to *Dangerous Intentions* but the tourists got it back every night.

On the perimeter of the square, another sign of the twenty-first century served as a harsh reminder of the passage of time: a caravan of trailers, housing computer equipment, equipment for sound and lighting, food service, makeup and hair, wardrobe, props, and one star "dressing room." Of course, that belonged to none other than Chelsea.

Cass sat alone amid the organized chaos on a classic director's chair, in the middle of the action.

The sun rose, a huge orange ball, over the canal. Electricians and carpenters shed too-warm clothing layer by layer, mopping their brows and fanning away the heat. The temperature was nearly sixty degrees, unseasonably high for winter. The technical director gave Cass a thumbs-up sign, signaling they were ready to go. Cass checked her watch and wondered when the cast would arrive. It was 6:45, and she had called for a 7 A.M. shoot. A production assistant handed her a cup of strong Italian coffee. She settled back to wait. Her body ached. Her mind was a bit weary—still, she could feel the adrenaline rush racing blood and energy through her veins.

She was thankful for the adrenaline rush because physical exhaustion had begun to set in. Since arriving in Venice two weeks earlier, the entire crew—including Cassidy—had worked nonstop, fourteen-hour days. The only downtime she had managed was a nightly hot bath and dinner in bed, but even then she was returning phone calls and taking a quick glance at the scenes on the next day's shooting schedule. With luck, she could get five, maybe six hours of uninterrupted sleep.

After the devastating fire, Cass had felt so overwhelmed that she had considered walking away from the project. How would she be able to complete filming on time, and keep within the budget, when they had to construct a brand-new set? It was apparent that someone didn't want *Dangerous Intentions* to be completed. The fire marshal's report had called the fire suspicious, and further alarms were triggered in Cass's mind when she saw in the report that Jack claimed to have left the studio at seven P.M. Cass was positive she'd seen his office lights on and his car parked in its place when she'd left after eight. Memories of Jack's cold, piercing gaze and his "I told you it couldn't be done" smirk in the days after the fire had set her mind racing.

It was already dawn when she arrived back at Whispering Winds that night. Jonathan was waiting for her in the library. He told her about his car crash. He looked bruised, even a little contrite. But there was a touch of phoniness in his apparent concern about how the fire had destroyed the set.

When Cass was safely up in her room, the door locked, the shades drawn, she laid all the documents pertaining to the film's schedule and budget across the unmade bed and studied them for two hours. The only solution was to rebuild. But she couldn't afford the three weeks it would take and *still* bring the project in on time.

Cass paced the floor and weighed her options. She pondered the what-ifs and why-nots and inventoried what she had to work with and what she needed to get back on track. In the eleventh hour, just before dawn, she came up with a plan.

If Mohammed couldn't go to the mountain . . .

Flying the entire cast and crew to Venice was probably more economical at this stage than starting over from scratch on the back lot. She had to forge ahead.

Still without sleep, she marched into Jack's office at nine A.M., provided all the necessary paperwork, complete with facts and figures, and announced to all involved that departure to Venice would be immediate.

To her astonishment, Jack approved all of her requests without the least question or hesitation.

Cass had always been good at pulling things together at the last minute. The immediate deadlines of weekly television train a person for that. And the ability to crunch numbers to the satisfaction of those network bean counters had proven helpful, too. Pulling this particular magic out of the hat would finally put to rest all the questions about her ability to make a success out of *Dangerous Intentions.* She thought again of the image of Jack sitting behind his desk, a look of dumbfounded amazement spread across his face. That moment alone had been a victory.

Cass felt even more triumphant when she found one dozen lavender roses waiting at her hotel room when she arrived in Venice. The card enclosed read:

You amaze me, Bellissima!
Best of luck, Jack

And so far this luck was holding out. The city provided a magnificent setting, needing little work to go back in time to meet the script. Even Mother Nature was cooperating. They had lost no time to bad weather.

Once shooting began, Cassidy realized she was totally at ease in her new element as a hands-on producer of feature films. Without meaning to, she had upstaged Rudolpho as director several times. Though producers were meant to pull things together—keep an eye on the big picture—while directors choreographed the acting, Cassidy, like other brilliant moviemakers, naturally assumed both roles. The uncanny ability to charm that she'd inherited from both her mother and father was serving her appropriately with the actors as well. She worked them like magic, getting performances from them that made the picture come alive. Even Chelsea was cooperating. She arrived on the set each morning promptly and fully prepared. She wasn't distracted, temperamental, or abusive. So far her performance as Ophelia had been stellar. It showed up in the dailies.

Cassidy watched as Chelsea studied the script every day while on the set. Chelsea had learned every line and character nuance and, for all intents and purposes, had *become* Ophelia, never breaking character. Gone was the bitch Cass had met in Los Angeles. Here in Venice, she was getting to know a Chelsea possessed of a graceful innocence and tenderness. It was an astonishing transformation. More than once she'd had to remind herself, that's why they call it acting.

Maybe the potential Jack and Rudolpho had seen in Chelsea was real after all. Cass was willing to give them the benefit of the doubt, for now at least.

On this morning, as on others, Chelsea arrived on the set with her entourage at 6:55. Clutching her black Coach attaché case as if it were a prop, she approached Cass.

"The light is all wrong."

When Cass didn't react, Chelsea signaled for her band of lackeys to scatter, threw her bag to the floor, put her hands on her hips, and frowned. "It's too bright. I'll look awful."

Chelsea pouted, but Cass saw through this petulant demeanor. Chelsea's insecurity about her looks was sincere.

"Chelsea," Cass assured her, determined to head off a show of temper, "you look beautiful—perfect. The early-morning sun makes you look radiant."

"You're just pacifying me," she said, her frown deepening.

"No, I'm not, I'm being honest." And Cass was. Chelsea did look radiant this morning—hair perfectly coifed, makeup meticulously applied, costume shaping her already-enviable figure into an hourglass.

But this beauty was more than costume and makeup. Chelsea had developed an incandescent glow that Cassidy, even with her limited experience, recognized—Chelsea "had a fella," as Rae would put it. The man in question, Cass suspected with a twinge of envy, was Rudolpho—even though placating a temperamental leading lady was not in his job description.

Still, from the moment the company had boarded the plane, the two had made it clear that they had "chemistry." Cass couldn't figure out if what she felt was really jealousy. She had no claim on Rudolpho, despite their extracurricular couplings back in New York. Whether or not he and Chelsea were lovers, or were going to be lovers, wasn't at issue. Cass's real concern was how a fling between the leading lady and her director might affect the film. She hoped she was reading this wrong.

Cass also wondered if their constant flirting and public displays of affection were performed for *her* benefit. Nonetheless, Chelsea had been transformed. In a very brief period of time she'd gone from a terror to a soft-spoken and pliant actress, save for those few moments like now when her "insecurities" surfaced. It was obvious to Cass that whatever the craziness behind Chelsea's tough image was, her demons surfaced if she felt insecure. So Cass worked to give Chelsea a sense of importance—she got star treatment, big time.

A maid was assigned to tend to Chelsea's needs: her clothing, her toiletries, her trailer. She was a young Mexican woman, pleasant and efficient. The woman was sharp and had been employed by the studio for years. She spent her days racing around the star-sized trailer/dressing room, hanging up Chelsea's clothing, setting out her makeup, and fetching endless cups of coffee.

Cassidy stayed with Chelsea as she had her makeup touched up, managing to talk her down. By the time she emerged from her dressing room fifteen minutes later, every bit the superstar, the actress was satisfied. She waited patiently, professionally, on the sidelines for the usual excitement to begin. And within minutes, cameras were positioned, the assistant director was conferring with the technical crew, and Cass took her seat behind the cameras.

| | |

"Action!" Rudolpho called.

The first assistant director called, "Roll camera."

To this, the assistant cameraman responded, "Rolling."

"Speed," called the soundman, followed by the cry of the clapper holder: "Scene 534, Take 1."

With that, the assistant cameraman called, "Marker!"

The clapper holder, standing just off camera, held the marker board, with the scene and take numbers written in chalk, in front of the lens and slapped the striped top of the board shut. *Clap!*

The day had begun.

Chelsea fell to her knees to crawl through a puddle of "mud." The thick mixture of powdered clay and water was caked on her hands and her clothing and was streaked down her face. It took a number of takes to shoot the scene, and each time she had to wash off the goop and change her costume, wig, and makeup so they could start over again.

The male lead couldn't get his lines right, and Cassidy saw that Chelsea was becoming frustrated. The only thing stopping her from blowing her cool and walking off the set, Cassidy believed, was the knowledge that this movie could make her a star.

Rudolpho yelled "Cut!" again, and this time Cassidy called for a fifteen-minute break.

"It's not working." Rudolpho cradled his head in his hands and let out a long sigh.

Cass shrugged and said offhandedly, "Chelsea's great. What do we do about him?" Cassidy discreetly nodded to Bengino, the young Italian actor playing Ophelia's great love. Famous in Italy, he was relatively unknown in the U.S.

John, the assistant director, spoke first. "I had a talk with Bengino yesterday about his poor performance. Chelsea just doesn't excite him. He said he doesn't find her the least bit attractive. I reminded him that he was supposed to be acting, but something must have been lost in the translation."

Rudolpho shook his head in exasperation and said, "We can't very well replace him now. The ball is in your court, Cass. I think it's time you worked your magic on our disenchanted Signor Bengino."

He shot her a mischievous smile, a dare, to which she replied, "You think I can't do it, eh?"

John eyed them both curiously.

Cass jumped out of her chair, handed Rudolpho her script, and approached Bengino, who was busily signing autographs outside his trailer.

Wherever they went, the dark-haired man with incredibly exotic features and a dazzling smile was trailed by fans. This time, a bevy of local young women, mostly shop girls from the stores around the square, had clustered around the set in hopes of a glimpse, an autograph, perhaps even a kiss, from their favorite heartthrob. Cass waited apart from the crowd, standing where Bengino could see her. When he looked up, she waved for him to join her.

Disappointed, his fans followed him with their longing eyes. Some glared at the dark-haired American woman who took him away from them. Cassidy did not speak Italian, but she understood the sentiment in the words the women shouted at her as the actor excused himself.

Once they were in the shade, out of earshot, Cass turned to face the young actor. She idly fingered the collar of her blouse before speaking. "Bengino, what can I say to help you with your part?" Cass said quietly. She paused, then continued. "Have you ever loved a woman?"

The young man shot her a cocky grin, then said, "Of course, I've loved more women than I can count."

Cass removed her dark glasses. She eyed him suspiciously. "No. I don't think you understand me." She took a deep breath and brushed her hair from her face with both hands. "I'm not talking about sex. No. What I'm talking about is the kind of love that controls your mind, your soul. Do you know this feeling, Bengino?"

She waited for him to answer. When he didn't respond, she continued. "Have you ever known a woman who made you weak in the knees? When just the sight of her was enough to drive you into a passionate frenzy? You think about her every waking moment—long to touch her, stroke her hair, kiss her lips . . . taste her."

The young Italian's eyes followed Cass's fingers as she idly unbuttoned the top button of her blouse, then rested for a moment on her cleavage. He shifted his gaze to her waist and around the curve of her hips.

Cass was not unaware of her effect on the macho actor. She played the seductress, placing her hands on her hips, which were snuggled into a pair of tight white jeans. She lowered her eyes. In a husky voice she said, "Even if you close your eyes—no matter where you are—you can still see her, smell her, feel her."

Bengino moved closer to Cass, so close she could feel his body heat. She smoothed his collar, pretending to brush lint from his shoulder. Boldly then, she let her hands linger for a brief moment on his chest, which was hard beneath the short-sleeve shirt he wore. He emitted a soft sigh and Cass knew her magic was working.

"Do you find me attractive, Bengino?" she whispered.

He nodded and Cass seized the moment.

"Remember this feeling, like a snapshot in your mind. Can you do that?" She touched him lightly on his bicep. She kept her hand there, feeling the heat build beneath it.

"Sì, yes."

The actor's slip into Italian told her his mind was focused on what he was feeling in this moment.

"Can you do me a favor?" She lifted her chin so their eyes met. "When you're on the set in front of the cameras, speaking your lines, holding Chelsea, imagine in here"—she rubbed her index finger across his forehead—"and in here"—she flattened her palm over his heart—"that it's me."

The actor's chisled features, as well as his deep black eyes, were easy to read: He had become so enraptured by Cass that he would do anything she asked. She almost felt sorry for him, remembering fleetingly the power of falling in love. Only the very young still believed in the magic of that instant where love comes into being.

But there was no time to feel anything right now. The clock was running. She had to get *Dangerous Intentions* finished in time, at any cost. So the kid would be in puppy love with her for a few days—big deal.

"Now, let's get back to work." She gently guided him into the sunlight and toward the set.

| | |

The rest of the day went smoothly. Bengino performed with such passion, such hunger, that the entire cast and crew were beguiled. As he projected those emotions to the camera, his performance raised that of all the other actors—including Chelsea. She seemed to float through her lines, bringing an ethereal but realistic life to her words.

Her eyes had a distant look, her movements made it seem as if she were being propelled by an otherworldly force, and the result was pure magic. The setting sun in the background, the low lighting, the crisp evening breeze—everything was so perfect.

"Keep rolling," Cass whispered to Rudolpho. "Use whatever's in the camera. We can use the extra footage for publicity."

Rudolpho, mesmerized as well, nodded. "Breathtaking, isn't it?"

"Picture perfect."

"Ready to fade," the cameraman yelled out. "Want to shoot another roll before we lose the light?"

"Cut," Rudolpho yelled. "Print it."

There was a buzz as the actors filed off the set and crowded near the food services table for a last coffee while waiting to turn in their costumes to wardrobe.

Rudolpho let out an enormous sigh of relief. "I thought we'd never get through today."

Cass leaned into the chair and ran her fingers through her hair. "It's probably the best we've shot to date."

"Thanks to you," he replied. For a moment their eyes locked. "How about a quiet evening, just the two of us, in my suite? A bottle of champagne, some lobster, and the most incredible massage. Sound enticing?" he asked.

Cass smiled. She knew he was trying to be gentle, not pushy, and a part of her longed for the comfort of just being with him. "I'd better pass, Rudolpho," she said, hesitating. It was best if they kept their distance. She didn't know what was up between him and Chelsea, but she thought it was prudent to stay clear of becoming entangled again with her part-time lover. She knew better than to mix business with pleasure. Cassidy got up, gathered her belongings, and headed for the water taxi. Shooting might be over for the day, but there was still so much she had to get done for tomorrow and the day after that and . . .

"What about the dailies?" Rudolpho called out. "We should really view them together. We're a team, remember?"

Cass stopped dead in her tracks. "Yes."

"So, seven P.M, your suite."

"Rudolpho, no." She kept walking, not waiting to hear his answer.

| | |

It was nearly six when Cass arrived back at the hotel. She was tired and hungry. The nightly water taxi ride to her hotel did help revive her. It was next to impossible to feel too stressed in this oasis of stunning architecture and luxurious gardens. She caught a glimpse of the magnificent Cipriani Hotel on the island of Giudecca, across St. Mark's Basin from the heart of Venice. The famous hotel was a mecca for the wealthy Italians.

Once back in her hotel suite, she threw her bag and blazer on a chair in the living room, kicked off her shoes, and put on an Andrea Bocelli CD. As Bocelli's voice filled the suite, she glanced through the messages the concierge had handed her as she crossed the lobby. Four from Roger.

Hmm, I'll call him in the morning, she thought, calculating the time difference between Italy and California. Cass had come to enjoy talking about work with her father, but tonight she was so weary, she was afraid he would hear it in her voice. Already he had offered to fly to Venice to bring a case of costumes for extras left behind in the flurry of the crew's departure. She knew that he was as nervous as a retired racehorse, with too much time on his hands, but fortunately, she and James had convinced him that an air courier service could make the delivery faster and more economically than he could. Roger always did respect the bottom line.

She tossed the messages onto the cocktail table and headed for the bath, stripping as she walked, leaving her clothes where they fell. She ran a bath, slowly pouring lavender oil under the running faucet. She turned on the Jacuzzi, lit scented candles, and clipped her hair on top of her head. Then she slipped into the steamy cocoon, allowing the warm water and oils to soothe and massage her aching body.

Soon she successfully pushed the day behind her.

Cass smiled with contentment. She really *was* a natural filmmaker, and she didn't need her father's approval anymore. Now she was working *with* him, rather than for him.

| | |

She considered reading another excerpt from her mother's diary, now securely locked away in the closet safe, but her eyes were too heavy, her mind unable to concentrate.

It was difficult for Cass to see the past through her mother's eyes. There were too many painful memories and shocking realizations for her to take too much at one sitting. She had made a pact with herself to at least try to absorb one entry—one day's writing—each night before bed. She was determined to finish reading the diary before she returned to Los Angeles. There was a great deal she wanted to discuss with her father.

Last night she'd learned of Lana's affair with an actor, whose name was not mentioned. To Cass's chagrin, her parents seemed to have had an open marriage well before it was acceptable. Both took lovers—often, it seemed from Lana's narrative, more as ammunition to use against each other than anything else. But to Lana, this new relationship was the first to ever "threaten" her marriage. She was afraid she would be forced to choose between her lover and her husband. Each page described hurt, each word hinted at betrayal.

Cass flinched at the agony her mother described. She suddenly felt newly vulnerable to the deceit and treachery of the adult world, as if she were still that ten-year-old girl who knew little of the world.

Halfway through the journal, Cass had become acquainted with a Lana Turmaine different from the Lana she remembered or imagined. Her mother's entries sometimes reinforced the image Cass had cherished of a beautiful angel of a mom, but others told of Lana's profound hurt at Roger's betrayals. Or told of lovers she allowed to humiliate her, just to get back at him. And one lover, the last, who finally owned her in a way that Roger, the journal made clear, never had and never would.

| | |

At ten of seven, Rudolpho arrived at Cassidy's suite. He let himself in quietly and called room service to order a bottle of champagne and eight ounces of beluga caviar. "Send it up to the Royal Suite—right away, please." He replaced the phone receiver, turned up the volume on the stereo and followed the trail of clothing. The sight of her naked, perfectly toned body nearly drove him insane.

Whatever happened next was inevitable.

| | |

James sat in Jack's private screening room adjacent to his office and watched the latest dailies that had arrived by Federal Express earlier that morning.

"You were right. She's quite impressive," Jack said when the lights came up.

James knew it took a lot to impress Jack, and even more for Jack to actually admit it with such understated praise. James had watched Jack throughout the screening. It was clear that what he had seen had not just impressed him; he was *excited* about the movie.

"If it gets finished," Jack said, *"Dangerous Intentions* just might be a major moneymaker. It certainly has all the makings of Oscar material. And with Universal's latest string of flops and money guzzlers, as well as the budget problems at Columbia, Miramax, and Disney, this film could quite possibly put Desmond back at the top."

James nodded. "Would I lie to you?"

Jack walked to the back of the room and opened a cabinet, revealing an elaborate state-of-the-art humidor. He pulled out the top drawer and removed two Cuban cigars. "Join me?" he asked.

"Sure," James said. "Cass's success at Desmond is reason enough for a celebration."

Jack cocked his head to the side and offered a half-grin. "It's not over yet. There's still one more week, ten days tops, of shooting in Venice, then one week on the back lot and, of course, editing." He returned to his seat in the second row and pushed a button on the arm of his chair. Instantly the screen disappeared. "But I will admit, I'm quite impressed with Chelsea's performance."

James raised an eyebrow. "Cass deserves the praise."

"Don't forget, Chelsea was my choice. I knew exactly the limits of her talents. For certain, she's not a natural."

So why *did* he insist on her? James had assumed that Chelsea was talking to Jack, but spies planted on sets, in companies, armies, governments, everywhere throughout history, were always two-bit players—marionettes—you never made them stars. What did Jack know about her?

"From what I'm seeing," said James, "Chelsea could even get a nod from the Academy, but Cass is the one who got that performance out of her. And she's as good with the bottom line as she is with the actors. Have you seen the budgets and production schedule she developed?"

Jack nodded. "I, for one, am astonished. She's got balls—something half the men in this town don't. This project was shaky from the start. Why Roger ever optioned it is beyond me." Just mentioning Roger's name caused Jack's tone to change. He scowled, nearly sneered. His enmity was so toxic that even Roger's vision, the genius to resurrect the film and initiate its creation, didn't lessen Jack's distaste for him. "It was a risky project from the start. I was convinced it couldn't be done," Jack said, almost apologetically.

James raised his eyebrows. "And now you're not so sure you were right?"

"Let's just say I'm prepared for an upset." He paused. The bet between Cass and Jack was well known in the inner circle. It had become an in-house joke. "But only Cassidy English can take the credit."

Jack clipped the tip of the cigar, then struck a match, held it to his mouth, and lightly swirled the Cuban as he took a long, smooth puff. James did the same.

"Jack, is it possible for you to admit you were wrong? Are you afraid this is one bet you're going to lose?"

Jack blew smoke into the air. "You know how much I love a good wager." His tone was ebullient, but a moment later his entire attitude changed. He moved forward, rested his elbows on his knees, and clasped his hands. "Tell me more about Cassidy. She's not involved with anyone, is she?"

It wasn't a question so much as a statement. A warning sounded in James's head. "Why do you want to know?"

Jack's face twisted, turned nasty. Clearly he wasn't used to having his queries go unanswered. He resented being questioned. Suddenly he stood.

"I like to know as much as I can about my employees—you can understand that, can't you?"

"Of course I can," James answered. He felt his face flush. He was angry that Jack was snooping around Cassidy's personal life. What business was it of his?

"My sources tell me she and the director have been involved for quite a while. Back in New York. And, after all, she did insist on hiring him."

James was caught off guard. Cassidy and Durban. It was just the kind of information Chelsea, Jack's "source," would be capable of uncovering. James had suspected that Rudolpho was a sycophant, using Cass to get what he couldn't get for himself. He needed no proof of that, he just knew it. *Oh, Cass, how could you let him do it?*

James's face gave away none of these thoughts.

"I don't know what you're talking about," James said. "Perhaps your *source*"—his voice mocked the word—"should pay more attention to her performance instead of to Cass."

Chelsea walked out on the terrace and leaned over the ledge, a glass of wine in her hand. The sun had set, but the city still seemed caught by its light and the view was breathtaking. The lights below mimicked a thousand assorted jewels, sparkling and glistening. The sound of the city rose from below as tourists from everywhere around the world lent their voices, their varied races, to the cobbled streets, to the murky water of the river that traversed the city.

What Chelsea saw was a city of hopes and dreams.

Romance, like the rich red Italian Chianti in her glass, spiced the night air and soothed all her heart's ancient pain. The clock on the dresser read seven P.M. Bella was tucked into bed watching TV.

Just a few hours ago, Chelsea had fired the second nanny since Jesse took off to handle her "family emergency." The sixty-year-old, rigid, by-the-book Irishwoman was too judgmental—of Chelsea, of Bella. Too much like her own mother.

Chelsea needed a nanny who would simply make all the decisions concerning Bella. Chelsea had neither the time nor the inclination to be involved in her child's day-to-day life.

Not while she was making the film of her career.

Besides, after a busy day of filming, Chelsea wanted to go out. She had no time to play Mommy. This seemed to anger the nanny, which puzzled Chelsea. The way Chelsea saw things, with her out of the picture, the nanny would have less to deal with. Instead the uptight Irishwoman had the audacity to criticize her employer's parenting, saying Bella was in danger of growing into a spoiled, selfish, and shallow brat like her mother. The nerve of the old bitty!

Chelsea had "suggested" that the woman pack her things and escorted her, none too politely, to the door.

Now Chelsea was back to square one. In the morning she'd have the concierge get someone from another agency to take care of Bella. So far no one from Desmond even knew the child was in Venice.

So there was no way she'd let her daughter cramp her style. She knew she shouldn't leave her alone in the suite, but it would just be for a couple of hours. What could happen? She'd been working her ass off every day since they got on location. She needed to let go of some pent-up energy. Besides, she had something else she needed to accomplish.

Chelsea left the veranda and checked on Bella, who had fallen asleep with the TV still on. Then Chelsea went into her bathroom, where she popped open her trusty bottle of pills and mulled through the assortment. She put a handful of them in her mouth all at once and washed them down with the wine. Soon she'd be flying high. She adored each flight of fancy and loved how the pills enhanced it. In fact, since the lithium the hospital insisted on prescribing cut into her high, she had stopped taking it altogether.

She slipped into a black Versace—a short number, silky and clingy. Still in full makeup from the set, she added a touch of frosty pink lipstick. She lined her blue eyes with a charcoal pencil and then donned a long, silky black wig. Her disguise was complete. Chelsea knew that, from a distance, she could easily pull off the charade.

Suddenly she felt extremely powerful and in control.

One last look in her vanity mirror and she was ready to play the role for which she'd trained her whole life.

Satisfied with her appearance she grabbed the room's key card and headed down the hall to the house phone near the elevator. She picked up the receiver and dialed the concierge's desk.

"Pardon, signore, could you arrange for a water taxi to meet me right away?"

"But of course," the young man replied. "What is your name, please?"

And with an incredible burst of confidence, she said, "Cassidy English."

| | |

Chelsea—as Cassidy—received VIP treatment. The doorman broke into a huge smile and gave her an approving nod. The driver helped her into the private launch. Everywhere she went people stopped and stared. Chelsea reveled in Cassidy's fame, even though she thought it was somewhat undeserved. The bitch had only been *raised* as the daughter of famous people. She hadn't earned it for herself, Chelsea reasoned bitterly.

Just wait until the film was released. The whole world would know who she was. Chelsea Hutton would be famous on her own. She would make sure of it.

On an earlier foray, Chelsea had already learned that Venetian nightlife was just as she had imagined, uninhibited and sophisticated— the clubs were so unlike the watering holes she frequented in the States. The people were warm and friendly, the men all eager to please. Chelsea asked the driver to take her to the Grand Canal for dinner, a restaurant in the Monaco Hotel overlooking the island of San Giorgio Maggiore. She had chosen the restaurant for its visibility and made a reservation for one earlier in the day. Women dining alone were a rarity in Venice, particularly beautiful women, and most certainly the recognizable. Chelsea didn't have to do anything but be seated to immediately become the center of attention.

The restaurant's rose-colored lighting emphasized her dramatic coloring, heightening her sheet of dark hair, her fair skin, and sparkling blue eyes. She had requested a table in the middle of the room. Dining alone, treated like a princess by the waiters, she was definitely seen.

From the Grand Canal, she directed her driver to Harry's Bar, the legendary watering hole frequented by Hemingway, Maugham, Onassis, and legions of others. People lingered for hours over one of Harry Cipriani's Kir Royales or Bellinis. Chelsea knew she could count on at least one or two celebrities to wander in here.

The sedate beige-on-beige decor might seem boring at first, but on closer inspection the "pictures" on the walls upstairs—windows whose vistas looked out on spectacular Santa Maria della Salute—easily compared with the finest scenic paintings. The atmosphere was the antithesis of that of L.A.'s politically correct nightspots. Men smoked cigars and swigged the driest martinis in town, while the women, most in elaborate makeup, artfully styled hair, and expensive designer couture, sipped heavenly champagne and smoked long thin cigarettes.

Chelsea made her way into the jammed space and squeezed onto a corner stool at the bar. From the corner of her eye she spotted Georgio

Valine, Italy's most notorious, not to mention most read, gossip columnist. She made a mental note of each man and woman seated at
his table. The bartender, a young brown-eyed bodybuilder type with
slicked black hair and a face bronzed by wind and sun, waited for her
request.

She eyed the man seductively. "My name's Cassidy English. And
yours?" She pretended to strain to see the brass name badge pinned to
his vest. She watched his eyelashes flutter in recognition of her name.

The young bartender clearly knew who she was, or pretended to.
"Vincenzo," he said, his voice husky.

A few compliments, some well placed flirtation, and a generous tip,
and she would have him eating out of her hand. "Vincenzo," she purred
smoothly. "I like that name. It's so rugged, *soooo* sexy. So . . . Italian." She
leaned in closer, resting her elbows on the bar and cupping her chin in
her hands. "So tell me, Vincenzo, what's your day job?"

And just as she'd presumed, he answered, "I'm an actor."

She had his full attention now. His eyes roamed her face, her shoulders, her partially concealed breasts. A delicious shudder rocked her
body. "I'll have a whiskey sour."

She was lonely tonight. What she needed was a good time, with
someone she'd never see again. Someone who'd give her exactly what she
wanted and help set her plan in motion, then disappear. Chelsea felt the
familiar floating feeling overtake her. From this moment, the night could
go anywhere Cassidy English took it.

Vincenzo reappeared with her drink and set it down on the bar
before her. He lowered his eyelids and, in a husky whisper, said, "I go on
my break in twenty minutes. I would love to buy you a drink." His
accented English was luscious, almost musical. He leaned over the bar
and his hands slipped up her arms, bringing her closer.

Chelsea stifled a delightful laugh.

He followed her eyes across the dance floor to an empty table in a
dark corner across the room.

"I'll be waiting," she said as she slithered off the stool. Another
patron arrived at the bar, and before Vincenzo could leave, Chelsea
touched his arm, not moving her eyes.

"Isn't that Georgio Valine over there in the corner booth?"

The young man didn't have to look. He nodded. "He's a regular here."

Of course, she already knew that. "I'll bet people in the business would do just about anything to be mentioned in his column."

Vincenzo nodded seriously. "*Sì*. Just about."

"I absolutely loathe gossip columnists. Parasites." Chelsea toyed with her straw. "There is one thing, Vincenzo." She turned her attention back to Valine. "Before we spend any time together, you must promise me something. Whatever you do, please don't let word get out that I'm here. I'd simply just die if my name turned up in his column."

She reached inside her bag, pulled out a hundred-dollar bill, and slapped it down on the bar.

From Harry's Bar, Chelsea and Vincenzo made their way to a hip after-hours club, where wealthy Venetians and savvy Americans could dance till dawn. Chelsea had watched as Valine, the gossip columnist, walked into the club, obviously following her.

Now Chelsea was floating—so high she could touch the moon, the stars. The blend of alcohol and Quaaludes was exhilarating. Her body felt numb, her mind free and clear. The music was so loud she was blown straight to heaven—or was it hell?

Her body rocked back and forth rhythmically as she was helped onto a tabletop by two men she'd been dancing with. She thrust her hips forward, then back, forward, then back. The crowd—mostly men— cheered and Chelsea thrived on the excitement. She kept her balance on top of the table with perfection and precision despite her drug-and-alcohol-induced stupor.

Through half-closed eyes she spotted Vincenzo standing beside Valine, whispering into his ear.

Through her chemically induced euphoria, Chelsea recognized that everything was going as planned. All she had to do was party the night away, make a spectacle of herself, drink, drug, dance—whatever it took to tear up Venice in Cassidy's name. And each time the crowd screamed, it was as though an electrical current shot through her. The warm, dopey feeling was stealing over her. She moved in slow motion. The crowd became a blur and the ever-present voices egged her on.

Tomorrow, when it was daylight and everyone had sobered up, they would look back at tonight and wonder whatever had come over them. Who was that trashy American woman? And then they'd open up the newspaper.

| | |

Cass stood under the hot needles of the shower, rinsing the shampoo from her hair. Then she stepped from the exhilarating warmth onto the cold marble floor, sending a shiver through her body.

She slipped into the warm terry-cloth robe and wrapped her long, thick hair in a towel. She stood over the hand-painted porcelain sink, turned the golden faucet, and reached for her toothbrush.

This project is *killing* me, she thought. But she was motivated and driven nonetheless. Her intent was to win—at any cost.

She brushed her teeth, hit the light switch, and opened the bathroom door.

Rudolpho was sound asleep, his well-toned form entangled in mounds of satin sheets and velour blankets. She stood in the doorway for a moment, unable to move, experiencing the same guilt she always did after they made love. Rudolpho both attracted and repelled her—or, rather, she had the urge to have him and then push him away.

It was wrong—she knew that, of course. Their arrangement was a thing of convenience. She cared about him, enjoyed his company, and found him fun and attractive. But as far as deep, erotic love went, it simply wasn't there. Yes, she loved him. But as a dear friend, whom she happened to sleep with on occasion. Yet she hadn't turned him away this evening when he'd turned up naked in her bathroom, carrying two glasses of champagne. Lately, everything seemed so complicated. Perhaps it was the stress of completing *Dangerous Intentions*—perhaps not.

She sat on the edge of the bed to think things out.

Rudolpho stirred, and without opening his eyes, he reached toward her and said, "Chelsea, is that you?"

"What did you say?" Cass asked, at once standing.

Rudolpho opened his eyes, suddenly, startlingly, awake. "I didn't mean that. You know I didn't, Cass."

"So you are sleeping with her," she said, her voice filled with disgust.

Rudolpho said nothing and Cass interpreted his silence as an admission of guilt.

"Damn you," she hissed.

She was angry but not crushed. Her pride was injured yet her heart was intact. She never imagined Rudolpho would actually succumb to the erratic actress. That he had chosen Chelsea as her competition drove her wild. "How could you? Goddamn it, Rudolpho, how could you jeopardize my project? I trusted you, you bastard."

He was sitting up straight now, shaking his head. He reached for Cassidy, trying to get her to sit down next to him. "It means nothing. She literally threw herself at me—just showed up in my room."

He was covering himself with the sheet, she noticed. A sign of embarrassment? Vulnerability? Shame? Part of her felt sorry for him. But the female side felt fury.

"Honest to God, Cass, it meant nothing. She means nothing to—" He looked up at her, this time directly into her eyes. Cass knew it wasn't for effect, he really meant it.

He leaned over and gripped her shoulders.

"I love *you*. You're the only woman I've ever said that to."

"So why did you sleep with her? I think you wanted to hurt me." She was calm, controlled, the anger dissipated. He was the one in an emotional frenzy.

"And I was wrong. But what the hell did you expect?" He let go, got up, and walked over to the window. Turning his head away, he said, "You've been stringing me along for more than two years. This game that you're playing is getting old. It's got me crazy. I don't know where I stand with you, Cass." He turned to face her. "You have to make a decision— do you want me in your life or not? I can't wait for you forever."

| | |

The child woke with a start. From down the hall came the rustle of room service, trays rattling, then a loud banging. The cold breeze from the open window sent shivers through her small frail form. She tossed and turned but couldn't find a comfortable position. The room was cold and dark, with only the small trickle of moonlight filtering in.

The fear and the cold consumed her and she began to shiver. She eyed the opened window but dared not close it. Her mother would be furious. When Bella was left alone, which was often these days, she was forbidden to move. Her mother was very specific about her instructions: "Don't touch the windows, never turn on the lights, and don't get out of bed unless it's an emergency."

The banging grew louder. Bella bolted upright, kicked the blankets back with her feet, got up and slipped into her robe and slippers. At the door, she stood up on her tiptoes and peeked through the keyhole. It wasn't her mother. Bella recognized the pretty woman even from the little bit she could see through the peephole. Her picture was in Mommy's box, the one in her dresser drawer. Mommy *couldn't* be mad if she let the lady in. She wasn't a stranger. Maybe the pretty black-haired lady needed help.

| | |

Was she at the right room? Who was this beautiful child shivering in her nightgown at three in the morning?

"Do you speak English? Are your parents here?"

The youngster shook her head. Yes. Then no.

"You're here all alone?"

The child nodded again. Her delicate features were familiar. Suddenly Cass knew. "Is Chelsea here? Do I have the right room?"

The little girl nodded her head up and down, then shook it side to side, and her long blond hair fell well past her waist in a cascade of curls. Her expressive green eyes regarded Cass with fear.

"Does that mean a yes or a no?"

Cass knelt down to the child's level and smiled warmly. She reached out for her hand, but the girl pulled back. "I'm not going to hurt you," Cass assured her. She peered over the child's shoulders, into the suite. She couldn't see a thing. It was dark. A rush of cold air burst through the open door.

"Are you alone?"

Instead of answering the question, the child said, "I'm not supposed to talk to strangers. Nanny Jesse taught me that."

"Is your nanny here? Can I speak with her?"

The girl shook her head. "Mommy got really mad at her and told her to go away."

How could Chelsea have left a young child alone in a hotel room? It was three in the morning! Cass tried to contain her fury.

Neglect. She knew how that felt. Sure, there had always been someone home, but no one ever nurtured her. Not after Lana was killed.

Cass knelt on the carpeted floor. She considered how best to reach Chelsea's little girl. "I'm Cass. What's your name?"

The enormous sparkling green eyes welled with water, and soon tears were streaming down her rosy cheeks. Her little body started twitching, shaking. The poor child was terrified. "Please . . . please don't tell Mommy I opened the door. She'd be *very* angry."

"No, we'll keep it our secret. I know your mommy. Her name is Chelsea. She's in a movie and that's why you're here, right?" Cass reached her hand out slowly, and this time the child let her touch the top of her head before moving away.

"I'm looking for your mommy. Can you tell me where she went?"

"I don't know."

"When is she coming home?"

Still the same response: "I don't know." Cassidy forgot all about why she'd come here in the middle of the night. Suddenly her rage at Chelsea and Rudolpho had vanished, leaving in its place only feelings of deep empathy for this young girl.

| | |

Chelsea groped around in the dark for her clothing. Her mouth was as parched as a desert. Her head was pounding so hard she thought it would explode. She looked at her watch. It was just past five-thirty in the morning. Vincenzo's spare, untidy studio was a far cry from the luxurious accommodations she had so quickly grown accustomed to. No, this reminded her more of Maria Hutton's pitiful apartment, where she lived as a child.

She reached under the bed for her shoes and tiptoed to the door. Vincenzo stirred, though Chelsea was sure he wouldn't wake. He'd tried to match her drink for drink. Chances were he'd be unconscious for hours.

He had surprised her. For a young man, he was an ardent, experienced lover. Not part of the plan, but a delicious plus. Once she'd made sure her performance at the club would create a gossip fest, Chelsea had celebrated by giving herself the gift of all-night, riotous sex with this sweet young man. Vincenzo had surprised her with some Ecstasy, and after that there was nothing, no conceivable sexual act, that she didn't explore with him. The only downside was his pathetic apartment—that, and the raging hangover she had from the cheap champagne he picked up on their way home. She paused in the doorway and took a good look around the garret, letting her eyes pause on Vincenzo one last time. Last night was little more than a memory now. A fast-fading blur.

| | |

Still disguised as Cass, Chelsea took pains to make sure the concierge and doormen noticed her entrance. Slightly disheveled, she pretended that she did not see the paparazzi lying in wait for her until the flash-bulbs were popping. Cassidy English was about to make tabloid head-lines, thanks to a tip Chelsea had phoned in to the news services when she slipped off to the ladies' loo at Harry's.

Once the elevator doors closed, Chelsea removed her wig and stuffed it into her large leather bag. She fluffed her hair and checked her reflection in the mirrored elevator wall. And by the time she reached her floor, an imaginary clock struck twelve. For Cinderella, the ball was over.

| | |

Roger was in his home office. He'd read yet another article about Cassidy shooting *Dangerous Intentions,* and his anxiety had reached an all-time high. He picked up his old-fashioned rotary phone and dialed James's number.

"We have a problem," Roger said grimly, gripping the receiver tightly. "Rae told me Cass found the diary. It won't be long before she puts two and two together. We have to get to her first."

A moment of silence, then: "What are you suggesting?"

"I'll have my secretary book me on the next flight to Venice."

"Hold on a minute." James's tone turned angry. "You're in no con-dition to be traveling. The doctors—"

"Fuck the doctors." Roger shut his eyes and squeezed the bridge of his nose. "You aren't in any position to give me advice. You're my lawyer, not my psychiatrist."

"You swore to me a long time ago that if it ever came to this, you'd tell her the truth. I know what's best for you . . . and for Cass."

"Don't you see, James? If Cass finds out the truth, I'm finished."

Roger hung up and immediately summoned Rae. "Book me on a flight to Venice—ASAP."

| | |

The tan Bentley pulled up to the entrance of the Beverly Hills Hotel. The driver jumped out and opened the passenger door. Jack stepped from the car, looking neither right nor left as he crossed the main lobby to the elevator bank.

When he reached his penthouse suite, he knocked gently and a pretty green-eyed brunette opened the door. Even though Chelsea was long gone, still it seemed to him that the suite was redolent with her scent.

"Jack . . . I've been waiting for hours. Why are you so late?" Her voice was a deliberate sex kitten's purr.

He shot her an icy look that said "You know better than to ask me questions" and pushed past her into the parlor. He removed his Armani jacket and tossed it over the arm of the sofa, then walked straight to the wet bar. He poured himself a shot of brandy, swirled the snifter, inhaled the pungent aroma, then sipped the amber liquid. It went down smooth. Jack enjoyed the momentary warmth. He set the glass on the bar and turned to eye the pretty young actress approvingly. Domi—Dominique Drake—had a continuing role on an afternoon soap. Definitely not Emmy material, but she sure was a looker. And she knew her way around the bedroom.

She had his full attention now and used each moment wisely. Slowly, seductively, she disrobed, revealing full, firm breasts, long, lean legs, and a small, trim waist. They dated occasionally, so she knew the plan. She stepped out of the robe and walked slowly toward him.

Jack unbuttoned the cuffs of his white shirt and rolled up the sleeves.

"Shall we move to the bedroom?" Domi's voice was husky, barely above a whisper. She leaned across the bar, put her hand behind his head, and pulled him close to her. At first he resisted, pulling back, breaking her strong grip. He had to let her know who was in control.

She stared back at him, her eyes begging. And when he knew she couldn't hold on any longer, he led her into the bedroom, into the forbidden pool of desires.

| | |

Jonathan's court-ordered stint at the Betty Ford Center wasn't nearly enough to sober him up. Oh, he was chemically free of drugs and alcohol, but his mind was still mulch. How was he ever going to "resolve" his feelings about killing a young girl? But that wasn't what he dwelled on. Mostly he worried that despite Roger's powerful connections and endless bank accounts, the Senator and Mrs. Williams would insist on making a real issue out of the "unfortunate accident."

And it was an accident, he kept reminding himself. He never intended for anyone to get hurt. Of course, climbing behind the wheel after seven martinis and a couple of lines wasn't the brightest thing to do, but who could have predicted the slippery conditions on the Pacific Coast Highway?

He had relived the accident many times with the therapist assigned to him: He slammed on the brakes, then the car spun out of control and smashed into a tree. Carina Williams died on impact. He was sure of it. He remembered pulling back the pretty red silk scarf tied around her neck and staring into the mask of death. Her face was covered in her own blood, her eyes open wide, the look of horror still evident in her expression.

He had stumbled out of the vehicle, climbed up the embankment, and walked two miles to the nearest town. Four hours lapsed before a rescue crew arrived on the scene. Of course, there was nothing they could do.

Despite what everyone—namely his father—thought, Jonathan really was sorry. He did feel remorse. But what was done was done. There was nothing he could do to change it.

Jonathan could remember only once before seeing his father cry, at Lana the bitch's funeral. And he knew, in this case, Roger's tears were for Carina Williams, not him. Ultimately, dear old Dad made "it" all go away—just like he always did. There would be no investigation, no charges, and no bad press. All Jonathan had to do was check himself into Betty Ford. Again.

The place was like a country club, except for the fact that he'd been expected to attend several AA and NA meetings a day. And he couldn't score any "real" drugs. But he now felt better, not so strung out. He'd done the one-on-one therapy thing, and "group," plus the obligatory twelve-step meetings. He'd also swum laps in the Olympic-size pool, worked out a few times, and watched newly released movies Roger's secretary obtained for him.

But he had to admit, the therapy had not gotten to him; it never did. There was no cure for an empty heart. Only alcohol, drugs, and sex ever satisfied him.

He had to figure out a way to win back his father's trust and at the same time make some good money fast. The groundwork had already been laid. Per his father's strict instructions, he was on his way to Venice. His luggage, packed for the trip, was delivered to the clinic the morning he was released.

Jonathan had received these instructions via a phone call from James. Roger wouldn't speak to him, he knew, until he'd "proved" himself, whatever that meant. From now until his father's precious masterpiece was wrapped up, he was to be at little sister's beck and call. *As if she'd ever call.* Maybe Roger thought this would teach Jonathan some humility, or at least keep him busy—whatever. He couldn't have planned things better himself.

But first he had to make one stop that was not on his father's itinerary.

| | |

Jonathan had called for a cab. His father's driver had not stayed to take him to LAX but had instead left him with an envelope of cash to pay for the ride. He threw his bag into the trunk, hopped in, and gave the driver an address.

The beat-up Chevy roared down Sunset Boulevard and screeched to a stop in front of a dilapidated apartment building, one of the few, bleak structures left standing in that part of L.A.

The cabbie was no fool. He kept the engine running.

Jonathan unlocked the rear passenger door and climbed out. A warm breeze licked at his face. A brown paper bag, some candy wrappers, and crumbled cigarette packs pinwheeled down the street.

He paused briefly outside the orange-painted door and glanced up and down the street. He had to be careful. Undercover cops were everywhere these days. The one thing he didn't need was an arrest for possession. Then again, the way his luck was running lately, it wouldn't matter.

Reasonably certain he wasn't being watched, he ducked inside the building, walked down a long hall that stank of urine, and bounded up the stairs. No sense staying longer than he had to.

In his early years, when Jonathan was still someone with promise, the dealers all came to him—to his hotel room, the country club, a hip watering hole, even home, to Whispering Winds. And no one was the wiser. These days, though, his funds were limited, and his old dealers—the ones he owed so much money to—wouldn't even take his calls, so he had to hunt his highs in places like this.

Jonathan made his way to the second landing, stepped over a strung-out teenage boy, and tapped lightly on the door. After ten minutes and much scrutiny, he was invited in. He entered quietly. The apartment was dark, and except for a card table, four folding chairs, and a box of drug paraphernalia, the place was empty.

The guy in charge, a husky black man who answered to the name of Streeter, approached Jonathan cautiously, cornering him.

"You got money?" A small pistol peeked out of a holster underneath the man's massive arm. Slowly, so as not to alarm the dealer, Jonathan slipped his hand in his pants pocket.

"Yeah . . . yeah, don't worry. I have cash," Jonathan said nervously.

The other man relaxed, pointed to an armchair so old and filthy that the upholstery's original color was unrecognizable. "Whaddya need?" In the dim low light, only the whites of the black man's eyes were visible. His lips pulled back into a predatory smile. He grabbed at the crumpled bills in Jonathan's hand.

"Won't be much longer you be able to cop the good stuff. The way I hear it, you're all tapped out."

It always annoyed Jonathan, how these street guys "heard" things. Silently, he wondered how long before he really would be tapped out. No—he couldn't even let his mind go there.

After getting what he'd come for, he left the apartment. Outside in the hall, he unwrapped the snowy white powder, lined it up carefully on a compact mirror, and using a rolled-up dollar bill, snorted deeply. And the image of Cass jumped into his head.

If he had his way, the bitch would finally get what she had coming to her.

| | |

Jack gave one last thrust as she cried out. When she stopped, he rolled onto his side.

"That was very nice, darling." She turned on her stomach and started stroking his chest. "You're such a skillful lover. You aren't selfish like most guys I know."

This wasn't empty praise, Jack knew. Domi "knew" many guys.

"A girl could get used to this." She planted soft, teasing kisses from his throat to the middle of his chest.

"Get in line," he joked.

"What's so bad about settling down with one woman?" She eyed him intently. He pushed her back, bolted upright, and reached for his silk robe at the foot of the bed. Once a lady started talking commitment, he knew it was time to move.

"I'm hungry," he said. "Be a sweetheart. Call room service and order us something to eat."

He made his way to the suite's living room and poured himself another shot of brandy. This place gave him the creeps. Chelsea's intense presence clung to it and brought back memories of the night he'd had to get her home from the psych ward. Jack wanted to go back to his apartment beneath his office at the studio. He thought about all the work piled high on his desk. Instead he would go through the proper motions, do what was expected of him.

Domi came out of the bedroom wearing only a transparent black peignoir, no doubt bought with his money from one of the high-end boutiques on Rodeo Drive. The smell of her heady perfume suddenly repulsed him.

"The food will be here in about twenty minutes." She came up beside him, wrapped her arms around his neck, and planted a gentle kiss on his cheek. "Why don't you come back to bed until it arrives?"

He forced a smile and gently but firmly pulled her arms off his neck. He glanced down at the newspaper on the bar. The lead article in the *Daily Variety* read:

> Cassidy English, daughter of notorious Hollywood bad boy Roger Turmaine and his murdered wife, the legendary Lana Turmaine, will soon debut as one of Tinseltown's powerhouse Generation X producers. Inside sources insist the beautiful and highly qualified Ms. English is set to take Hollywood by storm after inheriting *Dangerous Intentions,* a small-budget, no-name love story from her ailing, high-profile dad. Industry insiders say despite setbacks with the film, including a devastating set

fire, the beautiful blue-eyed brunette will not only come out triumphant, but may even be on a quick journey to the Oscars. Meanwhile, the international press hangs around the set, hoping for crumbs of information, a glimpse of her private side, but so far she has remained a mystery.

There was a flattering photograph of Cassidy exiting a posh L.A. eatery. Even in the grainy photo, her image drew him to her. He intended to surprise her in Venice, use the excuse that he was looking after his interests. Chelsea's information about Cassidy's liaison with the director worried him. He wanted it stopped. Location love affairs were bad for a film crew's morale, creating a tense dynamic on the set, no matter how discreet and professional those involved thought they were. Jack looked forward to the confrontation, anticipated a protracted one-on-one meeting with her. They had much to discuss.

"Actually, Domi, I have an important matter that needs my immediate attention. Why don't you take a ride to Rodeo and break in that new credit card I gave you." He set down the drink and picked up the telephone. "My driver is out front. I'll tell him you'll just be a few minutes."

She started to pout. "If I didn't know better, I'd think you were trying to get rid of me."

Ignoring her, he made a quick call to his driver, then punched in the switchboard downstairs and requested an overseas operator. He checked his watch: ten o'clock. That would make it six A.M. in Venice. He didn't care whether or not Cass was asleep. He wanted to speak to her now. He was the boss—he called the shots.

As far as he was concerned, Domi was no longer in the room. She caught on quickly and disappeared into the bedroom. He heard the bathroom door slam and the shower go on.

The operator returned and connected him.

"The Hotel Cipriani." Click, hum, click, hum. Over and over. The netherworld of hold, he thought. Jack wasn't a man who was used to waiting for anything. Then a high-pitched voice boomed over the line.

"Extension 3716, the Royal Suite, please."

He was put on hold once again. There was soft, classical Italian music, a click, then ringing. The thought of waking her aroused him. He could almost picture her stretched across the bed asleep, clothed in a simple black nightie, or a bra and a pair of cotton pajama pants. She wasn't the type to fuss and primp. God knows she didn't need to.

"Hello?" The sound of a man's voice, obviously roused from a sound sleep, jolted him back to full awareness.

"Hello?" the voice said again.

Jack gripped the receiver. "Who is this?"

"This is Rudolpho, who is this?"

Jack slammed the phone down.

| | |

Cass and Bella sat on the floor. As the two went through Chelsea's cache of mementos, Cassidy was both amazed and a little bit frightened at the vast collection of photographs and newspaper clippings the little girl removed from a box in Chelsea's dresser drawer. There were photos of Lana—hundreds of them—as well as yellowed newspaper clippings from long ago: Lana as a young bride in 1965, a new mother in '66, at premieres, the Brown Derby, the Polo Lounge, Grauman's Chinese Theatre. There were even reviews of some of her performances, clipped from *Variety* and the *Hollywood Reporter*, as well as rare photos of Cass as a child.

It all seemed terribly eerie. Bizarre. The clipping about Lana's death jolted Cass, but it was the last few items that truly shocked her.

A color photo from *Life* magazine showed Lana receiving the Oscar for Best Actress for her performance in *Beauty*. Next to her mother's stylish image stood Chelsea, as she appeared today, dressed much as she had at Roger's party. Not content to simply paste her image next to Lana's, Chelsea had apparently hired a professional to doctor the photo with a little computer imaging—the image of Chelsea next to Lana *had* to have been created digitally; there were no seams, nothing artificial about the coherence of the image. The two women stood side by side, smiles chilling in their similarity. The woman Cassidy saw every day suddenly seemed otherworldly, definitely weird, maybe a little crazy.

Was it possible that Chelsea had known Lana? She couldn't have, Cass reasoned.

Cass pulled herself away from the grotesque collage when she realized the child was talking to her.

"Mommy keeps them locked away. She'd be real mad if she finds out I showed them to you. I'm not supposed to know about them . . . but sometimes I like to look at the pretty lady."

Observing the child's nervous mannerisms and relentless anxiety, Cass remembered the segment on abuse she'd produced for *Up to the Minute*. This poor little girl revealed the classic symptoms of an abused child. Whether it was emotional neglect or physical mattered little. Chelsea's daughter was in danger. Cass's heart went out to her and her fury at Chelsea flamed.

Cass reached out and clutched at Bella's hand. It was ice cold and trembling.

She flashed her a warm smile.

Cass then closed the box, placed it back in the drawer where they'd found it, and sat back down beside her. She had to think of a way to get through to her without scaring her away. She had to find out the truth. "Does your mother leave you alone often?" she asked.

Bella fixed her gaze on a bright-colored painting on the wall. Cass asked again, but the child remained silent. She had tuned her out. She was completely detached from the situation, idly stroking her nightgown hem.

Cass stared at Bella long and hard, until the little girl's face seemed to disappear. In its place she saw herself, the terrified child she had been; the little girl who unknowingly sent her father to prison. The vivid emotions of that horrible day in the District Attorney's office, when she was questioned—no, interrogated—rushed back to her. Fear, anxiety, and loneliness.

Cassidy's own hands were trembling now. She struggled to fight her own feelings of despair. She had to concentrate on the child. What would she have wanted in Bella's place? Comfort, security, unconditional affection.

"Would you like me to stay with you until your mother gets back?" Cass was careful not to press, treating the child like a stranded infant, a wounded animal. In a way that's exactly what she was.

This must have been the right thing to say because Bella snapped back. Her eyes filled with gratitude. Something that resembled a smile appeared on her face.

"Come with me. You must be exhausted." Cass stood and held her hand out to Bella. "Climb back into bed and try to get some sleep."

Cassidy knew what it was like to be ten and look forward to the escape of sleep, how all fears and worries could vanish for a while when the child she had been pulled the covers up and willed herself to leave real life behind for the innocence and dreams of make-believe.

She walked Bella to the bed and tucked her in. "Close your eyes and think wonderful thoughts." She bent and gently kissed the child's forehead.

A real smile this time. Bella closed her eyes and wiggled under the covers. Within minutes she was fast asleep.

Cass watched the child, listened to her breathing as it became slow and regular before she went back to the sitting area. She plopped her tired body onto the sofa. The reason she'd come to Chelsea's suite to begin with seemed so petty compared to what she'd uncovered once here.

She checked her watch—nearly six A.M. Outside the sun was rising, birds were chirping, traffic sounds on the street below intensified. Still no sign of Chelsea.

What made that woman tick? Even after weeks of working together, and studying Chelsea's emotional depths in order to get a decent performance from her, still she knew nothing about her, only that they shared a lover, and even that seemed so unimportant now. What mattered was that Cassidy was working every day with a woman who kept secrets: Her child was hidden away—she'd even had the little girl and her nanny come to Italy on a separate flight—and her attachment to Lana was a mystery that made Cass's stomach knot just thinking about it.

The click of a card key in the lock, followed by the opening of the door, snapped her back to full awareness.

Chelsea stood in the doorway, looking strung out and haggard. Shock registered on her face the moment she laid eyes on Cass. "What the hell are you doing here?" she spat.

Cass squeezed her eyes shut, trying to slow the cascade of images behind her eyes: Bella's face when Cass found her; the doctored photograph of her mother and Chelsea that never could have been created by a rational person; and last, the picture of Rudolpho and Chelsea, naked under soft, hand-embroidered sheets, their bodies making the same music she and Rudolpho had made earlier tonight. Cass willed herself to remain collected.

Chelsea had an oddly distant look in her eyes. Her pupils were like pinpricks, her face drained of color. She was rambling on about invasion of privacy, hurling accusations at Cass. "You shouldn't have barged in. You have no business here. What do you want? Get out before I call the police."

"Don't you want to know if Bella's all right?" Cassidy asked sharply.

Chelsea forced herself to contain her rage and turned on the master manipulator inside her. She loved to play with other people's minds, to confuse them with the quick change in personality, and then to kill them with kindness. Instantly she turned her demeanor upside down. "I . . . I'm sorry. . . ." Her hand flew up to cover her mouth. "I . . . I had an emergency. I had to run out. . . . Normally I wouldn't leave her alone, but . . ."

"She was frightened. I put her back to bed."

The two women stood face-to-face, eyes locked. The silence was palpable. It was a showdown and neither flinched. Somewhere in the room, a grandfather clock ticked loudly. Outside in the hall, elevator doors opened and closed and the clitter-clatter of breakfast trays could be heard.

Cass moved first. "I came by late last night. I needed to talk to you. I found Bella all alone."

Chelsea's expression remained passive.

"It's not her fault," Cass went on. Her gaze swung to the door. "I was banging. I must have scared the daylights out of her. I sat with her awhile, put her back to bed, and decided to wait for you."

"How very kind of you." Chelsea forced a smile. She would keep the charade up for however long it took. No sense alienating her now. "Well, you must be exhausted. I can handle things from here on. Why don't you go back to your suite and get some rest?"

Cass eyed her suspiciously. Judging from her appearance—skimpy black Versace dress and perilously high-heeled stilettos, smeared lipstick and disheveled hair—Chelsea's "emergency" didn't fall into the life-threatening category. Not unless pursuing instant gratification could be considered urgent. Cassidy almost felt sorry for her. Obviously Jack and Rudolpho could not provide enough of whatever Chelsea needed. It was Cassidy's guess that one hundred—no, one thousand—men to love her would not be enough.

"By the way, what brought you here?" Chelsea asked suddenly.

"Actually, I came to see you . . . to discuss you and Rudolpho." Cass waited for a reaction. When there was none, she forged ahead. "He told me all about the two of you."

Again she searched her adversary's eyes. Still nothing.

"He told me how you just *showed* up at his hotel the night he said he was leaving if you were Ophelia. Why? Why did you go there? For that matter, how *did* you know where he was? He stays out in Santa Monica just so actors and actresses *can't* track him down."

Chelsea waved her hand in the air as if swatting away a fly. "Oh, hey, I'm really sorry about all that." She wiggled out of her shoes. "It was nothing, I can assure you. I don't know what he told you, but I didn't just 'show up,' as you put it, demanding sex." Chelsea tossed her stilettos into a corner and curled into a comfortable spot on the sofa.

"I went there to speak to him. Jack told me there was a problem with my read-through. We started talking, and one thing led to another. I swear it wasn't intentional. I did not deliberately seduce him. In fact, if truth be told, it was the other way around."

Cass found herself angry all over again, or maybe jealous. While Rudolpho would never be the man of her dreams, she did not respect a woman, or a man, who poached on others' lovers. "That's not what he said."

"Did he?" Chelsea chuckled. "He's a man. God knows, they all lie. Look, no offense, but he's not my type. Oh sure, he's handsome enough, but truth be told, he's a bit of a bore."

"Just stay away from him." Cass realized as she said this that it was the idea of any hassles during shooting that bothered her. That, and the thought of losing to Jack.

Chelsea hopped up from the couch and crossed to the foyer, leaning into the mirror to remove her false eyelashes. She kept her back to Cassidy. "The casting couch isn't a myth, you know. It really goes on . . . and it's a two-way street. What's so terrible about sleeping with a director who's just won two Emmys? I hardly see how my affair with Rudolpho will affect the movie, except in a positive way. If it's intentionally leaked to the press, curiosity alone could sell movie tickets." She looked quickly at Cass over one bare tanned shoulder. "Oh, unless you mind sharing him, that is." Her smile was baiting.

Cass couldn't summon up the energy to be angry. She was exhausted. If she had the set manager delay today's shoot until eleven and climbed into bed right now, she might get three full hours of sleep. "I'm going to get some rest. You look like shit, so you'd better do the same."

With her hand on the doorknob, Cass paused and looked back at Chelsea. "And don't leave Bella alone. If you don't want to hire a sitter, bring her to the set. If you have to kick up your heels"—at this Chelsea's eyes flared—"the studio will pay for whatever help you need."

Breakfast in bed was a luxury Cass afforded herself only on rare occasions. Yesterday's shoot had left her totally drained. Working on three hours' sleep had been horrific—not to mention dealing with the uncomfortable coldness between Chelsea, Rudolpho, and herself. The tension was thick, settling around them like heavy, wet cement.

At least one good thing had come out of the whole sordid mess from two nights ago. Chelsea had brought Bella along with her to the set. At first Chelsea seemed to dodge questions about the little girl until her press agent, Philip West, decided he could milk her being a widow, trying to raise her child singlehandedly. This might be an asset to her image.

Cass didn't really care *how* Chelsea handled Bella's presence, so long as the child wasn't spending the day languishing alone in a hotel room in a foreign city.

And as for Bella, the little girl had come to life, as if suddenly she were Dorothy in *The Wizard of Oz* and everything around her had just been bathed in Technicolor. Bella was clearly fascinated by all the activity on the set. Cassidy wondered how Chelsea had allowed herself to deny her daughter access to this part of her life.

Thirty minutes after the day's shooting was completed, Cass was in bed, and that's where she remained until nine the next morning. When she awoke, she still didn't feel any better. She picked at the plate of scrambled eggs and bacon and took one or two sips of chamomile tea. Even that, she could hardly keep down. She was weak and emotionally spent. No amount of rest or relaxation would ease that.

Cass pushed the breakfast tray aside, climbed out of bed, and stumbled to the bathroom. She caught a glimpse of her reflection in the mirror, observing once again the ghostly coloring and prominent dark circles under her eyes that no amount of makeup would hide. She splashed cold water on her face, patted it dry with a terry washcloth, brushed her teeth, then stepped into a hot shower.

A knock on the door interrupted her just as she was drying off. Throwing on a terry-cloth robe, Cass went to answer it.

"It's me, Ally," Cass's assistant said from behind the door. When Cassidy opened the door, the young woman raced in, waving a newspaper back and forth.

"Have you seen this?" Her petite size belied her militant nature. Anger seemed to fuel her as she thrust *Oggi,* Italy's major newspaper, into Cass's hand.

Heading the gossip page was a photo of Cassidy taken at an awards ceremony in New York earlier in the year for the *Up to the Minute* special about Venice. She could read enough Italian to understand the headline:

AMERICAN FILMMAKER LETS LOOSE IN VENICE.
ENTERTAINS PATRONS AND EMPLOYEES
WITH A TABLE DANCE AT HARRY'S BAR

Stunned, Cass sat at the foot of the bed. Then she began to read what she could of the article quickly. Looking up at her assistant, she said angrily, "This is bullshit. I was here . . . in bed. . . . I didn't go out."

Ally studied her curiously. "All night?"

"Yes," Cass was quick to add, "except when I went to Chelsea's room." She had told her assistant briefly about the visit. "But that was almost three A.M. This is completely fabricated."

Ally looked wary.

That's when Cassidy realized that no one from the studio, her able young assistant included, knew her well enough to consider whether or not the gossip might be true.

"Oh, come on, surely you don't believe this?"

The woman shot her an I-won't-judge-you-it's-none-of-my-business look and replied, "Do you want me to call the editor?"

"No, you'd better get Legal Affairs on it. They'll have more clout," Cass spat. "And you might want to give the corporate press office a call, too, and let them know . . . if they haven't seen it already. I want a retraction or I'll sue their asses off."

| | |

Chelsea, too, studied the brief story. Those words she didn't understand sent her to the Italian-English dictionary she kept on hand, mostly to decode any press she received or compliments from fans. Chelsea couldn't help but smile. Cass must be livid. Chelsea couldn't wait to get on the set to check out her boss's reaction. The story must be ricocheting from cast to crew. And ultimately to Jack, of course.

Chelsea shivered with delight just thinking about it.

She stared at her reflection in the mirror, critically studying the fine lines around the corners of her eyes. As soon as she returned to the States, she would have them done, and her lips as well. She applied a second coat of lipstick, powdered the shiny areas of her face, and fluffed her hair. Satisfied, she grabbed her dark glasses and Coach bag. To Bella she said, "Gather up your crayons and coloring book, whatever it is that keeps you occupied. We have to go."

The ringing phone startled her, and for a moment she debated whether to let the voice mail pick up or answer it herself. She opted for the latter.

"Hello?" she said, not bothering to mask her irritation.

"I'm proud of you." The sound of Jack's voice jolted her.

Her knees felt weak and her heart skipped a beat. She tried to catch her breath. "For what?"

"Not only did you manage to pull it off, you're doing a great job as well."

"Has someone been whispering good things in your ear about me?"

A pause, then: "No. But I've seen the dailies. I must admit, Cass is doing an incredible job."

Cass once again. It was always about Cass. Chelsea felt as though she might vomit. How dare the bitch steal *her* thunder.

Chelsea considered whether or not to mention the article. Something told her to keep quiet. Let him discover just how "incredible" his precious producer was. Instead she dropped her voice to a sultry whisper, oblivious to the child watching her. "When will I see you? I've been so lonely. I can't wait till I'm back in L.A."

"I'm here—in Venice—at the hotel. I'll see you on the set."

Chelsea started to say something, but he cut her off.

"Good-bye." There was a click, then silence.

And then the familiar cacophony began. *He's here to see her. She's trouble. Get rid of her. No, kill her.*

The voices had been escalating since she'd stopped taking her medication. Until this moment, they were simply white noise, indecipherable background chatter, but now it was as though somewhere in her brain the tuner had been moved. *Cass this. Cass that. He admires her more because of the work you've done. Stop her. Stop her.*

Bella followed silently behind her mother as they headed to the elevator.

| | |

Cass arrived late at the set.

She and Ally had stayed in Cass's suite, using the private line that Ally had had the foresight to request when she reserved the suite. Calls flew back and forth from the legal department at the studio and the *Oggi* publisher, Oleg Mancini. A three-way conference call brought in Desmond's head of Legal Affairs, who began a litany of accusations and threats. Mancini was standing by his star reporter, Georgio Valine. Cass would not, could not, leave the room until she'd been assured the magazine would investigate Valine's sources, even though she was told the entertainment reporter had never erred before.

Cass noticed that Chelsea had also arrived late. The prima donna arrived in a fury, the beautiful Bella struggling to keep up with her mother's usual entourage. Chelsea was now emerging from her trailer, already berating half the cast and crew, including her own dresser, hairstylist, and makeup person. The lighting was all wrong, the cameras were too close, the coffee was too hot.

Cass suspected that Chelsea was playing a game, trying to pay Cass back for ordering "her majesty" around the day before. Had it been only yesterday morning? All the days were one long blur punctuated by either crisis or the rush of a perfect scene, an artistic piece of footage, whatever perfection might be contained in the evening's review of dailies.

"I'm not leaving my trailer until someone fixes this damn corset." Chelsea's voice was demanding, shrill. A flock of pigeons scattered at the sound, making Cass smile for the first time that day. Who cared about lying gossip? She had a film to finish.

Cass went over to speak with her. "Chelsea, I'll send Hilary to your trailer," she said, referring to the head costume designer. "You've got ten minutes to either work the problem out or wear the corset as is."

"But . . ." Chelsea lowered her Armani sunglasses to stare at Cassidy, but her attempt at intimidation didn't work.

"Now, Chelsea. Either that or your body double does the scene."

"Well!" was all the actress said. The actress turned abruptly, making sure her ass, in tight white Lycra Capri pants, was pointed toward the omnipresent paparazzi, and she and her entourage, except for Bella, hastened back to the actress's trailer.

"You stay here with me, sweetheart," Cassidy said to Bella. The little girl settled into the empty canvas director's chair beside Cass. One of the assistants handed her a chocolate doughnut.

Chelsea's daughter smiled.

But there was still tension when Chelsea reemerged from her trailer.

Cass had to admit that she couldn't quite ignore the awkward stares she was getting from the crew. No one had mentioned the newspaper item. No one had to. But Cass could tell everyone had their questions, and their suspicions.

Finally, two hours later, convinced the scene was perfect, Rudolpho called for a half-hour break. Chelsea returned to her trailer, while Cass remained slumped in the director's chair. At that point Rudolpho approached her.

"Look, about the other night." Rudolpho looked almost nervous. "I never meant to hurt you, Cass."

For a moment, Cass hesitated. She didn't want him to feel worse than he already did. Besides, who was she to get jealous when she couldn't even commit to anything other than the relationship they had forged through the years? She didn't know what to make of all the feelings swirling around inside of her these days. "Forget about it, Rudolpho."

He was hurt. She could see it in his eyes. He had wanted her to feel jealous, to pout. He always wanted more from her. More than she could ever give him, or anyone. Cassidy softened her tone. "Listen, this is hard on all of us. I haven't slept a wink these last two days. I really need to just focus on the film now."

She sighed and continued, "Why couldn't you have chosen one of the extras? Any one of them would jump at the chance to sleep with the director. And now"—her eyes welled up despite her efforts to control her emotions—"with these lies being written about me, I am close to my breaking point."

Of course, Rudolpho mistook the reason for her tears. Instantly he was out of his chair and crouched next to hers. "Cass, if I had known . . ." But he stopped. "We've never had that kind of understanding. I just get so frustrated, never knowing what you want."

She looked away and focused her gaze on Bella, now sitting at a table sketching. To her dismay, Cass could not stop the tears. Desperately she tried to focus on what was going on right now. She couldn't drag this ridiculous business out with Rudolpho. *Dangerous* was what mattered right now. She couldn't let anything, or anyone, set her back. Not the lies about her and certainly not any nonsense on the set between her and Rudolpho.

"I'm being silly." Cass smiled. "It's just that we're so close to the end." She held up two fingers and crossed them. "One more week and I'm home free. This pressure is driving me mad. There's so much riding on it."

"Performance anxiety?" he asked. "You?"

Cass nodded. "Funny, isn't it? A month ago I would have given my right arm to get away from this thing, and now I'd give everything just to pull it off."

His eyes opened wider; a slight smile curled the corners of his mouth. "You'll do more than that. I have no doubt." A brief pause, then: "The movie is stunning, Cass. You've pulled off the impossible. And it's going to come in on time."

She returned the smile and for a moment their eyes locked. "And under budget!" she added.

"Do we have a truce?" he asked. "At least until after the film's complete, at which time, if you still want to, you can rake me over the coals."

Despite the pressure sitting on her lungs, she laughed. Rudolpho always found a way to make her laugh. Perhaps that's where the attraction began and ended. It was hard to tell these days. "I've been behaving like a child," she said.

There were issues that needed to be worked out between them, but now was not the time. Cass held out her hand. "A truce until further notice?"

Rudolpho's eyes told her he expected more than that. But she'd worry about that when the film was finished. "A truce," he replied as he accepted her hand.

| | |

He couldn't take his eyes off her. Jack eyed every move she made with great approval.

The director leaned in close to her, whispered something in her ear. Her eyes danced, her mouth smiled. She was more beautiful than any woman he had ever known, and he'd know thousands.

Maybe it was the way she'd looked into his eyes the night of Roger's party, or the way she moved or smiled, that made him want to touch her, hold her, kiss her, possess her. Certainly none of that would come easy. She was the ultimate conquest.

He chose to watch her, as he'd done once before, from a vantage point that kept him hidden. From his place behind the curious crowd always surrounding the set, Jack studied Cassidy English—how she moved, how she thought before she spoke. Beauty, poise, brains, talent, all in one woman. And she still didn't even know he was in Venice.

Cassidy was splendid, talented, and an enigma even to him. Her tall, graceful body promised delicious secrets. Mysterious women usually held no appeal for him. Jack was impatient and expected full disclosure from his partners—employees, lovers, friends. But Cassidy's mysteries drew him in.

And besides all that, she was Lana Turmaine's daughter. Her animated eyes, the vibrancy exuded by Cassidy's every move, was not only perfection, but they were qualities that echoed her mother's, and evoked Lana's memory.

A light breeze blew past him, a moment of cool, brisk air that sent her hair blowing in the wind. Long, lush, lavish. Incredible.

This was one challenge he would thoroughly enjoy.

| | |

Chelsea didn't move when Jack entered her trailer. She'd been waiting for him, and now she watched as his eyes took in the elaborate furnishings and expensive knickknacks, expertly appraising their value.

"I don't believe I've ever seen a boudoir that can compare to this. My company's money is being well spent," he said sarcastically.

Chelsea pouted. "Would it make you happy if I were terribly uncomfortable?"

She let him see her stretching her body like a cat. Then she let her eyes roam his body. As always, he was impeccably groomed—hair well styled and neat, face and body lightly tanned, clothed head to toe in Armani. Black jacket, pants, and T-shirt.

Jack found a comfortable spot on the olive-green camelback couch. "So tell me what I've missed."

Chelsea knew he meant only things pertaining to Cassidy. That was their agreement, after all. She would be cast in the lead in exchange for inside information—all part of his plan to upstage Cassidy, come in and save *Dangerous,* and be done with Cassidy's old man, Roger Turmaine, once and for all. This plan worked for her as well. By the time *Dangerous Intentions* was released, she would have Jack back where she wanted him. And Cassidy would be better than gone; she'd be history.

Chelsea sat down beside him. She pushed the costume underneath her. She could barely breathe, her already-slender waist cinched in to a mere eighteen inches. Her ample cleavage spilled forth over the bustier of the heavy white lace gown with yards and yards of crinoline and lace skirts. She was in full makeup and wore a wig that piled hair on top of her head, loose curls falling coquettishly down the sides of her heart-shaped face.

Jack found her costume and coif amusing. "Even I could mistake you for a virgin bride. And I certainly know better!"

He had a good laugh and Chelsea joined him. She knew the game. First she had to humor him, then make him do her bidding.

But with the passing of just a second, his expression changed. He grew serious—all business. "So fill me in on the director. I understand our Ms. English has a thing for him."

Chelsea rolled her eyes. "I'd hardly call it a thing. . . . More like an arrangement."

This tidbit of information intrigued him. "So they're not heavily involved?"

"He is, no doubt. She, on the other hand, seems to want only friendship and the occasional lay."

His eyes grew dark now and Chelsea realized that she'd hit a soft spot. He was jealous. And that hurt.

"If you want to get ahead," she said, "I'd suggest you move fast."

Her words had jolted him and he eyed her suspiciously. "What are you talking about?"

"Oh, come on, Jack. I can see it in your eyes, your expression, every time her name is mentioned. You're captivated by her."

Jack jumped to his feet. Good, she had gotten to him, Chelsea thought. Let him know what it felt like to be played like a dummy, a marionette. Yes—she could still push his buttons.

"That's ridiculous and you know it. My interest in Ms. English is purely professional, I can assure you. If *Dangerous* crashes and burns, Turmaine's out."

"Turmaine, maybe, but what about *Ms. English?*" She hoped her eyes did not reveal how tortured she felt. Was he really in love with Cassidy?

Jack pulled off his jacket and tossed it over a chair, then walked over to the small lunch table, picked a ripe apple from the bowl of fresh fruit, and toyed with it, tossing it back and forth as though it were a ball.

Maybe Jack would discard Cassidy, too. Perhaps she had misconstrued his feelings.

Buoyed by this thought, Chelsea stood, crinoline bouncing, hips swaying. She joined him at the window that overlooked the Piazza San Marco. She held him gently around his waist, resting her head on his broad back, which was warm beneath his spotless silk ribbed T-shirt.

"I've missed you terribly."

He moved away from her embrace.

"Let's get back to business, shall we?"

She wasn't used to rejection. "Business—meaning Cassidy." She seethed with anger and humiliation.

They stood close, just a few inches of air separating them. His eyes locked with hers, but she was sure he was looking right through her. Their romance was suddenly over and she'd had nothing to say about it. She saw with painful honesty that she had been good for an occasional romp, but that Jack didn't really take her seriously. Jack seemed obsessed with Cassidy English. But she'd get his attention another way. With that realization, she moved to Plan B.

"I have an idea that may expedite our both getting what we want out of our little deal." His green eyes bore into hers. She now had his full attention. She walked over to the dressing table and found a pack of cigarettes. She took one out and offered the pack to Jack.

He shook his head. "Those things will kill you."

She barely heard him around the voices going on now inside her head. Blood pounded in her temples.

"So will a lot of other things. Of course, that doesn't mean I'll abstain from them."

She brought the cigarette up to her lips, struck a match, and inhaled deeply, letting the smoke out in a long drawn-out breath—and giving herself time to calm down, get ahold of her rocking emotions.

"I have a plan, one that I've thought out very carefully, that will get us both exactly what we want—now."

"I thought you had what you want."

She shot him an icy stare. "Do you really believe I wanted this role only to further my career?"

His expression told her yes.

She let out a soft chuckle. "No, it goes way beyond that."

He hung on to every word and she relished the attention.

"The only way to get closer to Cassidy is to make her fall in love with you. Make her trust you with all her deep, dark secrets—her life."

Jack, still confused, said, "What the hell are you talking about?"

"She's the original Ice Princess, Jack. There's no way she'd let anyone get within a mile of her heart. No man can penetrate that invisible concrete wall she's built up around her." She looked him right in the eye. "No man except you."

He started to protest, but she held her hand to his lips. "I know, I know, you're not interested in winning the mysterious Ms. English's heart. Okay, but if you did so anyway, if you used all that wonderful Cavelli grace, charm, power, intelligence . . . should I go on?"

He smiled. "How about the things I can do to a woman in the sack?"

Chelsea forced a smile. "That, too. So you pour it on, she falls for you, and if she's tripping all over herself for your affection, your approval, you'll not only keep your hands on *Dangerous,* but you'll also get the skinny on dear old Dad." *Oops, a Freudian slip.* She caught herself and bounced back quickly. "On her dear old dad as well. That ought to make taking over Desmond a snap. It's for certain good old Roger has tons of bodies buried, and five will get you ten Ms. English will learn pretty quick where those skeletons are."

"And what do you get out of this?"

"Oh, Jack, for such a smart man, you can be so dumb at times."

He stood directly in front of her now, his hands gripping her shoulders. He squeezed so hard she nearly yelped.

"What the hell are you up to? What connection do you have to Cassidy? What has she done to you to make you this vindictive . . . this twisted?"

Chelsea couldn't keep herself together for one more second. The part of her ruled by raw emotion, the place from where the voices came, took over as he shook her.

"She stole my life. Now I want it back." A sudden, piercing chill hung on the edge of her words.

| | |

It was nearly six o'clock and both cast and crew were exhausted. The setting sun took away most of the natural light and it was hard to get a good take. Both Chelsea and Bengino were exhausted. Next to her, Rudolpho sat slumped in his chair, his head cradled in his hands. The only one filled with energy and enthusiasm was Cass. Chelsea had given a riveting performance of a woman scorned, robust with melodrama—real tears, real anger.

Still Cass wanted more.

As she was struggling to determine just what to try in the next scene, Jack appeared from behind the gawking crowd on the set. Instantly the cast and crew grew silent and still, no one moving. They all knew who he was, it was obvious to Cass. Without thinking, she grew irritated. This was her production, her set, her cast and crew. How dare he come along and disrupt it? What on earth was he doing here, anyway? Checking up on her, no doubt.

He walked toward her, green eyes meeting blue. The closer he got, the more nervous she became. Or perhaps it was intimidation. She couldn't be sure.

He, on the other hand, couldn't have appeared more at ease. From his casual dress to his confident manner, Cavelli was making a grand entrance. He was boss here, his expression said, make no mistake about it.

And he was handsome. No matter how pissed off she felt at his surprise "invasion," Cassidy could not stop her eyes from greedily exploring him.

He came to an abrupt halt about two feet from her and flashed her a devilish grin. "I'm impressed," he said, removing his dark glasses.

Cass was aware that every female between the ages of seventeen and seventy-five was studying him. There were men on the set who were lots better looking—Bengino, for instance—but Jack's essence, the core of his character, was as irresistible as true north, the magnetic pole. Mentally, Cassidy tried to put up a shield between herself and Cavelli's forcefulness.

Jack began to speak again. "I don't believe I've ever seen a producer so involved in the nitty-gritty of every shot." He turned his eyes on Rudolpho. "I thought that was the job of director?" His words were full of sarcasm.

She stood and, because she was tall, nearly matched his six feet. "We . . ." She turned briefly to Rudolpho, then back to Jack. "We didn't expect you."

Jack flashed both of them a pretend smile. "I bet."

Rudolpho, always a man who knew when to cut and run, removed himself quickly from Jack's attention. "Later," he muttered. Cass nodded.

In what seemed only moments, Cassidy realized, the set was clear. Everyone gone. Even Chelsea had dematerialized. Cassidy hoped that Chelsea had actually taken her daughter with her this time so Cass didn't have to add that to her worries.

"So tell me, Jack, are you here to check up on me?" Cass was blustering, the way she'd seen her father do so many times, fighting the jittery nervousness that had landed in her stomach. She bent over to get her belongings stashed behind the canvas chair—a beige leather knapsack, a straw hat, and a pair of sunglasses.

His laugh was barely audible. She could feel his piercing green eyes on her.

"Here, let me help you." He reached for the knapsack and slung it over one shoulder.

Her first instinct was to protest, but then the sight of the high and mighty one catering to her was suddenly appealing.

They began their way back to the hotel, taking their time in the early-spring night and making small talk about the production. Jack had hired a private launch to cross the lagoon to the set. Clearly he had already instructed the driver to take the long route back to the Cipriani.

From what he said, Cass could tell that Jack was up to date with the film's progress from the dailies. Production costs were checked by the studio's accounting department and he'd clearly seen all their reports. All essential information was stored in his head. And, of course, he knew about the article in *Oggi*. But he addressed none of this directly as they walked through the streets of Venice. Jack kept the conversation flowing with news and gossip about the goings-on in Hollywood. The Academy Awards ceremony had taken place. "We'll be there next year," was the only reference he made to *Dangerous Intentions* that suggested what he truly thought about how things were going on the shoot.

Have I made a mistake about this man? Is he actually a human being after all? Cassidy was afraid to let down her guard. Her father had warned her that Cavelli wanted to kill Desmond and get rid of him— and her—forever. But her father had told her many things that weren't quite as he said and there was something about Jack Cavelli that she couldn't quite put her finger on.

Instead of talking further about the film, he asked about Venice, offered information about the ancient city, its violent history, its myths and legends. Although Cass had heard a lot of the information before, she felt as if she were listening to Laurence Olivier give a monologue from *Hamlet*. She felt absolutely transported.

Once inside the lobby, she managed to compose herself. In fact she reverted to her role as the serious producer and bid him farewell. "I have to go. Thank you for the walk. I must say, I thoroughly enjoyed it," she said a slow smile creeping onto her face, unbidden.

He was staring at her. Then she remembered his eyes. Yes, it was at Roger's party, the brief time she spent with Jack, looking deep into her, her eyes, penetrating her soul, and suddenly she'd felt naked. As though he could view her inside and out. As though he knew all of her fears and secrets with just one penetrating glance. She grew visibly uncomfortable, fumbling inside the knapsack for her key card, pressing the elevator call button at least half a dozen times.

"Here, let me help you." He reached down for her bag and held the flap open, exposing all of its contents. "It's much easier when you can see what's inside."

Cass found the key. She reached for the bag and accidentally brushed his hand. An electrical current, the same one she felt when he held her in his arms the night of the party, shot through her body.

Finally the elevator car arrived, the doors opened, and Cass stepped inside. Jack held the door before it closed.

"Have dinner with me."

"Oh, no . . . I couldn't possibly."

Then he was inside the elevator and the doors closed. They traveled upward toward the penthouse. Cass was incredibly nervous now; beads of perspiration formed on her brow and nearly slid down her face. She started to speak, but he set a finger on her lips and stopped her. He kissed her gently on her mouth and she felt the heat of his lips ignite the passion she did not want to feel.

His soft lips nuzzled her throat and he whispered, "Be ready at eight. . . ."

One last ounce of reason remained in her, told her not to let feelings rule. For a single moment she was able to compose herself.

"I . . . I can't. I'm sorry. . . . But I'm really exhausted. And I need to prepare for Monday's shoot."

He rolled his eyes and let out a soft chuckle. "You've already done that preparation. I know that because you're like me—meticulous, ambitious." Now he leaned his head close to her.

She smelled the complicated odor that compelled her lips to lean toward his.

"And most of all—I know you want to win our bet. However, it's Friday night. You have the whole weekend to prepare for the shoot. The rest of the cast and crew are planning a weekend of nonstop partying." He shook his head. "I'm afraid I won't take no for an answer."

| | |

"Are you in?" Chelsea asked Jack. They were in his suite to discuss their new "deal."

He paused. "You haven't told me what you hope to gain. You said Cassidy 'stole your life.' What the hell does that mean? Explain yourself."

She stood in front of the fireplace, dressed only in a black mink wrap. Her eyes scanned his body and immediately she felt a sexual thrill go through her. She waited for a sign, some gesture of encouragement on his part. Jack was cut from a traditional cloth. He fancied being the aggressor. In fact, women who took the sexual initiative turned him off completely.

"In time," she purred, then she removed the wrap, let it fall to her feet. His eyes remained fixed on hers. He seemed unfazed by her action.

"Put your clothes back on," he countered sharply.

But she ignored him. Instead she moved closer, until her lips were nearly on his.

"Not now . . . that part of our relationship is over." He looked away from her, so she could not read his eyes.

Chelsea pushed her body up against his; her breasts were pressed against his chest. Her hips slowly gyrated in a semicircular motion as she ground her pelvis into his. She wrapped her arms around his neck and attempted to pull him closer. *Give up, she's won. The bitch has won. Now she's taken Jack, too . . . and she's going to pay,* the voices ranted. But something was still moving through her, urging her on. She kept on moving against Jack, trancelike, as though she were split in two.

Jack's fingernails dug into her flesh as he gripped her shoulders. "Listen, Chelsea, I want to know *exactly* what you have against Cassidy. Don't hold out on me. You have information, and I've paid for it. Now give. I mean it. Now."

She brushed back a lock of hair and smiled, feigning nonchalance. "It's this way, Jack. I owe you nothing." Her blue eyes glinted like steel. She won their brief staring contest. "If you think you'll win Miss Cassidy's heart, you're wrong. You've met your match. I would have helped you, taken Rudolpho out of the picture, let's say—and other things."

At this Jack gave a sardonic chuckle. "You really are crazy, Chelsea. You don't have the power or the brains to keep Cassidy English, or any other woman, from falling for me. Not when I put my mind to it."

Okay, Chelsea thought, let him go to hell right along with her, but all she said was, "We'll see, Jack. I'm going to use what I know to strip Cassidy English. I'll rock her world right out from under her. Then we'll see who's crazy."

She was trembling, close to the breaking point. She needed to get away, be alone to medicate herself. Any moment she could lose herself and her black side would emerge. Her life force would dissipate and she'd lose her will to fight Cassidy, fight Jack. To get back what was hers. But Jack had slipped away from her into Cassidy's arms. It was written all over him. And now she'd never bring Cassidy down—so she would never reclaim her life.

Chelsea quietly dressed and departed without another word.

| | |

Cass pushed open the door of her suite, hit the light switch, threw the key card onto the ivory fossil table in the hall, and kicked her Prada loafers into the corner. She tossed her navy blazer and leather knapsack over the arm of the sofa and headed straight for the minibar. Her mouth was dry as toast.

She twisted the cap off a bottle of Pellegrino water and headed for the bedroom, relishing the thought of a long hot bath. One thing was certain, she'd better get her head together by eight o'clock. Maybe she'd read a few more entries from her mother's diary. Maybe not.

But now as she groped for the bedroom light switch, an intense fragrance swept over her. Her weariness dropped away and she felt light enough to dance, to fly. On top of the wall-length bureau, on each night table, along the mantle above the bedroom's fireplace—crystal vases filled with dozens upon dozens of lavender roses, redolent of spring, of romance, of love, enveloped her. She went from vase to vase in search of a card. But found nothing.

Then she knew. They had come from Jack.

The pealing of the telephone startled her and brought her back to earth.

"Hello?" Her eyes still scanned the room, absorbing the breathtaking view. She rocked back and forth on her heels.

"I guess it's safe to assume you've discovered my surprise?" His voice was smooth and low.

Cassidy sank onto the bed, fumbling her words. "I . . . I . . . they're simply magnificent. I'm a bit overwhelmed."

"I thought you'd like roses."

"Yes," she whispered. It was that voice again.

"Because you have to be certain to keep me at a distance. Isn't that so?"

"Maybe," she said, though her heart objected. Since the roses were from Jack, she had all the more reason to stare, smell, touch each delicate petal.

"I have a meeting outside the hotel so my driver will pick you up at eight."

For a moment Cass thought she'd heard him wrong. "Your driver?"

"Yes. Is that a problem? Do you need more time?"

Blood rushed into her face and hammered in her ears. She saw red and couldn't speak. Something inside her slammed shut. "Has it occurred to you I'd rather not be sent for, well, like an escort? No, I won't be ready at eight. In fact, I just remembered I've made other plans."

She slammed the receiver down.

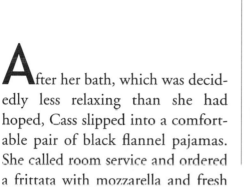After her bath, which was decidedly less relaxing than she had hoped, Cass slipped into a comfortable pair of black flannel pajamas. She called room service and ordered a frittata with mozzarella and fresh basil, a semolina roll, and chamomile tea with honey, then pulled back the comforter, climbed underneath the blankets, and reached for the diary.

Perhaps reading about her mother's rocky life might not seem like the best way to unwind, but compared to the storms Jack's attentions were creating, Lana's words were soothing. She wasn't sure why his sending a driver to pick her up had angered her so, but it had, and she didn't have to explain it to anyone. Who did he think he was to treat her in such a cavalier manner?

Where did he come off thinking he could get to her by filling her suite with flowers? If he thought roses would blind her to his flaws, he could guess again.

Cass shook her head to clear her thoughts and turned to the diary she held tightly to her chest. Settling back against the downy pillows, she opened the book and leafed through the pages until she came to one with a dog-eared corner.

SEPT. 16, 1975 ————————————————————

He makes me feel so alive, so wanted. When we're together, nothing else matters. There are no insecurities, no pressures, no inhibitions. Only mutual respect for each other. We are soul mates, cut from the same cloth. Two insecure actors with needs, wants, desires. My lover is like no other. Sometimes I just sit and stare at his magnificently sculpted face or long to run my fingers over his exquisitely carved body.

I'm not a fool. I am fully aware that he can have any woman in Hollywood he wants, yet he wants *me*. The real Lana. Not the plastic, make-believe, wind-up doll my husband has created. I often think about Roger, about what he would do if he ever found out. No doubt it would destroy him. But I can't think of that now. I think only of my lover. All I see is him, all I feel is his touch, all I hear is his soft comforting voice. In his presence I feel euphoric. In his arms I feel security. In his bed I feel pleasure.

I'm a queen—his queen. No one can take what we have away. We were made to be together. Somehow we'll find eternity.

Cass could hardly catch her breath. Her mother's passion was no shock. Every biography Cassidy had read, and there were many, claimed Lana Turmaine had been Hollywood's number-one party girl during her early days when she was a struggling starlet who worked days at a law firm between acting jobs. The studio system that paid potential stars a salary while providing training and the occasional bit part was no more. Now even the most talented and most beautiful—or handsome—newcomers were relegated to working jobs *outside* the industry to pay for classes and clothes. Often they "dated" agents, directors, producers, actors, and others on the periphery of the film industry in hopes of getting seen and getting a break. Even after the esteemed Roger Turmaine had *tamed* this classic beauty into marriage, Lana made sure that she was seen at all the right parties and premieres.

Like Harlow or Monroe before her, Lana needed to be admired and loved, and that need drew her into unsavory, even inappropriate, situations. But to read it in Lana's own words was startling and, Cass had to admit, embarrassing.

Cassidy slammed the diary shut, kicked the blankets off, and bolted from the bed. She locked the little book back in the room's safe and stepped out onto the terrace. She desperately needed air. Outside a chill spring wind slapped at her cheeks and sent shivers up and down her spine. A storm was coming. Two storms: one outside, and the other in her heart.

Who was this man who had so captivated and compelled her mother? Lana worshiped him, enough so that she was willing to walk away from her marriage, her career, her child. Though the diary recorded other liaisons, other men, Cass would guess that it was this lone affair that had brought on the fateful end, the awful days she still remembered when only silence, disrupted by bouts of screaming and yelling, filled the mansion.

A knock interrupted her thoughts. *Ah, room service.* Good, she was famished.

Cass slipped into her robe and slippers and opened the door. She froze. Instead of a waiter with her dinner, it was Jack. He stood in the middle of the hall, squarely in front of the door. Dressed in a handsome tuxedo with highly polished evening loafers, he clutched a beautiful white orchid, its stem protected in a water-filled glass vial.

She stepped back. Her eyes examined first the fine suit of clothing, then the corsage.

"Is this old-fashioned enough?" Again, his voice was soft, dusky. He smiled sheepishly.

Cass pulled at the belt on her robe to make it even tighter. "I was in bed."

Her body began to sweat, almost shiver, as she felt his eyes roam over her. The small slit down the front of her robe, revealing minimal cleavage, seemed to attract him the most.

"Well, aren't you going to get dressed?" His eyes danced and there was a mischievous look on his face. "I plan to make this a night you'll remember, but I'm afraid I've only hired the car until midnight."

| | |

Nothing in her wildest fantasies could have prepared Cass for the evening that lay ahead. Jack wasn't kidding.

A vintage Rolls-Royce convertible fit for royalty waited at the door. The doorman helped Cass into the open passenger section and spread the lush sable blanket across their laps to keep them warm in the crisp night air. The driver, already behind the wheel in the enclosed chauffeur's compartment, started the motor and eased silently into the narrow street, off to the Venice airport, where Jack's private Gulfstream jet was waiting.

The smartly uniformed pilot greeted them at the bottom of the ramp and then an attractive flight attendant escorted them on board, where champagne was chilling in a sterling-silver bucket embossed with the Colossal logo. Elegant Lalique champagne flutes and a bowl of sugared long-stem strawberries waited on a small table that was covered with a fine linen cloth, edged with embroidered cutwork.

"Where are we going?" Cass whispered.

Jack smiled and said, "Paris."

"Oh." Cassidy settled into the soft leather seat as the plane taxied down the runway.

Once they landed at Paris's Orly airport, they were whisked into the center of the city by a gunmetal-gray Mercedes limousine and dropped at the doors of Les Ambassadeurs, in the famed Hotel Crillon. Cass was dazzled by its magnificent frescoes and marble halls, furnished with authentic antiques. Formerly a palace, the ultra-chic hotel and its stunning restaurant were a gathering place for many savvy Parisians, visiting heads of state, and very wealthy tourists.

"I hope you don't mind," Jack explained as they were seated. "I asked Jean-Jacques to order for us."

They dined on a light Langoustine Soup au Cognac; Moules Marinère—mussels poached in dry white wine with shallots, garlic, and parsley; Foie Gras de Canard—duck liver pâté, garnished with escargot and chanterelle mushrooms; warm house smoked salmon slivered and served on almost transparent slices of toast, and a delicate trout stuffed with fish mousse. Dessert was an elegant blood orange sorbet, served in a meringue shell and dusted with dark chocolate slivers, *and* a perfect crème brûlée. "I couldn't decide," the flamboyant chef laughed, with an expressive Gallic shrug.

Of course, the sommelier served a different wine with every course. Vintage all the way.

Cassidy was sure that she had slipped beyond the camera and sets and landed in one of Hollywood's classic love stories, one with Ingrid Bergman, Carole Lombard, Natalie Wood, or Vivien Leigh. And she— well, right at this moment, she was luckier than any leading lady Hollywood had ever created.

Jack held doors, pulled out chairs, listened attentively, and stared longingly at her. He paid attention to details. At one point he even requested that the small jazz combo, fronted by a lanky blond singer in a strapless red sequined dress that was slit up to her thigh, play the Billie Holiday classic "God Bless the Child"—one of Cass's favorite.

As they sipped espresso and hundred-year-old port, Jack brushed her hand with his fingertips and said, "Come . . . let's go."

Now the limousine traveled like a luxurious modern magic carpet through the City of Light, along the Seine, weaving through the city's heart—past the Eiffel Tower, a seven-thousand-ton marvel of iron latticework and lights, looking every bit like a big golden candle against the dark night sky; the Champs-Elysées, a magnificent example of Napoleonic grandiosity; and, of course, Notre-Dame, the great Gothic fourteenth-century cathedral standing mystically on the Île St.-Louis.

At one point—Cassidy didn't know exactly when Jack took her hand. He sat close to her in the back of the limousine. His black silk suit jacket felt soft against her bare arm. He leaned down, lips close enough to graze her neck. The Donna Karan "perfect little black dress" hugged her body and clung to her curves. But it was Jack's attention that was making Cass feel so sexy. Her body throbbed as her blood raced through her veins. She tried to keep her palms from sweating in Jack's firm but gentle grasp.

"Have you had enough of Paris yet?" he asked.

Cass leaned her head into the supple leather seat, stared out the half-open window, and let out a long, deep sigh.

Jack chuckled softly, then said, "When you told me you'd never been here, I thought you were kidding. But now seeing you like this . . ." His eyes were still on hers, penetrating. "Well, I'm only glad that I was lucky enough to share in your first time."

The driver pulled the car past the Place Vendôme and came to an abrupt halt.

"Come with me. There's something I want to show you."

Outside the night air was turning cold. A light rain was starting to fall, adding glitter to the streetlights and causing the traffic to come to a standstill outside the hotel.

Cass pulled her velvet cape around her shoulders.

Cars and taxis whizzed by, while pedestrians—mainly tourists—scurried along the sidewalks, heads bowed against the chill.

Despite the encroaching midnight hour, Paris was still very much alive. Like New York . . . with grace.

Jack struggled into a raincoat, then gently took hold of her elbow. He led her past a very couture, very of-the-moment boutique, even further past a small quaint café, till they came to Boucheron, the jewelry store Cass had read about. The window sparkled with replicas of the magnificent jewelry, each piece museum quality—not only an accoutrement but also a work of art. The centerpiece of the window was a carefully orchestrated display of finely cut glass, each piece modeled after one of the famed store's rare diamonds.

"Eye-catching, isn't it?" Jack said over her shoulder, leaning in close—so close, she could feel his hot breath along the nape of her neck. "Monsieur Lareaux keeps one of the finest collections of diamonds in the world inside the safe."

Cass leaned in to get a closer look at a pair of sapphire-and-diamond earrings, but Jack tugged at her arm.

"Hurry, Monsieur Lareaux is waiting."

"But it's nearly midnight."

Jack smiled as he opened the door and ushered her into the showroom as though it were perfectly natural for a world-famous jewelry store to be open at this hour.

A small, squat man with frail features, olive skin, and closely cropped salt-and-pepper hair stood waiting. He was dressed in an elegant black tuxedo.

The two men embraced, shared some small talk, then Monsieur Lareaux locked the store's doors, checked his alarm system, and led them to the back of the showroom and through a set of intricately carved wood doors. The viewing salon, as it was called, was for appointment viewing only. They were offered seats on a plush burgundy sofa. A finely dressed younger gentleman appeared carrying a tray of Dom Perignon and two champagne glasses. Before she could ask Jack just how he had arranged for this unorthodox private viewing, the man handed each of them a glass, then filled it with the bubbly golden liquid. He bowed slightly and backed out of the room. Monsieur Lareaux quickly followed.

Jack turned to Cass, held his glass up to her in a toast, and said, "To us."

His eyes, mysterious and magical, gave away nothing.

She watched him raise the glass to his lips and sip the rich bubbling liquid. Jack leaned back, resting his head on the back of the sofa, and let out a comfortable sigh. He never once took his eyes from hers. His intense stare burned straight through her, once again turning her inside out. Cass waited for his next move, holding her breath.

Suddenly everything was happening in slow motion, yet every sense was rich, alive.

Jack Cavelli, one of the world's most eligible bachelors, a big-time player-playboy, could have any woman in the world. Why was he wining and dining *her?*

Embarrassed, she felt her legs quake. Her wraparound dress fell open, gracefully exposing one thigh. Could he see her tremble? His smile stayed the same; his eyes never left hers. The shaking wouldn't stop, the champagne was going to her head. She was sure it was the reaction he'd hoped for. She was totally out of control and it terrified her.

Just then Monsieur Lareaux returned, and this time he was escorted by two armed guards, in full uniform. The jeweler was carrying a black velvet pillow. Whatever gem was on it flickered in the salon's low, soft light.

Jack leaned forward, set his champagne glass down on the cocktail table, and reached for the velvet pillow. Carefully he held it up in front of her, revealing the most exquisite emerald-cut diamond Cass had ever seen. The chandelier's prisms picked up the brilliant blue hue of the unset stone, refracting the light like fireworks. The diamond was so precisely cut that, had she wanted to, Cassidy was certain she could study each separate facet.

Jack pushed the stone toward her. "Here, have a look," he said. Then he handed her a jeweler's loupe. "Go ahead. Look."

With shaky hands Cassidy reached for the gem. Its icy feel reminded her that diamonds are the toughest stone on earth.

"Well, what do you think? Is it worth bidding on?" He smiled and she couldn't help but wonder how many hearts that smile had broken.

"I . . . I don't know. I guess it all depends on how much you're worth." She had no idea what made her say that; it just rolled off her tongue.

His smile changed into a mischievous grin. And for a second he reminded Cass of a little boy with an awfully big secret.

He reached for the champagne, took another sip, and said, "Actually, it's mine. I bought it several years ago."

Cass was too stunned to speak.

"It's one of the world's finest diamonds. Monsieur Lareaux has been kind enough to let me keep it safe and secure in his state-of-the-art vault."

Lareaux nodded appreciatively.

Cass placed the diamond back on its pillow. Jack set it back on the tray and Lareaux and his men disappeared, taking it with them.

"I like to check up on it from time to time."

"Why would you buy such an amazing, expensive stone? Are you a collector of rare gems?"

Jack shrugged his shoulders. "No, not a collector, just a hopeless romantic. I made up my mind years ago never to marry unless I was one hundred percent sure. My bride would be a princess—not one born of royalty, I assure you, but one in every other sense of the word. She would be flawless, like a perfect diamond—brilliant and exquisite—and I bought a stone that would be worthy of her."

He stared intently again and she couldn't help but fidget.

Slowly he continued. "I never believed marriage to be a temporary union based on fleeting passion, want, need." His gaze drifted now, darting around the room, encompassing his surroundings. "I truly believe marriage should last forever. Don't you?"

"I honestly have never given it much thought." She turned slightly and leaned forward to place her champagne flute on the table . . . and to put some distance between her and the man beside her. This wasn't a lie. She never had. Marriage meant commitment, trust, years of happiness, pain, joy, and babies—lots of them. All the things Cass could never offer any man. Sure, she wanted them—what woman didn't? But Cass had her own version of a perfect world. And Prince Charming would play a pivotal part. He was someone who could love her, give her a house with a white picket fence, a home filled with laughter and promise. Her prince would be someone who would take care of her if she got sick, someone who would say after a hard day's work, "Darling, you look tired, let me draw you a hot bath." Someone who at any given moment might come up behind her in a crowded room and whisper, "I love you." Someone she could count on in good times and in bad, trust with her life, her future. In short, someone who didn't exist.

He stared at her with disbelieving eyes. "I can't say that I've ever met a woman who didn't want commitment—marriage."

"You have now." Cass smiled.

Her words piqued his curiosity even more.

"Oh, come now. Tell me you've never envisioned yourself in a magnificent white wedding gown, surrounded by flowers and candles, beautiful bridesmaids and handsome ushers. Tell me you've never fantasized of dancing around a fabulously decorated ballroom while hundreds of people worshiped you as Queen for the Day?"

Cass nodded only slightly, and looked away. "Once . . . a long, long time ago."

"What happened, Cass, to send you underground?" He paused, studying her. "I can't believe it was Lana's death that put you so out of reach."

He took her chin in his hand and turned her face to him. She wished she could flee. Instead she remained passive, held hostage by his probing eyes. All the therapy in the world couldn't erase some of her demons, or her secrets.

"Some poor stupid fool did you an ugly injustice? It's the age-old story: Boy meets girl, boy and girl fall in love, boy promises girl the world. Stability, romance, financial security—like an old Brando movie—then the ultimate betrayal. Boy breaks girl's heart. Am I getting close?"

She didn't answer, only stared.

Jack continued, "You can't spend the rest of your life taking it out on every man who comes along."

Cass desperately fought back tears. If he didn't stop, she was sure her heart would break all over again. Making the first offensive strike worked in war, in football—and in love, she thought. Recovering some of her composure, she said in a steady voice, "That's very good. Do you use it on every woman who isn't immediately smitten by your charm and good looks?"

She watched to see how her unkind words affected him. But he didn't react, not the way she'd imagined.

Instead he chuckled. His warm eyes embraced her. "All men are not alike. There's one or two among us who are considerable gentlemen. One or two who would never mislead or deceive."

"Look," she said, checking her watch. "It's late. I really have to get back to Venice. I'm afraid there are some script changes I need to go over first thing in the morning."

"On a Saturday? Nonsense. The night is young. There are still so many surprises to be discovered."

Cass continued to protest. "No, really, I must get back. There's work that has to get done on the final scene."

"Nonsense," Jack said just before he leaned over and picked up the house phone to let the concierge know that they were ready to leave.

Monsieur Lareaux returned with their coats.

Jack helped Cass into her cape and said, "Yes. We'd better get going. The Moulin Rouge awaits."

Still reminiscent of Toulouse-Lautrec's posters of the famed cancan girls, the Moulin Rouge was the embodiment of Parisian after-hours glamour and energy. From there, they caught the late show at the Lido, one of Paris's most famous cabarets. Their final stop was the Crazy Horse, where the striptease was elevated to an art form.

It was now after three-thirty A.M. As they left the club, practically running through the downpour, Jack said, "I don't think it's a good idea to try to fly back to Venice in this weather. At least not until daylight. My plane's too light."

Cass cringed, the cold wind shooting through her thin wrap. They were steps from the waiting limo. And with rain splashing against her cheeks, dripping down her face, she replied, "What do you suggest? Perhaps that we get a room? Because if that was your plan all along, I can assure you, you've made a terrible mistake."

He eyed her incredulously. "Do you think I arranged for this horrific weather? Rest assured, even *I* am not capable of that."

"Let me guess, is this the part where we show up at some fancy hotel only to find out they've only one room left with one king-size bed?"

As he pushed her inside the car, he said, "That was *It Happened One Night* with Gable and Colbert. No, I'm afraid, Ms. English, this is real life. And this situation was most definitely not planned."

The driver fired the heat up high and Jack struggled out of his sopping-wet Chesterfield coat.

"As for your theory, you are right on two accounts. The hotel is fancy, but it's not one room, it's an entire floor." He turned to her; a smug smile covered his face. "And yes, you might say I planned it ahead of time, if you consider reserving space all year long at the Ritz premeditation. The executives of my company—Roger included—spend a lot of time in Paris, Cassidy. Sorry to burst your bubble. It's good corporate economics to have a place for them to stay at a moment's notice."

Cass couldn't identify the uneasy feeling inside. Was she angry or insulted or embarrassed or perhaps a little of all three?

They drove to the Ritz in silence. Cassidy missed the warm connection they'd built through the night. What an ass she was to pull it all apart in a moment.

| | |

Chelsea had just slipped a ten-thousand-lire note in the bellhop's jacket. The swarthy young Italian had told her that he'd observed Ms. English leaving the hotel sometime between eight and eight-thirty P.M. She had not been alone. According to the bellhop, Ms. English was escorted by none other than Mr. Cavelli, whom the bellhop knew by name.

The young Italian had also managed to slip her a spare key to Cass's suite. It was amazing how far money got one these days.

Chelsea paused in the foyer of Cassidy's suite. She glanced into the living room, taking in the magnificent splendor of the space, comparing it to her own, of course. But the furnishings and the elaborate floors, walls, and decorations held no real interest for her. She had other things on her mind. Chelsea moved through the suite, floating, pulled by an unimaginable force, until she reached the bedroom. The temporary heart of the princess. The private abode where Cassidy retreated each evening and carried out her mundane, pathetic ritual, which some might call work.

Chelsea crossed the threshold and, immediately, she was enveloped in envy. Lavender roses, hundreds of them, filled the room. Their heady scent was sweet, powerful, and overwhelmingly thick. She didn't have to see a card to know they were from Jack.

Her eyes took in every detail as she made her way around the room. The lace canopy enveloped a queen-size bed which, though hardly different from the one in Chelsea's own room, seemed to her eyes more regal. The room was cream colored with white moldings and the bedding and curtains continued the white-on-white theme—a satin quilted bedspread, four pillows in hand-stitched embroidery perched against the bleached oak headboard. Lace draperies, left slightly parted, whispered in the cool night breeze. Spiral-bound pads, no doubt filled with notes for the movie, and scripts—lots of them—were piled high on the night table.

There was a Louis XIV desk, on top of which was an old photo of Lana in a beautiful silver-and-gold frame. The image was grainy, its edges yellowed, but the legendary movie star's indisputable beauty shone through. The light from overhead fell through the glass and seemed to illuminate her perfect features.

Chelsea looked more closely at her mother's image, searching for similarities, recognizing certain characteristics. They shared the same nose and eyes. But the resemblance of Bella to her grandmother precluded any doubt that Lana was Bella's blood.

Chelsea set the photo back down and went over to the bed. Had she and Jack slept together yet? How far had Jack gotten in his plan?

Chelsea sat and pushed back, sinking into the soft comforter and mounds of pillows.

Her presence was most powerful here. Chelsea could smell Cass's scent, sweet and floral, lingering on the delicate fabrics. Her outstretched arms roamed the mattress, imagining for a moment what it felt like to be on top of the world. Soon, she thought. First Cassidy had to suffer—had to experience the pain and heartache she did.

She was floating in a state of peace, her body now at ease, but her mind was in overdrive. As she stared up at the ceiling, a million different scenarios of Cass's ruination shuffled through her head. A broken heart perhaps? Professional demise? Something drastic, devastating had to happen.

First things first. At the moment, *Dangerous Intentions* meant more to Cass than anything on earth. But sabotaging the film would be like cutting her own nose to spite her face. Chelsea wanted and needed this role and the accolades it would bring. If everything went according to plan, she would be as big as Pfeiffer, Sarandon, even Gwyneth Paltrow.

The old adage "Give someone enough rope and soon they'll hang themselves" would definitely work here. Cass was going to self-destruct.

The very thought sent Chelsea's mind racing. And Jack was going to help Chelsea in bringing about Cassidy's demise. God knows, there was no one who could take a woman down more sweetly and with such savagery as Jack Cavelli.

The throbbing in Chelsea's temples came on all at once and quickly intensified. The all-too-familiar feeling of mania suddenly came over her. She bolted from the bed and began pacing the room, moving swiftly from one corner to another and back again. The voices began, softly at first, then became loud and abrasive.

Staring at her reflection in the mirror above the dresser, Chelsea watched her features morph, becoming ugly and distorted, with that same faraway gaze now in her eyes.

Are you scared? Of course you are. You'll never win. Not against him . . . or her.

"No!" Chelsea shouted. "No, no, no, no . . ." She massaged her temples in a practiced semicircular motion. But her efforts to ease the pounding failed. The next dip in her emotions was as predictable as worms rising from the earth after a spring rainstorm. She felt propelled by anguish to act, do anything, until the bad side of her was satisfied and the voices ceased.

Thirty-three years of ridicule. Don't you think the time has come for retribution? That bitch stole your name, your being, your life.

The voices now dominated her own ability to reason. An alien being had invaded her body. The strengthening force propelled her into the bathroom. She opened the medicine cabinet and rummaged through its contents—nothing to assuage the spirits in her head.

Then her eyes rested again on the picture of Lana. Running now, Chelsea slammed the old photo down on the nightstand and ran out the door of the suite.

| | |

Jack and Cassidy had returned to the Place Vendome. The Ritz was, without doubt, the most exquisite gem of all Paris hotels. Festooned with gilt and ormolu, its halls, swathed in heavy silk and tapestries, dripped with crystal chandeliers. Here the world's rich, those beyond celebrity, chose to stay in not just glorious surroundings, but in the hands of the most skilled and discreet hoteliers in the world. Here the patrons chose anonymity; in fact, they demanded it. And the Ritz knew exactly what to supply.

The moment Cassidy and Jack arrived, they were whisked through the nondescript and well-secured lobby into the elevator and up to the top floor, where Jack owned one of the penthouse apartments.

Jack had promised her rooms to choose from, but Cass certainly hadn't expected to find at least a dozen of them, five of them bedrooms, each bedroom sealed off from the others except for two: The master suite opened onto a bathroom that included a Jacuzzi and sauna; this bathroom led to a dressing room, which in turn led to another large bedroom.

While Cassidy's heart jumped into her throat, her legs headed directly for the second master bedroom, what was sometimes called the "mistress" room. After a brief look around, during which Cassidy willed herself not to even glance at the bed, her fear propelled her out of the exquisite bedroom.

Instead she chose the smallest, coziest guest room. Finely decorated with early baroque furniture and fine raw silk fabrics in delicate hues of peach and pale blues, it had windows with magnificent, panoramic views of the city. Here she'd make her stand.

She removed her wrap and shoes, both sopping wet, and headed straight for the bathroom. Her reflection in the mirror confirmed her suspicions. Her hair was flat and stringy, and her makeup had run down her face. The delicate silk-and-wool blend of the new Donna Karan dress was beginning to pucker.

She washed her face and dried her hair. Warily, she eyed the soft terry-cloth robe hanging behind the door. She couldn't help but wonder what other women had worn it—and how many? Not that it had any bearing on *her* life.

Never mind the fact that she had spent a most intoxicating evening with the man she might have cast as the hero if ever there was a romantic movie in her future. Assuming, of course, that she had a future in the film business.

Was Jack vindictive by nature or just ruthless? Because whatever switch she'd accidentally tripped by doubting him had slammed shut the opening between them. As soon as they arrived here, he'd locked himself behind the two massive mahogany doors of the private master bedroom suite.

This was turning out to be a terrible ending for a nearly perfect night.

What if her unwillingness to fall for his ploy caused Jack to scrap the movie?

Cassidy's gut told her that as long as *Dangerous Intentions* lived up to the word of mouth and came in on time, and under budget, Jack would not stand in her way in Hollywood. In fact, she was certain that, insulted or not, he'd honor his guarantee to deliver Desmond into her hands. All she must do was focus on these last critical days of shooting. No sweat. Now all she needed, craved, were a warm bed and a few hours of sleep. She stepped out of the bathroom and hung her dress and undergarments over the radiator.

There was a knock at the door and Cass nearly jumped out of her skin.

The butler, a middle-aged Englishman named Nigel, stuck his head inside and asked, "Can I get you a cup of hot tea, perhaps some warm milk, madame?"

Cass gave him a warm smile. "Actually, tea would be wonderful. Thank you."

He started to leave, but she continued talking. "Is Mr. Cavelli . . . asleep?"

"No, madame." The Englishman bowed his head slightly. "Mr. Cavelli is having tea in the salon."

Cassidy was surprised that she felt slighted by not being invited to join her host. She wondered if Jack was now punishing her for accusing him of setting her up, of trying to get her into bed.

"On second thought, I've changed my mind. I'll be joining Mr. Cavelli in the salon."

"Very well, madame," he replied, then left.

When the door closed, Cass scrambled about in search of props and preparations to enhance her dreadful appearance. She emptied her black evening bag on the bed, finding a tube of pale pink lipstick, a blush compact, and a miniature perfume atomizer. She was thankful that the room came equipped with a new brush and comb, toothbrush and paste. This was not enough for a complete makeover, but it would have to do.

Fifteen minutes later she emerged, recharged and refreshed. Her hair and dress were now dry thanks to a blow-dryer the hotel provided. Her face was clean, with just a dab of lipstick and blush, and she wore a hint of her favorite scent.

Cass practically tiptoed down the marble hall to the salon. Without taking time to absorb the opulent surroundings, she focused immediately on Jack. He sat in a dark velvet armchair, his back to her, staring at the fire that crackled in the mammoth fireplace that was the focal point of the room—a simple dark wooden mantle-and-slate hearth, reminiscent of Frank Lloyd Wright's Usonian designs.

It was clear that the dark, brooding man before her was not going to acknowledge her presence.

Cass stood in the doorway for what seemed like an eternity and then turned around a matching armchair so that she could sit down next to him. The silk embroidered fabric swished against her dress. For a few moments that was the only sound in the room. That and the crackling fire.

Finally she spoke. "I'm sorry. I was very hard on you. I jumped the gun."

He didn't respond, only listened. He took a sip from his tea and set the cup down. Silently.

"You were right . . . what you said earlier tonight about my not trusting men."

Jack tilted his head slightly and raised an eyebrow. Another moment of silence, then he said, "Go on . . . I'm listening."

Cass became nervous. Other men, including Rudolpho, had expressed interest in what made her tick, but she'd known instinctively that their concern was only a ploy to get intimate with her. Jack's interest was sincere. She was certain of that. She had read that Cavelli was curious about the people around him, and those "people" now included her.

"Remember that awful scene Jonathan made when we were talking at my father's party?"

Jack nodded. He evaluated her every word.

"Well, he was referring to something that happened a long time ago, to a different Cassidy English. I was young, barely eighteen. I fell in love with someone who broke my heart."

She looked far beyond Jack, remembering those horrible years after Tom. "He devastated me."

Jack started to speak, but she held up a hand to silence him. "The specifics don't matter. What does is that I was betrayed. I made another person the center of my universe because I was young, stupid."

"And lonely?" he asked.

Cassidy nodded.

He continued, "And living like some foster child who nobody cared about?"

Her thoughts left the past and returned to the present. *How did he know these things about her?*

Jack had tapped the door that slammed shut when she left LAX, abandoned, all those years ago. He had loosened the pile of painful memories she'd stacked so neatly and put away on a shelf in her heart labeled "Cold Storage." Her cries came from a cave where feelings had hibernated. The tears seeped out at first, then they flowed.

Jack stood up and moved toward her. He reached for her hands and pulled her up. They faced each other, their bodies just inches apart. With his hand he gently wiped away her tears. And then he kissed her. He placed his hands on either side of her face, framing her gently, then he lowered his head, brushed her mouth with his. Their lips barely touched.

"Tell me what you want," he whispered. He ran his hands over her shoulders and down her arms to her hands, never once taking his eyes off of hers.

Cass closed her eyes, imagining his hands roaming her body, pulling her closer. The heat radiating from her heart's core was intense. She fought hard to hold back the desire that had been let loose. She realized that she was embarrassed by her longing and felt her face flush.

And without thinking, she replied, "You."

He brought his lips down on hers again, this time with much more force and aggression. His lips parted, his tongue mingled with hers. Then he pulled back teasingly, playfully biting her lower lip.

The losses and betrayals, past and present, were swept away in that moment. Jack made her forget Tom, the abortion, the abuse heaped upon her by her vicious aunt and uncle . . . her father's quest for control, Rudolpho's deception, the stress of completing *Dangerous Intentions,* and the unbearable loneliness she'd grown so accustomed to throughout her life.

Then suddenly and abruptly, Jack pulled back, taking her newborn happiness with him.

"It's awfully late. . . . You really should get some rest."

Confused, not able to speak around the lump in her throat, Cass remained silent.

"Nigel will bring you something to sleep in." He reached for the poker and stabbed at the burning wood, causing sparks and crackles. And with his back now to her he said, "I'm afraid I have nothing frilly and feminine. But I'm sure one of my silk pajama tops will do."

"Is that all?" she replied.

He turned to face her; his finely chiseled features, lit from behind by the fire, appeared unreadable, unearthly. He spoke almost in a whisper. "I just think if we let things go any further, we would be making a mistake. There's too much at stake. Each of us is vulnerable, in our own ways. Your needs are personal, mine are professional. To mix the two would be a mistake."

Cass nodded and feigned a smile.

He gently took her arm and led her to the door.

"I think you are an incredible woman—beautiful, intelligent, and filled with so much passion. The very thought of spending the night with you, making love to you over and over, is enough to drive me wild with want—need." He cupped her chin in the palms of his hands. "You do understand, don't you?"

Despite her disappointment, Cass had to agree. In fact, she applauded his honesty. He could easily have taken advantage of her. She would have allowed him to. But he didn't and for that she commended him.

"You're a true gentleman." This time her smile was genuine.

He lifted her chin just a bit and stared at her long and hard. "Don't tell anyone, you'll ruin my reputation."

They shared a laugh.

He leaned down and brushed her forehead with a gentle kiss.

"Good night."

| | |

He sat in front of the roaring fire sipping his tea. All he could think about was the young woman sleeping down the hall. Blurred images of Cassidy played out in slow motion in his head. He was so close to possessing her, it stunned him. Chelsea had planted the seed, but it had grown into something huge, beyond even his intention. Make Cassidy fall in love with him and then it would be easy to grab total control of Desmond away from Roger.

Great idea, except Cassidy was his fantasy woman. She was beautiful beyond belief, witty, sophisticated, and so unaffected by the razzle-dazzle world that surrounded her. Everything she did was sincere, every emotion she expressed was genuine. There was nothing fake, nothing make-believe, about her. Never before had he known a woman so tenacious, so passionate. He was swept up in his yearning for her.

And also he was afraid. This need and passion were stronger than he was.

Having her only as a fantasy wasn't enough. He longed to observe her during her most private moments—even in sleep. He couldn't help himself. Knowing she was mere feet from him, just imagining her legs tangled in blankets and sheets, her wild mane tousled about the pillows, was too much for him to bear. So he tiptoed silently into her room to watch her.

Then quietly he returned to the sitting room. She was so much like her mother. Jack did not want to need Cassidy the way he had needed Lana. Could he survive another onslaught of that magnitude?

Just one kiss had won her over, he was sure of that. He easily could have had her tonight, but it was her soul he wanted, her very being. He needed for her to trust him, to open up and let him inside.

Sometime during their night together Cassidy had moved into his heart, and now she possessed him; not the other way around. This was not what he had intended. Jack was losing control.

When you got right down to it, this wasn't personal, it was business. *All* business. He held the sole minority block of Desmond stock—forty-two percent—yet Desmond represented roughly fifty percent of Colossal's holdings. From the beginning, Jack had set his course on gaining *total* control of Desmond, wresting it away from Roger Turmaine. For Lana. That had been his sole motivation in getting involved with Turmaine in the first place. Now Turmaine was old and ill, and it was apparent that his son, Jonathan, was not equipped to run the company. He hadn't counted on Cassidy English to factor so strongly into the picture.

The Colossal umbrella was already a power to be reckoned with in the industry. But were Jack to take total control of Desmond, it—*he*—would be unstoppable.

All barriers needed to be destroyed for his plan to work. For this to happen, he had to get to Cassidy . . . and get over his memories of Lana.

She still lived under his skin. The love of his youth, Lana Turmaine had been his mentor, a star who was his inspiration. Mother and now daughter. Both were fiery and exciting and not easily controlled; both left him weak, even humbled. His intense desire for Cassidy was making him question his own motives. The game was nearly over. That was good. He couldn't hold out much longer. It was too debilitating, too time consuming. And it took him away from reality—his work.

James was staring at the setup in one of the conference rooms at the Hotel Cipriani. He and Roger had flown in only two hours earlier. Both had called Cass's suite, but either she was not answering her phone or she had left the hotel for the day.

James had insisted that if Roger was going off to Venice to "check up" on Cassidy, then he was joining him. Cassidy and her father's telephone calls had been warm, even productive, yet an undercurrent of tension had been building over her refusal to follow *all* of Roger's advice about the filming of *Dangerous Intentions*. At least James stood half a chance of keeping their meeting, which was destined to become confrontational, from reaching a distasteful crescendo.

However, neither man could have predicted the seismic effect of seeing the rough cut of *Dangerous Intentions* in its entirety—or, more specifically, the leading actress's impact.

The character of Ophelia, played by Chelsea Hutton, had brought a face from the past into heart-wrenching reality.

James remembered the face and, he knew, so did Roger. Somehow this strange woman, the intruder who had claimed to be Roger's daughter, had manipulated Cassidy to win the lead in *Dangerous Intentions*. James wondered whether Chelsea knew that her likeness to Lana would come through in this way. Was that what she'd really been up to? Had he underestimated Chelsea Hutton? Had she outmaneuvered him? Clearly she was using Cass and *Dangerous Intentions* to get what she wanted. And he was helpless to stop her. Once *Dangerous* was released, she'd have the public's sympathy and ear. Cass couldn't possibly have a clue as to what she was up to. James was sure of that.

James had the technician stop the film and asked that he and Roger be left alone.

"You recognize her?" James understood Roger's tone. He was look-ing to his friend to dispel his fear. But James couldn't give him that relief now.

"I recognized her at the party, then again when I saw the first dailies with Jack. I guess I was distracted enough not to realize *how* I knew her."

Roger called the technician back and had him roll the film again. The actress moved about the screen like a cat, and James and Roger watched the woman's familiar feline grace. As soon as the men were alone again, Roger said, "I need to talk to Cass. If this Hutton woman gets to her first, she'll be lost to me forever. I couldn't live through that now."

James looked at his old friend. "I'll see what I can do." He thought of a dozen different scenarios to present to Cass, but she was no longer a child. She would easily see through his disguise. "I think we should stick to a conventional story. You were young and foolish, did some cat-ting around, and your irresponsible behavior may have produced a child—you couldn't be sure. Then we can assure Cass that you would never intentionally hurt her. No, you love her far too much. In the end she'll believe you—she'll have no other choice."

Roger turned to James. "Arrange for Ms. Hutton to have dinner with me in my suite at eight o'clock."

| | |

Cass was sipping chamomile tea in bed when the butler knocked on her door and delivered numerous bags and boxes from all the finest shops in Paris.

A bit confused, certain someone had made a mistake, she said, "These aren't for me. . . . I didn't order—"

The butler interrupted her midsentence. "Mr. Cavelli asked that they be delivered before noon." He checked his watch, even compared it to the antique clock on the night table, and smiled. "Fifteen minutes to. I like to carry out orders precisely." He removed an envelope from inside his jacket pocket and handed it to her. "Mr. Cavelli also asked that I give you this." She thanked him, and as he left the room, she eyed the pack-ages: Chanel, Prada, La Perla, and Dior. Her heart raced as she tore open the envelope.

I awoke a bit earlier than usual this morning, and instead of sending out for the trades or waking my secretary in L.A. and driving her crazy dictating memos and ordering everyone around from here, I decided to use my extra time wisely—shopping for some clothes and accessories that I know you need since I couldn't get you back to Venice when I promised. I must admit it was quite a challenge to find items dazzling enough to complement one of such beauty as you.

Please accept them not only as my apology for not getting you "home" last night, but as a token of my affection . . . and my invitation to join me for dinner on the Riviera.
Hoping this evens the score.
Warmly, Jack

P.S. I must admit I had to consult the young lady at the salon off the lobby about the maquillage. *If the colors aren't right or if you need anything else, please call and ask for Jeanne-Marie.*

One minute Jack could easily convince her he was driven by ego, and then the next that they should stay clear of each other, and now *this*. Cass felt pushed and pulled, confused and conflicted. She had no idea what to feel: joy, confusion . . . fear?

Her head told her to get angry—he was toying with her emotions, and at a time when it was imperative for both of them that she maintain her balance. But maybe he was confused, too. He was used to the complications of business—did that make him ready for life's complications?

As he had pointed out, they both had to be careful. She couldn't allow herself to be hurt again. She had to remain in full control.

She pondered what to do about the gifts. Should she do the right thing, remind him of his own caution and return them? It wasn't as though no one had ever showered her with expensive clothing. Once Rudolpho had sent her an entire wardrobe because, he said, he was tired of seeing her in "perfect black Chanel suits." (She'd pointed out that she also owned one in navy blue.) And Roger had done the same for her when he convinced her to remain in L.A. So why return these?

Cut the bullshit, she thought, and went to the telephone to call Jack before she lost her resolve to say thanks but no thanks.

"Does it feel like Christmas morning?" he asked before she could say anything. His voice was all honey.

"Well, honestly, I haven't—"

"Don't say another word. I have a definite motive for sending you those clothes. As I said in my note—you *have* read it, haven't you?—a very influential business associate of mine has invited me to the Riviera tonight. Dinner parties bore me to death. Can you find it in your heart to accompany me for dinner, dancing, and whatever?"

"Whatever" could mean a hundred things, but she didn't care. Cass was instantly under his spell. "But I thought you wanted to separate our business and . . . whatever."

"Are you listening, Ms. English? This *is* business."

She didn't have to think any more about it. Bags of beautiful gifts beckoned. "Then it would be my pleasure."

"Well, I suggest you try on your clothing. You might need tailoring."

"No, I'm sure they'll fit." She could scarcely speak. Her heart was on a seesaw with her brain. *Dangerous* with its final details seemed a million miles away.

"Then I'll call for you at seven." He paused. "Notice I'm not sending my driver!"

"You're a quick study. I'll give you that." She laughed lightly, but inside she felt like a total wreck.

"Au revoir." Jack rang off.

In a Chanel bag she found not one, but two pairs of shoes. The pair meant for this evening were incredibly sexy high heels—off-white *peau de soie* T-straps with rhinestone buckles. The second was a pair of low-heeled black pumps made of glove-soft leather. She found a note card that read, "Comfortable shoes to help you run faster making our movie!" She smiled and moved on to a second Chanel bag. Nestled in tissue paper was a delicate off-white silk pleated clutch. Wrapped neatly in a packet of tissue were three pairs of gossamer silk stockings—cream, nude, and black.

Next she opened the Lagerfeld bag and found an elegant sweater set—a jewel-toned draped-neck pullover with a solid amethyst blazer with rolled collar and raglan sleeves. The next tissue-wrapped bundle contained exquisite black silk trousers with loose straight legs. Other packages revealed a classic Prada shoulder bag, a simple lightweight wool-and-silk slip dress with matching three-quarter-length double-breasted jacket, and a skirt and blazer in soft glove-leather the color of fresh butter, with a matching silk shirt, loafers, and clutch, also from Prada. Oh, he *had* been busy.

Cass saved the Christian Dior garment bag for last. Inside the beige bag were layers of tissue that crinkled and rustled as she tore it to find an off-white, backless tank dress made of diaphanous silk and cashmere crepe, draped slightly in front to expose just a bit of cleavage. She tried it on. The handkerchief-hemmed skirt flared ever so slightly so that it moved gracefully as she twirled before the mirror. Usually Cassidy couldn't be bothered with evening clothes, resenting the concept of formal dress and the functions that went with them, but this dress changed her attitude in a minute. How could this man who hardly knew her select a gown she'd have bought for herself?

The bias cut and body-clinging fit of this obviously handmade gown precluded the wearing of undergarments. "Mmm, what would Edith Head have given Marilyn to wear with this?" she mused.

Jack—or whoever he had engaged to shop for him—had chosen an assortment of lingerie, so beautiful they would fulfill the fantasy of any woman, or man, on earth! In addition to a pearl-white satin La Perla nightgown with matching peignoir and slippers, she found the sexiest, most exquisite bras, panties, camisoles, and teddies she'd ever seen—and she'd seen plenty, since beautiful "under-things," as Nanny Rae always called them, had always been her passion, ever since she played dress-up in Lana's closet.

| | |

When Cass opened the door to him, Jack's eyes roamed her body. Exquisite, he thought, but dared not say. Instead he smiled. "The dress fits as if it were made for you."

His voice quivered. The moment seemed an echo, a repeat from a long, long time ago. Lana, the night she was murdered dressed in a similar gown. Jack had managed, without meaning it, to summon feelings better left buried. What had possessed him to buy this sensual, evocative gown for her? Was he losing his edge? After all, his goal was to *dissolve* Desmond, not fuse with its new executive producer.

Cass nodded her thanks with a half smile.

As he helped her on with the light lace wrap, also from Dior, Jack studied her from behind: the long, luscious hair, the bare shoulders that begged to be kissed. Purposefully, he let his hand linger for a moment on the small of her bare back. To feel her skin made his resolve crumble a little more. He had to gain control of this game he had started.

His own history had taught him this lesson. The past is prologue, he reminded himself. Cassidy had to think she was reading him, leading him. But he had to keep the delicate balance even between them. He could lose his business, his future, even himself if he wasn't careful to stay one step ahead of her—and his heart.

| | |

It was dusk when they landed at Nice airport. They were whisked by limo along narrow and winding coastal roads until they reached Monaco, a virtual paradise by the sea. The Hotel de Paris, with its enchanting snow-white filigree and sculptured facade, lit with thousands of lights and overlooking the Place du Casino, was positively breathtaking. The red carpet welcomed them as if they were royalty, and the Baccarat crystal chandeliers sparkled like millions of lightning bugs on a summer's night.

So enraptured by the lights of the casino, Cassidy was slow to realize that she and Jack were the object of what seemed like hundreds of cameras. Microphones appeared out of nowhere to invade her space. She felt sudden panic. Just then Jack grabbed her elbow and ran like a quarterback, steering her away from the chaos.

"We're safe here," he said once they'd reached the bank of elevators. "The staff at the Place de Casino is more difficult to get past than the entire French army."

He smiled down at her, apparently unfazed by the commotion. She drew strength from his calm eyes. Then something—a storm, a black moment—flashed across his face, his eyes, then Jack was saying something to her.

"By tomorrow the tabloids will have us already at the altar," he said, laughing mirthlessly.

Suddenly she felt a flash of confusion. Her emotions dipped and rolled. For an instant, it was as though she were standing on shaky ground.

"Would that be so terrible?" he asked. "You look terrified."

She had no time to answer, for just then a dark-haired man, dressed in a top hat and tails, greeted them warmly at the elevators. "Monsieur Cavelli, it's so good to have you back."

Women, bedecked in elaborate evening gowns and expensive jewels, accompanied by handsome gentlemen, all in black tie, moved in and out of the lobby as though choreographed.

The elevator opened directly into a glorious suite with a breathtaking panoramic view of Monte Carlo through a glorious wall of windows.

Before this moment, Monaco had been a vague locale, a fairy-tale principality—James Bond, Princess Grace. . . . For Cass, the name signified only the terrible death of the beautiful, blond princess, Hollywood's own Grace Kelly. And, of course, the casino and its history, which overshadowed all other gambling houses in the world.

Behind her, she heard the bellman arrange their luggage, the maid begin unpacking, polite questions to ascertain that everything met Mr. Cavelli's approval. Then the door shut and she was alone with Jack.

"Let me show you to your room," he said and led her through the suite, which contained a living room with a fireplace, a dining room, a library, two bedrooms, and three baths. The suite was the size of a small house!

Unlike the Ritz, it wasn't grandiose or ornate, but rather warm and intimate. The floors were covered in plush apricot carpeting; the walls, pale peach moiré fabric. The draperies were luxurious silks and soft tapestries, inspired by the floral needlepoints of the beloved late Princess Grace.

Cassidy's bedroom was in the back, where a large balcony overlooked the port. The room's decor was softly feminine and incredibly romantic. Sheer ivory silk was draped from the ceiling over the bed's four posters, then puddled onto the cream-colored carpet. One of the maids had turned down the bed already, exposing off-white Frette sheets and silk-satin pillowcases.

Jack left her standing at the window as the enchantment of Monte Carlo went to her head. Cass stepped through the French doors and onto the balcony, where she found herself standing above the Mediterranean Sea. A warm wind blew and she put aside the lace wrap to let the friendly air embrace her. Beneath the sheer gown, she felt her nipples harden, responding to the sea wind, which touched her like a lover. She breathed deeply, wanting to capture the moment. Electricity passed through her being as she became aware of Jack's presence behind her. She wished she knew what he was thinking.

"We should get going. Dinner is called for eight-thirty." His mellow voice penetrated her thoughts.

She spun around to meet his gaze. Her eyes opened wide with excitement, and a smile curved the corners of her mouth.

"I take it you're pleased with the accommodations."

"Very," she replied with just the hint of a giggle in her voice.

"Good. I promise I'll have you back in Venice, hard at work, by noon tomorrow."

She wanted to say, "Please don't take me back, not yet. . . ." The truth was, she didn't want the weekend to be over, but all she said was, "Very well." She started for the door, but his words stopped her.

"There is one thing I forgot. . . ."

Cass had a puzzled look on her face. "Yes?"

He reached inside his suit jacket and produced a black velvet box.

"Just one more gift."

"Oh, no," she started to protest, but he hushed her.

"I insist. . . . It will complete the magnificent package." He handed it to her. "Open it. Please." His voice was insistent.

With trembling hands she removed the lid. Inside were the sapphire-and-diamond earrings she'd seen when they visited Boucheron, the ones she'd admired in the window.

She spoke. "No . . . Jack . . . really, I can't."

"You have to," he replied. "The ladies downstairs are dripping in diamonds. You'll feel terribly out of place, I'm afraid."

Still she hesitated.

"Well then, take them on loan. Celebrities do it all the time."

Jack wasn't used to not getting his way, so she indulged him.

She clipped them on, even though her hands were still shaky. She glided to the large baroque mirror in the hall and stared at her reflection. The brilliance of the gems was dazzling.

"The sapphires are as brilliant as your eyes," he said, leading her to the door, his hand gently placed at her waist. "You'll be the envy of every woman there."

"And what's more important to you, Jack, than being noticed by every man?" She spoke not with sarcasm but with a hint of mischief in her voice.

| | |

The other guests were already socializing over cocktails when Jack and Cass arrived at the private dining room off the lobby. At least twenty round tables spread with white damask cloths encircled the room, each set with the most regal china and silver imaginable—dinner plates on gold chargers, baroque gold-washed flatware—around exquisite candelabras and beautiful white lilies.

Servers, dressed in starched white shirts, black trousers, and white gloves, served champagne from trays and offered the guests hors d'oeuvres. As they watched, the servers disappeared and several chefs stepped forward.

"I see Anton's decided to go casual tonight," Jack whispered into Cass's ear, indicating the three serving stations positioned around the room. "Buffet."

Indeed, the tables were laden with entrées—lobster, Chateaubriand, pheasants, perfectly blanched vegetables, glorious salads, fruits, and delicious cheeses. At each, a toque-clad chef carved and served meats to order, while waiters provided impeccable white glove service, right down to carrying the plates, filled to order, to the table.

Jack was not surprised that everyone in the room found a moment to study Cassidy—discreetly, of course—though he found it amusing to catch one or two of them and embarrass them by breaking their gaze.

He actually overheard one woman whose blond hair stood out in clumps like an aging club kid's say, "Guess she's the new flavor of the month."

One of the women with her, younger though rather homely, responded haughtily, "No doubt another aspiring actress or model."

"By midnight she'll be yesterday's news," retorted another.

Jack was enjoying the eavesdropping. It was better than actually having to make small talk with these people. The men, of course, had a different take on Cassidy.

"Jack's caught himself a keeper this time," said a silver-haired gentleman with patrician features. Jack knew this man, Claude DuPrey. They had invested together in a London play.

Jack caught Cass's eyes. She looked up at him and her eyes said everything: *Get me out of here, this makes me crazy.*

Whispering in her ear, he said, "An hour, tops—I promise. Then we'll leave."

She nodded, and seconds later he was swept into the crowd, working the room like a diplomat.

Cass, Jack noticed, did her share of mingling as well. She was polite and charming, graceful and witty. Her presence seemed to throw the room into a tailspin.

Jack couldn't help but feel proud. He stood in a corner, where powerful businessmen and women would crowd around him, each one vying for his attention. He glanced Cass's way every now and again and gave her a warm smile. He had known she'd be an asset as his date, but he had not realized she'd actually steal the show. At one point he excused himself, sneaked up behind her, placed his hand delicately on the small of her back, and whispered, "You're magnificent. Look around the room. Everyone is under your spell."

The party ended just before midnight. Jack decided the night was still young and so he insisted they visit the casino.

Cassidy English had traveled to many places. She'd spent her childhood as a princess in a Hollywood mansion. She'd been to the Taj Mahal, the greatest castles of Scotland, England, and Ireland. In China she had toured the sacred Imperial City. She thought there was no grand display of enormous wealth on the entire planet that had escaped her, but she was wrong. There was Monte Carlo.

The crystal and marble lobby was decorated with subtle opulence. Not for Monte Carlo was the glitter, huge children's games, and loud thumping music of other casinos—no, this was no theme park. Here, gambling was gracious; gamblers might be drunk or they may have made their fortunes in distasteful ways, but the trappings bespoke elegance.

Cass was not a gambler, although she had been to Las Vegas on a number of assignments. But Vegas and Monte Carlo shared as much in common as, say, Jupiter and Earth. This was the international elite. Quite a few of the guests had titles: counts from Eastern Europe and knighted Englishmen. Sheiks in custom-made suits, shirts, shoes, played baccarat, and one look at the chips stacked on the table told Cass the stakes were high.

They walked around a bit as Jack busily greeted old friends and well-wishers. Cass was engrossed by the sight of gentlemen and women, young and old, standing by piled stacks of chips on the green roulette tables. The wheel was spun, the ball found its numbered slot, and the chips were swept away by skillful croupiers.

An impeccably groomed floor manager swooped down upon them, arriving at Jack's side with a huge welcoming smile on his face. "Monsieur Cavelli, what a pleasant surprise."

Jack returned the smile. "Good evening, Albin. Have you an interesting table for me tonight?"

The gentleman nodded. "Of course, sir. Right this way." He gestured across the opulent casino.

Jack escorted Cass across the floor to the *salons privés* and into an elegant gaming room— a glittering jewel-box casino within the casino, where the minimum bets began at one thousand francs.

A couple of the tuxedo-clad gentlemen seated around the table looked up; one acknowledged Jack with a slight nod. They had placed their bets, ready for play to begin.

"Perhaps I should wait outside . . . since I'm not playing," Cassidy whispered.

"That's impossible. The game has started. Place your bet," Jack replied with a sly smile. He pulled out a red velvet chair and gestured for her to sit.

Cass looked him straight in the eye. "You're kidding?"

He offered no response.

"You're *not* kidding." The croupier pushed a stack of chips in front of her. "But . . . I don't know how to play. . . . I've never . . ."

He stared back. "Then I'll teach you." He directed his attention to the other players and asked politely, "I'm sure all of you won't mind if I take a moment to teach the beautiful lady to play?"

The other players and the croupier, a stunning red-haired woman dressed in a raw silk Armani tuxedo, all gave the go-ahead.

Jack and Cass played for two hours and neither of them came out a winner. But throughout the entire evening, Jack could feel Cass by his side. When he leaned into her, to direct her play or explain the different nuances of the game, he inhaled her scent. It was all he could do to stop himself from whisking her out onto the balcony that overlooked the cove below.

He tried to concentrate on his game. He had to keep his cool. One step at a time.

After they were finished playing, they waited in a candle-lit bar as Albin cashed out Jack's account for the evening. Then they strolled back to their hotel.

Jack saw Cass to her room. He hesitated, not wanting to push too far. All he said was, "Good night, Cass. Thank you for such a wonderful evening."

| | |

The thought of going about her nightly ritual—taking off the dress, cleansing her face, putting away her jewelry—struck Cass as bizarre, surreal under the circumstances. So, having removed her shoes and stockings, she found the night wind blowing in from the terrace irresistible. Barefoot, she went through the doors onto the balcony. There, suspended over the sea, she watched the lights in the distance—Cap d'Antibes, where night never ended but, instead, melted into the next day's party.

Suddenly she was startled by a sound to her left, but Cass didn't have to look. Her body told her that Jack was there. How stupid of her not to realize that he, too, might want to step out onto his own terrace. Well, there was nothing to do but try to slip back into her room in silence. As she moved inside, Cass looked back to find Jack's eyes. Without saying a word, he seemed to call her, commanding her to come closer.

Now, her back against the French doors, she closed her eyes in anguish. Never before had she felt such an overwhelming lack of control. She had lost all ability to direct her behavior, her actions, her desire. She stepped back into the room and poured herself a glass of champagne from a bottle the staff had left chilling by the terrace doors.

She sipped the champagne and approached the armoire. Rifling through the clothes, she found what she was looking for. Had he planned this all along when he selected this seductive nightgown for her?

No matter. To her astonishment, she did not feel frightened or threatened. She wanted to let go, she had to.

Cass sat at the dressing table, fluffed her hair, freshened her makeup, and applied a touch more perfume to every part of her body that she wanted to be kissed. Barefoot, she slipped out into the hall and stood outside Jack's door.

Drawing on all her courage, she summoned up the nerve to knock.

Mere seconds elapsed before he opened the door. Cass sensed he'd been waiting for her. The look in his eyes was less commanding than before. Now the green mirrors to his soul spoke of warmth and solace. She stepped inside. Across the room, she saw his jacket and tie flung across a black-and-gray-striped velvet Empire couch. A fire was blazing in the tiny fireplace—so European, so romantic—its flames dancing to the languid tones of Billie Holiday.

"Are you sure?"

When she nodded in the affirmative, he held out his arms and she walked into them.

His first kiss took her with an urgency close to anguish. But then he slowed, his lips exploring hers, his tongue tasting her very being. She stood so close she could feel the heat of his body. She could feel he was fully aroused.

Slowly, he ran his hands over her shoulders, slipping his fingers under the straps of the nightgown. He let the thin fabric fall, freeing her body.

Cass dared not protest. Every pleasure point in her was alive now. She trembled with desire.

Despite the fire-tingling sensation that coursed through her being, Cass felt safe, shielded from the usual fears that haunted her, that had always prevented her from letting go. Who was this man, the virtual stranger who had come along and taken such a powerful hold over her emotions? Jack left her euphoric, terrified, and safe—all at once. And she felt as if she might cry.

Perhaps to slow himself down, Jack stepped back. His breath came faster, louder. His eyes searched her body, the look so intense that she felt he could see straight into her heart and beyond to her essence, her soul. He taunted and teased her breasts, first with his lips, then his teeth, his tongue. She could not hold back the tremors, then the seismic waves that followed in the wake of his caresses.

His hands gently yet firmly probed her body, working, exploring. He ran his fingers through her wild mane. His mouth strayed from the fragile skin of her neck to her lips.

Jack led Cass to the bed with one hand, the other working the buttons of his shirt.

He sat on the edge of the bed and pulled her close to him. She was still standing as he buried his face in her softness, planting delicate kisses across the smooth skin along her stomach and pelvis. His hands gently, so gently, caressed her buttocks.

As he moved, Cass ran her hands along the rugged lines of his shoulders. She followed the thin line of hair on his chest . . . down . . . past his waistline. His body was hard, well toned. He moaned softly. The thought of pleasing him made her dizzy.

Jack lay back on the bed and pulled her gently toward him. Cass brushed her breasts against his chest as she straddled his waist, her knees slipping into the soft velvet bedspread. She hugged him with her thighs as she waited for him to make the next move. But he remained still, watching her face. She closed her eyes and smiled.

Then Jack whispered, his voice husky and low, "I've waited so long. . . ." Cass knew it was time: He was ready.

Jack gathered her close to him. Now he was on top, his eyes holding hers for a long time, as if memorizing them.

He entered her slowly.

"Now," she whispered, convinced the desire, the anticipation, was going to kill her. She couldn't stifle her moans.

As Jack's pace quickened, Cass's body merged with his as they pumped rhythmically together. Her eyes fluttered. Her arms snaked around him, pulling him deeper inside her. Her body flushed; her breath quickened until she could no longer control it.

Jack's face showed the same triumph, and together they experienced a mutual explosion of passion, need, and pleasure.

Chelsea squeezed herself into the dress, a little black number that was both revealing and suggestive. Good. Give Daddy Dearest a peek at the fine merchandise he tossed aside thirty-three years ago.

She grabbed her purse, made her way to the elevator, and rode it to the top floor. She stood outside his suite, took a deep breath, then knocked.

They were waiting for her, the great Roger Turmaine and the lawyer who had made it big by hanging on to her father's coattails. Both men looked smug, confident.

Not for long, you bastards, she thought.

Roger stared at her, studying every feature.

She assumed he was looking for similarities. She certainly was. No matter, there would be time enough for that later. Her head pounded; the Valium was easing its way out of her system. Now she had to act fast. She couldn't chance "losing it" in front of him.

"I resemble you both, don't you agree?"

Judging from his stern expression, Chelsea surmised Roger wasn't amused.

"What is it that you want, Ms. Hutton?" James walked toward her. His voice was heavy with disapproval.

"First, I'd like the dinner you promised me," she said as her mood pitched downward, threatening to send her into one of her episodes. In fact, as Chelsea tried to maintain composure, a scarlet curtain of rage throbbed behind her eyes. She willed herself to stay calm with every breath she took.

"Let's settle this first," Roger said as he pulled out his checkbook and Montblanc pen. "How much will it take to get you out of my life? Name your price."

James stepped behind him. Shoving a handful of papers toward her, he demanded, "Sign these and the money is yours."

Her rage reached full boil, ready to bubble over. Did he genuinely believe he could buy her silence?

"When I came to your office that time, all I wanted, all I expected was acceptance."

"Well, that's right. Just money won't do for you." Roger turned to James, his tone sardonic, grating her nervous system like a violin bow stabbing clumsily at fragile strings. "We had forgotten, James. . . . Ms. Hutton is now a star, ready to become a superstar, I bet, thanks to *Cassidy English.*"

Roger looked straight at Chelsea as he spoke Cassidy's name.

She tried to avert her eyes, but it was so hard. His stare was unnerving.

James remained still, expressionless. He seemed the less predatory of the two, so Chelsea directed her final appeal to him. "Explain to your client the seriousness of this situation. If this leaks out, his career, his life will be in shambles. Once the public, not to mention the authorities, learn what he did"—Chelsea shifted her gaze to Roger—"he's finished."

She was nervous now, but struggled to keep her emotions well hidden. She dug her fingernails into her palms, needing the physical pain to divert her attention from the emotional agony. Nevertheless, her eyes were filled with water. She opened them wide to hold back the stinging tears.

Now it was she who stared, looking at Roger with hate-filled eyes, *willing* him to look at her, to demonstrate the respect she deserved. She knew, however, that he would continue to give all adoration to the princess, even though Cassidy was not his biological daughter. The one. The favorite. The only. Cassidy was strictly made-to-order. She was perfect, beautiful and healthy. Roger would never accept Chelsea as his blood. So it was up to Chelsea to destroy them both. That's exactly what she planned, first by exposing him publicly. She had all the documents now, and she would hire an attorney to take the legal steps necessary to force Roger Turmaine to submit to a DNA test.

Then she would take to the talk-show circuit, do some print interviews, maybe even write a book about her horrific experiences as the unwanted, unloved child of Roger and Lana Turmaine, discarded to live in a hell managed by Maria Hutton.

The ultimate prize would be hers. The world would embrace her, long to love and protect her. America's very own Princess Diana. Fame, power, acceptance—three things Daddy's money could never buy.

Chelsea took a deep breath and, inwardly, she smiled. Judgment Day had arrived.

James positioned himself between Chelsea and Roger. "Won't you consider the money? You could live comfortably for a very long time. All you have to do is sign these papers."

"By this you mean relinquish any claim that he is my father."

There was a long pause. She waited for an answer, even though she knew there wouldn't be one. She could tell that James was sympathetic. It showed in his face. But like every other attorney—or right-hand man—he was the flunky, the go-between who did all the dirty work for his boss.

It was time to leave. Chelsea had to get out of there before she exploded. She turned to the door, intentionally brushing past Daddy. "Sorry it has to end this way. But then, destroying you and your fake daughter—that's precisely how I planned it all along." Every word dripped with venom.

Roger grabbed her arm with such force that she nearly tripped. Instinctively, Chelsea swung around to face him, doubled her hands into tight fists, and wildly pounded his shoulders. His touch shook loose a lifetime of violent feelings waiting at the surface.

She exploded, shrieking into Roger's face, "I hate you! I hate you both," she cried. "You *all* will burn in hell for what you've done to me."

| | |

Safely back in her suite, Chelsea stripped off her clothing and rolled everything into a ball, which she tossed behind the sofa. She marched into the bedroom, her steps swift and purposeful, and got her makeup bag from the bureau, then dumped its contents onto the bed. Her hands trembled as she grabbed her trusty bottle of pills. She strained to focus, challenging her mind to remember her last dose of lithium. Two, maybe three weeks ago. Ordinarily, she managed to regulate the severity of her mood swings by taking the pills on weekends when she wasn't working, but the last few weekends they'd continued to work. No wonder she was spinning totally out of control.

Now her moods whirled; her mind raced, urging her to do crazy, obscene things. The need for drama was great. God, she loved the feeling, each and every bit of the euphoric bliss. But she had to stay rational, at least until shooting was over. She needed to stay—what did the doctors always call it?—"balanced."

If Jack, or anyone else, picked up on even the slightest change in her demeanor, she'd be finished. Jack had made that absolutely clear before he let her keep her part in the film. She was supposed to stay on the damned medications—that was the deal.

Chelsea swallowed three lithium capsules, two Depakote, and one Valium with a glass of water. She stood in the doorway, holding on to the frame on each side, and breathed deeply. Give it time, she told herself. Once the mood stabilizers kicked in, she'd be okay. They'd tide her over until the lithium got into her system.

Sleep. That would help.

Chelsea tiptoed past Bella's room, assuming she was asleep. She'd do *anything* not to wake her. She didn't have the presence of mind to deal with her daughter right now. The arrangement she'd worked out with Miss Perfect was working pretty well: Days, Bella came to the set whenever Chelsea had a call. At night, hotel staff was paid to stay with her, amuse her, feed her—in short, nurture her.

The only better arrangement Chelsea could hope for would be that the child disappeared.

Once in a great while, Chelsea would see herself in Bella—the unclaimed, unwanted child. And tonight Chelsea felt a surge of those feelings. *Poor Bella. Poor me!*

Her father, her *true* father, had done worse than disappoint her: He had disavowed her existence; he had annihilated her. Roger Turmaine had made it clear that, to him, she did *not* exist. He had his daughter and her name was Cassidy and there wasn't room for another.

With bare feet, Chelsea padded across the carpet to the bed. She knelt down, reached under the bed, and pulled out a shoebox filled with her most valuable possessions: proof of her identity. Her true identity.

She sorted through the uncashed checks, a letter demanding Maria's release of all claims on "Baby now known as Turmaine" in exchange for payment, and then a second letter, also from James, asking Maria to respond. How stupid, Chelsea thought. Two presumably smart, successful men, leaving such a paper trail. She fished through the papers to the bottom and retrieved her pièce de résistance: the hospital letter.

She clutched it to her breast.

Sleep was washing over her, stealing her consciousness. She stuffed the contents back into the box, replaced the lid, and pushed it under the bed. Then she hoisted herself from the floor and, in catlike movements, made her way across the comforter. The dark cloud was still upon her, swallowing up her ability to reason.

Her surroundings suddenly became black and dreary. She didn't recognize the room or its furnishings. She was confused and no longer knew where she was.

Outside, heavy rain pounded the windows. Lightning darted across the sky and thunder roared through the rapidly encroaching darkness. The weather fit her mood: dark and angry. Chelsea's inner turmoil roiled. Reality against fantasy; good fighting bad. This time, though, she was terrified that she would lose. She was in pain, unbearable, inexplicable agony.

Chelsea's head was pounding so hard that she took another Valium. Still, oblivion refused to come. She was so weary that pulling her legs onto the bed required that she break the action down into tiny steps and order her body to respond: Sit on bed; bend knees; lift legs; roll over on left side; put head on pillow . . . and so on. Yet once her whole body was in one place, she could only stare at the ornate molding that outlined the ceiling. Horrible images filled every thought: What if she couldn't convince anyone to believe her? What if she lost out to Roger and Cassidy and never worked again? What if she was wrong? Or crazy? When would she be happy? When would she ever see light again? Thoughts of suicide enveloped her, but she was too weak, too immobilized.

Time passed. She didn't know how long.

Then Chelsea felt a tiny spark of resolution rise to the surface. She bolted upright, swung her legs over the side of the bed, and dropped to her knees. On all fours, she pulled the box from under the bed once again. She slipped her hand under the lid and reached into the box, groping among the papers and pictures, searching until she felt something cold and abrasive. She started to moan. Then the moans turned to sobs. They were loud and piercing, the sounds of a wounded animal.

She picked up the .38, turned it over in her hands, and ran her thumb over the hard, cool metal of the barrel. The knowledge that she didn't have to live in so much pain suddenly gave her strength. Her "demons" urged her on. *Do it. Once people find out that Turmaine's real daughter killed herself because of him, he'll be ruined.* Chelsea raised the gun and pushed the end of the barrel to her temple. She squeezed her eyes shut and pulled back the hammer. Then she heard the shrieks.

"Mommy, don't! Please, Mommy, don't do it!" Bella stood in the doorway. Her eyes were filled with terror, a look that Chelsea identified with entirely.

Everything stopped. The voices grew silent. Chelsea knew that this little girl was her child, but beyond that, all else was a void. She free-floated somewhere between sanity and suicide. She dropped the gun to the floor and reached her hand out to Bella. Pulling her daughter down beside her, Chelsea sobbed.

"Go back to bed. Mommy will be all right." As she drifted into a deep, drug-induced sleep, Chelsea whispered, "Someone, please help me."

| | |

Jonathan had always suspected that Venice was a lucky city. He'd had his first sexual experience here as an adolescent, scored dope from a Carbinieri, gotten drunk on one-hundred-year-old red wine. All of these first lucky breaks. So it was no surprise to him that he happened to be passing his father's hotel room when the rising voices—his father, James, and a woman . . . ah, Chelsea Hutton—compelled him to check the side service entrance to the suite. And it was unlocked! Bingo! More good luck!

Was he ever glad he'd opted to take a nap rather than paint the town red with the young exotic dancer he'd met at a bar the night before. If he had, he would have missed all the action. So, the horny old devil had a love child. This little tidbit could come in handy.

He stood silently in the butler's pantry. He heard the door slam and knew the actress had left. Then he listened, closely, straining to hear everything Roger and James were saying.

"Do you believe her?"

"I don't know," Roger replied. "But there's one way to find out."

"How?"

"I want a DNA test done. Confidentially, of course."

"Do you think she'll agree to the test?"

"If she's gone to all this trouble to impress me, there's no doubt in my mind she'll submit to a test. If she refuses, it affirms that she's a fraud.

As always, be discreet. If this ever leaked out, the media would have a field day—never mind what it would do to Cassidy."

Hmmm, Jonathan thought. This could be *very* useful. Good ol' Dad will do anything to keep *this* quiet. Even send Cass packing if . . .

A plan took shape: He'd break into Chelsea Hutton's suite, search for the documents, or anything else that would link her to Roger, and destroy them. There was no way she would inherit any of the Turmaine estate. Jonathan already had his hands full trying to get Cass out of the picture, and he wasn't about to let this bimbo cut his inheritance by one more dollar.

But what if the DNA test was positive? Then an even grander scheme popped into his head.

| | |

With a little help from the maid, a young, round Sicilian woman who responded well to flattery and a few American dollars, Jonathan entered Chelsea's suite. A duplicate of his on the opposite end of the hall, it was dark and cold. The French doors to the balcony off the living room were open, and there were traces of dishevelment, revealing a woman in confusion. Even in his perfunctory sweep of the darkened living room, lit only by a low-wattage sconce in the entryway, he glimpsed piles of clothing, obviously dropped wherever Chelsea happened to be when she took it off.

Jonathan was all too familiar with the telling symptoms of psychic fatigue, when a person was too spent, too used up, to close pill bottles, which in this case lay at random about the room. Jonathan had been there, often. Nevertheless, identifying with Chelsea Hutton's inner turmoil gave him the creeps. Jonathan did not want to know her life story, just enough to hurt his father . . . and get *her* out of the Turmaine family picture.

He tiptoed quietly past the sitting room and into the first, smaller bedroom. He peeped inside and, making sure the tiny form wrapped in blankets and sheets was fast asleep, he entered.

The child stirred, and for a moment, Jonathan panicked. Her body grew still again and he felt himself relax. He tiptoed back into the hallway and made his way to the master bedroom. Inside, things were a mess. Blankets and pillows were strewn about the room; papers were scattered all over the carpet. The woman he recognized as Chelsea was curled up into a ball on the floor beside the bed, peacefully sleeping. Something glinted and caught his eye. He nudged it an inch or two with the tip of his shoe and realized it was a gun. Obviously he had missed quite a pity party.

Perhaps she *was* suicidal—not a terrible thought. Maybe even homicidal—an even better one. What if she killed Roger . . . and then herself? Now, *that* would solve a few problems, Jonathan mused. With Roger out of the way, Cass would be easy to handle.

He knelt down beside the woman's unconscious form and quickly scooped up a stack of papers, examining each page carefully in the dim light from the hall.

Each piece added to his pile of pay dirt. Definitely it was time for a celebratory drink—maybe even a snort of the "tweet" he'd smuggled into the country.

| | |

By noon, Jack and Cassidy were flying back to Venice on the Colossal jet. Jack rode in the cockpit, chatting knowledgeably with the pilot about the new technology that made flying this plane as simple as operating his young nephew's remote-controlled model.

Inside the plush interior cabin, Cass rested on the daybed, made available by the flip of a switch by the attendant. She relished each ache of her body, reminded of a night spent making love in every imaginable way. She and Jack had broken away from each other only to talk—about everything, the passion they shared for work, failed loves, broken dreams, and, now, the magic they could create together.

She must have fallen asleep for a while. Awakening, Cass felt Jack's comforting presence. When she opened her eyes and caught him staring, her lips curved into a smile.

He took her hand, brought it to his lips, and gently kissed her fingers.

Jack leaned forward, brushed a stray hair from her face, and cupped her chin in his hand. "Well, I promised you a memorable weekend. Was it?"

Cass placed her two hands over his. "Very, very memorable."

She moved to the soft leather seat beside Jack and pushed the call button. When the attendant responded, she asked her to convert the bed back into a seat. They were entering the Venice airspace, and *Dangerous Intentions* was suddenly very much on her mind.

And Jack's, too, apparently, because he cocked his head to one side and a huge grin spread across his face. "When will you finish shooting?"

She put on her producer's face now. "If we stay on schedule, we should be able to plan a wrap party for Thursday."

Jack seemed genuinely surprised. "Really? I wasn't aware you were that close to the end."

"Perhaps you're afraid I'll still hold you to our bet. Remember, you wagered I'd never bring it in on time?"

Jack's grin turned back into a smile. "Or within budget. Hey, I never pull a bet."

"Even if the stakes are Desmond? We're talking about your live-lihood."

"*Part* of my livelihood, dear lady." His expression turned impish. "Perhaps my livelihood will become ours."

Cass ignored this comment. Surely he was teasing. The thought of a permanent relationship with this dynamic man was enough to threaten the peace she had just found.

Sensing her reaction, he changed the subject.

"What kind of party do you have in mind?"

Cass shrugged. "I'm not sure. These past weeks have been so crazed, and so draining, I hadn't really given it much thought. I'd really like to do something fun, something wild. The cast, the crew, everyone, really pulled together to make this work. A lavish party would be a reward for all their hard work . . . and a farewell party to Venice."

"How about a masquerade ball?" Jack flashed one of his incredible smiles and waited for her response.

Thinking of the movie's budget, she hesitated momentarily. "That's a bit extravagant, don't you think?"

"Nonsense. Today's the first day of Carnevale in Venice. This is like Mardi Gras in New Orleans and Carnevale in Rio, only more grandiose. More rooted in history. It started in the eleventh century, I believe, only it fell out of favor, so to speak, in the eighteenth century, but then was revived in 1979—no holds barred. There are costumes, parades, pageants, game, balls—any festivity the imagination can dream up. It used to last for two months, but now it's just ten or twelve days. We'll be here right in the middle of it!"

Cass nodded in amazement.

"Cass, everyone involved in making this movie happen could be there, coming together as equals. No stars or gofers, just a whole bunch of people who've worked their tails off."

Once again, Cass was stunned by how, despite his supreme success, he could remain at heart so simple, so real. Was this all true? Could she have found the man of her dreams?

"It sounds incredible, Jack, but how on earth could I pull together a masked ball between now and then *and* finish filming?"

Jack grinned. Cass should have expected what came next.

"Consider it done."

The seatbelt sign lit up and the aircraft began its descent into the Venice airport. The attendant collected their champagne glasses and magazines, then disappeared to the tail of the aircraft.

Jack leaned forward and took Cass's hand once again. "You know I meant what I said before."

From what she knew of Jack, Cass readied herself for anything— well, almost.

He pulled a small velvet box with the distinctive Boucheron logo out of his jacket pocket.

"You recognize this?" he asked, opening the top of the box.

Cass sat paralyzed, pulled in two directions. *The perfect diamond— brilliant and exquisite, he'd called it; a stone worthy of his bride.* This exquisite stone, now mounted in a classic platinum solitaire ring setting, was more than a gift of jewelry. Jack was holding out his love, his life, to her, and she wanted to grab it—and him—and hold on forever. But the rational, practical Cassidy English held back.

An evening in Paris and a night of magic in Monte Carlo—these memories were indelible, but they didn't add up to love. It wasn't logical. She couldn't explain how such strong-minded, independent spirits could mesh so quickly. How could she trust her *own* feelings, never mind his?

"Please." His voice was insistent.

"Jack . . . no, no I can't."

"Yes you can."

"No, really . . . I can't."

He took the ring out of its satin cushion and slipped it onto her finger. "It was made for you."

Cass was shocked. She could swear he was nervous.

"Please. Say yes."

Like a car stuck between two gears, she was stalled.

"You're moving so fast. I'm confused. I don't know what to say."

He made it all seem so natural—falling in love, committing to the future. Without meaning to, she had slipped behind the steel gate that had contained his love. And she knew he had gotten inside the stone walls around her heart. There was no denying it.

But could they really say "forever"? Did he mean it? Could she?

"Say something." Jack held her hand and the diamond flashed yellow-blue lights of love in the sunlight high above the clouds over Venice.

"I'm afraid."

He leaned back in his seat, cocked his head, and grinned. "Then don't say anything now. Sleep on it. Give me your answer at the ball. If you're wearing the ring, I'll take it as a yes." He paused for a moment. His eyes bore into hers. "If you're not, then it's no."

| | |

Cass returned to the Cipriani still in a state of bliss. She collected the dozen or more messages left for her at the front desk and headed upstairs. She was on a cloud, floating in a whirl of happiness and pleasure.

Blissfully, she opened the door to her suite, fully intending to take the longest, most heavenly bath of her life. Bubbles, candles, soft music—the works. Each time she thought about Jack, her skin tingled with excitement.

"I've been worried sick."

His voice startled her out of her happy haze. Cass turned and saw her father rise from the sofa. There was nothing warm in his tone.

Taking a moment to collect her thoughts, Cass put her suitcase down and looked quietly, calmly, at her father. How was it possible that this man could *still* make her feel like a disobedient child? Not this time. Cassidy knew in that instant that she was the stronger one. She felt a twinge of pity for her ill, aging father, an old lion whose roar had diminished.

She spoke calmly. "Hello, Father. Do you mind telling me how you got in here?"

"The gentleman from the concierge desk said you left Friday night with Jack Cavelli." Roger's eyes focussed on the Louis Vuitton suitcase. "Do you mind telling me where you've been for two days?"

"As a matter of fact, I do. It's my private life. It doesn't concern you."

"Like hell it doesn't," he fumed.

Cass had never seen him so disturbed, so angry. His face twisted into a grotesque mask. He stood with arms at his sides, fists clenched. Memories of Roger's terrifying tirades against her mother invaded her thoughts. And she suddenly wondered what it was that Jack had done to make her father loathe him so much.

"Jack and I went to Paris and Monte Carlo," she replied. She picked up her bag and crossed to the bedroom.

But Roger was still quick and grabbed her arm as she charged past him. "You listen to me, young lady. You remember that this is business. There will not be anything else between you and Jack Cavelli. I forbid it. Do you understand me?"

For a man who had had a heart attack recently, Roger was amazingly strong.

Cass saw, again, the father who had shattered her childhood, not the man she had come to love and respect when she stepped into his shoes at the helm of Desmond. She could never forget what damage he had done. Perhaps now was the time to remind him. "You forbid me? Since when do you have any say in my life? You think you can just erase all those years you were absent—even after you got out of jail? *You* excluded me from your life. And you expect me to sweep these memories under a rug and pretend they never existed?"

His daughter's words had an impact on Roger, for he let go of her arm and, lowering his eyes and his voice, said, "He's no good for you, Cass. Trust me. I, of all people, know what he's capable of. He'll . . ."

He stopped talking and stared, lost in thought.

She stared back at him, willing him to leave, but, of course, he didn't.

Twenty years ago, she would have given anything to have him involved in her life, but not now. And there was no way she'd let him keep her from Jack—whatever the reason.

He must have picked up on her thoughts because he backed off and switched gears. "I came here, to Venice, to discuss something of great urgency with you. Something I feel must be addressed."

He was serious. More serious than Cass had ever seen him before.

"Maybe you should sit." He led her to the sofa and sat beside her. He dared not look at her. Instead he stared straight ahead.

"What's wrong?" she asked. Gone was the scolding father. In his place was an obviously troubled man.

"I'm afraid we are about to be hit by a scandalous rumor."

"What rumor? Is it Jonathan?"

Roger placed his hand on her knee and squeezed gently. Still he did not look at her but only shook his head.

"Chelsea Hutton. How long have you know her?"

"Not long at all." She remembered their "accidental" meeting in the cemetery. But that probably didn't mean much, so she said, "We met at your party."

"Then you must know that she was Jack's date." Roger studied her face. "What made you give her the lead? Your decision to recast that part wasn't based on her experience or talent."

Cassidy was determined not to feel defensive. "Jack insisted."

Roger shot a sardonic smile her way. "Didn't you wonder why? Jack's role in this mess is actually the least horrible part."

Not to Cassidy. Her mind drifted: A room filled with lavender roses, an overnight trip to Paris . . . a diamond ring so large it could compete with the stars. Words like, "Perhaps my livelihood will become ours." Where, exactly, did Chelsea Hutton fit into the equation? The knot twisted tighter.

"How much worse does this situation get?" she asked, noticing that her own caustic tone was so much like Roger's.

"Some months ago, Chelsea came to my office. She claimed to be you, my daughter, so Security assumed it was okay to pass her through the checkpoint and let her come upstairs. She barged in. I asked her to leave. I even threatened to have her thrown out. She refused. She was raving, saying she was my daughter and how the two of us could be together."

Roger watched her expression change from confusion to disbelief.

"She was crazed, right? The accusations are false, aren't they?" Cass was afraid to hear his reply.

"Probably."

Her heart sank. If she hadn't been sitting, she was sure she would have fallen.

"Look, it's possible I made a mistake. These days, one can't be one hundred percent sure. It was the sixties; everyone was promiscuous. On the other hand, these crazy paternity suits are turning up right and left. It's quite possible she's a fake, a phony."

"And quite possible she's not." Cass's voice quivered. She suddenly flashed on the pictures Bella showed her, especially the one with Chelsea's picture digitally added to a photo of Lana. And the chance meeting at her mother's grave. Was it really by chance?

"I'll handle it, Cass. I just wanted you to hear about it from me, in case . . ."

"In case what, Dad?"

Roger took a deep breath and rubbed his hands through his hair. "I've offered her all kinds of money to leave us alone. Astronomical amounts. She's refused. I'm convinced it's not money she's after."

"What, then?"

"My public humiliation, perhaps. Publicity to further her career . . . Who the hell knows?"

"Does she have any proof, any paperwork to back up her claim?" Cass spoke like a detective now.

"She says she does, but she won't let me or James see it."

While Cass absorbed the information she had just heard, he continued talking.

"I'm not perfect, Cass. I've made many mistakes in my life. One of them was loving your mother too much." He held her full attention now. "And I never, ever, stopped loving you. You were . . . always have been the most important part of my life. I've done some stupid things. I . . ."

Roger paused. He shuddered, then continued to speak. "I see that ring on your finger, and the love you feel is brimming. You're glowing with it. So I have to tell you the rest. The truth."

A part of Cass had waited her whole life to hear those words; the other part was terrified. She felt a surge of emotions, love purging the anger and fears of a past gone wrong. She listened with an open heart.

"In a way, I'm glad you insisted on reading your mother's diary."

Cass looked sharply at her father. Before she could speak, Roger continued, "Rae told me you had it. She wanted me to know. In a way, it makes this a little easier."

Cass's first impulse was to cover her ears and run. She could sense that some terrible secret was about to be revealed.

"I don't know how much you've read. Obviously your mother and I had a very volatile relationship. We weren't always good for each other," he said softly. "Your mother was insecure about her beauty—hung up, really. She needed constant reassurance and praise. I wasn't able to give her everything she needed. No one could have. Lana's need was bottomless. So she turned to other men. They made her feel good about herself. I think they made her feel needed, something she never felt with me."

He hesitated and cleared his throat before continuing. "She had problems, serious mental problems. She saw a psychiatrist. Took pills . . . medication."

Cass straightened in her seat. Roger was right; the diary *had* prepared her to hear what he had to say. Many of the journal entries were hysterical. Lana often wrote of suicidal thoughts. She had a fixation, an addiction, to love. How hard that must have been for Roger. Cass realized with new insight how difficult it must be for him to tell her this. So what was driving him? Something terrible was about to be said.

"She would do bizarre things . . . lock herself in her room for days, crying, withdrawing from me and from the world. Then she would emerge and it was like she was someone else, a different person." He turned to her now, gauging her reaction, then continued. "Lana abused booze and drugs—marijuana, Valium, speed. She was fully involved in the party scene, adventurous and daring . . . and promiscuous."

Cass saw the hurt in his eyes.

"There were lovers, so many I lost count. I can't tell you the embarrassment, the indignity I suffered being cuckolded in front of the whole world like that. Everyone knew."

The tone of his voice changed. He was no longer angry or wistful. He seemed, for lack of a better word, pathetic. Words tumbled out of his mouth, all mixed up.

"I was no angel. God, her behavior caused me such grief. It made me do unspeakable things. . . ."

Cass sensed he was leading up to the murder, to a confession, and she didn't want to hear it. She couldn't bear the thought. Everything inside her suddenly began to rumble and shake at the terrible memory of seeing her mother's lifeless body after she heard the loud gunshots. Cass was seeing shoes—gray wing tips. The police questioned her for hours about what she had seen through the keyhole, but she never could remember. Except for the shoes.

Her eyes searched her father's face. "Stop," she whispered. "I don't want to hear anymore." Cass covered her ears with both hands. Her face twisted in horror. "Stop it! Stop it!" she yelled again and again.

Roger dropped to his knees before her, cradling her in his arms. "I'm sorry. You needed to hear this from me. I couldn't let you read it in her diary."

Cass was sobbing now, her face and hands wet with tears. His face was next to hers. The smell of liquor on his breath filled her nostrils. She fought the urge to vomit. Maybe that was why he was talking like this. Maybe he was drunk and rambling.

Grabbing her hand, Roger rocked her world even harder with one last statement. "Jack was one of her lovers. He was obsessed with her."

| | |

Cass pressed seven on the telephone and listened to the voice-mail message for the fifth time.

"Hi, gorgeous, it's Jack. I hope you found some time to relax, maybe even nap. You looked so tired this morning, but at the same time so adorable. I hope you're giving my question much thought. I'm holding my breath, hoping for good news. Anyway, all the preparations for the wrap party have been made. You can expect the grandest, most elegant masquerade ball Venice, Italy—the world—has ever seen. I've booked the Madrid for the night—the whole place. It's an amazing castle, very eighteenth century . . . right on the Piazza San Marco. It's the place to see and be seen during Carnivale, and it's all yours for the party. Invitations have gone out to the cast and crew, and as *I* speak into this infernal telephone, *they* are starting to search for their costumes—doges, Casanovas, Clementines . . . plague doctors, aristocratic dandies . . . perhaps a unicorn or a seven-foot flowering tree."

His voice stopped for a moment, and she could hear him laughing.

"I can't wait to see you again, baby. Get a good night's sleep."

Then a beep, a click, and the automatic voice—first Italian, then English—came back with more options. She almost played it again but decided not to. She was torturing herself.

Through tear-filled eyes, she studied the magnificent ring Jack had given her not even a day ago. She turned it over in her hands, ran her finger over its sharply defined edges. She held it to the light and watched the rainbow-hued prisms dance around the room.

A part of her, the left brain, felt sorrow and loss. The right brain felt angry and betrayed. How could he be that cold and calculating? How could *she* have been that naive and stupid? The manipulations, the intricate machinations, the emotional games—what else could all of it add up to? In a moment, her father had opened the window on her future, on Lana's past. Jack's reasons for replaying his love affair with Lana was clear: He wanted to hurt Roger. Cassidy was simply his instrument, a vehicle in his cruel scenario to destroy Roger, especially now that her father was down, sick and unable to complete his final project. This knowledge stripped her of every magic moment since her arrival in Italy.

Everything was coming together now. Jack had been insistent that Chelsea be given the lead role because he needed a spy. Possibly he was even in on Chelsea's plan to invent some claim on Roger. He had destroyed Lana—emotionally and now his plan was to destroy her. How had she let herself be swept away by his charisma, his charm? Cass could no more believe in Jack's love than in Chelsea being Roger's daughter—her half sister. At least she found out in time.

Still, that notion did little to lessen the blow. She felt betrayed, foolish, empty . . . as if there were a huge hole in her very center. She closed her eyes and her mother's likeness was everywhere, like an ongoing slide show or a mental photo album, the last image being her lifeless body, sprawled out on the carpet beside her bed. Then the shoes again. Shiny, fancy. Her father had at least a dozen pairs just like them in his closet. The gunshots, then the shoes, then Lana's body. Back and forth, round and round.

Then a terrifying thought crashed into her consciousness: Jack—was it possible that *he* murdered her mother? Was he that obsessed? That devious?

Cass checked her watch. Chelsea had been in the makeup trailer for two hours now and she was growing impatient. "I asked that Chelsea be made up to look haggard and upset. That shouldn't be too difficult."

"Meow." Rudolpho laughed, shooting her a wicked grin.

"What's taking so long?"

This was the last day of shooting. The B unit was out, collecting extra footage—mood shots, exteriors—just in case the editors needed it. All costumes, lights, sound equipment that weren't needed were being packed up to be shipped back to Los Angeles or returned to the agencies here in Venice that had leased it to the film company.

The day before, Cass and Rudolpho had given everyone, cast and crew, who wasn't needed a day off. Today's scene required everyone's best—makeup, wardrobe, lighting . . . everyone. Of course, the most demanding work would be needed from Chelsea. And Cass.

Rudolpho handed her another cup of coffee—her third this morning. "Here, sit back and relax. All of it'll happen in time. We've done our best. Just let the pieces come together, fall where they may. In just a few hours it will all be over, and tonight we'll celebrate." He placed his hand on his friend's shoulder and squeezed gently. "Which reminds me, I think it's great to throw such a lavish party for everybody. It's definitely well deserved. What better theme than masquerade, during Carnevale? Brilliant. And a lot better than steaks on the back lot."

Cass didn't flinch. She didn't dare tell him the idea was Jack's. She was humiliated enough as it was.

The sound tech fired up the background music—a romantic ballad of love and loss—to set the mood. Cass could identify with its meaning this morning, but she refused to get caught up in it again. Instead she turned off all emotions, steeling herself against any other feeling other than triumph.

Chelsea finally appeared, all pouffed and primped, a gorgeous bride, but haggard, frantic, disheveled, just as Cass had specified. At that moment, Jack and his entourage arrived on the set.

For a second Cass wondered if it really was a coincidence, but dismissed the thought as absurd. He looked relaxed, dressed in khakis and a tan and blue polo shirt.

Jack made his way over, kissed her lightly on the forehead, and said, "I waited for your call last night. By midnight I realized you must have fallen asleep. You did get my message, didn't you?"

Cass forced a smile. "I was really tired. I . . . I guess I crashed."

He shrugged, a bit confused. "Okay, but you could have called this morning."

"I was in a rush. . . . I had to get to the set. My mind's on the film." Her voice was flat. Cass didn't dare look at him. She managed to tune him out completely.

Jack's voice grew tight. He stepped back. "Should I leave and come back? Perhaps we can start over."

She turned to face him. "You'll have to excuse me. We're about to begin. Would you mind stepping off the set?"

Cass signaled Rudolpho, who passed the command on to an assistant who bellowed, "All quiet on the set!"

The energy was charged as camera positions and lights were checked and adjusted. Hair and makeup people were standing by and Rudolpho conferred with the tech crew. Chelsea took her place behind Bengino.

When planning how this scene would be shot, Rudolpho and Cass had decided that she would direct it. Bengino *still* considered her his muse, and even after all this time, and all her craziness, Chelsea never failed to deliver when Cass suggested a movement, or asked her to say a line a different way.

The previous week they had shot the final scene of the film—when Ophelia flees the church where she was supposed to marry the doge her father pledged her to, only to find Carmelo dead, with the jeweled sword of her father's sentry embedded in his chest. The farmer who owned the cottage that the production company had rented to use as the trysting place of Ophelia and Carmelo needed it for his foreman. Rearranging the shooting schedule had not been a problem; the scene before that heartbreaking finale was set in the Piazza San Marco.

Now Cass was faced with the task of drawing out the love and passion of these two disparate actors who, even after spending weeks in each other's arms, *still* had no affinity for each other. She had to get every ounce of anguish out of Chelsea/Ophelia when Bengino/Carmelo tells her that he has married another, even though he still loves her as much as life.

He—Carmelo—did this, he explains with great passion, to prove to her father that he would not interfere with her marriage. The two lovers part—she, returning to the glorious chapel to marry the sadistic doge; he, presumably, to go home to wait for his own bride to return from the wedding of his true love. As Ophelia starts down the aisle to marry a man she abhors, she turns and flees, this time never to return. She discards her veil and flowers on the cathedral steps and runs through the piazza. She rips a gold medallion from a ribbon around her neck and hurls it toward a startled farmer who has been selling vegetables off the back of his cart. "For payment," she cries, hopping into his cart and whipping the horses to a frenzied gallop. With little time to get away, to safety, to her beloved, Ophelia speeds away, certain that her beloved has gone to the cottage where they were lovers. In the last shot, Ophelia's bridal train flies dramatically behind her.

Played correctly, the scene would be absolutely operatic, filled with passion and drama. Done wrong, it would be hokey, a caricature of the story Roger had almost given his own life for to get to the screen.

Cass had already checked with her camera crew, so now she spoke briefly with Chelsea, who was waiting to make her entrance from the cathedral doorway. She knew she needed to get every ounce of anguish out of this obviously unstable woman. It was there, hidden beneath the layers of deceit and anger. After speaking with Chelsea, she went to Bengino, who stood beside the fountain. Satisfied that both were on the same page, with the same energy, she signaled Rudolpho that she was ready to go.

With everything—and everyone—in place, Rudolpho yelled, "Action!"

The wide-angle shot focused on Ophelia—Chelsea in the twenty-five-thousand-dollar wedding dress Valentino had created for the film—growing tighter as she walked across the stone piazza toward Carmelo, who stood anxiously at the fountain.

Cass's decision to have Chelsea made up to look a bit insane was on the money. The blond actress with the wild eyes and loosely upswept hair walked hurriedly, not bothering to protect the skirt of her gown as it trailed through the leaves and puddles.

"Carmelo," Chelsea/Ophelia called furtively.

"I'm here, behind the fountain," the actor responded. Cassidy had worked forever, it seemed, to pull the right performance from the man, but she was not satisfied. She stopped the scene and they tried again, but still without success.

Finally she approached the actor. "Bengino, you have experienced a broken heart?"

He nodded. Makeup people fussed around him. Someone put more gel in his ponytailed hair. "Certainly. I told you."

"Tell me again. Tell me about it."

For five minutes, the actor recounted the story of his first, devastating love affair.

"Think back now. How did you feel?"

"I wanted to kill the man who stole my lover."

"And what did you feel about her?"

The actor reached some memory. Cassidy could see his luminous black eyes begin to burn.

"Okay, let's take it from Ophelia's entrance again." Cass called to Chelsea, "Chelsea, you're ecstatic to see him. You've come to him with the news that you have left your betrothed at the altar. You were afraid he would not be there to take you away. Now you are anxious that he act quickly so you both can flee."

Chelsea stood trancelike when in character. It was amazing, even a little scary. She barely acknowledged Cass's direction.

The scene began again. When Ophelia reaches Carmelo and places her hand on his shoulder, she speaks urgently. "We must go immediately. My father, no one, knows that I am gone. We must leave everything. Start over as we planned."

When he does not turn to her, Ophelia reacts with fear. "What is it? Tell me, Carmelo, why do you not look at me? I came as I told you I would. I am yours."

"It is too late."

Ophelia moves to face her lover. The cathedral-length train of her gown—helped a bit by a well-directed fan—swirls around them. "Listen to me."

Carmelo stands still, not reacting. "No, my love. It *is* too late."

Ophelia holds her hand for him to see. "Do you see? No wedding band. I am free. I am yours. We must get away before Father discovers I am gone."

Carmelo slumps against the fountain wall and struggles to meet her astonished stare. Cass signals the cameraman to move in closer—a two-shot.

"I married another. Sophia. I could not help it. Your father . . ."

Ophelia stands frozen. The wind—another, larger fan—blows across the fountain, catching both the spray of the water and the lace-edged veil and train. Ophelia/Chelsea reaches to catch the veil, which instead blows free. Chelsea's blond hair has been styled so that it immediately falls in sweet curls, framing her perfect, heart-shaped face.

This is going beautifully, Cass thought. She gave a thumbs-up sign and moved over to a few feet behind the cameraman.

And at that moment she saw it—the resemblance to Lana. A photo of her mother as Ophelia crossed her mind. Cass squeezed her eyes tightly and blocked out everything *but* the scene being shot before her.

"Sophia! Impossible. She is my maid of honor. She is there at the chapel right now. Waiting."

Carmelo shakes his head. "That matters not. I . . . I was so angry. Your father . . . we . . ."

"So you married my best friend?"

The scene called for a pause while Ophelia absorbed these words and supposedly got in touch with her emotions. For the first time since shooting began, Cass concentrated on Chelsea and what she was doing. Not only was she *not* in any anguish, but the actress was obviously working very hard not to smile. Or, more correctly, not to smirk.

At the same time, Chelsea focused her attention on Cass, who stood beside the camera. Her gaze never wavered.

Suddenly a noise, a sound like the low growl of an angry, wounded animal, rose from Cassidy's throat. As she walked, then ran, from the set, she heard Rudolpho call after her.

"Cass, what the— Where the hell are you going?" he screamed. "Cut!"

The assistant director stammered, "Uh . . . take five, everybody."

| | |

Cass almost made a clean break, but as she was about to step aboard the *vaporetto,* someone grabbed her arm. She spun around angrily. Jack's grip was not gentle. His green eyes were hard, the color of emeralds.

"What the hell is going on?" he demanded.

"Nothing. I'm fine. I'm just tired."

"What about the shoot? An hour or two and the filming's complete. How can you walk away now?"

Cass looked at him cruelly. She had played his game. "Oh, so now you want me to win? Is that it?"

Jack's eyes opened wide now. He released his grip. "What are you talking about?"

"Make up your mind, Jack—win or lose? You can't have both. I walk off the set now and we don't finish shooting by midnight. Sure, Rudolpho can direct the scene. We've talked it all out. But it's going to take time to get everything reset and everyone back on track, so we still wouldn't finish by midnight. Then you win, right?"

Jack stepped back, not sure what to say. "Well, yeah . . . but all of that—"

Cass wouldn't let him finish. "And if I go back now, we could still finish on time, and I win. Which way puts you in a better position?"

"A better position for what?"

"To fuck me royally!" she shrieked. She held nothing back. She wanted to slap him across the face. She fought the urge to pound her fists into his chest, rip his hair out of his head, or, even better, claw his deceitful eyes out of their sockets.

Instead she swept past him, flung her knapsack over one shoulder, and headed back across the piazza. Jack followed just steps behind.

"Will you please calm down and tell me what this is about instead of acting like a spoiled brat?"

This last remark sent Cassidy over the edge. She swung around, intentionally smacking him with her bag.

"Your goddamn plan! That's what this is about. You, Chelsea, the devious plot the two of you concocted against me—and my father."

Despite his healthy tan, Jack paled. His eyes darted away from hers. "That vicious bitch," he muttered. "She couldn't wait to tell you."

Cass couldn't contain her tears. She let them fall from her eyes, stinging her cheeks and trailing lines of mascara.

"At least you have the decency to admit it."

He reached out for her and touched her shoulder lightly.

Cassidy recoiled in revulsion.

"Please, Cass, let me explain." He reached for her again.

"Leave me alone. Don't touch me."

"Relax." He held his hands up in surrender and stepped back. Translating the pained look in her eyes, he continued, "I admit that sometimes my tactics are a bit devious. I wanted to win, but that was before you and I—"

"Don't." She put her palm up in front of his face. "I don't want to hear it."

Jack, shocked into silence, stood still, watching the woman he loved. His heart broke, piece by pitiful piece. Finally he spoke. "It's no secret Roger and I are adversaries, enemies. I *did* want him to lose Desmond. It's a vital part of Colossal and I wanted it all."

He paused. "And when we made that bet, I assumed you would feel that was my plan. Chelsea was the perfect choice to spy on you. She'd already told me she wanted the part. Also, I was sure she would make the film a disaster. You might say Chelsea was my Plan B." Again he reached toward her. "But much to my surprise, you got the best out of her. Roger can be proud to retire with *Dangerous Intentions* as his last film. And you're three hours away from winning our bet. So, you see, both Plans A *and* B failed."

"You're lying," Cassidy spat, pulling away from his grasp. "Not only did you try to destroy my father's hold on Desmond, you also cooked up that cockamamie story about Chelsea being my father's daughter."

"What? I don't . . ." He was completely shocked, and Cassidy could see this.

Still she accused him. "You're lying."

"Cassidy." He reached to tilt her chin up, but she resisted. "I don't know what you're talking about."

Cass stopped in her tracks but did not look at him. She was certain he was telling her the truth, but she could not let him read her feelings. It seemed prudent to change the subject.

"That may be true, but the rest of it—"

He interrupted quickly. "It started out one way and ended up another. You were a direct link to Roger. When it comes to you, in case you hadn't noticed, he's defenseless. I knew I could get to him through you. But as I got to know you better, something happened. First you had the talent to step in and do this very difficult job, and then I fell in love with you. It didn't seem the least bit important for me to hurt Roger anymore—or to take his studio—because I had you."

Cassidy made certain Jack was looking directly into her eyes when she said, "Is that what you said to my mother?"

She did not wait for a reply. There wasn't time. Her feet did the thinking and she followed them right back onto the set. There was no point in letting *anyone* stand in the way of *Dangerous Intentions*. She signaled Rudolpho that everything was okay, and picked up exactly where she had left off fifteen minutes earlier. There was just this one final scene to finish and the film would be done; Desmond, safe in her hands. To hell with Chelsea and Jack.

Cassidy English, daughter of the legendary Roger and Lana Turmaine, would prevail.

Then she could worry about the future.

"Sorry, folks," she called out to cast and crew. "Must have last-day jitters . . . You're doing great! Let's get back to work. I can't begin to tell you how much I appreciate the phenomenal work you people have produced, often against almost insurmountable obstacles and under less than optimal conditions. Most of you know the effort it's taken to get *Dangerous* off the ground." She looked from Rudolpho, to Chelsea, to Jack, then continued, "Some more than others." She shook her arms and wiggled her shoulders. "Bottom line is, you're the best team *anyone* could ever work with. I'll finish saying thank you at the party tonight. So now let's take it from where Carmelo tells Ophelia that he's married Sophia. Okay, let's go. This is the last scene. Give me your absolute best."

As technicians, actors, extras—everyone—scurried into place, the assistant director yelled, "Quiet on the set."

In unison, Cass and Rudolpho, standing side by side behind the main camera, called, "Roll camera."

"Rolling."

Thus work resumed, as though uninterrupted. Instead of perching on her chair behind the camera, Cass flew about, around and behind the cameras, coaxing, coddling, cajoling cast and crew, never once losing awareness of what was going on before the camera.

The church scene was already set and lit, so shooting the interiors—Ophelia's attendants helping her with her veil and flowers; the priest and acolytes at the altar; Ophelia's father, the evil doge, the musicians . . . close-ups and long shots—took only about an hour and a half. During this time, the cart and horses were brought in and the piazza was set for the final take of the scene. Lights and sound needed little adjustment since the first part of the sequence had taken place in the same area, at the fountain.

Chelsea's performance was flawless. Cass considered wrapping after one take of her escape, but prudence called for a second.

The minute Chelsea and the cart left the piazza and rolled out of sight, Rudolpho shouted, "That's a wrap!"

The silence on the set turned to applause, then joy. A cheer echoed through the ancient piazza. In that moment, cast, crew, and city were one unit—the team that had made this beautiful dream of Roger Turmaine's come true.

Cass and Rudolpho embraced jubilantly, and Ally raced to join them. Then Cass broke from their embrace and turned to her company. "Thank you, all, every one of you, from the bottom of my heart; from the bottom of my father's heart. We'll see you tonight at the ball!"

She had to get away from the set, the people, before she broke down. The emotions roused over the past week were churning. Fused with the unending tension that had been building since she left New York for Los Angeles—to be at her dying father's side, no less—the pressure was becoming unbearable. It had to be released. But not now. Not in front of everyone.

Feelings swept through the set as if there were another fire—this one purely figurative, of course, but just as real. They'd pulled it off!

She was certain *Dangerous Intentions* would be a hit, in the same vein as the great Merchant-Ivory historical films. Her gut instincts told her so, but for the moment, it didn't matter. Only harsh realities remained foremost in her mind: who she had been; how she'd gotten here; even who she had become. This had been a time for great emotional growth, great joy, and great pain. Only then did Cass realize that she had won her bet! Desmond was in her hands.

From across the piazza, Jack shot her a thumbs-up sign and smiled. But even from that distance, Cass could see that his smile was shot through with sorrow.

Shortly after returning to the hotel, Cass got a phone call from Rudolpho.

"I asked editing to put together a rough cut from the film we have," he said. "Why don't you stop by my suite before the party and we'll look at it together?" Rudolpho might want to pretend things had not changed between them, but Cass refused to go along with him.

"Maybe later," she replied, hoping that the anger and hurt she felt could not be heard in her voice. She had not forgotten that he'd had an affair with Chelsea. As much as she wanted to trust her longtime friend again, she couldn't. Especially not since finding out how perverted Chelsea was, how much she wanted to tear her father down. Exactly what was Rudolpho's part in her plan?

"Okay. But I have to say, Cass, it looks like we scored—big. So big I can see an Oscar on a shelf in Roger's office."

Cassidy didn't want to discuss the movie right now. In fact, all she wanted to do was push *Dangerous Intentions*, Jack Cavelli, Chelsea Hutton—even Rudolpho—far from her thoughts. All she had been able to think about since returning to the hotel was how fast she could get a flight back to Los Angeles. The party was the last thing on her mind. Of course, she would have to put in an appearance. If she didn't, the gossipmongers would begin to put two and two together, and it wouldn't be long before her life was being played out in the tabloid press once again.

"I could stop by tonight and pick you up. We could go together."

"No . . . I'm not sure when I'll be ready. I've got to return some calls before it's too late, and I need a nap. Let's just meet at the Madrid."

There was a short pause, then "Suit yourself," followed by a dial tone.

Cass replaced the receiver in the cradle. Wearily, she eyed the costume hanging on the closet door. It had arrived before she left for the set in the morning; still she hadn't the slightest desire to open the zippered garment bag and take a peek. Her hesitation was no doubt prompted by the fact that Jack had selected it and had it sent to her suite.

She sat motionless on the side of her bed and retraced everything that had happened over the past few weeks . . . especially her weekend with Jack. They were aboard his jet. Flying back to Venice. He suggested a masked ball and she squealed like a child. In fact, she couldn't wait to put on a fancy costume, sip champagne, and bask in the spotlight of *Dangerous Intentions.* By the time the night was over, she would have accepted his marriage proposal. That was then.

Now she fully intended to confront Jack, question him about Lana—about her murder. Then she would go after Chelsea. She would expose the lying slut, embarrass and humiliate her in front of her peers. In front of the industry. It was time someone else suffered the intense pain, the brutal betrayal she now felt.

Cass spotted the silver-framed photo of her mother on her bedside table and began to weep. In the rush to finish filming, she had completely lost track of the date. This was the twenty-third anniversary of Lana's murder.

Now, as then, she felt frightened, alone, and heartbroken.

| | |

Jack paced furiously around his suite, cradling a hefty tumbler of scotch on the rocks—his third. The image of Cassidy spewing accusations at him commanded the space. Her look of betrayal and the disappointment in her eyes were enough to bring him to his knees. These were feelings he'd never expected, or even considered, when he embarked on this delirious journey.

He stopped in front of the window and looked out, oblivious to the breathtaking view. "So that's Turmaine's message?"

James nodded. "More or less. Roger wants you to stay away from her. There are to be no more business dealings, no contact, no communication of any kind. From now until the movie premieres, any dealings between Colossal and Desmond will go through me. Then we'll see. Maybe it won't be a bad idea for Colossal to absorb Desmond after all.

That *is* what you wanted, isn't it? Let's get it done. Just stay away from Cassidy."

"Like hell I will!" Jack yelled. He spun around and looked James straight in the eye. Then he hurled the glass of scotch across the room, shattering it against the bar.

"I'm in charge. I own Colossal. Hell, I *am* Colossal." Jack jabbed a finger into his chest for emphasis. "Now Turmaine's going to decide what's best for Cassidy? Why now? He's ignored her for most of her life."

Ashamed of losing his composure, he methodically picked up each piece of shattered glass and threw it into the wastebasket. "Shit!" A tear of blood fell from his fingertip. Jack took an exquisite white silk monogrammed handkerchief from his pocket and wiped his index finger in it.

Then, from his crouched position, he looked up at the older man. James still stood close to the door, as if he couldn't leave fast enough.

"So . . ." Jack spoke solemnly. "Roger's going to run Cass's life just like he ran Lana's?"

Jack stood and moved over to James, getting right in his face, and said with deliberation, "My position, my money, my name—this means power all over the world. Do you understand me? Push aside all of my other companies and corporations; let's just concentrate for the moment on Colossal. Currently it's the largest studio in the industry. Number one. And I call *all* the shots. I can make any movie I want, hire any star, screenwriter, director, or producer. And I can deal directly, face-to-face, one-on-one, with *any* employee of *any* of my subsidiaries. Including Cassidy English. Do you get my point?"

James nodded silently.

"I am in control. Tell your client, your friend, I can rock his fucking world anytime I please. You tell him that if he backs me into a corner—"

"You can't blame Roger for losing it," James interrupted. "You're playing some sick, demented game and you're using an innocent young woman as the pawn. What happened between you and Roger happened a lifetime ago. Can't you both look past it? Isn't it time to move on? Haven't enough people been hurt?"

Jack did not want to think. He fought hard not to make sense of James's words. He was losing control. He had allowed his emotions to cloud his judgment and, as a result, he had lost his edge. For a moment he was struck by the irony that it was exactly twenty-three years to the day since the *Tamed* premiere party at Whispering Winds in Lana's honor. Twenty-three years to the day since she was murdered. But he couldn't dwell on that. He had to regroup, put everything back together the way *he* wanted it; the way it had to be.

Like it or not, an unbreakable bond linked them all: James, Roger, Lana, Cassidy, and Chelsea.

| | |

All his life, Jonathan Turmaine had felt like a victim.

Time and again, no matter what he did or how hard he tried, he ended up a loser, a bottom feeder on the food chain of life. But not anymore. Everything he had ever wanted, searched for, was right in the palm of his hand. He clutched the hospital letter tightly in his fist.

A mix-up at birth—of course, he thought. He'd known all along that Cass didn't belong, even when they brought her home. He always said she was an outsider, and now he had the proof. He held in his hand enough ammunition to finally bring down the domain that dear old Dad had worked all of his life to build.

When Jonathan was finished, *nothing* would be left of the great Turmaine dynasty.

His plan was simple. He made four copies of the documents he took from Chelsea's room. One would go to Cass, the second to Roger, the third he would hold on to as a souvenir for all his incredible detective work, and the fourth—that would be his insurance policy. If Roger or the bitch had any crazy ideas about not giving him exactly what he wanted, then he would go to the press: the *Los Angeles Times,* perhaps *USA Today,* Ted Koppel.

As for the clever and cunning Ms. Hutton, he would deal with her according to whether or not she went along with his demands. If she went away quietly, he might let her live. If not, then she was writing her own finale.

Good old James, he thought. He never went anywhere without his little fax/copier machine, making it possible for Jonathan to run off what he needed and put the originals back into the mess in Chelsea's room before the junked-up cow came to!

The only problem: The bitch woke up before he got the chance to return them. From outside her door, he heard her yelling at her kid.

| | |

Chelsea thrashed about the carpet and ripped the linens from her bed. The papers *had* to be here somewhere. She tried to rethink what had happened that night, and she always got stuck at the same place: the pills, then darkness. She couldn't remember beyond that point. The cold hand of panic had slapped her hard in the face when she discovered the papers were missing. And she had spent the days since acting, eating, existing in a terrified fog.

She had examined the room in search of signs of forced entry, for the smallest indication that someone had invaded her space in the middle of the night.

She pushed past Bella, who stood terrified in the bedroom doorway. The pathetic waif was crying again. So what else is new? Chelsea thought.

"That brat is becoming more and more of a nuisance," she muttered as she caromed down the hall.

She spun around to face the child. "I'm going to ask you one last time. Did you hear anything that night? After you went to bed . . . someone walking around, the door opening or closing?"

"No, Mommy. I was sleeping. . . . I promise. I, I, I," she sobbed. Terror registered on her beautiful face.

But Chelsea wasn't listening. She needed those papers. It crossed her mind that Roger, or his henchman, had hired someone to steal them. She wouldn't put anything past that bastard. The very thought sent her heart racing. What on earth would she do now? She had no copies—she'd never gotten around to making them. How careless she was!

With no proof, Roger would walk away, clean as a whistle, and she would be labeled a psychotic stalker. Unless . . . Suddenly another idea popped into her head.

Plan B: The papers could be stolen, shredded, even burned. It still wouldn't change the fact that she was the daughter of Roger and Lana Turmaine. She had all the proof she needed. It was a wonderful thing called DNA!

| | |

"You can't avoid the party. If you're a no-show, a red flag will go up. To hell with what the cast and crew think, what about the press? Reporters, TV cameras . . . an obscene number of paparazzi will be there. Hell, even *Entertainment Tonight* sent a crew from New York to cover the thing. They're already lining up at the Madrid, waiting to catch a glimpse of all the key players—mainly you and Cassidy." James was talking, though he was sure Roger was only *half* listening.

"It's only a wrap party, for Christ's sake. It's not a fucking premiere. The damned thing isn't even edited and scored yet." Roger sat on the sofa, dressed in burgundy silk pajamas with a matching robe. He leaned forward, cradling his head in his hands. "Besides, whose idea was it to throw this fancy bash, anyway—and tonight of all nights?"

James was already handsomely attired in a navy tuxedo with a faint pinstripe—very Saville Row. "Listen, it doesn't matter *whose* idea it was. The fact is, you're expected to show. The press will make—"

"Fuck the press," Roger fired back viciously.

James straightened the lapels of his jacket before the mirror in the foyer. "I'm not as concerned about the media as I am about Cassidy. How do you think *she* would feel if you don't attend?"

James watched Roger's image in the mirror. He saw that he now had his full attention.

"She's already been through enough. This business with Chelsea, and now with Jack—all I'm saying is, why add to her grief?"

The two old friends faced each another, eyes locked.

Roger let out a long sigh. After a few moments, he spoke. "Okay, I see your point."

His head raced with memories of Lana, intensified by the anniversary of her murder. No matter how much he thought about it, or how many therapists he consulted, he could not remember what happened that night beyond escorting her through the hundreds of guests who filled their home to celebrate the success of *Tamed.* He'd had a lot to drink and, beyond that, he had blocked everything else out. Everything, that is, until Lana was dead and there were police and he was arrested. And he remembered kissing Cassidy good-bye. "You'll be home tomorrow, Daddy," she had said. "I love you."

He remembered that Rae had pulled Cassidy close, shielding her as the police took him away in handcuffs and reporters ate up every second of the tragedy. Cameras flashed, microphones were shoved into his face.

For the longest time he thought that he really *had* murdered Lana. God knows he had reason enough, and he had been drinking pretty heavily in those days, especially near the end. As time went by, his lawyer—James—shot enough holes in the prosecutor's case to confuse Roger, so, in truth, he really wasn't sure if he had killed her or not. That's why he needed to proceed with a clear head tonight. This wasn't going to be a repeat performance . . . this time with Cass as the victim.

| | |

A mechanical dove soared from the bell tower of the Cathedral di San Marco, showering the crowd below with enormous clouds of confetti and a bounty of balloons. Street performers—mimes, clowns, jugglers, musicians, acrobats, and fire-eaters mingled madly with the brightly costumed revelers who filled the piazza.

Castle Madrid was an imposing dark brick structure at the far end of the square. Six massive windows fronted the facade, providing an astounding stage from which one could see and be seen. Its unrivaled sophistication made this the ultimate rendezvous spot for celebrants. Add to that the glitz and glamour of the visiting Hollywood—and European—film set and the paparazzi stalking their every move, and the entire piazza was overflowing.

How Jack had managed to book the Madrid for the private wrap party defied imagination! Indeed, the Cavelli name *did* carry clout.

As the masked and costumed guests lined up to enter, hordes of spectators, themselves masked and costumed, gathered to watch the ongoing festivities. Partygoers responded to the cheers of onlookers with candid poses, exaggerated mannerisms, and feigned arrogance and condescension toward the pesky peons who lined the way.

Traditional Venetian characters—medieval plague doctors dressed in long black robes and the traditional white-beaked mask, popes and cardinals, and exquisitely gowned Clementines, traditionally the only unmasked Carnivale character—romped alongside more contemporary creatures, such as a gigantic bright orange butterfly with deep purple spots and a trio of "little green men." A court jester did handsprings along the red carpet leading up to the guarded doorway, where four regal trumpeters heralded guests inside once their invitations had been checked and their names marked off the guest list.

Cassidy had taken advantage of the Cipriani security manager's hospitality and accepted his offer of a launch to take her across the lagoon and a costumed guard to escort her to the party. He'd even arranged for her to be admitted through a private entrance so that she wouldn't have to push her way, alone, through the hysterical throng.

Inside the great hall, Murano glass chandeliers sparkled with hundreds of candles. The result was movielike magic. At least a hundred outrageously costumed guests celebrated the completion of their film. The music was live, of course. A twenty-four-piece orchestra played from a crescent-shaped tier suspended above the castle's expansive ballroom floor.

Cass's immediate thought was regret that she hadn't planned to film the festivities. She'd have found a way to use it in *Dangerous Intentions*. Somehow.

Pausing at the top of a marble staircase that fanned gracefully onto the dance floor, Cass studied the exhibition of energy that played out before her. A garish skeleton, bones aglow in fluorescent paint on black leotards and tights, danced by with a six-foot flamingo—really one of the grips, wearing a huge bubble-gum-pink headpiece and tights with wrinkly yellow boots.

She scanned the merrymakers before her, searching for a familiar face. She felt absurd in the elaborate gold-and-ivory eighteenth-century wedding gown. Either it was Jack's idea of a joke or an extension of the head game he was playing on her, on them all. She had seriously considered showing up in her own clothes until she realized that the only evening gown she had with her in Venice had been his gift. Had the wardrobe not been crated for the return to California, she would have called Hilary Suazy and asked her to pull something together. The idea of *not* going had also crossed her mind, but Cass owed it to the entire team—Americans and Italians—who worked so hard to pull *Dangerous Intentions* together to be there with them.

Now that she was here, she found herself surrounded by unrecognizable bodies, and trampled by waiters with trays of champagne and canapés. Cassidy began to panic and she looked frantically around the grand ballroom for an exit. Unconsciously, she squeezed the gold-and-ivory evening bag around her wrist and felt the impression of the ring. She would return it before the night was over.

"Cass, is that you?" It was Rudolpho's voice she heard, but the Velveteen Rabbit she saw. "With that mask on I wasn't sure. Wow! Jack told me you'd be wearing a wedding dress dripping in ivory-and-gold lace. I had no idea!" He stepped back to get a better look. "I have to hand it to him, the man's got great taste."

Cass glared.

"I don't mean the costume. He told me I'd recognize you when I spotted, and I quote, 'the most elegant creature in the room.'" Rudolpho walked around her. "He wasn't kidding. You look great."

"Where on earth did you get that costume?" she asked.

"Jack, of course. Can't you tell? You get to be an exquisite eighteenth-century bride, and I"—he hopped back a step and spun around—"a stupid, ridiculous rabbit."

Cass couldn't help but laugh.

"Has my father arrived yet?"

"James and I bumped into each other at the bar about twenty minutes ago. I assume your father is not too far behind."

Her eyes continued to scan the room. "What about the queen? Has she made her entrance?"

Behind his adorable bunny face, Rudolpho laughed. "If you're referring to Chelsea—no, Her Royal Highness has not yet graced us with her presence."

Cass checked her watch. It was almost nine.

"Come now, Cass, you've been working with that diva for close to three months. Surely you realize that Ms. Hutton will wait to make a grand entrance. I'm surprised she didn't have that press agent creep of hers arrange for a pink follow spot and special music."

Of course, he was right. And Cassidy didn't dare leave before Chelsea grabbed the spotlight. Like it or not, she had to be there to witness the next stage of Chelsea's plan to disrupt and destroy everything she had worked for. Those who didn't know about Chelsea's deception would think Cass was showing respect for the actress for her magnificent performance. Those who did would agree that the best way to keep an eye on her and to avoid playing into her game was to be there for her entrance.

"So far the party is a raging success," Rudolpho continued. "Looks like everyone is having a great time."

Cass scanned the room again.

Rudolpho picked up on her nervousness. "Hey, relax. Like I said, when she arrives, you'll know about it."

He couldn't possibly know that she was thinking about Jack, wondering what costume he was hiding behind.

"Is there a quiet corner we could hide in?" Cass asked him. "I'm not ready to deal with all the noise."

Rudolpho cleared a path through the dancing throng and led Cass to a corner table, away from the noise. Already seated were John, the assistant director, who had flown his fiancée, a painfully thin Belgian model, in for the festivities. At the far side were Roger and James, the only two people in the room—probably in the entire city—not in costume. The two men rose as she neared the table. She chose the chair farthest from them, next to her personal assistant, whom she hadn't seen all day. Ally wore a silver satin sheath dress and evening gloves and a glittering headpiece that made her look like a sparkler.

Cass noted that James and Roger had stopped their intense conversation when they spied her heading their way.

"Can we discuss your schedule for L.A. sometime before the evening's over?" Ally leaned toward Cass, who immediately shook her head.

"No . . . absolutely not. No business tonight. We'll worry about L.A. when we get there. Which reminds me, when do we leave?"

Ally pulled a tiny notepad from her left glove, skimmed through a few pages, and announced, "Tomorrow night, eight o'clock."

Thank God! Cass thought with relief.

| | |

The buzz for the night was all about Jack and Cassidy and their "fling." Every gossiper seemed to make the same claim.

"Jack and I go back," proclaimed a chunky man in a Bill Clinton mask, dark suit, and Nicole Miller Clinton/Monica tie. "This is classic Cavelli. He made sure his money was protected and got himself a great piece of ass in the bargain. I'd bet big bucks he'll dump her once the premiere's over."

How pathetic Cassidy is, Jonathan thought. Did she really believe Jack Cavelli was capable of sustaining a meaningful relationship? In her silly fit of romantic bliss, she'd probably *assumed* the two of them would ride off into the sunset together. The fact that they wouldn't relieved him enormously. Ms. English had already had more than her fifteen minutes of fame. Merging with Cavelli would make her one of the most powerful players in Hollywood. That would be disastrous. Fortunately, Jack was a known womanizer. Thank God for small favors!

Jonathan's own machinations—and there were some great ones—had not scared her off, much to his dismay. Nonetheless, they had created enough trouble to keep Cassidy on her guard, and not a little wary of Jack. He smiled at the memory of the music he played the night she arrived from New York. Sort of a welcome home to get her juices flowing.

The singed photo, the mannequin in the attic, the "altar" to Lana . . . the bugs in her office. Now, that had been good. Learning about her bet with Cavelli had led him to think of setting the fire. That one had been especially sweet.

Still, none of his elaborate plans had driven the bitch away from L.A., off the movie. But he'd do it all over again if he had the chance. It was enough for Jonathan that he'd caused Cassidy anguish, insecurity, and brought up haunting memories of the past. Must have set her therapy back years!

Now, maybe, she'd learn what it felt like to be the victim, the loser, the bottom feeder in the family fishbowl, living on others' garbage. Now her final curtain was coming down. No more games.

A twenty-something babe, wearing only a toga and sandals and a glittery mask, cruised past him. For a moment their eyes locked. She gave him an inviting stare, but he fought the urge. No time for pleasure, that would have to wait. If things went according to plan, he'd never have to worry about money again. Parties, coke, beautiful babes, more coke—nothing would be out of his reach.

Chelsea—the queen of craziness—should be arriving momentarily. Jonathan was actually excited at the prospect of her grand entrance. He signaled for a waiter, a young man dressed in full costume, and handed him an envelope. "Get this to Ms. English—it's urgent."

| | |

Wisely, Jack maintained a considerable distance. Cassidy was hurting. Her wounds were still fresh. She'd come around, he was sure of that. It was only a question of locating the right button to push. He needed time with her to figure that out. That was all. Since gifts, apologies, and attempts to communicate with her had failed, perhaps staying away from her would work. Lying low, remaining a little detached. But that wouldn't be so easy, especially not tonight.

Cassidy looked incredible, absolutely dazzling in the glorious satin-and-lace gown, except for her eyes, where radiance once shone and sadness now reigned. Twice he fought the urge to sweep her into his arms, away from the crush of the partygoers and the din of the celebration. Pangs of guilt stabbed at his heart.

Jack never meant to hurt her. He just couldn't help himself. The same way he couldn't help himself twenty-three years ago. What he had felt for Lana had been animal. The lust of a handsome young actor. Her mere presence left him weak and out of control. But with Cass, her daughter, it was different. There was a connection; he wasn't whole anymore. He was no longer his own person. Cassidy, without realizing it, had brought something to him. She completed him. Now the thought of losing her threatened his survival. And what if she fell for someone else? Or went back to Rudolpho? These thoughts possessed him.

| | |

This should have been one of the most enchanting nights of Cassidy's life. Gorgeous orchids, glamorous costumes, romantic music, and a dazzling diamond in her purse, given to her by a gorgeous, charming man with overpowering magnetism who professed to adore her.

Instead it was a nightmare incarnate.

She wondered how he got the nerve to disguise himself as Errol Flynn—Captain Courageous. The mask of Hollywood's most infamous rake certainly suited Jack inside and out. He had painted his face with the signature Flynn mustache and wore the flamboyant swashbuckler's costume—eye patch, tight black pants, white silk shirt with flaring sleeves worn open to the waist, and red sash with a small sword.

Every once in a while, Cass had caught him staring, then he'd look away as though surveying the celebrants. Fame, money, and power *mingling* in one room . . . at his behest. Cass was sure this delighted him. Jack was driven by power; his need to control was incredible. And to think she believed for one moment that he was throwing this lavish party as a reward for the cast, to show appreciation for a job well done. It was all about control. It wouldn't surprise her one bit if he hadn't booked the Madrid and arranged for the gala the moment he okayed her plan to move the shoot to Venice.

The "spontaneous" trip to Paris and Monte Carlo, the ring inside her purse, his tenderness in bed that she had mistaken for caring—all of these things were Jack Cavelli's way of making certain she knew who was boss.

"Excuse me." A young waiter, dressed in black tie and holding a purple and red sequined Harlequin mask to his face, hovered over her. "Are you Ms. English?" He leaned in close so that she could hear him.

"Yes."

"This is for you." He handed her an envelope. It was marked *Urgent*. She looked around the table.

All talk stopped.

Cassidy felt Roger's presence. Suddenly he seemed to grow larger, cast a shadow over her from across the large circular table. I can't do this, she thought, and decided to read the note in private. But the moment she stood to excuse herself, a stir arose in the ballroom.

Partygoers rushed toward the base of the stairway, fighting reporters and photographers who had broken through the phalanx of security guards and entered the castle for a closer view of the celebrity who was making this intentionally grand entrance. Someone signaled the orchestra to stop.

Rudolpho stood next to her. "So now the queen."

Chelsea Hutton had arrived. Despite herself, Cass strained to get a peek. Her curiosity was getting the best of her, but the crowd made it impossible to see. Not wanting to miss the moment, she pushed her way through the throng, clearing a path that allowed her entry to the queen's circle.

The pandemonium of the party subsided, replaced by barely audible gasps, indecipherable whispers, and long, intense stares. First at Chelsea, then at Cass.

A short man dressed as Pablo Picasso came up to Cass. "Did you plan this? I think it's a great ruse," he said with a drunken leer.

On the edge of the crowd, Jonathan leaned against a pillar. A smirk crossed his face. Absolutely brilliant, my man, he thought. The best fifty bucks I ever spent, getting that horny little maid to take snapshots of the gown Jack had rented for Cass.

Chelsea was standing—no, posing—in the center of the dance floor, dressed in a costume identical to the one Cass wore. She stared at Cass and then turned to Jack, who stood at the bottom of the stairs.

Jack seemed ruffled, even embarrassed. There was a spark of some undefinable emotion in his eyes. Was it anger? Revenge? Cass couldn't read him, but he had to be part of this plan to further embarrass her. She was sure of that.

The crowd remained quiet, silence filling the thick, warm air.

Cass could not bring herself to run. Forgotten was the envelope marked *Urgent* under her arm.

"Well, well. It seems as though someone else wants to play the heroine," Chelsea said, with the full attention of the crowd. She took a step back. Her jaw tightened. She placed her hands belligerently on her hips. "Now, what is *that* saying?" Chelsea put her finger to her lips, lowered her eyelids as if deep in thought, and said, "Oh, yes. Imitation is the finest form of flattery."

She was smiling now.

Cass looked about the room until her eyes fell on her father. She saw definite sadness and pain in his face. She was sure he was as humiliated as she. Then she shifted her gaze to James—hurt, despair—and scanned the crowd, their eyes large, glittering orbs of repudiation.

The blood pounded in her temples. Her breath quickened. Her cheeks became warm. She was furious with herself for being embarrassed, *angry* that she'd allowed all of them to do this to her—Jack, Chelsea, even Roger.

Cass pressed her hand over her face, convulsively gasping for air. She prayed she wouldn't faint before she could get away.

Someone, probably Rudolpho, came to her rescue. The orchestra got the signal to begin playing again, the bartenders poured drinks, and waiters served food. The party resumed as though nothing had happened.

Cassidy found the nearest exit and bolted.

Like his daughter, Roger also exited the ballroom. Running away, however, was not on his mind. He wanted Jack. Now.

Finding his nemesis propped in a corner against one of the huge columns on the perimeter of the hall, Roger reached out to grab Jack by the shoulder but instead yanked the eye patch off.

"You're responsible for this fiasco, Cavelli, and this time you won't get away with it. I won't let you!" he roared.

Roger lunged at Jack, but James, who had followed only a few steps behind him, was quick to jump between the two men.

"Take it easy. Don't complicate matters." James was speaking to Roger, but his eyes never left Jack. "He's not worth it. Cass needs you. Go to her."

Jack, who had not said a word until this point, straightened his costume and stepped back. "Yes, go to her. I saw her heading toward the inner courtyard."

Roger dropped his clenched fists. "You've done enough, you son of a bitch. Stay away from my daughter." He stepped toward the exit, then stopped. He turned back to face Jack. "I'm going to make you pay for what you've done."

To James, he said, "Keep him out of my sight."

| | |

Jack came up on Chelsea's right side and grabbed her elbow. "Sorry, folks, you can talk to our star later," he told the gathered crowd with a dazzling smile. He forced her into a nearby corner.

"What the fuck are you up to? How did you get this costume?" He faced her, gripping her shoulders with both hands, and shook her into gasping silence.

Icy fear pierced her heart. Chelsea was well aware of his temper. When crossed, he was almost uncontrollable. Still defiant, she held her head high and said simply, "You . . . you sent it. The card attached was signed by you. . . ."

"You're twisted and dangerous," he spat. "I curse the day I ever laid eyes on you."

She shuddered. "You don't mean that, Jack. We're a team. You're . . . you're just angry, confused." As she fumbled for words, she felt her body tremble. The pain in her head was so intense she almost blacked out.

"You don't give a damn about who you hurt as long as you get what you want. Right?"

He squeezed harder, digging his nails into her flesh.

"I warned you not to play games with me. You knew the rules. You agreed to them. Then you deliberately broke them. Now you're going to pay the price."

| | |

Good. She was humiliated. From where he was standing midway up the grand staircase, he could swear he saw a tear or two. Jonathan couldn't have scripted a better opening himself. He had to give that psycho bitch credit. She was cunning. Getting Chelsea out of the picture might be harder than he expected.

No matter. He welcomed the challenge.

He tossed back the rest of his drink in one gulp, wiped his mouth on his sleeve, and headed for the men's room. He locked the door and pulled the black satin pouch from the pocket of his brocade jacket. A dandy in Napoleon's court. It was that or a scratchy, hooded brown burlap monk's robe. The robe had no pockets and the hood impeded his view. He couldn't have that. Tonight he had to see *everything*.

He carefully laid the white powder on the small mirror, also stashed in the pouch. Using a tiny white straw, he snorted the powder, first in one nostril, then in the other. One deep pocket of air and then the rush was incredible. Adrenaline surged through his veins, causing his heart to beat a rapid tattoo. His energy soared; beads of perspiration formed across his brow.

Ah. It was time to finish what he'd started. An intense burning sensation radiated from his chest throughout his body. He had to move fast.

| | |

Cass made her way through the corridor, inspecting each room for the perfect place to be alone, the perfect place to hide. She took a flight of stairs down one level and found herself out on a balcony. The air was brisk, the noise level minimal, and the view startling. The lagoon was smooth, the water sparkling like a black mirror reflecting the colorful Carnevale lights. Cass could see the marina, filled with private yachts bedecked with streamers and lights. The distant sound of laughter annoyed her.

| | |

The voices were getting louder, screaming. *You worthless fool! You've never done anything right!* Her head ached, pulsing at her temples and burning around her eyes. The need to flee was great. The look on Jack's face, the rage in his eyes, the coldness in his voice—how could she have been so stupid? It was obvious Jack loved Cassidy; obvious Roger chose her, too.

She broke free from the crowd. She couldn't bear their eyes boring into her. What would happen next? That *is* what the vultures wanted to know. Nobody loved a good scandal as much as Hollywood. And considering the history of scandal associated with her father and mother, what happened tonight would be in tomorrow's papers—and on everyone's lips.

Chelsea made her way down a quiet hallway, away from the noise—the laughter. *Listen to them! They're all laughing at you, you fool.*

| | |

Phew! He'd had some powerful blow before, but never like this. Pain gripped his chest like a vise, crushing his lungs and squeezing his heart. He was drenched in perspiration from head to toe. Every organ—every cell—in his body experienced its own, piercing pain. He gasped for breath with little success.

Jonathan pushed the bathroom door open and lunged into the hallway. He was lightheaded, dizzy. He braced himself against the far wall to get his balance, then staggered toward the ballroom. Suddenly the floor tilted sharply and the walls closed in on him.

Jonathan opened his mouth to call for help, but no sound came out.

The shiny marble floor raced up to meet him as he fell headlong, crashing his face into the cool, hard surface. The pain in his chest and head intensified, surging throughout his body like a massive electrical current.

Even as his heart struggled with one last pump, as he breathed one last breath, Jonathan thought about Cass. The bitch.

| | |

He could see that she was crying, even from where he stood in the doorway. Her body was wracked with sobs of pain and humiliation. Good. The blood that flowed through Chelsea's veins—Lana's and Roger's— could never allow her to stake a claim on Lana's legacy. The babies, lying side by side—one wan and motionless, and next to her, the perfect infant who he made sure became Lana Turmaine's daughter, Cassidy.

From the very beginning, Cass was beautiful, seductive, charming, and persuasive, just like her mother, her mentor. Lana had been an incredible teacher. Cass, as a young child, was the sponge soaking up Lana's style. Everyone, especially men, were caught completely off guard, mesmerized by her. Like a spider, she spun a web of gold, trapping, ensnaring anyone she chose to grace with her smile. One was powerless against her charms.

Yes, Chelsea shared Lana's genes. She did inherit her physical beauty, but who knew why she had inherited all of her mother's negative traits, too? The mood swings and mental instability; the promiscuity; the ruthless, deceitful behavior and, worst of all, the ability to manipulate beyond belief, she had shown them all.

He had watched both of the girls as they were growing up. He had been a surrogate father, a loving self-appointed uncle to Cassidy—especially when Roger was in prison. And he had kept a close watch on Chelsea, too. From a distance, he witnessed her painful path of destruction, the one born of a life lived in poverty and despair. There had never been any doubt to him: Chelsea was the incarnation of "the bad Lana."

Cass, on the other hand—now, she was regal. She was the *rightful* heir to Lana's legacy. He smiled with satisfaction.

He knew without a shadow of a doubt that he had made the right choice that night thirty-three years ago in the nursery of Cedars-Sinai Hospital.

A light rain had begun to fall as dark clouds rolled in from the bay and hovered over the piazza, a perfect backdrop for the finale he had planned.

For now he made no attempt to let her know that he was behind her. Instead he stood in the doorway in silence, to observe and study.

A gush of cold air whipped through the open French doors. He watched her shiver. Her arms were folded across her chest, as if she was holding herself together. She looked down as she drew into herself.

"Did you honestly believe you could waltz in here and take back your life?"

She swung around to face him, but he couldn't read her expression. The elaborate white-and-gold mask covered her eyes. She did not speak. Perhaps the shock of what he had said rendered her mute. She simply stared at him, eyes penetrating and defiant.

James took a step toward her. He pulled his gun from his pocket and held it in his right hand.

A street lamp above the canal created a hazy halo around her. She seemed to glow, like an angel, or an apparition.

"Oh, Chelsea," he said, quite seriously, "I'm afraid you couldn't be more wrong."

He raised his hand and aimed the gun at her chest.

"You're dead wrong. Your mother—your *real* mother, that is—was the same way. Headstrong. Single-minded. She was always too quick to make a decision. I never, in the whole time I knew her, saw her think anything through. Her actions never made sense. She was impulsive, difficult to contain."

His steely eyes served hers. He could see that she was crying. Was it from fear? Shock? It was impossible to tell with her mask on.

James's mind started to drift. He had planned—choreographed—every word, every movement of this moment. He knew it was inevitable. He had known that from the moment she had invaded Roger's office.

He had a story to tell, and he had to tell someone. It might as well be Chelsea. After all, she was a large part of it.

"I was an actor—bit parts, hustling my way up the Hollywood ladder. I lived a life of sin, excess, but I redeemed myself. I met an extremely wealthy woman, an attorney. She became my patroness. She put me through law school, then taught me the ropes of the entertainment industry and entertainment law. That's when I met Lana. It was thirty-six years ago. I was instantly captivated. She had that kind of power over men. I'm sure you know that from her films—no one was immune, least of all me. It was love at first sight."

His tone softened. He was hardly aware of the gun in his hand. "It lasted ten years—on and off, of course. She never could make up her mind: Roger or me, me or Roger, back and forth. I never knew what to expect from day to day. She told me she was pregnant and it was Roger's child. I thought I would die. I was brokenhearted. I hated you, even before you were born. And I hated everything you represented. She would have left him had it not been for you."

He focused his gaze on her face. Even though she was still masked, he could see that she was rigid with fright.

"I suppose the easy solution would have been to just let go, let God take over. But I couldn't let you destroy her. I was convinced you would be damaged from the alcohol and drugs in Lana's system. It would have destroyed her—sent her over the edge. Caring for, worrying about, raising a sick child was the last thing she needed in her life. And she would be forever far from my grasp. I couldn't let that happen, I had to come up with a plan."

He paused for a moment, let out a long sigh. Then a smile crossed his lips. "The switch was brilliant. Don't you think? Lots of money, little persuading and heavy maintenance. I suppose you don't know what I'm talking about, so let me explain. The late Mrs. Hanson, the delivery room nurse, was a snap. There's nothing like the offer of money to get a greedy drunk to make the switch. You must have figured by now that I killed her. Of course, when I learned that you had found out about her and that she was going to blab everything to you, I had to make sure she didn't talk. No big loss. She was sick and old—probably didn't have much more time, anyway. I couldn't let you get to her."

Did he just say that he killed someone? She felt herself becoming nauseated.

"Then, when you were about ten, the hospital contacted me with regard to a complaint initiated by Maria Hutton. I handled it on Roger's behalf, so I never told him about the suit. Why should I? He wouldn't have known what they were talking about. I realized it was only a matter of time before everything came to a boiling point. How wrong I was."

James noticed that Chelsea immediately looked away from him. For a moment he wanted to see her face, know if she understood what had happened. He needed her to understand so he could have closure, put this secret behind him.

But he thought better of that idea and dropped the notion of removing her mask. That would be dangerous. He could shoot her masked. But if he saw her face, this child he had watched from afar for so long, he might not be able to go through with his plan. He certainly couldn't risk that. No, he'd said too much now.

"So, Chelsea, your whole childhood would have been so very different. I really tried to work something out with Maria. But your mother—well, I mean, the one you thought was your mother—was a God-fearing woman. She thought like a peasant." He sneered with disgust. "Maria wanted no part of any deals. She wanted her real child back. But that was impossible, of course—rotten, silly fool. When you think about it, she had no leverage. How could she have brought a lawsuit? Still, when she refused, I realized I needed insurance. I sent your mother the checks, which she never cashed, so I never had to justify the expense to Roger. I'm responsible for the paper trail.

"If Maria ever did get to a lawyer, Roger would have been the suspect, of course. I'm glad to tell you this. I've felt guilty about what I did, not only to you, but to your father. If Maria had been able to get the case to court, all the evidence would point to him. I was his best friend. And not only was I screwing his wife, but I was setting him up for the fall in case the story of the switched babies ever came out. He didn't have a clue.

He staggered closer, and a quick chill raced up and down his spine.

"We always remained close, Lana and I. I was the one she ran to when Roger 'didn't understand' or 'didn't care.' I was always her knight in shining armor."

James was tired of talking to himself. Why didn't she say something? Maybe he could goad her into speaking. His smile turned into a grin now. "Of course, I knew about the others. But unlike Roger, I wasn't in denial. I dealt with it. I knew she loved me best. She proved that with Jack. Good old Jack really made a play for her, but she resisted."

She gasped.

"Oh, you didn't know? They worked together—a film, a huge project. Everyone saw the two of them as the next Taylor and Burton. Roger was directing, and when he saw the to-do about them, he was livid. He did everything in his power to destroy Jack. Your father never knew Lana had rejected him, and I didn't tell him anything different. Oh, he suffered terrible public humiliation over her 'flirtations'—that's what the columnists called them in those days. Once they got on the scent of the chemistry between Lana and Jack, they wanted to know *everything*. Oh, they couldn't find out anything specific. None of her other 'diversions' were celebrities or even in the business—an airline pilot she met in Hawaii, a bartender at the Waldorf-Astoria, an investment banker at the Fountainbleu in Miami." James's voice trailed off as he became lost in his memories.

"Roger knew Lana's infidelities were secret until Jack. Roger was furious, but not enough to let her go. So he had to get rid of Jack." Roger paused. "I came up with the successful gambit to break the studio's contract with Jack, of course—creative differences. How original."

She raised her hands.

He jumped back. "Easy now, Miss Hutton. You don't want this gun to go off accidentally, do you?"

Slowly, her fingers clasped the edges of the mask and tore it from her face. The shock of seeing Cassidy's face silenced James mid-sentence. He was very still and helpless for the moment.

And Cass seized it.

"You . . . you bastard! It was you." She was numb with horror, and her eyes were riveted. "You killed my mother . . . the night of the party. The gray shoes . . . Oh God, it was you!"

Sobbing loudly, Cass pressed her hands over her mouth. Her heart pounded in her chest. She could not move.

James started speaking again, but she couldn't hear him; her sobs swallowed whatever sounds he made.

A noise caused her to turn to her right. Roger stepped from the shadows. Silhouetted in the moonlight, he stood with his arms folded across his chest. In his hands he clasped the contents of the envelope she had given him earlier that evening. A silence both terrifying and ominous enveloped the trio.

Roger was looking at James, yet his gaze was far away.

James was stunned by Roger's appearance. Instinctively, he drew far back.

"I, I, I'm sorry. I didn't mean for you—" Clearly terrified, James looked from Roger to Cassidy, then back to Roger. "I thought I would find Chelsea out here alone. I followed her from the bathroom."

He turned to Cass. "I'm so sorry, Cassidy. I never meant to hurt you, of all people. Everything I've done has been for you. I gave you a fairy-tale childhood. . . ."

Add fear and weapons to a dangerous, disturbed mind and the possibilities for further disaster were high. Especially, Cassidy realized, since James held the gun. What else did she have to lose? "And then you took it away when you killed my mother." She stared him in the face. "It wasn't love you felt for her—it was obsession."

Cass moved closer to him, along the way brushing Roger's shoulder. Her father reached toward her, but she ignored him.

"Do you realize all the pain you caused? For my father? For me? Even for Chelsea?" Cass spoke strongly, steadily. Her eyes never left James's face. "Do you *honestly* believe you can justify what you have done? You loved my mother . . . so you killed her." Her voice remained steady. "I trusted you. You were like a father to me. I thought you cared about me, about my family, and all the time it was *you* who destroyed my family."

Cass turned to Roger. "All these years, I blamed you. And I blamed myself. It was my testimony that sent you to prison. I was convinced you killed Mother." Cass brought her hand up to her mouth.

Too numb to speak, Roger stared at the man he had trusted for so many years.

"Enough!" James broke the silence. The timbre of his voice became high pitched, shrill. "I can't bear this walk down memory lane." He checked his watch. "I'm running out of time. Someone's bound to come looking for us."

He abruptly turned and aimed the gun straight at Roger's heart.

"I never intended to hurt either of you," he mewled. "But now that's impossible. You leave me no choice."

"You can't kill us. You can't be that coldhearted." Terror swept over Cass as images of her murdered mother flashed through her mind. She heard the gunshots and heard her scream. James had killed Lana and now he was going to kill them.

"You don't want to do this." She lowered her voice, trying to sound composed despite the tears ready to pour from her eyes. "As bad as it seems, we can fix it."

But he couldn't hear her. James was lost in his own memories of Lana's death.

He pulled back and squeezed the trigger.

| | |

The deafening blast resonated a thousand times off the bare stone walls of the castle.

Jack, who was standing near the doorway, heard the report and immediately recognized it as a gunshot. Cass was in trouble and he had to find her. He was running out of time. He was convinced Chelsea was insane and capable of anything—even murder. What had she done?

"Please don't let me be too late," he prayed.

Then another shot exploded down the hallway.

| | |

Roger summoned up all the strength he could from his frail form. He lunged at James and pinned him to the cold, damp ground. Despite his poor physical condition, Roger fought like a man possessed, furiously wrestling for the gun with savage strength. He slammed James's hand against the ground several times, so hard the gun fired twice.

"You son of a bitch!" he yelled right before James broke free and slammed the pistol against the side of his head, knocking him unconscious.

James rolled out from under him, stood and aimed the gun at Roger's heart.

He looked at Cass again. "I'm sorry. This is not how things were supposed to end."

"Daddy!" she screamed.

Then the gun crackled. Cassidy froze with fear. Through her tears she thought she saw James stumble back. What had happened? Who was moaning? Which man was screaming? Cass had seen James raise the gun and take aim at Roger's unconscious form on the floor, but then *his* body fell forward, slamming into the ground. Blood poured from a gaping hole in his back.

A shadowy figure loomed in the doorway.

Cass squinted in an effort to make out who it was.

"I couldn't let him kill my father," Chelsea cried. "There's no way I will allow *anyone* to get between Roger and me anymore." She turned the gun on Cass, who stood between the French doors in a halo of moonlight. "You, too. You've had him for thirty-three years, only you didn't *want* him."

Chelsea had the familiar, faraway look that Cassidy had learned was a sign that she was slipping into madness. Then all the pieces fell into place: How many times had she seen her mother with the same mysterious look? How many times had she heard her mother rambling on and on, making little sense? Now she could see that the similarities between the two were startling. The resemblance was incredible.

"You bitch," Chelsea continued railing. "You took everything—my parents, *my* life!"

From where she stood, Cass was certain that James was dead.

How ironic that Chelsea would kill the one person responsible for everyone's misery.

"I know things look incredibly distorted," Cass said to her, "so far from reality right now, but we can work it out. We can try to—"

"Oh, shut up!" Chelsea shrieked. "Shut the fuck up." She squeezed her eyes shut and waved the gun about.

"Try? Try, you say?" Her voice grew louder. "You want me to *try* and forget the misery I grew up with? The things I had to do, the groveling just to get here? You're too damned late."

Chelsea stepped over James and lunged toward Cass, so close only inches separated them. Chelsea brought the gun up to Cass's face and traced the outline of her features with the cold metal tip of the barrel. Cass tried to turn her head to see if Roger was still breathing, but Chelsea pushed her head back so they were eye to eye.

"So beautiful," she murmured. "Perfect eyes, lips, nose, and . . ." She purposely twisted a lock of hair around the gun and tugged. "But of course," she whispered, "only the best money could buy."

"Please . . ."

"Don't speak," Chelsea said, her tone menacing. "It's my turn."

She smiled hysterically, opening her eyes wide. "I tried to fix things. I gave Daddy the chance to make things right. I thought he was responsible. . . . I thought he made the switch. Everything pointed to him. How clever James was." She continued rambling. She was hell-bent on revenge. And at that moment, all of her fury was directed at Cass.

"Maria, *your* mother, was pathetic. So good, so squeaky clean. Just like you. We were nothing alike. Not one similarity. I couldn't wait for her to die. It took forever."

Tears coursed down her cheeks, yet she still smiled. Then she spoke. "And now I'm going to kill you. This time nothing will stand in our way—not you, not James, not anybody. Daddy and I will live happily ever after."

Chelsea grabbed Cassidy, her arm around her shoulder, and pulled her closer. Her body felt like steel, heavy, rigid, immobile, not the least bit compliant.

In that moment, Cass grabbed the gun. As though operating independently of her body, her hand fast as lightning, she tightened her fingers around the gun barrel.

"I won't let you kill me," Cass stated defiantly. She elbowed her attacker and stomped on her foot. "No!"

Chelsea staggered but did not lose her footing, nor did she lose her hold on Cass as the two women struggled for control of the weapon. Chelsea's stamina was remarkable. She exhibited the maniacal strength of a wild animal.

"Good-bye, Chelsea Hutton," Chelsea whispered, shoving the gun into Cass's side.

A resounding gunshot brought both women to the ground.

The noise, the smoke, the unbelievable agony, and then silence.

EPILOGUE
One Year Later

The magic of Oscar night kicked into full gear the moment the celebrities exchanged the privacy of their limos for the excitement, glitz, and glamour of Hollywood's most celebrated event. The red-carpet arrivals, decked out in fabulous designer gowns and jaw-dropping jewelry, the men in black tie, sauntered past the throng of security guards and reporters down the most powerful fashion runway in the world. And hundreds of cameras and microphones stood at the ready.

Cassidy and Jack entered the Dorothy Chandler Pavilion right behind Gwyneth Paltrow, who was with her father, Bruce, and mother, Blythe.

They sat in the second row, carefully positioned among Hollywood's A-list: Spielberg, Hanks, Lucas, and Roberto Benigni.

Colossal had managed to garner five nominations. *Dangerous Intentions* had opened to critical acclaim and excellent box-office numbers. The smart money said it was a sure win for Best Picture.

Jack, considered this year's "messiah" for saving the studio, was content, and he owed it to Cass. *Dangerous Intentions* was her movie and this was her night. And it seemed as though everyone here tonight had come out to pay homage to her.

Jack could barely keep his eyes off his wife. She sat next to him, mesmerizing, dressed in a luxurious ivory silk organza gown. Her delicate porcelain face was framed by long silky curls, dramatic in the simplicity of the style. Her eyes, lips, and cheeks were kissed with just a hint of makeup.

The brilliant diamond solitaire she wore on the ring finger of her left hand sent the light from the chandeliers across the auditorium in a spray of rainbow stars.

Cassidy and Jack had been married in a small church in Beverly Hills one month to the day after their return from Venice. Cass wore an exquisite candlelight satin gown, encrusted with pearls. She glided down the aisle on Roger's arm with measured grace, her head held high. Her wild mane was tamed by a diamond-and-platinum tiara and what seemed an endless whisper of tulle veiling.

By the time she reached the altar, tears of joy were streaming down her cheeks.

Jack was completely dazzled by her beauty, and the joy that they were now joined for life.

Hollywood, this land of happiness and heartache, had been yearning for another powerful love story—a beautiful princess, a powerful titan, true love; life partners, destined to be together from the beginning. And Jack could not have cast the players better himself.

Even Roger seemed genuinely pleased by his daughter's newfound bliss. At one point during the reception, he stood and made a moving toast to the happy couple, referring to Jack as "my nemesis and my new son-in-law." The crowd laughed, knowing how far Roger and Jack had gone to put their grudge aside.

| | |

To Jack's left, Bella fidgeted in her seat, obviously bored with the evening's grown-up festivities. Her slight form rocked back and forth, her halo of blond curls danced about wildly. The lovely lavender dress Cass had picked out for her set off her expressive emerald green eyes. Bella felt Jack's eyes upon her and turned and smiled. Finally a look of contentment, confidence, and peace settled about her. Cass was a great role model and would be a perfect mother to this "little princess."

Jack had surprised Cass just that morning with the final adoption papers. By his going straight to the governor to get him to move the people at the Children's Services, the whole process was expedited. The fact that Bella's late father had no immediate family to contest this move helped. Of course, a few "white lies" filled in the void of so many unanswered questions, especially about Chelsea.

The tragic murder/suicide had rocked L.A., in fact reverberated around the world. Roger and Cass agreed that when the Italian police investigated, Chelsea should be protected; they gilded her image in the telling of her death. It was labeled a tragic suicide—anything else would have been too complicated. The papers Jonathan had stolen from Chelsea's room proved invaluable. The torrid story of Cassidy, Chelsea, James, and Maria Hutton was confirmed.

That story, of course, had the tabloids in a feeding frenzy. Chelsea was now a Hollywood legend. A real Cinderella.

With his left hand, Jack squeezed Bella's small fingers and Jack examined his new daughter's profile. She was watching the crowd. When Leonardo DiCaprio stopped to say hello, Bella fell in love at first sight. "He's awesome," she said as the handsome young star winked and walked away.

Jack thanked the stars above that he'd finally filled the void inside of him. He'd waited all of his life to feel complete. His position at Colossal, his vast wealth, the strong arm of power he possessed—all of it no longer seemed important. The past was gone. It was time to move forward. Even Lana, the only woman Jack was convinced ever captured his heart, was now nothing more than a memory—a silly schoolboy's fantasy. Cass was real. Yes, it was pure magic—this thing called love.

| | |

Roger straightened in his seat. Despite the fact that *Dangerous Intentions* was up for Best Director, Best Actress, and Best Picture, he wanted nothing more than to be at home on the sofa, watching the awards with Rae, eating microwaved popcorn. He'd had enough of Hollywood.

The story of this movie's wrap party tragedy had brought back memories of Lana's murder especially since it was on the anniversary of another Turmaine tragedy. The media had a field day; the people in Hollywood who envied him feasted on it. Enough. After tonight, no one in Hollywood would ever see him again. He'd be home enjoying his granddaughter. And if he did come back to this life, it was certain he'd never do this scene again.

Meryl Streep and Mel Gibson read the nominees for Best Actress and Chelsea Hutton's name drew the most applause. This was Hollywood, after all, and the players always rooted for the underdog. He glanced over at Cass, watching her reaction. He wished he could read her mind. He imagined she was still as shocked and mystified today as she was that dreadful night in Venice.

He knew the healing process would be a long one. Time was the only solution.

James had manipulated all of their lives like a mad puppeteer, just as he had been manipulated by his obsession with a myth: a goddess he confused with Lana. Her shame-filled life of privilege, Chelsea's piteous life of poverty, pain, and sin—Hollywood with all its traps, make-believe. James's horrific acts of desperation had left behind terrible heartache, unbearable pain for them all, most of all for Cass. The trauma of her own horrific childhood and now its aftermath was painful, but as hard as it was, he knew she would pull through. She was a survivor.

Then he thought briefly about Chelsea, and for a moment he understood her torment. What if he had been able to help her? She *was* his daughter in the biological sense. They shared a mixture of blood, of genes and chromosomes. But she was a complete stranger, an entity that belonged only to Hollywood, in its pantheon of goddesses. Just as Lana did.

A moment of silence, then: "The Oscar goes to Chelsea Hutton."

Roger watched Cass, studying her expression. There was sadness in her eyes, but a smile formed on her lips. He understood her mixed emotions but knew her well enough to see some pride—admiration and grief as well.

| | |

Cassidy accepted the statue, mouthed a polite thank you to the people around her and then made her way to the podium. Before she could open her mouth to speak, the crowd was standing. The thunderous applause nearly took her breath away. Standing center stage, staring into the sea of admiring faces, was all so like she'd pictured it in Lana's bedtime stories. And for one moment, she put aside the madness, the pain. She ignored the struggle to keep the past and the present separate; forgot the bad parts and only remembered the good.

She cleared her throat and began. "Chelsea Hutton wanted nothing more in life than to be an actress—a star. She longed for the world to see her as they did Monroe, Grable, Gardner, and Turmaine." Cass fought hard to hold back the tears. She held the statue close to her heart and for a brief moment remembered Chelsea's taut body pressed up against hers. They were struggling for control of the gun, twisting, pulling, hanging on for dear life—then the feel of her finger wrapped around the trigger, squeezing. It was self-defense, she managed to convince herself, but that did little to lessen the pain.

Cass stopped speaking; the room was silent.

She had thought a lot about the strange woman who owned a piece of her life. She had dug inside herself and found her connection to Chelsea. They had begun life in that nursery so long ago and ended up here winning this award together. She had searched for the real Chelsea Hutton—gone through her belongings, read her journals, even torn a small entry to read aloud tonight.

She placed the crumpled piece of paper on the podium and began reading:

"Life and death—mania and depression.

"My hell on earth.

"Forever clawing my way through the fire; the flames are licking my body—drawing me in.

"No one knows where I have walked better than I. I cannot feel, therefore I am unable to heal.

"The good I've seen, even the bad. I would do it all again—it was worth it.

"The price of fame."

Now she held the statue up, looked straight into the camera, and said aloud, "Chelsea Hutton has achieved her dream, to be nothing less than a *superstar*."